Jame recognized ██████████████
he hadn't left with ██████████████
indeed gone home. ██████████████
was all too clear.

Two of his followers remained in the pasture. Now they were trying to sneak up on the rathorn. Death's-head charged one. The other used the distraction to snake a rope around his foreleg. Tangled, he fell, plowing into the mud on his shoulder. A second rope snared another of his flailing hooves.

Jurik straightened, climbed over the fence, and sauntered toward the prone beast, a bridle with a cruel, spiked bit dangling from his hand. He might even have laughed, as if it had been so easy after all.

As he approached, Death's-head glared at him through a besmirched mask, panting. The prince was within feet when the rathorn hooked his nasal tusk under the ropes and ripped them off.

Jurik stopped.

Death's-head regained his feet. Head low, horns poised, he moved toward the prince. Stalking. One slow step, then another. Oh, never offend a rathorn's dignity.

Jurik dropped the bridle, turned, and ran.

Jame was running too, toward the enclosure, toward the watching, horrified Bashtiri. She slipped between them, between the bars, between the prince and his would-be prey, just as the latter charged.

BAEN BOOKS by P.C. HODGELL

The Kencyrath Series

The Godstalker Chronicles (omnibus)
Seeker's Bane (omnibus)
Bound in Blood
Honor's Paradox
The Sea of Time
The Gates of Tagmeth
By Demons Possessed
Deathless Gods

To purchase any of these titles in e-book form, please go to
www.baen.com.

Deathless Gods

By

P. C. Hodgell

A Baen Books Original

Baen Publishing Enterprises
P.O. Box 1403
Riverdale, NY 10471
www.baen.com

ISBN: 978-1-9821-9297-6

Cover art by Jeff Brown
Maps by P.C. Hodgell

First printing, October 2022
First mass market printing, October 2023

Distributed by Simon & Schuster
1230 Avenue of the Americas
New York, NY 10020

Library of Congress Control Number: 2022026488

Printed in the United States of America

10 9 8 7 6 5 4 3 2 1

Dedication

For Judy and George,
Deathless in Memory

RATHILLIEN: THE CENTRAL LANDS

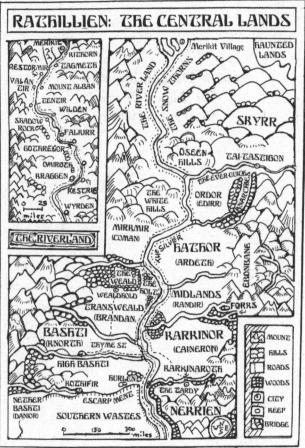

THE RIVERLAND

MERIKIE
RITHORN
RESTORMIR
TAGMETH
VALAN TIR
MOUNT ALBAN
TENTIR
WILDEN
SHADOW ROCK
FALKIRR
GOTHREGOR
OMIROTH
KRAGGEN
KESTRIE
WYRDEN
25 miles

Merikit Village
HAUNTED LANDS
THE RIVER LAND
THE SNOW THORNS
SKYRR
OSEEN HILLS
TAI-TASTIGON
THE-EVER-QUICK
SNARCKLES
ORDOR (EDIRR)
THE WHITE HILLS
MIRKMIR (COMAN)
THE SILVER
HATHOR (ARDETH)
EBONBAINE
THE WEALD
WEALDHOLD
THE BOLT
MIDLANDS (RANDIR)
FORKS
TRANSWEALD (BRANDAN)
BASHTI (KNORTH)
THYME ST
KARKINOR (CAINERON)
HIGH BASHTI
KARKINAROTH
KOTHIFIR
HURLEN
NETHER BASHTI (DANIOR)
ESCARPMENT
THE TARDY
SOUTHERN WASTES
NEKRIEN
0   150   300 miles

MOUNT
HILLS
ROADS
WOODS
CITY
KEEP
BRIDGE

P.C. Hodgell 2022

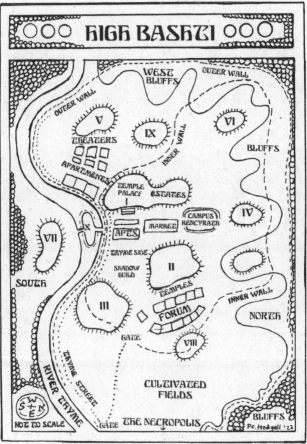

HIGH BASHTI

WEST BLUFFS

OUTER WALL

OUTER WALL

V

IX

VI

BLUFFS

THEATERS

INNER WALL

APARTMENTS

TEMPLE PALACE

ESTATES

CAMPUS KENCYRATH

IV

X

APTS

MARKET

VII

THYME SIDE

SHADOW GUILD

II

SOUTH

TEMPLES

INNER WALL

III

FORUM

NORTH

GATE

VIII

THYME STREET

RIVER THYME

CULTIVATED FIELDS

BLUFFS

S W N E
NOT TO SCALE

GATE

THE NECROPOLIS

Pc. Hodgell '22

HILLS: I FLOTEN II TIGGANIS III SANCTOR IV LEXION V TRESPAR
VI SCHOLA VII BELACOSE VIII ARTIFAX IX DELECTICA
X MERCANTY

Chapter I
The Muster

Gothregor: Summer I

I

IT HAD RAINED HARD overnight and well into the morning. By mid-afternoon, however, puddles reflected white canvas and blue sky even though tent lines still dripped. The camp at the foot of Gothregor had been churned into mud since the previous night when each of the nine houses had hosted its own party, however damp, and cadets had passed from one enclave to the next to greet old friends, to share news of the past year. If some had drunk too much hard cider in the process, well, what else were such gatherings for? That, at least, and for gossip.

Three years ago, some eight hundred of them had entered the randon college at Tentir—as mere children, it seemed to them now. Since then the best had spent their second year at Kothifir with the Southern Host where they had faced the Karnid invasion and lost some of their number. Throughout, they had been subjected to tests and culls. In their final, third year, each had been tasked to learn what he or she most needed to know. What that was, however, had not always been made clear, nor whether in the end they had passed. Now all anxiously awaited judgment, in hopes that by the end of Summer's Day they would be promoted to an officer's collar.

In the meantime, they were dimly aware that this was no ordinary muster. For one thing, far more of the senior staff were present than usual, including the entire Randon Council of Nine. Even the current Tentir commandant was there, although the college had its own ceremonies on this day which he would be missing. What were they all doing here, and why did they gather by twos or threes or fours to talk so seriously, in such low tones?

"They're worried about the summer campaign," a Danior cadet wisely told a Brandan, who with half a dozen others had gathered outside the Knorth tents, unconsciously mimicking their superiors. "Now that Kothifir says it can't afford us anymore, we have to go back to the Central Lands to find paymasters to get us through the winter."

A Coman snorted. "Everyone knows that. I hear that we have your precious lordan to thank."

"Jameth lost us King Krothen?" said the Danior scornfully. "Don't be silly."

The Coman flushed. "She went into the Wastes with a caravan, didn't she? And how many came out? After that, there were no more trade missions or goods, ever. Kothifir's wealth was cut off, just like that. What did she do anyway, destroy an entire city?"

Others laughed, but with a nervous edge. They had

noted before that the Knorth lordan often brought about results beyond her intentions.

Indeed, another point of nerves was the presence of three lordan in the graduating class—Jamethiel, Gorbel, and Timmon: Knorth, Caineron, and Ardeth. On one hand, they were rivals by house and by blood; on the other, they were also friends, bound by their shared experiences at the randon college and Kothifir. How would that all sort out, and what would it mean for the rest of the Kencyrath?

"Anyway," said the Brandan, "it isn't as if we've never dealt with the Seven Kings before. Most of the time we've been on Rathillien, we've been in their service. They gave us the Riverland."

"Yes, and then we found out that it couldn't support itself."

"Well, there is that. After the White Hills, though . . ."

For a moment, no one spoke. They were all remembering the stories they had heard about that dire battle.

"Fell he came from the slaughter,
Red his women on the floor.
Rage he swore 'gainst the slayers,
Madness, he chose the wrong foe."

The Jaran cadet's quiet voice hung over them, a lament, an indictment. Ganth Graylord and the White Hills had nearly shattered the Kencyrath. A powerful Shanir could possess his followers that way, not that Ganth had ever recognized himself as such. The Shadow Guild, not the

Seven Kings, had slain the Knorth women—Kinzi, Telarien, Aerulan, and those other few of an already nearly extinct house. Many still wondered who had bought the assassins' services and why.

However, the cadets' own concerns turned continually back to the day at hand. If this was the last cull, who had passed, and what had they been tested for, anyway?

"I never could master the kantirs of wind-blowing," said the Danior, looking nervous. "My Senethari said that I was too scatterbrained."

"I can't maneuver troops out of an ambush without losing half of them," said the Coman. "And, mind you, this is still only in practice."

"Me, I'm hopeless with heights."

The others laughed; the Caineron were notoriously bad at such. The cadet from Restormir blushed and turned to the Knorth.

"What about you, Char? Did you ever learn how to obey orders?"

Char glowered. He had had to repeat his third year, mostly because at Kothifir he hadn't been able to accept the Knorth lordan (then a second year) as his superior. Since, he had spent a year under her command at Tagmeth.

"Ask Ten," he said.

The group turned as Brier Iron-thorn emerged from the tent, closing its flaps behind her. A lance of sunlight kindled the smoldering red in her hair. She regarded them out of the teak brown face of a born Southron as if out of a mask.

"Well?" she said.

Several cadets fell back a step.

"Nothing," they muttered, and scattered.

"You'll have to tell someone sooner or later," said Char. "Gorbel and Timmon have already asked."

"And what should I tell them?"

That was it: their lady and one-hundred commander, Jame, had disappeared seven nights ago, without a word. She had known how close the muster was and how much depended on it for her newly established keep. Without her, would her brother Torisen be able to support Tagmeth's claim to legitimacy? Yet she had gone. Where, and why?

Betrayal, said Brier's unblinking malachite eyes, without speech. *How like a Highborn.*

Char met her glare and countered it. He hadn't trusted Jame either at first. Did he now? She had set him to herding cattle, as his father had done before him—he, a randon cadet, who had hoped never to step in a cow-pie again. Yet he missed the familiarity of the herd, especially that lumbering, affectionate yack-calf Malign. And he missed Tagmeth. A year had changed much for him. Now he felt as if he had stepped off the edge of the world.

A murmur spread through the camp and heads turned. Then a cry arose:

"The weapons-master is here!"

Cadets streamed between the tent lines, their boots sucking in the mud, splashing in puddles. Over the past few days Randiroc had been sighted at odd moments, in odd places, whenever he let his guard down. For someone who had spent years on the run, in the wilderness, he must have found the teeming muster a trial. Worse, whenever he appeared, someone challenged him. His evasions, thus, had taken on the inadvertent air of hide-and-seek.

He now stood in a cleared circle surrounded by a growing mob of eager cadets. As usual, he wore green-mottled hunting leathers with a hood pulled down to protect his eyes from the strengthening light. White braids hung to his waist. His shoulders fluttered with the flexing wings of jewel-jaws which, being the breed known as crown jewels, had changed their color from azure to match their more somber perch. He waited for whatever might come next, his rueful smile somewhat askew.

In a way, he was the fourth lordan present at the muster, sometimes known as the Lost Heir, although he had been cast out of his house and was pursued by it through no fault of his own. Merely, he had stood between Rawneth's son Kenan and lordship. Also, he had developed into an undeniable Shanir who could only live on blood and shunned daylight. Beyond that, those few who had met him declared him to be quiet and rather shy. Also, he was a randon.

"Did you hear what he did in the storage room?" one cadet eagerly asked another. "Several Kendar surprised him there. He flailed one half silly with a half-sack of potatoes, blinded another by slapping him across the face with a salted herring, and pinned a third to the wall with assorted cutlery, including spoons."

"That's nothing. Did you hear that explosion? On the way out, he filled the air with flour from a slit bag and set a spark to it. Then there was the wet noodle fight in the kitchen."

"Why do I get the feeling that he might just be hungry?"

A nervous cadet stepped out of the crowd, holding his jacket wrapped tightly around him.

"That's Gari, a Coman," Char said to Brier as they stood watching from the crowd's edge, as if Brier didn't know. "He binds insects. Now what . . ."

Gari opened his coat. Out flew an emerald swarm of locusts.

The jewel-jaws launched to meet it. Wings whirred and fluttered; legs tangled in mid-air. The 'jaws dropped, wrapped around their prey in struggling bundles. Then they fed. Their wings turned bright green, veined with milky white. What they left, when they rose, were tiny chitinous casings as intricate as toys, sucked dry. Gari sighed and closed his coat.

"What can we learn from that?" one cadet asked another.

"Never bring a bug to a jewel-jaw fight?"

Randiroc turned to go, but paused when a slight cadet emerged from the crowd, nervously wringing her token scarf as if about to choke herself with it.

"Please, ran, my aunt won't come out of the closet. May she have her mask back?"

The weapons-master smiled. Reaching into the shadow of his hood, he withdrew a lacy visor that he apparently had been wearing.

"Oh, thank you!" said the cadet, receiving it.

As her peers craned to see what she held and to wonder at it, Randiroc slipped through their ranks in a flurry of changing wings. A thin, dark girl followed him, her outline also seeming subtly to shift.

"Shade," commented Char. She was their classmate and Lord Randir's daughter, but she was also half Kendar and as such casually dismissed by her house.

"Their mistake," Jamethiel had once said.

It had been well known at Tentir that Shade would have sworn herself to her cousin Randiroc if he had permitted it but how, living as he did, could he support a follower?

"This is the first time that the Heir has been seen in the camp," said Char. "I wonder if he came to visit our guest. Maybe they were at Tentir together."

"Huh," said Brier. "It wouldn't surprise me. Did you stake out his mount in the picket line?"

"See for yourself."

One horse loomed above all others at a good twenty-two hands, a chestnut gelding with blonde mane and tail. As they watched, he ducked his head to snuffle at a snowy, heavily feathered fetlock above an enormous hoof.

"Big," remarked Char. "Not one of our remount herd."

Brier grunted again. "He was at Tentir. She"—no need to say who that was—"rode him into the wilderness one summer solstice but came back without him. 'Chumley' is his name."

The crowd broke up before an approaching senior randon. This individual stopped in front of Brier and attempted to look down his nose at her—not easy, given that she was half a head taller than he.

"The Randon Council requires your attendance. Immediately."

"Well then, ran," said Brier. "I suppose I should go."

II

THE KNORTH CADETS had been quartered at the foot of Gothregor in the mud to demonstrate that they were shown no special favor at the muster. The Council, however, had been given lodgings in the keep itself, on the second floor of the northern barracks, with a common room in which to meet.

Brier hesitated just short of the threshold. Voices spoke within, although from this angle she could only see the Caineron war-leader Sheth Sharp-tongue as he leaned against the wall by the door, an elegant figure in a long coat of black brocade. He glanced at her sideways and flicked a white finger:

Wait.

"Why is he here at all?" demanded a peevish voice, surely belonging to the Coman, currently the commandant of Tentir by rotation. "No one invited him."

"Need they have?" That sounded like the Brandan—Lady Brenwyr's choice, some said, as if there had to be an excuse to choose a woman war-leader. "He's a randon officer too, like you or me, and this is a meeting of family. Everyone who could come, has."

"Surely you don't believe what some say, that this may be the last muster. Things aren't that bad."

"Yet."

"Is Randiroc truly one of us, though?"

This voice was smooth, with a smile in it.

The world is so amusing, it seemed to hint, *for those of us clever enough to appreciate it.*

Brier hadn't heard her speak before, but guessed that this was the new Randir war-commander. The old one, Awl, had died at Urakarn and was sorely missed. No need to wonder if Rawneth had chosen her replacement.

"His collar was bestowed in his absence," that light, mocking voice continued. "Why, he didn't even attend his own graduation."

"Huh." A rough grunt from the Knorth Harn Griphard. "He was on the run by then, chased by the Shadow Guild, and well you know it."

"He threatened his lord."

"You mean that his existence threatened your lady, Rawneth. He was and still is the true Randir heir. Anyway, politics don't affect his randon status, or shouldn't. Then some fool put out the rumor that after so long away he had to prove himself. Now the cadets won't leave him alone."

The Edirr laughed. "Not just the cadets. Did you see that sargent, stripped naked and re-inserted into his clothes backwards, who keeps falling over? No one will help him with his buttons. They just laugh. Then there was that officer suspended by his boot-straps from the catwalk. And the lady who tried to seduce Randiroc, or so I hear. Funny, how all of those were Randir."

"And they were all armed to kill," Sheth added mildly.

"Yes, even the lady. With a razor-edged fan. I understand that he disarmed her and shoved her into a closet."

"It's not amusing!" the Coman burst out. "You Edirr think that everything is a joke. Yes, even raiding our lands, if only for the fun of it! How long before someone gets killed?"

"Now, now," murmured others.

The Coman and the Edirr had been at odds recently more than usual, the latter seeing fit to tweak their neighbors' stuffy noses. Kendar on both sides had hoped that as they matured the Edirr twin lords would settle down. If anything, however, they had grown more outrageous.

From the sound of it, Harn was stomping back and forth over groaning floorboards.

"You fools!" he roared. "Can't you see? Whatever our house politics, we randon are supposed to stand together. What have we to do with politics, especially when dealing with each other?"

The Randir spoke almost gently, as if to soothe an agitated stallion. "Now, now. When has that ever truly been the case, whatever pretty words we preach at Tentir?"

"Commandant, say something!"

Harn had turned to Sheth.

"*I* command the college now." That was the Coman, taking umbrage. Brier realized that he was jealous of both Sheth and Harn, whose reputations so much overshadowed his own. Would anyone address him by the honorific of commandant after his tenure at the college? Probably not. Nonetheless, he blundered on. "Who should speak for Tentir but me?"

"Then speak," said Sheth blandly.

The Coman stuttered. "W-we tell the cadets that the randon are one family to keep them from killing each other. You know how the young Kendar of all houses fight when first thrown together. It's instinctive. There must be discipline."

"Are you saying that we lie to them?"

"No! That is, not exactly."

"'Not exactly,'" mused the Randir, and she could be heard to smile again as if to say, *How naïve some people are*. "Honor and lies. Lies and honor. Sharp-tongue, what is this we hear about your lord going back on two of his three contracts in the Central Lands? We expected to see your troops in the Transweald and the Midlands as well as in Karkinor."

Brier had heard rumors of this upset and had wondered about it as others obviously also did. A contract was one's sworn word, based on one's honor. How could Caldane renege?

Sheth shrugged. "Who am I to speak for my lord? We must have misunderstood the arrangements."

"Did we also misunderstand your lord's comments at the last High Council meeting about his new contracts?" That was the Jaran Jurien, speaking sharply. "Has he truly left out the hidden clause?"

"The what?" asked the Danior, confused.

"Ah, you are too young to know. In the old days, before the White Hills, we always included a clause that forbad the Kings from ordering us to kill each other. There were accidental deaths, of course, and bloodshed, but no mass slaughters. Our scrollsmen saw to that."

"I've always heard that the Kings were free with blood not their own. They agreed to this?"

Jurien laughed. "Mount Alban buried the clause deep in a forest of verbiage. It was different each year, and for each house. The Kings knew it was there, somewhere, but rarely found it until they stumbled across it in practice. A game of wits, if you will. Also, they didn't like to admit that they had been fooled, again, and so were less free with certain demands. That was when we still had some leverage with them."

"And this is what Caldane referred to as a trifle? Why would he leave it out now?"

"Presumably he has his reasons. Mostly, at the Council meeting, he seemed to be striking out at you, Commandant."

Sheth shrugged again, dismissive. "He and I tend to disagree. I must confess, it puzzles me somewhat that I am still his war-leader."

"The bigger the foe, the greater the fall," said the Randir flippantly.

"Perhaps. We are gathered here, however, to discuss another matter, namely the qualifications of the Knorth lordan."

"She isn't here," said a new voice, older, mellow, dismissive. That was the Ardeth Conillion. "What else is there to say?"

"Much, I hope, and here is someone to tell us."

Sheth gestured for Brier to enter. She did, aware that her face had frozen even beyond its usual wooden expression. Her salute to her assembled superiors was stiff and wary.

"Ten-commander Iron-thorn, you have spent a year at Tagmeth under the command of the Knorth Lordan Jamethiel, whom her house sent to learn leadership. What can you tell us?"

Brier felt her mouth go dry. What could she say?

Harn lurched up to her and glowered into her face.

They were of similar height, but he was twice her width and he loomed. "Speak! You and a one-hundred-command were sent into the wilderness, to survive on your own for a year in a half-ruined keep. Did you?"

"Yes, ran, with only a few casualties."

"Well, go on. Obviously, you found food."

Thankfully he didn't ask her how as that would have involved the gates, those portals into different parts of Rathillien. Torisen knew about them. Brier suspected, though, that he didn't want that knowledge to spread, nor did Jame. Her sense was that neither quite knew what to do with them yet.

"There was a yackcarn stampede," she said. "That hunt gave us enough meat to last the winter. The Merikit helped."

"You had dealings with the hill-tribes?" asked the Jaran Jurien, clearly fascinated, his home keep being closer to the hills than any house except the Caineron.

Brier realized that this must be the first most of the Council had heard about Tagmeth except perhaps for vague stories. No wonder they were interested.

"Yes. Jamethiel established a relationship with them."

Sweet Trinity, she had established an entire new family complete with a wife and child, but Brier didn't mention that, not yet being sure what she thought about it herself.

"Marc Long-shanks was with you," said the Danior, a young woman from an old but diminished house, with an equally young lord. "The Merikit slaughtered his entire family at Kithorn. How did he feel about that?"

"He and the Merikit queen made peace."

The Ardeth fastidiously brushed straight his

embroidered sleeves. "The Merikit, after all, are mere savages. Did Jameth maintain discipline?"

"We obeyed her," said Brier, but the thought lurked: *Most of the time*.

What leaped into her mind was her own rebellion about the gates. After all, she had gone off through one of them into the Western Lands on her own, nearly getting her ten-command killed in the process. Jame had saved them. Brier remembered turning on her when they were back at Tagmeth, furious that she had risked herself, being slapped back by that flare of cold berserker rage.

"There are some things that only I can do," Jame had said, almost purring. Brier's spine prickled at the memory. "Remember the old songs. Think of yourself living the worst of them. Certain people stand between you and that fate. I am one of them. Be glad of us."

"Has she learned to delegate responsibilities?"

Had the Ardeth picked up on her hesitation? Brier suddenly felt cold. She could say enough, if she wasn't careful, to damn Jame and ruin Tagmeth. That, especially the latter, was the last thing that she wanted. But she must also be truthful, as a lie was the death of honor.

"She sometimes takes more on herself than she should. Must one always lead from behind?"

"We have often debated that," said Sheth. "Sometimes yes, sometimes no. Did she foster a sense of belonging among her people?"

Autumn's Eve. The Tagmeth garrison had gathered for the annual feast to remember the dead. It had always been a somber affair, but more so in this place so far from home, facing possible starvation in the season to come.

Why were they here, anyway? So that the Highlord's sister could prove herself with their lives? Then Jame had entered, dusting snow from her sleeves. She had looked thoughtfully around the room, meeting their wary eyes with the twitch of a wry smile.

"She remembered all of our names."

And that had won them.

"Did she lead by example?"

That startled a laugh out of the cadet. "To do so, we would have had to be like her. Instead, she let us be ourselves."

"Has she your loyalty?"

Brier's anger returned in a rush. *Betrayal*. If her face could have, it would have darkened. Perhaps it did anyway; they were all staring at her.

Discipline, she told herself, and took a deep breath.

To be fair, she didn't know why Jame had left. There might even have been a good reason (Sweet Trinity, though, what?). There were so many reasons why she should trust her lady, and would have, if only she hadn't been a Highborn.

That thought brought her up short. She had considered such things before, but then had shrugged them off. Now, they returned. Was that all there was to it? Was she simply prejudiced?

"She has earned my loyalty," she heard herself say through stiff lips. "She is loyal to Tagmeth. If she is confirmed as a randon, her brother has promised to let her bind more of us to her service."

A ripple ran through her audience. Backs straightened. Eyes sharpened.

"I told you things would become serious," the Ardeth said, with a disdainful sniff. "We have played this game long enough."

"Is Tentir a game?" barked Harn. "Are our traditions child's play to be out-grown? You agreed to accept this girl as a cadet, female, Highborn, and Shanir though she be. You cast the stones that made her one of us. Would you go back on that now?"

"She is also the Knorth lordan," said the Jaran Jurien. "I support her as such."

"You would," said the Coman with a sneer. "Your house is on the brink of accepting Kirien as your liege-lady. Pardon us if we hesitate to follow your example."

"You can't stop us," said Jurien, unusually blunt for one who, besides being a randon, was also a scrollsman. "You can't stop the Highlord either, if such is his will."

"Besides," said the Danior, waxing pugnacious, "you ask what the Knorth lordan has learned over the past year. What about the Caineron and Ardeth? Gorbel has gotten fat out of sheer boredom. Timmon was given a pretty uniform to serve as a palace guard."

The Ardeth rose, shaking out his sleeves. Perfume puffed from them. "Does either house really expect one of them to become its lord? We have Dari. For that matter, we still have Adric. You Caineron, answer for yourselves. But neither of them is the Highlord's potential heir."

The Edirr stifled a laugh. "Have you considered what will happen if we don't graduate this girl? What can Torisen do but drop her back into the Women's Halls? The Matriarchs barely survived her the first time."

"That," said the Ardeth, "will then be their problem. In the meantime, we need to speak to Torisen. Agreed?"

A mutter answered him, more of a reluctant growl from some. They filed past Brier, out of the room.

Sheth touched her sleeve in passing. "Nice job," he murmured with the glint of a crooked smile. "At least they didn't ask where your lady is."

III

BRIER GAVE THE COUNCIL TIME to get ahead of her, then followed. At the door they turned left and walked purposefully in twos and threes around the inner ward toward the old keep that housed Torisen's quarters. Did they really expect to find him there on such a day as this? At least they skirted the newly planted vegetable garden that the ward had become. Gothregor also had its worries about the coming winter.

Brier turned right and started back toward the campground, not really paying attention. She was still shaken by the discovery of her blind prejudice. Ancestors knew, though, it had been there all this time, her constant companion. How could she not have noticed? Brier Iron-thorn didn't consider herself clever, but she also didn't think that she was stupid. How could an emotion twine itself so deeply into her being that it had remained virtually invisible? Had she been duped by mere feelings?

Then too, it was the Caineron who had abused her for most of her life, not the Knorth. Torisen had offered her an escape. Jame had offered a home. Now, perhaps—oh, bitter thought—she had thrown both away.

A familiar figure emerged from the western barracks—short for a Kendar, tow-headed, clad in a cadet's coat.

Brier cut across the garden without even noticing it and grabbed Rue by the jacket.

"Where is she? Where have you been?"

Rue blinked up at the Southron. Her face was wan, her eyes bruised with exhaustion. "We went. We came back. Can't tell you where, ten. She will, if she wants to."

Brier barely restrained herself from shaking the girl. "Where is she now?"

"In the old barracks. We slipped in before dawn. She's barely slept in six days, or has it been seven? Don't wake her."

Brier looked hard at Rue, who appeared to be half-asleep herself. "What about you?"

"Oh, I slept some, but not since we left Tagmeth—was that just yesterday? It was a wild ride through the folds in the land, over two hundred miles in a night." Rue shuddered, eyes momentarily unfocussed, then shook herself. "Must see to my post pony. Death's-head is around somewhere, probably terrorizing the local poultry."

With that, she wobbled off.

What old barracks? Oh, of course, where Jame's ten-command had been quartered last year, from whose door Rue had just emerged.

Brier stormed in. On the ground floor were the rows of empty beds (what, they couldn't have slept here instead of in the mud?). At the end of hall was a room, sectioned off.

Brier stopped short in the doorway.

Jame lay curled up on the bed. She was fully clothed and shod, boots shedding mud on top of the blanket. Her stiff garments looked as if they had molded, wet, to her form, and there had partly dried. Black hair straggled across her pale face, its fringe stirred by the deep breath of *dwar* sleep. Other than that, never before had she appeared so unnaturally still.

Brier stared down at her. Hands opened, hands closed.

Suddenly she became aware that Torisen was sitting on a chair next to the bed, watching her. He also looked exhausted.

"Neither of us could sleep," he said, speaking very softly. "Long days, longer nights. But I am more experienced at this game than she is."

"Do you know . . ."

"I don't. She will tell me—us—when she is ready. Will you trust her?"

Hands shut. Hands opened.

"Yes," said her gruff, grudging voice.

"Good."

Brier cleared her throat. "The Randon Council is looking for you. They heard that you mean to let her bind more Kendar."

He rubbed his eyes. Despite the white threading his hair and beard, he looked very young, very vulnerable.

"Oh. That is . . . unfortunate. I should meet them, I suppose." He started to rise, faltered, and sank back. "But maybe not quite yet."

Brier left them both fallen again into sleep, breathing as one.

As she paused on the barrack's threshold, she saw the Randon Council coming back from the keep. It hadn't taken them long, it seemed, to discover that the Highlord wasn't in his quarters. Where would they look next? Then, as one, they paused. Someone had emerged from the gatehouse onto the verge of the inner ward. He was stocky, but not as tall as a Kendar. Moreover, his coat was finer than most that Kendar wore. He saw the Council, and his face split into a wide, white-toothed grin that identified him: Tiggeri, Lord Caineron's youngest established son, last seen by Brier when he had besieged Tagmeth, and after that at an improbable breakfast.

Someone emerged to stand unsteadily behind him, surreptitiously raising a cider jug to drink as he did so. Fash had been a randon cadet but had given it up on the eve of his promotion to serve a new master—one, he thought, who could offer him more. Now, it seemed, he had made it to the muster after all.

But what was either Highborn doing at Gothregor on this of all days? Traditionally, those who weren't randon stayed away out of respect except for the Highlord, who acted as host.

"Hello, hello!" Tiggeri cried, with a cheerful wave.

The Council awaited his coming drawn up in stiff, unresponsive ranks.

IV

AFTERNOON dwindled toward evening.

Clatter and cheerful talk arose from the kitchen as

cooks set about preparing for that night's feast. Even with all available hands at work, though, Gothregor could never have fed everyone. These days it strained to supply its own garrison augmented as it was by those troops returning from service at Kothifir. And now the keep hosted some one thousand extra guests. Most of the other houses had sent supplies with their randon to be prepared in mobile kitchens for daily use. Tonight, however, would be a communal feast for which both the keep and the camp made ready. Moreover, there were spaces to prepare in the empty, half-ruined halls behind the old keep, behind the Women's World, which in better days had housed a much more prosperous Knorth. Fire now bloomed there in pits, and haunches of meat began to turn—beef, pork, venison, yackcarn. The savor of roasting wafted over broken walls, into the ward, down the hill. Cadets below sniffed, then continued to wander about the camp, nervously chatting.

They wouldn't know until that night whether they had graduated or not. Most did, they reassured each other, but there were occasional exceptions.

"I hear that this time our houses decide who passes and who doesn't," a Brandan remarked to an Ardeth. "Well, it makes sense. We have to be useful to our lords. Presumably they've had their eyes on us all of this time."

They both glanced side-ways at the Ardeth lordan, Timmon, as he passed by in a cloud of glory made visible by a glimmering coat of silver and gold thread.

"Would your lord deny him?" asked the Brandan.

The Ardeth turned up his nose.

"D'you mean Adric or his grandson Dari?" asked the

Caineron, looking snide. "They say that Adric has gone as soft as a rotten peach. Dari rules in all but name. What time d'you think he has for his precious, fancy-pants cousin?"

"For all of that," said the Brandan, "Timmon is one of us. He proved himself at Kothifir during the Karnid invasion. For that matter, what of Gorbel?"

The Caineron turned huffy. "He proved himself there too, even if his lord father can't stand the sight of him. The Commandant likes him, though."

He meant Sheth Sharp-tongue. Even the cadets tended to overlook their current Coman superior, which infuriated him.

"But then Sheth also favors the Knorth lordan," said the Ardeth, "and where is she? His credit is at stake here too."

The sun set. Cadets began to drift up the steep stair to the keep, drawn by tantalizing smells. Surely it was the first watch of the night by now, which began at sunset, but no signal had yet been given. Where were their officers? Had the feast started without them? Was this another test, as if to say "Are you too stupid to find your next meal?" They filed onto the walks surrounding the garden that was the inner ward. Here were the gates on either side of the old keep that opened onto the Women's World. No man was said to be welcome there and, besides, what dire sorceries might brew within? But how else did one pass into the empty halls beyond?

"You go first, lordan."

"No, you. It's your keep, after all, and you're female."

"How nice of you to notice."

That was Timmon speaking to the Knorth Mint, with whom he had absentmindedly been flirting, to the distress of her partner Dar.

"Oh, for Ancestors' sake," said the Knorth cadet Damson, and stumped through the gate.

Small masked faces peered down at her from the classroom windows above like a school of guppies. Such young girls, brought here from eight houses to be molded into proper ladies. Jame, the sole surviving female of the ninth house, was said to have given them collective fits.

"Well?" said Damson, glaring up at them.

They withdrew. A face, or rather an eyeless mask, seemed to float up out of the gloom within as if out of dark water. Hands rose in welcome, gesturing her forward. Damson took it to be a general invitation.

"Come on," she said to the others. They edged in on her heels, by instinct forming into defensive ten-commands as they passed.

Beyond the maintained halls, the watching eyes, was a wilderness of roofless ruins. Could there ever really have been so many Knorth? Yes, although all who had lived here had been Kendar. Then nearly every lady had been slain by Shadow Assassins in the north-eastern mural quarters now called the Ghost Walks and their lords had gone to their deaths in the White Hills. Some cadets found this open desolation unsettling. Others were reassured that Torisen Blacklord felt strong enough to display his family's weakness.

Here was an inner courtyard surrounded by flaring torches with three trestle tables set up down its length and one at the far end, across its eastern head. No one yet sat.

Opening off of it were nine roofless halls within which firepits blazed, each tended by the randon of a different house with choice provisions brought from home, each trying to out-do the others. They were laid out according to the barracks at Tentir, three by three by three, also according to the old keep's High Council chamber, or so said those who had seen it: Randir, Coman, and Caineron to the north; Jaran, Knorth, and Ardeth to the west; Brandan, Edirr, and Danior to the south. Cadets scattered each to their own house's fire where their officers waited.

Timmon and Gorbel hesitated on the yard's threshold.

"Well," said the former to the latter. "Here we are, already divided."

"Huh. Be reasonable. There are over seven hundred of us in this class alone. Did you think the Council would call us up one at a time to collect our collars?"

"How many d'you think will be assigned to the Central Lands?"

"A lot. The Seven Kings are setting up a mill fit to grind us all to pieces."

Timmon shuffled uneasily. "You say such things, but do you know? Does anyone?"

"Call it a hunch."

Someone cleared her throat behind them. They turned to face a slim young woman with hair ornately braided in the Merikit style, wearing a white, lacy court coat into which a diary of her days at Tentir had been stitched, except for the ugly repair of a weld in the back where Killy had tried to stab her. Not all of her college memories were pleasant.

"What have I missed?" asked Jame.

V

"YOU LOOK AWFUL," Gorbel said, peering at her.

"Such kind words. Not as bad as I must have merited a few hours ago, though. *Dwar* sleep is a wonderful thing. And no, I won't tell you where I've been."

Timmon grinned. "You're here now. That's the main thing."

Jame regarded him thoughtfully. He seemed more relieved to see her than she would have expected. Timmon had always been haphazard in his attention to duty, putting his pleasure first, but since she had known him he had started to pay more attention. It hadn't previously occurred to her that he might be taking his cue from her, and maybe in part from Gorbel. At least, her absence seemed to have rattled him.

"I like your coat," she said, brushing the gold and silver threadwork with gloved fingertips. "Gorbel, you seem to decorate with gravy stains."

The Caineron slapped his bulging belly. "Too much food, too little work. An end to that soon, eh? Well, see you at the feast, assuming we all make the cut."

He tramped off, turning left toward the Caineron's designated hall where Sheth waited for him on the threshold.

"Conillion should be as glad to greet me," said Timmon with a wry smile. "See you later, I hope."

Jame turned right along the court's western side toward her own house's temporary camp.

Within the ruined hall, firelight flared against stark walls pierced with darkening, empty windows. There was the pit, there cadets throwing logs under a huge, dripping carcass. Yackcarn. Again. Tagmeth had lived on the spoils of that hunt all winter, preserved by the Merikit queen's little bag of spices. It would be a novelty here, though. There were also roasting vegetables and fresh sliced fruit, totally out of season for the Riverland. Brier had brought a good assortment from the gates, more than Jame might have risked. She wondered, yet again, how the Kencyrath could best make use of such bounty. It had served Tagmeth well, but come winter other keeps might lack even the basics. She and Torisen needed to talk.

The Tagmeth cadets gathered around her, their relief evident. Rue was there too, still looking dazed. Something stirred a tremor of unease deep in Jame's heart, something to do with water, but she shoved it away as others from Tentir also approached if a bit more hesitantly. They hadn't seen Jame in a year. Some had begun to question their college experiences as stories had grown about them.

Brier loomed up against the flames.

"You came," she said gruffly.

"As you see. Sorry I'm late."

"You're here now," said the Kendar, in grudging acceptance, unconsciously echoing Timmon. "That's all that matters."

Jame felt her eyebrows rise. If Brier had really brought herself to believe that....

"We have an unexpected guest," the Kendar said, gesturing aside.

Turning, Jame first saw the shambling bulk of Harn, then someone behind him even larger.

"Bear? He came with you?"

"Yes. On Chumley. From just south of Tagmeth. This muster has drawn all sorts of people. Randiroc is here too."

Grease spattered on coals. Trenchers baked, steaming, on flat rocks around the firepit. Jame heard her stomach growl. She couldn't remember when she had last eaten. Oh yes: in the saddle, before . . . before . . .

Harn clapped his hands. "Time to get started. Gather around."

Beside him was a rack thick with silver collars reflecting red firelight, enough to have kept Knorth craftsmen busy all winter. From most hung a small enameled plaque representing graduation from the randon college at Tentir. Others in addition sported a pendant for service at Kothifir. There were more emblems as well related to individual third year cadets, including one for Tagmeth. All were modest affairs, as befitted newly minted officers. Harn himself wore a heavy collar densely hung with the honors of a lifetime, all chiming together as he moved.

One by one, he called forward the cadets, lifted the appropriate award, and clamped it around each neck while their mates cheered and craned, looking for their own among what remained. There seemed to be no order to these presentations, no way to tell if one's place had been bypassed ignobly without comment.

Rue was called forth. So were stone-faced Brier and a flushed Char.

The last cadets watched with growing apprehension,

including Jame, until only one collar remained. Harn picked it up.

That must be mine, thought Jame, surprised at how dry her mouth had gone. If so, three years of hard work had gone into this moment.

"This," said Harn, "is for our one-hundred commander and lordan, with thanks for not getting us all killed."

The ranks answered with applause and nervous laughter, some clearly asking themselves, *What, we came so close?*

"Jamethiel Priest's-bane, stand forth."

The shadows behind him moved. Bear emerged also to grip the collar with the tips of his massive claws. Four big hands fumbled over the slender silver band. Would they shatter it between them? Jame touched Harn's arm.

"Please, ran, this is my Senethari. Let him."

Harn scowled down at her, nodded grudgingly, and let go.

"You taught me the Arrin-thar," she said, looking up into Bear's hirsute face, "and that claws don't make a monster."

He stood there turning the collar over in his hands, inspecting it. Firelight tinged his gray hair as it tumbled down into the crevasse in his skull left by an axe in the White Hills. They had put him on the pyre. Then his younger brother Sheth had seen him move in the flames and had pulled him out. Jame remembered first meeting him in his cramped, noisome quarters at Tentir where he had become known to generations of cadets as the Monster in the Maze, then again later in the Pit where he had taught her how to use the Shanir attribute of which, for so long, she had been ashamed. At length he had escaped and come to Tagmeth which, bemused, had taken him in.

He fumbled with the collar's clasp. Like Torisen's Kenthiar, the circlet was hinged on one side. Belatedly Jame wondered if, like that other dire collar, it would defend itself against the unworthy. The snap closed around her neck. Bear grunted.

"My heart," he said, then roughly cleared a throat unaccustomed to speech and spoke again. "My heart is full."

He backed up in a stunned silence, turned, and shambled away.

Jame stared after him. Was she dreaming, or had the cleft in his skull begun to close?

He had ridden in on Chumley. Did that mean that he had met the Earth Wife, to whom she had given that enormous beast? Mother Ragga was many things. A healer too, perhaps?

The tension snapped. Former cadets, with a cheer, broke for the food and carried heaping trenchers out into the courtyard. The Danior already waited, seated at the middle table, and greeted their Knorth cousins boisterously.

Not long afterward the Coman and the Edirr emerged. These went to the northern and southern extremes of the yard, glowering across it at each other. The Jaran joined the middle.

Then there was a pause. No one felt like starting without the others, however hungry they were, especially with the high table still empty.

The Brandan went to the middle; the Randir, to the Coman. The Ardeth, drawn by Timmon, drifted toward the Knorth. Finally, the last and largest house appeared, Gorbel first, wearing his new collar. He joined Jame and Timmon. His house, however, split, some backing their lordan, others edging uncertainly toward the Randir and Coman. Now that, thought Jame, was about as clear a picture of Riverland politics as one was likely to get, their college bond be dammed.

Randiroc slipped into a seat at the foot of the middle table, Shade a ghost on his heels. Everyone ignored them both.

Finally, just in time to avert rebellion among the hungry cadets, the Randon Council took their seats at the high table. Besides the nine there were two guests—the Highlord and Tiggeri, with Fash standing in attendance behind the latter. Last to appear, to the chagrin of many, was Bear. His brother made room for him so that he settled with a grunt between Sheth and Tiggeri, shoving them both farther apart. Tiggeri did not look pleased, but he also didn't flinch.

Jame remembered, watching him askance, how Caldane's son had attacked Bear at Tagmeth, alone, armed only with a boar spear. As little as she liked Tiggeri, she had to admit that he was brave.

Sheth rose. His collar, if anything, surpassed Harn's with awards and formed a glittering breast-plate against the somber field of his black coat. It seemed wrong that the Coman and not he wore the commandant's white scarf. Still, he ranked highest on the Council.

"Fellow randon," he said, spreading his hands.

"Welcome to these tables and to our ranks. May you serve both well."

The former cadets laughed. Many of them were still absorbing their new rank after the uncertainties of the day. It seemed that everyone had passed after all.

"Well, we would have to, wouldn't we?" a Danior asked a Jaran, wise in hindsight. "After all, it would embarrass the randon to fail us at this point."

"It may be that we face dark days," said Sheth, "but now is not the time to consider that. Eat. Drink. Rejoice. Tomorrow is another day."

He spread his hands as if in invitation and resumed his seat. Attendants ran to supply each of the Council and their guests with the best that each house had to offer. Shade served Randiroc, who seemed bemused by the attention. The new randon officers noticed where the servers went. More than a few slipped off to gather special tidbits from neighboring fires while they lasted. The Knorth hall was soon crowded.

"Was it wise," Gorbel asked Jame, "to be so free?"

Jame cursed herself and Rue, who had served the Caineron fresh figs during his recent visit to Tagmeth. Timmon looked blank. Could it be that he hadn't noticed the gates' bounty when he also had been a guest? Now everyone with any wits would be talking.

Tiggeri rose, smiling. "Ahem."

At first, no one paid attention. Fash reached around him and smashed a glass. Before he could draw back, Bear caught him by the wrist. Fash twisted, trying to break free, failing. His master ignored him. So did Bear, except to maintain his iron grip.

"Thank you all for this hospitality," said Tiggeri with an expansive opening of his arms as if to embrace the entire assembly. "So many bright faces. So much hope. Your lords will be proud of you, no doubt. For the first time in decades, you will be going back to the Central Lands as proud representatives of your individual houses, and I include here my own. Hello, Cainerons!"

Fash lost his balance and fell, his arm still trapped in mid-air. He thrashed about, futilely prying at Bear's fingers.

"This will be a special time for us all," Tiggeri continued, ignoring the commotion beside him, "and not just a series of bloodless, boring war-games. There used to be a practice of writing in a secret clause to prevent you from fully proving yourselves. This year, there was even a competition at the scrollsman's college to write the cleverest one and a panel to judge it. I ask you, which do warriors need more, brains or bravery? My lord father didn't think this was fair, either to your employers or to you. When he happened to find out what the clauses were, for all nine houses, he generously shared that information with the Kings and left it up to them to decide what to do with it. The White Hills showed them what we are capable of. Will they abide by such cowardly restraints now? What do you think?"

His smile had grown into a bearing of wet, white teeth and gleaming eyes. "This time, oh brave children—I mean, of course, oh brave officers—you will earn your pay."

The Council had listened to this, appalled, but it was Torisen who spoke, quietly:

"Why would Caineron do such a thing? He puts his own troops at risk too."

Tiggeri grinned at him. "Oh, he was well paid for it. I

understand that the Kings will pay less the longer you lords mull this over. Of course, you don't have to sign the new contracts at all."

"Yes, and starve come winter," growled Harn.

Tiggeri shrugged. "As you wish."

The former cadets were murmuring. Most of them had never heard of these clauses before, and they had expected to go into a dangerous profession. Why was the Council so upset?

"Look at it this way," said Jame. "You might die, yes, but you might also be asked to kill each other."

Friend looked at friend, from table to table, from house to house.

"Oh," said someone.

"You can let go now," Sheth said to Bear.

Bear did, looking surprised to find Fash still in his grip. Fash stumbled back. He drew a knife, but the attendants on either side seized him before he could stab Bear in the back.

"You embarrass me," said Tiggeri over his shoulder. "Come back when you have learned some manners."

Fash floundered away. Obviously he was very drunk.

"Well, that was informative," said Timmon. "Is that what the Commandant meant, about dark days?"

"I should think so," Jame said. "Gorbel, I heard you and Timmon talking. You had some idea this was coming, didn't you?"

"I do my homework. What, you don't?"

"Tori may never have heard about these hidden articles. Remember, he came to power years after the White Hills."

Timmon pouted. "And what chance have I had to learn? Cousin Dari doesn't take me seriously about anything."

Gorbel glowered at him. "You have to make him. D'you think my father confides in me? I learn what I can the hard way, like tearing flesh off a yackcarn's sour flank."

Fash wandered past between the tables, between worlds. He tried to look down his nose at the feasters, once his companions, but only succeeded in looking lost. No one called for him to join them, not even among his own house. Jame almost felt sorry for him, until she remembered the knife in his hand behind Bear's back.

At the foot of the tables, Randiroc suddenly broke into a rare laugh, perhaps at something that Shade had said.

Fash jerked as if slapped, and his pale face flushed. The knife was in his hand again.

"Don't you dare laugh at me!" he screamed, and started running.

Jame found herself on her feet, close on his heels. Anger flared: The attendants had seen his state of mind. Why hadn't they disarmed him?

Randiroc and Shade saw him coming. They rose.

The Randir Heir slipped past Fash's charge with a wind-blowing move and stood aside, looking bemused, as his assailant stumbled past. He touched his chest, white fingertips coming away red. The blade had slashed through his hunting leathers, cutting skin. Even a master, the saying went, should fear the instability of a drunkard. Shade stood aside, a ward against interference; so she must have done all day, trusting the Heir to fight his own battles. Fash staggered, recovered himself, and came back.

Randiroc threw pepper in his face.

Fash careened into the nearest table, occupied by Caineron who scrambled out of his way. He rubbed furiously at his streaming eyes. Beyond were the Coman and the Randir, several on their feet.

"Help me!" he cried to all three houses. "This is your enemy too!"

They hesitated. Some Randir had been attacking the Heir all day, but never in the open. Now the rest faced the same choice that the Caineron had at Tagmeth when called on by Tiggeri to kill Bear, house loyalty against randon honor. No one moved.

"I don't understand you people!" Fash cried in frustration.

Sheth Sharp-tongue had risen at the head table. "That is evident," he said. "Go."

Fash bared his teeth and swung wildly on Randiroc. Jame stood in his way. As he lunged, she caught his arm and threw him. He landed in a heap and didn't get up. It soon became clear that he had fallen on his own knife.

"I'm sorry," said Jame, rising from his body. "I was clumsy."

"Just as well," growled Harn, sitting down again with a thump. "He would never have made a good randon."

VI

"IT WAS AN ACCIDENT," Jame said later that night to Torisen in his tower study. Muffled singing came to them from the courtyard to the keep's rear, around many corners:

"We faced the foe in classrooms dire.
On lesson fields did oft we meet.
Who stood by you in winter's fire?
Contrarywise, who stood by me?"

"I should have pulled his arm clear of his body as he fell," said Jame, turning a shoulder to the song. She knew very well where Fash had stood.

"'Some things need to be broken,'" said her brother, quoting something she oft had said.

"Well, yes. Like Harn, I don't greatly mourn him. He supplied Merikit skins to furnish Caldane's apartments, you know. So, what happens next?"

On went the song:

"Then on we went to battles new
In southern climes or on the steppe.
The Karnids came, we battled same.
Contrarywise, who stood by you?"

Torisen restlessly stirred the message scrolls piled high on his desk. "These do mount up," he said. "I've finally read through yours from the past year, though, put aside when I thought that I was dying. You suggest that the gates might help us in future. How certain is that?"

Jame adjusted herself in the visitor's rarely used chair. "Well, the potential is there. We already have access to an oasis, orchards, and grasslands. Fish too, if we ever get the knack of building boats, or even of baiting hooks. Then there are gates not yet opened and gates within gates, not yet explored. A lot of Rathillien seems to be unoccupied. At least, that's where the gates lead so far."

"You haven't met any residents?"

Jame shifted uneasily. "Every time we open a new area, we send out scouts to look for neighbors. So far we haven't found any, which is rather odd. I wonder if the original architects somehow staked claims that nobody else has yet contested."

"By said architects, I take it that you don't mean our mysterious Builders."

"Not primarily. They got the idea from Rathillien natives who came before and, frankly, did a much better job. Our Builders' oasis colony might still help, though, moving forward, especially if they can regain control over their pet trocks."

"What will you do if you find someone who's since laid claim to these lands?"

"Try to make friends, I suppose, and establish trade. It could get messy, though, if we end up competing for the same resources. In short, I don't know. What we need right now are more Kendar to develop whatever we find. These lands have lain fallow for a long time."

"You mean, we can't count on this for the coming winter."

"No."

He sighed. "Too bad. That leaves us with Caldane's betrayal and the kings' ultimatum."

The song continued, plaintive now:

"New foes, new lands, now do we seek,
Our lords to please, in worth our trust.

But doubt stands forth within our ranks.
Contrarywise, who stands by us?"

"Huh," said Jame, listening. "Good question. What will you do?"

"I'm thinking about it. At worst, I accede, send Harn, and hope that he can keep us from disaster for the coming year. Another White Hills' debacle would shatter us. Sheth will work with him, I think, but they will be on opposite sides of the Silver. Then too, the Kings are unpredictable. As Tiggeri said, it took Ganth's madness to show them what we were capable of. They've played at war through us for millennia. After thirty years of abstinence, what might they not ask?"

"What do you want me to do?"

"I agree that we should develop the gates. That will take Kendar who might otherwise have gone south to earn us winter wages. It's too early, though, to invite the other houses to participate."

"I agree," said Jame, who was already having nightmare visions of Tagmeth overrun by strangers. "About having me bind more Kendar . . ."

"First, tell me what happened to Rue."

Jame blinked. A nervous tremor returned to the core of her being.

"Who . . . what . . ." she stammered, and stopped.

Water.

"I met her before I saw you," he said, patient, inexorable. "Before even that, there was a shudder in the bond between us. I also felt that when you bound Brier at Kothifir. This time. . . ."

"I'm beginning to remember." Jame rose and started to pace the small room, three steps one way, three steps back, arms clasped around her. "We had ridden all night, after days awake. I was nearly done in. Death's-head stopped halfway across a creek near Gothregor to drink. I-I groped for the food sack, and then I was in the water. I'd tumbled out of the saddle, asleep, and there I was face down, drowning, in barely a foot deep. I woke up on the bank. Rue was bending over me. She must have dragged me out."

"That's not so bad," said Torisen.

"You don't understand. In my mind, I was still drowning. I couldn't breathe. I panicked and grabbed her. She was there. Her strength drew me. I think she expected to be bound. That, she might have welcomed. Instead, I nearly ripped out her soul. That's what demons do. I was just in Tai-tastigon. I saw it happen."

"You were in the Eastern Lands?"

"Yes, by way of the gates. I have friends there who were in trouble."

"Oh. Well, that explains everything. Have you ever fed on Graykin or Brier?"

"No," she said, glaring at him. "Have you on your own people?"

"Never. Whatever else I am, that doesn't seem to be part of my Shanir nature."

"But is it part of mine?"

Jame continued to pace, more and more agitated.

"Understand: Brier and Gray both came to me; so did Jorin and Death's-head. Their need drove them, not mine. I gave. They took. This time, it would have been my choice to take. Tai-tastigon taught me that the one unforgivable sin is to prey on another's soul. The Master does. So does Perimal Darkling itself, on the essence of entire worlds. It's the main trait that defines a demon."

She didn't put into words what worried her most: Was that what she was becoming as she edged toward That-Which-Destroys, whatever her god's intent? Had she been a demon, in embryo, all along, thanks to her tainted blood and darkling training? Trinity, think of all the times she had nearly used the Great Dance to reap a soul, but not quite. Was that what she had nearly done to Rue now?

Torisen seemed to be thinking along similar lines. "If you might hurt Kendar, there can be no question of you binding more of them voluntarily," he said, and his voice was that of the Highlord, implacable. "They are too vulnerable. At the very least, we owe them protection."

"I know that," Jame snapped, then bit her tongue. After this, who was she to chide him?

He blinked, as if waking. "Of course you know," he said, in a gentler tone. "What we both need is more sleep. At least I do. Tomorrow we will make plans." A wry smile cracked his weary lips. "To ask questions, eh?"

⟨⟨⟨ Chapter II ⟩⟩⟩
Days of Summer
The Riverland: Summer 5–63

I

Summer 5

FOUR DAYS AFTER THE MUSTER, the Highlord of the Kencyrath walked at dusk in Gothregor's apple orchard. White blossoms tinged with pink cascaded around him, clinging to his shoulders, carpeting the ground at his feet. Through the mass of fallen petals gnarled tree roots surfaced here and there like the backs of so many subterranean serpents. His boots stirred subtle hints of decay from last year's windfalls. From overhead, however, fragrance drifted down and bees hummed, heavy with pollen. Hopefully, come winter, there would be a good supply of hard cider. Other crops were usually less bountiful.

At least, thought Torisen gloomily, *as long as the cider lasts, we can always get drunk.*

With longing, he considered Tagmeth's gates and what

might pass through them. It would be such an elegant solution to so many of his problems, but Jame was right: first the land must be cultivated beyond her keep's narrow needs.

Blossoms swirled. Through them came his sister, darkness emerging from the glimmer of twilight. Why had they both chosen to favor black clothing? At least it suited Jame. True, she was too thin, but she carried herself with such supple grace that one hardly noticed. His servant Burr, ever tactful, claimed that it made him look gaunt and gloomy. Blacklord, indeed, and "Blackie" to his friends.

"Hello," said Jame. "Are you pleased to have Gothregor back to yourself?"

If only that were true.

The last randon had departed the previous day to consult with their lords about the lost safeguards and the new contracts which they expected to arrive momentarily. Indeed, that very afternoon the Kings' representative had appeared at Gothregor. His visit seemed timed to take advantage of the confusion sown by Tiggeri's announcement, and his choice of the Highlord's keep first deliberate. If Torisen signed, after all, the other lords would have little course but to follow his example. So far, Torisen had put off seeing him, wanting one last chance to think through possible alternatives. Soon, however, he must make up his mind.

"About the gates," he said, to forestall the evil hour. "I've talked to my husbandry-men."

"Discreetly, I hope."

"Of course. It wouldn't do to raise false hopes."

"And Restormir is Tagmeth's nearest neighbor. Can you imagine how Caldane would react if he were to hear of such a temptation? Luckily, Tiggeri didn't notice anything the last time he came to call. I don't want the Caineron descending on us again."

"Of course not," said Torisen with a shudder. Given the chance, Caldane would happily rape his way across all Rathillien if he believed that it was to his benefit. "In terms of preparation, it helps that you've already been getting reports from Farmer Fen. His opinion, you tell me, is that it will take at least a year to put the land you've already discovered into heart. My Kendar agree. I propose an initial force of one hundred with tools, livestock, and provisions. The man to lead it, I think, is a Kendar named Rush. At least I hear good things about his determination. In the meantime, the Riverland will just have to survive. Do you still plan to leave tomorrow?"

"Yes. I need to get back to Tagmeth, especially if you're about to send us reinforcements. Also, Trishien has requested our escort back to Valantir."

That surprised and dismayed him. Just to have the Jaran Matriarch at Gothregor had been reassuring as she was the only senior lady to whom he felt he could turn for advice.

"I understand that the Jedrak has recalled her for consultations," said Jame, looking at him warily, askance. "You hadn't heard?"

"No."

And he should have.

Trishien was his guest, after all, and he her host as he was to the entire Women's World—not that many

Highborn ladies chose to remember that. Most of them considered part of Gothregor to be their exclusive property, as often as the Jaran Matriarch corrected them.

Moreover, this sudden news reminded him of a conversation several days ago in his study when Jame had chided him for not keeping better track of current events.

"Haven't you forgiven Burr yet for spying on you for Adric?" she had asked.

Burr had been working in the room at the time, pretending not to listen. After all, Torisen told himself, he could hardly order his servant to be deaf.

"Of course I have," he had said. "You know that, Burr, don't you?"

"Of course I do," Burr had replied, with a blank face.

"Then it's Lord Ardeth whom you continue to blame," Jame had said, and he had known that she was right.

He now turned toward her, glowering. "I still decline to use spies. What, should I employ someone like your precious Graykin?"

She grimaced. "Gray can be a pain, but he learns things. You could too, if you just asked questions. For instance, did you know that quite a few ladies are leaving? They say that they don't feel safe here anymore."

That came as a second jolt. All winter Torisen had had the sense of things slipping away, but then he had been deathly ill with lung-rot and had expected to die. Now, cured, was it any better?

"How is Rue?" he asked abruptly.

Jame blinked at the change of topic.

"The same," she said, "as the last time you asked. I didn't hurt her, Ancestors be praised. Death take me, darkness break me, if I ever do. She, Brier, and Marc could be the Kendar rolled up as one. How does Rue feel? I'm not sure."

Did Torisen believe her? His father no longer muttered behind the door in his soul-image—that door, in fact, now stood unnervingly open—but it was hard to dismiss a lifetime of instilled prejudice. Was it part of her Shanir nature to prey on others, as she had half suggested? Could she even help it? Yes, he loved her, but the fact remained: she was dangerous.

"Nonetheless," he said, more harshly than he had intended, "I don't want you to bind anyone else."

"So you said before."

He began to pace, impatient with himself as much as with her. Why did their conversations always turn so prickly?

"Has it ever occurred to you," he said over his shoulder, "that the whole idea of binding is just . . . wrong? Since I drove our father out of my soul-image, I have more scope there, but I don't want to use it to bind more Kendar. I just don't."

She had bridled at his tone. Now she looked thoughtful. "How long have you felt this way?"

"Oh, for quite a while, I suppose, but I didn't question it. That was just the way things were. Now you say that I may be turning into That-Which-Creates. I don't feel especially creative, except for random outbreaks of mold or thistles, but I am . . . dissatisfied. So much is wrong in the Kencyrath. So much needs to change."

"Now you sound like me. I think, though, that it's easier to break than to make."

Someone was approaching. Bright patches of color showed through the blossoms, jarring flashes of crimson and orange. A hand batted away falling petals and bumbling bees. The face that emerged was dark and vaguely familiar.

"Ah, there you are, Highlord," said the agent of the Seven Kings with a bland smile. What was his name? Oh, yes: Malapirt. "Your servants really should have told you that I had arrived."

"They did."

"So blunt. One might almost say, so rude, but we of the south are an understanding people. I have brought the new contracts for you to sign."

Torisen ignored the scroll presented to him.

"Your presence puzzles me," he said. "Traditionally, the Knorth serve at High Bashti's court. Prince Uthecon of Karkinor is your master, is he not?"

"Yes." Malapirt waved more bees away from his face, which they seemed to find attractive. Close up, it was apparent that he wore a rather strong floral perfume. "This year, though, once we discovered your little . . . er . . . game, their highnesses convened to write a new joint contract. I am the common emissary of Bashti, Hathor, and all the countries which they have become, including Karkinor."

"I recognize you now," said Jame, who had been staring at him. "You were here last Summer's Eve, come to collect Lyra Lack-wit."

He gave a start, pretending to notice her for the first time. "Ah, lady, pardon me. I did not recognize you with your clothes on."

Jame blinked, then smiled.

Dangerous, Torisen thought again.

"I'm usually wearing something," she said pleasantly, "if only sleeping ribbons. As I recall, you tried to kidnap me."

He bowed. "Oh, lady, I would not aspire so high. You were merely where we expected to find the princess. She will soon reach my prince through other means."

Jame looked momentarily taken aback. "I didn't know that. So her father has agreed to a new contract after all."

"She was, let us say, a cardinal clause of our general agreement. If you should wish to follow her example, something might be arranged. My prince has a nephew. Rumors that he is imbecilic and diseased are, no doubt, greatly exaggerated."

He slapped at more bees. They were beginning to swarm.

"Respectfully, I decline that honor. Please remind your prince: Lyra's father may have signed her away yet again, but she still has powerful friends. We will be watching."

He bowed yet again. "I have no doubt. My lord, the contract?"

Torisen had accepted and unrolled it, reading as the other two talked. "In the morning," he said, letting it curl up on itself. "I want to go over this more closely."

"As you wish. Remember, though: the longer you delay, day by day, the less it is worth."

"Huh," said Jame, watching him go, trailing bees, stumbling over roots. "The last time, you shouldn't have ordered him out of the Riverland by sunset. Fifty miles in a day. He isn't likely to forget that anytime soon."

"Let him remember. In the meanwhile, I have until tomorrow to see if there's anything in this precious contract of his that will help us."

"You saw something?"

"A glimpse. Maybe a glimpse."

II

Summer 10

QUARRELS at Mount Alban had festered ever since the Jaran randon had brought back the dire news about the contracts days before. Voices hissed from landing to landing up and down the wooden stair well that climbed the college's spine within the cliff face. Inkwells were thrown, quills hurled like darts, and books flew. Doors slammed against the assault, then were thrown open again to emit further heated rejoinders:

"You scrollsmen think you're so smart," someone jeered down the stairs. "You should have listened to us singers!"

"What," said a voice below, "and have used the Lawful Lie? I can just imagine how that would have worked."

"You begged us for poetic language!" shrilled another voice.

"Yes, to make the clauses more confusing. D'you think we came to you for sense?"

"Arrgh!"

Slam. Splat. Thud. Creak.

On a landing halfway down a tiny old singer confronted

a looming scrollsman and jabbed her forefinger into his stomach.

"It's a Trinity-be-damned mess, admit it. We have to figure out what to do next. Why can't you just write in new, even more obscure clauses?"

"Haven't you been listening, woman? Because the Kings have composed their own contracts, which we haven't yet seen."

"All right, all right. The question lingers, though: who betrayed the clauses to M'lord Caldane? I say that it must have been a Caineron, yes, from this very college."

The scrollsman, a Caineron himself, growled. "Nonsense. It could also have been a judge of that cursed contest."

"Not necessarily." The little woman rose on her toes and jabbed higher, eye level for her, breast level for her colleague. "You all talked freely about your precious articles. In fact, you bragged."

Other voices heckled back and forth, above and below:

"We did not!"

"Yes, you did, you did, you did! That's how you were able to steal each other's ideas."

"It isn't plagiarism if you improve on it. You singers do it all the time."

"In that case," piped the little singer on the landing, "if he learned one clause, he could have guessed the remaining eight, but he still had to learn at least one. Who told him? This argument goes in circles. Don't you dare try to put this disaster off on us, you . . . you great lummox."

Someone stepped between them and held them apart, one hand on a chest, the other on a forehead.

"Dunfause," murmured the stair-well. "Back from Restormir."

"Behave yourselves," said the newcomer in a tone of outraged authority. "Is this any way for Mount Alban to behave? How did the Director let things get so out of hand?"

"The scrollsman started it," muttered someone below.

"No, the singer did," came a snarl from above.

"Quiet!"

Kindrie leaned over an upper rail, listening. Mostly, he could see the top of heads, the top of doors, but the stair-well echoed. Kirien came up behind him. He knew from the warmth at his back and her sweet breath on his neck.

"Oh," she said. "Dunfause has returned."

"You know him?"

"We've been friends since I was a child and he a dashing young apprentice. In those days, you may laugh, but I idolized him."

Dunfause came up the stairs, smiling. He was middle-aged, with the fine-drawn features of a Highborn and an elegant scrollsman's robe edged with lace to match.

"My dear girl," he said warmly, taking her hands. "I hoped to find you here but then again, where else would you be?"

She smiled at him. "True, Mount Alban is still more my home than Valantir. There's some time, yet, before I come of age."

"Then the Jaran could have no finer lady, if it must have one at all. You know how I feel about that—the waste of an excellent scholar, I mean. Your uncle Kedan will be pleased to give up power and return to his academic role, though."

His gaze, shifting to Kindrie, hardened. "You. Still here?"

Kindrie bowed. He had only met this man once before and was unsure, then as now, how to take him. "As you see."

"In my day, bastards knew where to keep themselves."

"Kindrie is not . . ." began Kirien.

". . . unaware of such opinions," Kindrie concluded.

Hide, said long-entrenched instincts of self-preservation. *Deny*—but wouldn't that be a lie?

"Just so," said Dunfause, turning his back on him. "My dear." This, to Kirien. "Will you join me for dinner?"

Someone nearby, hoarsely, cleared her throat. There stood Singer Ashe, looking as haggard as usual—small wonder given that she was that rare thing, a sentient haunt.

"Lord Jaran summons you . . . to dine," she said. "The Knorth Lordan and Lady Trishien . . . have arrived."

"Oh," said Kirien, pleased. "Jame and my aunt are here? Now we shall have fresh news, I hope. Kindrie, will you sup with us? Dunfause, of course, you too. Supper at the college tonight is likely to devolve into a food fight."

Ignoring Kindrie, the scrollsman gave her a bow and departed, remarking that he would bathe and change his clothes first.

Kirien turned. "You didn't have to be so rude to him."

"I? To him?"

"Many people think that he should have been nominated director of the college instead of Taur."

"I expect that he thought so too," said Kindrie, then looked at her. "Why? What have I said now?"

She turned on her heel and walked away.

They had been having these irritable exchanges for some time now. Kindrie didn't know what they meant except that, perhaps, Kirien was having second thoughts about their relationship. He had never been in love before. Kirien said that neither had she. How were they supposed to know what they were doing?

Kedan, lord of the Jaran, was a fixture only until his grand-niece Kirien came of age. All Lords Jaran were also known as the Jedrak, meaning roughly One Who Has No Time to Read. As Dunfause had said, he was impatient to become simple Kedan again. That night, however, he obviously enjoyed using his temporary rank to entertain his guests at Valantir across the Silver from Mount Alban.

There, Kindrie greeted his cousin Jame with pleasure. What a long time ago, it seemed, since she had scorned him for his priestly training.

"Kindrie," she now said, smiling at him. Her eyes were silver-gray; his, pale blue. They still differed in that at least. "You look well."

So did she, in a patchwork court coat made up of rich, heirloom scraps such as Kencyr often carried with them to be used in their eventual death-banners, along with threads from the more mundane clothes in which they died. Her people, he understood, had gifted her with them in this form. How far she, too, had come since their first meeting on the River Road, in flight from a world that had rejected them both.

Kirien wore her usual dove gray coat, and it became her well. She probably would always look like a handsome boy, which endeared her all the more to Kindrie. Dunfause sat by her side, murmuring in the ear that she bent toward him. Was he, Kindrie, about to lose her? Was this wretched feeling jealousy?

"The Kings' emissary is on my heels," said Jame to the Jedrak and to Kirien. "I've told you that my brother has agreed to his terms." Here she paused, but bit back what she might have said next. "I stopped at Falkirr and Shadow Rock on the way here—not, you understand, at Wilden."

"Of course not," murmured the Jedrak.

Everyone knew that the Knorth and the Randir were at dagger's point, or should have been. Knowledge that Lady Rawneth had tampered with Torisen's soul-image was by now wide spread, although he had made no formal complaint. The Kencyrath wondered about that too.

"What of the Brandan and the Danior?" asked Kirien.

"Brant is upset, of course. He values his Kendar, which isn't always the case."

They all thought of the Caineron and possibly of the Randir, although no one quite knew how to judge the snake pit that Wilden had become.

"I think Brant will try to bargain," said Jame, "but I don't know how well he will succeed. He has his home keep to provide for, of course. The Danior even more so, with less resources. They will be assigned to Nether Bashti, I understand. At least not much happens there."

"They will be under Bashti's shadow, though," said Dunfause, fastidiously stirring his cream of turnip soup, so far not deigning to taste it. "That is to say, they will depend on your troops to the north."

"I didn't know that," said Jame ruefully. "Truth be told, I haven't gotten it all worked out in my mind yet who goes where or what their relationships will be with each other."

"Highborn women seldom worry themselves about such matters," Dunfause said, eyes still on his despised soup.

Trishien, across the table, regarded him thoughtfully.

She takes him for a fool, thought Kindrie, and was obscurely reassured.

"In fact," said Dunfause to Jame, "has the Highlord consulted you at all?"

"Sometimes he thinks out-loud."

The Caineron dismissed her, turning to the Jedrak. "What are your plans, my lord?"

The Jedrak leaned forward, earnest. "We hope for a different approach. Everyone knows that the Central Lands are obsessed with history. Some of our scrollsmen are experts on that region and our singers have many songs. We propose that they travel the west and east banks of the Silver with randon escorts, bartering such information."

Jame considered this. "It's worth a try. You, at least, have special skills besides fighting."

The main course arrived, borne by the twin boys Tomtim and Timtom whom Kindrie had helped rescue from the Priests' College at Wilden, who were now the Jedrak's pages. Dunfause greeted their burdens—galantine pie and pike pudding stuffed with oatmeal—with evident relief.

"What I don't understand," said Lord Jaran, sopping up gravy with spiced toast, "is who betrayed whom first. You say that Caldane was rewarded with concessions. But who told him?"

Dunfause grimaced. "Such an unpleasant topic. Must we?"

"It will keep coming up," said Kirien. "After all, it's unpleasant to think of a traitor in our midst."

"Need it be so?" He looked around the table. "Others are here besides scrollsmen and singers. One sits among us even now."

It took Kindrie a moment to realize whom he meant. "Me? Why would I do such a thing?"

"Why would anyone?" Dunfause leaned forward.

His eyes, Kindrie thought, had a feverish glint. The healer in him wondered: what is wrong with this man?

"What but someone who doesn't belong and never will?" Dunfause continued. "What price acceptance then?"

"I-I don't know what you mean," Kindrie stammered, although he did. A lie, but surely a minor one. But did that excuse it? For a moment, he thought that they all looked at him askance. He was the outsider. He always had been.

"During my recent absence," said Dunfause, "you were seen talking to a Caineron agent. What did you talk about, eh?"

"Nothing to do with this."

"Tell me."

"No."

Dunfause had the Shanir trait of command, but Kindrie's word dropped like a stone into the room, waking them all.

"We do not question honor here," said Trishien, with a finality that even the Jedrak did not question.

Afterward, Kindrie and Jame walked to the door, following their host and his other guests.

"You know," said Jame, "I really don't like that man."

"Kirien thinks highly of him," Kindrie said unhappily, watching the two precede him, their heads bent together.

"He certainly seems smitten with her. I gather that they're old friends, come to the next potential step. Mind you, I'm no expert. Tori and I have problems of our own. It seems to me, though, that Kirien has to decide that she wants, the past or the present, with the future at stake. What can you do about that? How should I know? I have to leave in the morning. If you would like to talk more, though, visit me at Tagmeth."

III

Summer 24

THE TWENTY-FOURTH of summer arrived, a fine, hot day now tending toward sunset. Soon would come supper and ease after the day's work. Before that, Jame and Brier met in the lordan's quarters to discuss what needed to be done next.

"Are we still expecting Gothregor's one hundred tomorrow?" asked Brier, deliberately ignoring Rue, who was repairing a smashed shutter.

When Jame had first returned from Tai-tastigon, she had found the rooms torn apart—clothes shredded, furniture torn apart, holes punched in the walls. No one had admitted to the destruction. Her own belief was that Brier herself had done it in a fit of unconscious rage at her disappearance, hag-ridden by a dream-stalking Gerridon who had haunted the keep in Jame's absence.

Gerridon.

Jame had tried not to think about him since her return, which might yet prove to be a mistake. After all, she had left the Master in his own soul-image, stripped of the larder of souls that fed his life, in dire straits. He would try to do something about that, but what, and when, and where?

Admit it, she thought. *You aren't ready to face him again. Will you ever be?*

Shaking off doubts, she turned back to the matter at hand.

"According to the latest messenger," she said, "they should arrive some time tomorrow or the day after. Our number here is about to double. You've warned the kitchen, the barracks, the latrine squad?"

Brier nodded. "All should be ready by then. How soon before they take to the gates?"

"Quickly, I hope. We need to start supplying the Riverland or at least Gothregor as quickly as possible. Anything to break this dependence on the Central Lands."

"Fen thinks it will take at least a year."

"Hopefully he's wrong. It sounds as if you have doubts."

Her marshal moved restlessly around the room, still avoiding Rue. Could she be jealous, thinking that Jame had indeed bound the former cadet? No, that didn't make sense: Brier wanted Jame to bind as many Kendar as possible to strengthen Tagmeth. Jame hadn't yet told anyone about Torisen's prohibition. That news would be hard to break, especially to Marc who had waited so long for her. To Rue as well.

Brier echoed her with an impatient shake of her head. "Doubts? About the gates? How could I not? We don't know what lies behind most of them or what it will mean to exploit them fully, much less so rapidly. Don't tell me that you are certain."

Jame couldn't, because she wasn't, but now she was committed to try.

"What about the rest of our new randon officers?" she asked to change the topic, also because she wanted to know.

Of her original ten-command, so far only Dar and Mint had asked for reassignment to the Central Lands.

"We don't want to leave for good," Dar had said, looking embarrassed, "but, well, both of us are getting a bit restless at Tagmeth. We'd like to see more of Rathillien before we settle down."

If she had offered to bind them, would they have stayed? How many more, eventually, would want to exercise their new rank on a wider stage? Of course, she had given them permission, and now wondered if she would ever see them again.

From outside, muted by the tower's stone walls, came a horn's blast.

"Visitors?" said Brier, listening to its wavering note. "From the south. A lot of them. You don't suppose . . ."

They descended to the courtyard. Soon afterward into

it rode a small Kendar on a dusty horse, at the head of a one-hundred command on foot, looking exhausted.

"Here at last," said the Kendar—Torisen's Rush, presumably. He swung down with a grunt on hitting the ground. His legs bowed, then straightened. "When do we eat?"

"We didn't expect you until tomorrow at the earliest," said Jame mildly, although her smile was tight.

He grinned. "Best not to keep your lord brother waiting, eh, lady?" His eyes slid past her as if in search of someone more responsible and settled on Brier Iron-thorn. "Marshal, where do we sleep?"

"Rooms will be cleared out to accommodate you," said Brier in a stony tone.

The command sagged against the walls.

"I have a bad feeling about this," Jame murmured to Brier.

IV

Summer 30

SEVERAL DAYS LATER, Jame went out in search of Death's-head. The rathorn colt hadn't been seen since their return to Tagmeth and she was worried, given how hard the ride south had been. Moreover, recently her blood-link with him had been unusually chaotic. She had wondered before how stable he was considering all of the times, accidentally on purpose, he had tried to kill her. What was wrong with him now?

Behind her, likewise, she left a keep in disarray. Rush had dispatched his Kendar to the gates already opened except for the one leading to the oasis, which she had forbidden. Rush had scowled at that.

"My lord said that all doors would be open to me."

"I doubt if those were his exact words. This is my keep. I determine what happens here."

"Humph. He is your lord as well as mine. Who are you to deny him?"

"And you, of course, speak for the entire Kencyrath."

Such sarcasm, she suspected, was lost on this diminutive Kendar. One said that, but actually he was bigger than she was and moreover tended to balance on his toes when they talked, the better to tower over her. On the last of these occasions, Brier had come up and put him in her own intimidating shade. Jame was beginning to hope that Brier meant what she had said at Gothregor about accepting her, Highborn or not. She would trade any amount of aggravation for that.

Now here she was, on the top cliff above the keep, on her stomach, having crawled to this vantage point under tangled boughs. To the north, the Silver roared down the ravine from the escarpment, throwing up a spray that, even at this distance, flecked her face. Below, the river frothed southward. In between was Tagmeth on its teardrop of an island. Her bond to the rathorn had brought her here. Where was he?

The branches behind her rustled. Something snuffled. Before she could edge away from the drop, her boot was seized and she was jerked backward.

Jame twisted over onto her back and lashed out with her

free foot. The first time, it tangled in undergrowth. The second, it made contact, answered by an enraged snort.

One jerk more and she was out in the open, looking up into a pair of furious red eyes. Fangs bared. A white nasal tusk brandished before her face. She kicked again and caught her assailant below the horn, in the nose. Her foot was dropped. Hooves drove down, barely missing her head as she rolled aside. The other reared, black against the sky, and struck again. Jame scrambled back between dancing hooves, noting in passing that this was a mare, but she had already guessed that.

Kindrie's voice came back to her:

"The Randir were riding thorns—you know, those female offspring of horses and rathorns, yes, just like the ones that the Karnids rode to attack Kothifir. Well, one of them escaped just south of Mount Alban. . . ."

And that, Jame reckoned, was what she faced now.

The thorn wheeled on her haunches and charged back at her. Such speed, so much power on the hoof. Terrifying.

A rushing wall of white cut between them as Death's-head shouldered the thorn aside. They circled Jame, the mare outermost, the stallion blocking her, snapping at each other, until she subsided with a grumble and a glare. Jame suddenly wondered if she was in foal.

"So now you have a mate," she said to the rathorn, who snarled at her over his shoulder. "All right. That's your business."

After all, she thought as she walked away, deliberately not looking back, he had been lonely for a long time. She should be glad for him. But sweet Trinity . . . !

V

Summer 35

KINDRIE HESITATED outside the door. Did he really want to do this? No. However, Kirien had asked him to.

"He spends more and more time in his room," she had said, looking worried. "It's been nearly a week since he last joined us for a meal. Then, yesterday, he got into a shouting match with a fellow scrollsman. They nearly came to blows."

Someone spoke within the room, seeming to plead, and a voice answered with a laugh. Kindrie's skin crawled. Surely, he knew the latter with its smug undertone, its not so subtle reminder of pain and despair, but what was it saying? The door muffled any words.

He can't be here. He can't. Run away. Hide.

No. Kindrie was a healer with a duty.

He knocked, too softly at first, then louder, although the noise made him wince.

"Well?" snapped the first voice. "Come in, if you must."

The apartment was one of Mount Alban's best, located near its upper observation deck with windows chiseled out of the cliff face's living rock. Late afternoon light streamed through the latter, the sun having declined to just above the opposite peaks. Dust motes danced in its shafts. These last also illuminated the apartment's furnishings, which were rich and comfortable but in a state of disarray. Clothes lay strewn on the furniture, dirty dishes on the table. Over all was the faint but unmistakable stink of sickness.

Dunfause sat behind the table, indistinct in the shadow of a window, cut off from the rest of the room by the light lancing through it. He was alone.

"Oh," he said. "You."

Kindrie blinked against the glare, collecting himself. "Er . . . Kirien sent me to ask if you are coming down to dinner. Also, if you are all right."

Fabric rustled as the Caineron huddled deeper into the folds of a heavy robe. "Of course I am. It's just a chill."

Kindrie didn't point out that such things were rare for a Kencyr. "I am a healer, you know," he said. "Would you like me to examine your soul-image?"

"No! But I thank you." Dunfause was trying to be gracious. It came hard. "Can't a man indulge in a little privacy? Life at Mount Alban can be so . . . contentious."

"You at least have found it so."

"Some people are fools. All of this talk about those wretched clauses . . . The harm is done. Can't they let it go?"

Hard, thought Kindrie, *when so many lives among the Host remain in danger*. Nothing dire had happened yet, though, as far as he knew. *Ancestors, please, let that state continue*.

"I'm sorry that you find it distressing," he said.

"I? What about you? Still won't tell me what Lord Caldane's agent said to you, eh?"

"That was personal. Besides, his agent came while you were still at Restormir. He didn't tell you either, did he?"

"When m'lord speaks, it is for the good of his house. You served him once. You owe him now."

Sweat beaded Dunfause's face. Perhaps he spoke for himself too.

How well Kindrie remembered his own temporary, ill-fated connection with the Caineron. He had been fleeing the Priests' College at Wilden. Any rescue from that hell-hole had looked good at the time. Then he had met Torisen and had realized where his true loyalty lay, even before he had recognized the blood tie between them. He and Caldane had not parted on the best of terms, given that m'lord had nearly flayed him alive.

"I follow my honor," he now said.

Dunfause sneered. "You are a bastard. You have no honor. What lies did you tell Kirien to seduce her, eh?"

Kindrie bit his tongue. What lies had led to the quarrel between them? Rather, what truths? Kirien urged him to declare his legitimacy, to support his lord cousin and Jame. Why couldn't he?

The sun set. Shadows crawled up the walls, chasing the dying brilliance. In gathering darkness, Dunfause began to cough.

"Oh, go away," he said, weakly flapping a hand. His voice broke. "You sicken me."

VI

Summer 35

"THE EDIRR are still bedeviling the Coman, either by cattle raids or by hunting on their land."

Steward Rowan shifted scrolls away from the visitor's

chair in Torisen's study, but otherwise seemed hesitant to sit down. How often, after all, did her lord ask her for Riverland gossip?

"Boys' pranks, I would say," she added, trying to be judicious, "but that doesn't explain it: the Lords Edirr are both grown men, if young."

Torisen listened. Jame had said that he should ask questions, but it still came hard. This felt damnably like prying—behind the lords' backs, too.

Then: *Don't be childish*, he told himself.

In his father's day, the Coman would long since have brought a formal complaint. They might even have done so to Torisen himself before his illness. Instead, the Coman were trying in their ham-handed way to cope on their own, which only made the Edirr laugh harder. How many more houses now made do without his judgment as Highlord? For that matter, how well had he judged before with so little information?

A night breeze blew through the open window, cool after the day's heat. The summer was passing quickly. There was enough at Gothregor, Ancestors knew, to keep him busy—the keep to run, the crops to cultivate, news from the south to sift . . . but he wouldn't think of that last just yet.

Rowan caught another scroll as it rolled off the chair. Rush, his chief agricultural agent at Tagmeth, had been sending him a steady stream of notes, all complaints. The lands beyond the gates were too diverse, or had been neglected too long, or the seasons there were wrong, either to plant or to harvest. Under this ran a current of insinuation: the lordan didn't know what she was doing, no, nor did her precious Farmer Fen. The latter criticized. The former interfered. Why had m'lord sent him, Rush, if not to take charge? Jame's letters listed problems and minor triumphs but said nothing about Rush, which in itself was telling. Well, let her cope with him. It was her keep.

"What about the Ardeth?" he asked, reaching for a boot.

Rowan looked almost embarrassed. Who, after all, was she to bring him such tales? Was he being fair, he wondered, even to ask her?

"We only get rumors from Omiroth. Lord Adric is sound some days, rotten with age on others. Dari rules in his stead, at odds with Lady Distan—Timmon's mother, you know. My impression is that she is much more ambitious than her son."

"The Brandan?"

"Still a strong ally. The word is, though, that Brant is worried about his sister."

That sounded serious. Brenwyr was a maledight, a Shanir whose curses could kill. They might call her the Iron Matriarch for her self-control, but Torisen had always found her terrifying.

"The Randir?"

Rowan shook her head. "I thought we would hear more, what with the Heir back in the Riverland, but they keep things as tight there as Lady Rawneth's smile. M'lady may have a new councilor. At least, there are reports of someone whispering in her ear, a pale presence that wasn't there before. And there are also strange rumors about Lady Kallystine's pregnancy. Apparently the baby is moving around inside her body at will." The steward's expression didn't change, nailed in place as it was with scars, but her face flushed. "Sorry, Blackie."

"Why? Because she was my consort once? That's long over."

Was it? There were still occasional dreams, and there had been no one since.

Rowan collected herself. "My sense? Wilden is on the edge of explosion. Lord Danior can't be happy having it as his neighbor."

"Poor Holly," said Torisen absently. He tended to forget how vulnerable his cousin was, just across the river from Wilden. For tiny Shadow Rock to have survived so long, the Randir must assume that the Highlord would stand behind it. What could he do, though, if they attacked Holly? There were certain points at which he felt his weakness with special keenness. This was one of them.

Rowan fidgeted with another scroll, this one from Harn in Bashti, newly arrived there with the Knorth troops. Nothing terrible had happened yet, as far as Torisen could tell. Harn seemed obsessed, though, with local politics, and he was oddly scatter-brained. If—when—trouble came, would he be able to handle it?

"The Jaran have their own interests," Rowan continued. Now that she had adjusted to his curiosity, she seemed determined to satisfy it. "They may be the only house that's managed to alter that damn contract, although their arrangement may yet come back to bite them. The Caineron seem happy too, in a strange way. Lord Caldane laughs a lot, I hear, but there's been a rash of suicides at Restormir."

All in all, it was more information than Torisen had expected from what he judged to be idle chatter, but it still raised more questions than it answered. Where had he been while all of this was happening? Dying, he had thought. No more.

"Look," said Rowan. "Blackie. Do you really want to try this?"

She meant his experiment that night. Some of the cattle had come down with blisters in their mouths and on their feet—a murrain, his herdsmen called it. This had happened before and wasn't always fatal, but no one seemed to know what to do about it except to keep the afflicted cows apart.

On a side table was a somewhat more orderly stack of scrolls and books which he had borrowed from Mount Alban. It was not enough to ask questions, he had learned. One had to know what questions to ask. His correspondence with the college had been erratic at best. They kept demanding what he wanted to learn. How was he supposed to know, though, until he stumbled across an answer?

One of the books that had come his way detailed native remedies for bovine diseases, noted by the recording scrollsman as "a compendium of superstitions, some oddly effective."

Torisen grudgingly accepted that some of Gothregor's recent woes had to do with his perverse experiences as That-Which-Creates. Mold. Fungus. Weeds. Disease. If the cause lay in him, though, might not also the cure?

"Ask questions," Jame had said.

"Ask the right questions," he now would have answered her.

"The Merikit swear by this," he said, taking the scroll from his steward. "Can it hurt to try?"

Rowan looked dubious.

So too did the other Kendar as he descended Gothregor's steps to the strip of land on the valley's floor that edged the Silver. The crescent moon had set, leaving a star-spangled sky. Midsummer it might almost be, but a breeze blew off the heights of the Snowthorns and breath clouded the air, both of the herders and of the restless herd. It looked as if all the latter had been brought, a sea of eyes and tossing horns over dark shoulders. Those afflicted, at least, came first.

Close to the Silver and again closer to the keep, two fires sparked to life. Kendar had been quickening them since sun-down, twirling spindles into the notches of fireboards. Needfire, it was called, and sometimes force-fire. By rights, all hearths above should have been quenched, but Torisen hadn't gone quite to that extreme. As it was, by now the herdsmen's hands must be blistered, if not themselves smoking.

Torisen felt momentary guilt. *I asked them to do this, out of faith in me.* Well, if it worked . . .

Flames started, fed with tinder, then with kindling, then with sticks. Bovine eyes gleamed uneasily in the flickering light and horns tossed. Brush was added. Smoke began to rise, full of darting embers. The herdsmen urged their reluctant changes forward. The idea was to drive them between the fires, through the cleansing heat. It seemed an odd idea, but perhaps no stranger than that spores could rise from the roots of plants to infect Kencyr lungs. What if the cows, likewise, were surrounded by tiny agents that passed disease from the sick of the herd to the well? Fire was said to purify. Let it do so now.

The breeze had died. Smoke billowed up into the chill air, merging between the fires, shouldering its way into starlight. It started out white. Then a shadow seemed to gather within it.

"What's that stench?" asked Rowan, standing beside Torisen, sniffing. "Has someone fallen into the fire?"

The darkness moved, defined by rolling clouds, by dancing sparks. Here might have been a broad back straightening; there, arms laced with veins of fire. It seemed to bend over those gathered at its feet. Deep sockets peered down. The ghost of a hand reached out.

"Sweet Trinity," said Torisen, staring up. "It's the Burnt Man."

Rowan pushed him out of the way, then staggered as her jacket burst into flames across the back. Torisen wrestled it off of her, scorching his fingers in the process. Others rushed up to beat it out along with a dozen other small conflagrations caused in the dry grass by falling sparks.

The herd surged back and forth, likewise stung but held in check. Then something dark rushed through its midst, nipping at flanks, yelping. The cows stampeded. Some charged straight through the smoke. Others, shouldered sideways, blundered into the two needfires and scattered them. All stormed on, bellowing, pursued by their tenders.

The shadowy image overhead wavered. As the breeze returned and the smoke dispersed, it disappeared except for a lingering charnel reek.

A gray wolf trotted out of the shadows, rising onto his

hind-legs as he came, his fur subsiding into that appropriate for a very hairy young man.

"Just what did you think you were doing?" he demanded of Torisen, when his mouth was the right shape to form words.

"Not what I expected, apparently. Hello, Grimly. What are you doing here?"

"Starving," snapped the wolver. "First, food. Then answers."

They retreated to the keep's mess-hall where Torisen scrounged for left-overs from dinner for his friend. Bread, cheese rinds, stew.... Grimly tucked in voraciously, with a tendency to slobber the latter's gravy.

"I've been on the road for nearly two weeks," he said, after licking the bowl clean and then his chops with a red, alarmingly long tongue, "mostly hunting small prey as I went. One gets tired of raw rabbit, though. And are my paws sore? Woof!"

They had last met over a year ago at Mount Alban, when Torisen had fought and killed the wolver king known as the Gnasher. The Gnasher's daughter, Yce, had been there too, and when it was over she had left to claim her father's place in the Weald. Grimly had gone with her—as an escort, he had said, and then had laughed.

"As if she needs one!"

Yce was young but fierce, like most deep Weald wolvers. To call them feral was to slander true wolves. Their kin in the Grimly Holt were gentle by comparison, most of them dedicated poets much given to the cadences of howled song. Torisen had wondered how his old friend would fare among his savage cousins.

"Have you been in the Deep Weald all this time?" he now asked.

Grimly grinned, then shuddered. "Most of it," he said. "I watched Yce fight her way to power, and I do mean fight, tooth and nail, against both males and females. Real wolves would have had the sense to roll over and give in. These had to be killed, maimed, or driven out. She bears scars now, our lady. She still speaks of you often."

Torisen had thought about her too. Yce had come to him as an outcast pup in flight from a father who devoured all of his potential heirs. But she had grown. He remembered her arms around him at the scrollsmen's college, her rough tongue as it had licked his cheek.

"I will miss you," she had breathed in his ear.

"And I, you."

So he had, if with a certain relief that she was gone.

He now regarded Grimly askance. "What aren't you saying?"

The wolver ducked his head, looking away under shaggy brows. "She came into power. She came into heat. We of the Holt practice courtship. Many of our best songs are about it. We also can control our mating cycles. Being around my cousins, though, and especially around her... She was overwhelming. It was madness. I think, now, for the first time, that I understand how you felt about Kallystine."

Torisen rose. "Kallystine was poison," he said over his shoulder. "She made me crave her against all reason. She used her aunt Rawneth's witchcraft to manipulate my senses. With her, love was a ravenous thing."

Grimly cringed. "I'm sorry. I didn't mean to pry."

Torisen stopped himself, conscience struck. "I'm sorry too. We Kencyr have some odd practices, I think. You were saying?"

"Only that, from then on, I had to fight to keep her. Against every male in her pack. I have my scars too, now. Even so, I only survived by engaging them in songs and riddles and jokes. They are our kinsmen, after all; we have some things in common. But it got to be too much. How often can you make a bully laugh and not feel like a fool or a coward yourself? I went back to the Holt. Even there, though, what could I say about such things? My own kind are too superior to understand. I wish I still was. So I came here."

Torisen gave him a crooked smile. "And glad I am to see you, however rough your welcome."

"About that. To repeat, what did you think you were doing just now?"

Torisen explained. Grimly groaned.

"You can't just conjure up other people's gods!" he exclaimed.

"Is that what that was?"

"Well, not exactly. The Deep Weald wolvers claim that he is their progenitor. A confusing story, that. They say that he was originally a Bashtiri prince who killed his father and then fled to the Weald—a template, as it were, for the Weald's subsequent patterns of parricide and infanticide, Yce and the Gnasher in a nutshell. His brothers tracked him down there and burned him alive. The heart of the Weald is a blackened ruin to this day. Of course, this was after he mated with a she-wolf to sire the first of my kind. We of the Holt have some good songs about that. I hope to learn more of them."

"So you do believe in the Burnt Man."

"I saw him. So did you and not, I think, for the first time."

"Seeing is believing?"

"On some level. As to what we saw, ah, that's a different matter."

"Jame said something similar about the gods of Tai-tastigon. Your world has given us monotheists much to think about."

Grimly grinned. "Still, you Kennies have a hair-raising disregard for local powers."

"Sorry about that. Here. Have some more stew. And stay as long as you like. I, too, could use someone to listen."

VII

Summer 40

MARC HESITATED IN THE DOORWAY under whose lintel he had ducked so that his bald pate entered first. "You sent for me, lass?" he asked, looking up at her from under tangled brows.

Jame rose from her desk and the letter she had been scrawling to her brother. Torisen, as usual, was proving an unsatisfactory correspondent, although he had informed her that Grimly had come to visit and moreover had passed on an interesting story about the

Burnt Man being the progenitor of the wolvers. Also, the needfires apparently had worked: the sick cows were on the mend.

Rather than talk about himself, her brother tended to relay stories about other people or things—he, who couldn't stand to rely on spies.

What to make of the latter report about the Burnt Man she still wasn't sure.

Good, she had thought about the former. Despite his friendship with the Kendar, Tori needed a companion.

Just the same, he might at least answer her own missives in more detail.

She would rather prod him once again, though, than go through with the conversation that lay ahead.

"Come in," she told her old friend. "Rue has brought us some of the last wine."

"Well, now." Marc sank into a mended chair, which creaked alarmingly as it took his weight. He was in his nineties now, on the edge of old age. His own legs must ache from stumping around the keep all day, helping to make everything work. This was his home. He cherished it perhaps even more than she did. "You know that cider is good enough for me, lass. What's the occasion?"

Jame hedged. "How are Torisen's people settling in?"

"Well enough," he said, accepting a cup, regarding it dubiously, much as he did her. "Most of them are encamped beyond the gates. Sometimes they come back to report. Sometimes Master Rush goes out to them."

Rush had taken the first floor of the tower as his headquarters after Graykin had moved out, in part driven away by Rush.

"He has no respect for my profession," Graykin had complained. "Neither has his lord, he says."

"Tori's opinions are his own. It occurs to me, though, that, thanks to them, we are largely blind in the Central Lands. If I send you there, can you remedy that?"

Graykin had drawn himself up, the hem of his shabby court coat lifting away from scrawny ankles. He had taken to stitching extensions onto it as each robe in turn wore out. While these were all gaudy, Jame had realized, they weren't of very good quality. Annoying as her servant could be, he deserved better.

"I have my allowance from Aerulan's dowry," she had said, "and, so far, not much else to spend it on. I can send you to Bashti."

She had read the conflict in his face. He wanted so desperately to belong to the Kencyrath, but Tagmeth was too primitive to suit his pretensions. Then there was Rush, sneering.

So he had gone.

Jame wondered now if he could really help, cut off from all of his accustomed sources. Well, he was a spy. That was his choice, and his chosen job.

"Most of the newcomers seem like decent folk," said Marc, taking a cautious sip. How long since he had last tasted wine? The gates could provide many things but, so far, not that. "Farmer Fen says so too, when Master Rush lets him speak at all. Lass, what's wrong?"

"Oh, Marc. I nearly bound Rue on the way to Gothregor and . . . and then almost fed on her soul. Now Tori says that I can't be trusted to bind any more Kendar."

He sighed. "I thought something was up. You didn't hurt her, did you?"

"No!"

"I didn't think so. We always knew that you were dangerous, but also compassionate. Both seem to be your nature. Don't fuss."

"If I could have bound anyone . . ."

"It would have been me. I know that and appreciate it. But, lass, can we really be closer than we already are?"

He put down his cup, barely tasted, and opened his arms. She walked into them. Oh, the thump of his strong heart, the honest smell of his sweat. This was the father she wanted. Ganth had been a pale ghost by comparison.

"Commandant," a guard's voice called from below. "Master Rush is here. He wants to talk to you."

"'Commandant'?" Marc raised an eyebrow.

Jame laughed, a bit unsteadily. "It's the first time I've been called that. Will Sheth Sharp-tongue be annoyed with me?"

"He will always be *the* Commandant to those who know him. Otherwise, it's primarily a title of respect rather than of appointment. He should be pleased that you've earned it."

It seemed to her, on descending, that her guard had spoken in counterpoint to her guest. Rush waited below, looking impatient. He had clearly come from the field, with dust on his riding leathers and horse sweat staining his knees.

"About those hills," he said pugnaciously, as if blaming her for them.

Jame thought first of the Haunted Lands, but that gate

had been sealed ever since it had unleashed a horde of haunts on Tagmeth the previous year. She had come back to the keep one day not long ago to find Rush poised to break it open.

"You really don't want to go there," she said.

"What? This is where you deflected me."

Oh. He meant the next gate to the east, unopened until now, which she had offered him as a sop.

"What about it?"

"It would do for pasturage, but we already have the savannah. Now there are interlopers. Riders, watching us from hilltops. Savages, judging by their leather and furs. Then yesterday one showed up all decked out in gold and silver plaques. Fair dazzling, he was, by all accounts. I reckon this land is rich in more than grass."

Each gate tended to face in the direction of its destination. She should have considered that before.

"I think," said Jame, "that you may have come out in Skyrr, north of Tai-tastigon. That certainly sounds like Skyrr armor. They are nomadic herds-people, but their wealth lies in metal and minerals."

Rush grinned. "I was right, then. Think of it! With resources like that, we can buy anything we want from the Central Lands, things that the gates can't provide, without bartering our blood. Our lord will be rich! And here I was beginning to think that this keep was a waste of time."

Jame had come downstairs absentmindedly carrying her cup. He seized it and drank. Wine splashed, unheeded, on his chest.

"Listen," she said, trying to recapture his attention. "We can't just seize their property. You call them 'interlopers.' Rather, we trespass on their land. Oh, Tori warned me about this possibility and I shrugged him off because it hadn't happened yet. Now, apparently, it has."

Rush stared at her. "What are you saying? We should just walk away? We are better warriors than that. Send enough troops and we can fight off any barbarian who dares to challenge us."

"Arribek sen Tenzi, the Archiem of Skyrr, is a friend, and a very impressive man."

"Impressed you, at least, did he? But then I hear tell that you've spent most of your life away from the Kencyrath. Gone native yourself, some say, north of Kithorn. I wouldn't know about that. Consider this, though: as we speak, our Kendar are at the mercy of the Seven Kings, Trinity damn them, and all may yet end in a second White Hills massacre. That would break our lord, your brother."

"I hear you," said Jame grimly. "I ask you, though: is survival everything? Would you choose it, without honor?"

"What does that have to do with this? These are savages, not our own people."

"There speaks the likes of Lord Caineron. I think, Rush, that you are in the wrong house."

He went beet-red. While he sputtered, Jame took back her cup, which now was empty.

"Enough," she said, putting it aside. "Withdraw our Kendar from that gate and never go there again. Be still. Do it."

And she walked away.

VIII

Summer 56

AS TORISEN APPROACHED the bake-house, voices sounded within it. One belonged to Grimly, the other to bake-master Nutley.

"How do you keep your balance?" the former was asking.

"Much the same way I always have," replied the latter cheerfully. "It still comes a surprise sometimes, though, to glimpse them out of the corner of my eye. 'What are those?' I ask myself, then remember and smile."

"Truly, you never regret them?"

Nutley laughed. "Why should I? They are a new experience. Besides, my lady Rowan likes them."

Torisen looked in at the door. "Grimly, don't tease. Nutley, good morning."

The baker straightened from the kneading board and brushed a lock of raven hair out of his eyes with the back of a floury fist. His beard was neatly braided. His bosom had all but burst its bodice with his recent exertions. His proud breasts, also flour-speckled, resembled the two newly risen lumps of dough on the table before him. Well they might, thought Torisen, given that Kindrie had kneaded them out of Nutley's chest in an effort to save his life after he had been attacked by a batch of sour dough gone rogue.

"Good morning to you too, my lord," he said, grinning.

"I have a batch of those sticky buns you like due out of the oven momentarily."

"I thought that I smelled something good. Your stores are holding up?"

At this time of year, between harvests, that was always a question.

"The winter wheat crop was adequate. Meanwhile, the cooks are devoutly grateful for these mysterious supplies that your lady sister sends us, although they say that more would be better."

"We're working on that."

Munching fresh, hot buns, Torisen and Grimly left the fortress and walked down its steep steps toward the valley floor. The sun shone bright in a midsummer sky, catching glints off the swift-flowing Silver. Butterflies danced over the flanking fields.

"Having breasts really doesn't bother him," said Grimly, still amazed.

"Why should it? The Kendar are very adaptable. Male Kendar have even been known to breast-feed babies in times of need, not that they can bear them. As far as I know."

What would he say if Rowan asked him for permission to have a child, if only to please her mate? That acceptance would be a promise that he would take the infant into his house, just when he had decided that binding Kendar was wrong. Rowan and Nutley were both bound to him, and seemed pleased to be so. Everyone had always thought that that was just the way things were. And now? Eh. A problem for another day.

"I mean," said Grimly, still fretting, "what does it signify to him to be a man?"

"What does it to you?"

Grimly squirmed. "I'm confused. And, anyway, I'm also a wolf, most of the time. I would have said that we wolvers of the Holt didn't put as much stock in such things as those of the Deep Weald, but that was before I lived among them. They have a prime male and female, but their leader can be either. That's Yce. I don't think, though, that she really recognizes me as her peer or a proper mate. That would be you, Tori, but I was as close to you as she was going to get. Then. Let's hope she never chooses to fight Jame for your affection."

"That," said Torisen, "is quite enough. Grimly, behave."

The wolver giggled. "I'm trying to. Just tell me how."

Here was the field which the Burnt Man had visited. Beyond was the bridge over the Silver, which had to be rebuilt nearly every year due to the gnawing of the River Snake. Beyond lay the hayfield, set in the lower meadow.

Soon the Knorth cadets would return from Tentir to help with the Minor Harvest. Torisen had already sent out gleaners to cull the hay of false timothy. No one else, he was determined, would suffer from either hay-cough or lung-rot as he had. This time, despite their protests, the reapers were supposed to wear masks to protect them from the spores that the false timothy stems ejected from their chambered roots when severed. No one, so far, had gotten sick. That at least had been one good guess.

Now he saw these select gleaners at work, under direction of the bad-tempered harvest-master who had already shouted himself hoarse at them. He wasn't wearing a mask.

"Why not?" Torisen asked him.

"Huh. Are we to believe in tiny demons who try to drown us from the lungs out? Highlord, give us credit for more sense than that."

"Nonetheless, you heard my orders. Follow them."

The man snorted, but then his eyes fell before Torisen's steady gaze and he backed off, muttering, fumbling for the cloth that hung from a string around his neck.

Near the edge of the field, the Kendar Merry watched her child Bo while her mate Cron labored amid the crops. Bo crowed when he saw Torisen and toddled eagerly toward him.

"He's missed you, lord," said Merry, smiling.

Torisen hadn't seen the little family much of late. He still felt guilty for almost killing Bo by coughing lung-rot spores in his face, thereby giving him a near fatal case of hay-cough. If Kindrie hadn't seen it happen, though, he might never have guessed how the disease was spreading, Kencyr as a rule not being prone to infection. Torisen was relieved to see that the child was now wearing a scrap of cloth as a mask, but worried to find him so close to the original source of contamination.

"Let me walk with him for a while," he said to Merry, picking up the toddler.

Merry agreed. "I'll be glad to join Cron in the field," she said, "for what's left of the morning."

With Bo in his arms, Torisen departed, Grimly at his side. Ahead, stretched across the rising ground, lay bright, terraced ribbons of flax, barley, oats, and wheat, all ripening toward the Great Harvest at summer's end. Workers' paths led upward, cutting across the furrows to the wooded toes of the Snowthorns.

As he climbed, Torisen kept glancing back down the valley and the River Road.

"It's been a while since the last message from Harn," he said when Grimly noticed his abstraction. "He didn't seem very happy then."

The wolver grinned. "I pity anyone who causes that man trouble."

"He has his weaknesses too, you know. You've never seen him in the grip of a berserker fit. If there's one thing he fears, it's losing control."

And, thought Torisen, that was what he had sensed behind Harn's last few scribbled scrolls—an incipient panic. What could have upset him so much? For years he had been the Knorth war-leader and, during that time, also the commandant of Tentir, neither easy jobs. He was, as Grimly said, a formidable man. With potentially fatal weaknesses.

"Around you, though," said Grimly, "he seems to be all right."

"That might be because of the bond between us. On the other hand, Jame's presence also seems to steady him. I don't entirely understand that."

Grimly looked at him sideways. "About messages, nothing new from your old mentor?"

"These days, Adric doesn't send messages. The last was from his steward and grandson, Dari. I told you about that. Adric seems to be getting more erratic, which isn't surprising. Highborn tend to go suddenly soft in old age. Dari wants to be recognized officially as lordan regent to House Ardeth."

"But Adric favors his other grandson, Timmon."

Torisen grimaced. "Half of the time, he thinks that Timmon is his son Pereden."

He had fretted that the other houses were not bringing him their problems for judgment. Then this had happened, a situation in which he had no desire to meddle. Unlike Jame with Marc Long-shanks, he had had two failed fathers, Ganth and Adric. Ganth had warped his life for years, only to disappear, as it were, in a puff of miserable smoke. Alas, that his feelings toward Lord Ardeth were still so mixed.

"And then," he said, "I've also heard from Timmon's mother, the Lady Distan, pleading her son's case, with some justice."

"A mess," said Grimly solemnly, not understanding. His father had died while he was still a pup. What memories he had were good.

They were in the shade of trees by now, winding around brush and the occasional ravine. Sound still rose from behind them in the field, but it was more and more muffled, even the irate shouts of the harvest-master.

"Goo!" said Bo, waving small fists. One hit Torisen in the nose. The other dislodged the child's mask. Torisen removed it—they were far enough from the field by now—and shoved it into a pocket. Grimly walked more and more slowly, his ears pricked through the unruly thatch of his hair.

"Listen," he said softly. "Do you hear that? Do you smell it? Stay back."

With that, he dropped to the ground in his complete furs and charged through the undergrowth. On the far side, someone grunted in surprise, then gave a wordless shout.

Torisen followed as quickly as he could, hindered by Bo.

Beyond was a clearing. In it, Grimly circled a big man nearly as hairy as he was himself. The stranger held an axe in one hand, a piece of kindling in the other. He shifted them as if unsure which to use, if either.

"Grimly, stop!"

The wolver lunged. Blocked by the kindling, he locked his jaws around it and tried to wrest it free, ignoring the axe with which the other could easily have split his skull.

Bo bounced in Torisen's arms, gurgling.

The big man raised the stick with Grimly still clinging to it.

"Huh," he said, looking at Torisen.

Torisen put down Bo, stepped forward, and tapped the wolver on the shoulder as he swung in midair.

"Grimly, let go. This is Bear."

The wolver's eyes swiveled toward him. He let go, thumped to the ground, and backed off, rising to his hind legs as he went, retracting his claws and some of his hair. "He's who?"

"One of my sister's randon *Senethari*."

"Oh," said Grimly. "What is he doing here?"

"At a guess, chopping wood."

Torisen looked around. Across the clearing a door gaped open, and out of it rolled a fog of cold air. The door seemed to stand by itself among the trees. A shift of position, however, revealed a low wall framing it, sunk into the earth, decorated by a band of *emu* faces.

"And that," he said, "appears to be the Earth Wife's lodge."

"What, here?"

"She and her lodge can be anywhere. The last time I visited, both were in the middle of a volcanic eruption. Today, the interior appears to be someplace cold, hence that firewood."

He turned. Bear sat on his haunches before Bo, playing a clapping game. His hair still tumbled into the crevasse in his skull, but not quite as deeply as it had before. He chuckled. Jame would be pleased to know that he was happy.

A horn sounded in the distance. Torisen listened.

"That signifies a post rider," he said. "I said that one was due."

When he looked again, Bear was gone. So was the wall. And the door.

IX

Summer 60

ON MIDSUMMER'S DAY, Jame visited the Caineron and the Randir *yondri* in the oasis. She had been there before, on a similar errand.

"We understand," said nurse Girt, cradling Benj, who for once was peacefully asleep. Perhaps the Builder Chirp had recently been there; no one else seemed able to pacify the infant. "Our lady Mustard wanted your house to accept us. She had no greater ambition for herself. But now we have her child. He will be our new lord."

Jame bit her tongue. Benj might be Tiggeri's son and

Caldane's grandson, but Must had been half Kendar. There had never been a lord who was not pure Highborn, nor an unsanctioned cadet house. She knew what Caldane would say. What about Torisen, though? Even if he wanted to, had he the authority to make such a drastic change in the code that had ruled the Kencyrath for millennia?

The Randir *yondri* spoke through their youngest member—why, Jame wasn't quite sure, unless it was because he seemed the least afraid of her. The others, after all, had had a lifetime of their Lady Rawneth, who was enough to scare anyone.

"We have decided to wait for Lord Randiroc," the boy now told her, with an air of consequence. "After all, he is the true Randir heir."

So he was, if he survived Rawneth and her precious son Kenan. That was another affair where Torisen might eventually have a voice, if he could muster the influence. More and more, she didn't envy his fate.

On the way out of the oasis, she stopped by the Builders' low-slung lodge. No one appeared to be there, but then they never did. When she turned, however, a small, gray-robed figure sat on the shore before the lake, his back to her. She approached and settled down on her heels behind him. They watched the sunset. Flickering patterns of red light played across the water. Date palms rustled. Birds called. It was all very peaceful.

"This is a nice place," said Jame.

"It is home," said Chirpentundrum. "Now."

"The special bread is still delivered every other day? And you still eat it?"

"Of course. How else can I share my dear wife's memories one last time?"

"Oh. I didn't realize that was what you were doing."

"You give the ashes of your dead to the wind. We consume them, a bit at a time, baked in bread. Which way is better?"

"I suppose that depends on what you want. We think of it as freeing them. You think of it as communion. Some memories of the dead I would not want to share."

The sun set behind the western bluffs. Shadows crept over the lake, over the garden. Bats flitted from grove to grove. An olive tree rustled.

"We are being watched," said Chirp.

Jame stifled the urge to turn.

"Does this happen often?"

"Only recently. It is, I believe, just one person. He has never offered us harm."

"Bad enough," said Jame, "that he knows anything about you at all."

Who could it be, she wondered as she left the oasis. The slyness of it worried her more than anything else, although mere curiosity might make any observer shy, not to mention the Builders' unique appearance.

Back at Tagmeth, an unusual number of workers from the gates milled about the courtyard carrying tools as if not sure what to do with them. The garrison cut through their ranks with amused jibes ("Looking for trouble?" "What, there's not enough work for you afield?"), bound for the mess-hall and the evening meal.

That reminded Jame: she had missed lunch yet again. For that matter, she couldn't remember breakfast either.

Rue always chided her for such lapses. Now, however, she was hungry. As she approached the mess-hall, Rue emerged from it carrying a tray loaded with food. She passed Jame without seeing her and entered the tower. Jame followed. Rush awaited his dinner, as usual, in his quarters.

"Go away," he told Rue.

Rue, turning, met Jame in the doorway but stifled her surprise at a gesture from her lady.

Rush took a handful of dates from his pocket and garnished his plate with them. He looked pleased with himself. Jame stepped forward and picked one up. He started as her hand passed under his nose.

"Good," she said, eating it, "but then everything in the oasis is. I told you not to go there."

He tried to collect himself. "Is that what you call it? An apt name."

"Given that is what it is."

She saw that she made him nervous, and was glad. He rose, the better to loom over her. She smiled up at him, although anger stirred under her bland expression.

"Now see here," he said, attempting to bluster. "Matters have become unacceptable. You thwart me at every turn. I can't do the work to which I was assigned, and it's important, whatever you think."

"So?"

"Some time ago, I sent a message to the Highlord, explaining all of this. Either he was to give me a free hand or I would leave."

"And?"

He thrust out his chest, a glint of uneasy triumph in his

small eyes. "He has not replied. I take it, therefore, that he agrees with my position."

"Which is?" It was hard to keep her voice from sinking to a purr. Oh, how she wanted to lapse into a berserker flare. Insufferable man.

"We will send a force from Tagmeth's garrison into this land that you call Skyrr to seize whatever riches we find there. I doubt if your precious Archiem will give us much trouble. Now that I have seen it, we will also secure this oasis of yours. It was a mistake not to tell your brother about it, by the way."

"What makes you think that I didn't?"

"Well, of course he would have set our people to work there rather than leave it to such worthless folk as the *yondri* and those strange little people."

"And what future role do you see for me in these plans?"

He relaxed somewhat. "Someone has to manage this keep. Your second-in-command, Brier Iron-thorn, would be the most competent person for that job. You can go back to your brother's house where you belong. It will be more comfortable there, after all."

Her smile sharpened at the corners. "Oh, so generous of you to express concern for my comfort. I choose, however, to stay. It is you who will leave."

He laughed. "By now, my people will have seized control of the courtyard. Shall we see with whom they side?"

"Yes. Let's."

In the doorway, she paused. "By the way, have you been in the habit of sending my brother complaints?"

"Reports, rather, as is my duty."

"I think, in that case, that you haven't heard from him because he has stopped reading them. You can ask him when you see him."

With that she left the tower, leaving him with his mouth open.

Many of his people indeed milled about the courtyard, looking as puzzled as they had before, watched curiously by the garrison.

"Master Rush is leaving," Jame told them. "Your new commander is Farmer Fen, pending my brother's approval. In the meantime, please join us for dinner."

They looked at her doubtfully, then turned to file into the mess-hall. Jame hoped, watching them go, that Cook Rackny could scrape up the extra food on such short notice.

Rush stood behind her, aghast.

"You will want to pack," she told him kindly, "and, no doubt, to finish you own supper. Then go."

He turned, speechless, and reentered the tower.

Brier came up, slapping dust off her clothes. It would seem that she had ridden in from the fields in haste. Jame realized that Rue had slipped out earlier, no doubt to send a message.

"We wondered how long it would take you to drive him out," said Brier.

"And I did it without losing my temper."

The big Kendar regarded her, expressionless. "Congratulations."

Jame shivered despite herself. She felt from the pressure in her chest as if she had just swallowed something enormous. It was a step toward self-control, however, and away from her hated god.

"Just the same," she said, gulping down bile, "the experience leaves a bad taste. What I am. What I could become. How easy it would be just to give in. It's nearly the summer solstice. I think I'll spend it in the hills with the Merikit. They have a way of clearing the mind."

X

Summer 63

When Kindrie entered the library, Kirien was studying a scroll, or trying to. Her gaze lifted, blank at first, then focusing on him as he stood tentatively in the doorway. Their daytime encounters of late had all had this disconnected air, as if each was locked into his or her own thoughts which they dared not share. At night they met, starved for each other but wordless, in the dark. Kindrie missed their talks; however, he dreaded this one.

"You sent for me?" he said.

"Yes. It's about Dunfause."

"Again?"

Her voice sharpened. "Do you resent that?"

"I . . . may."

"You're jealous."

"I suppose I am. Is that foolish of me?"

"Yes. Very. We have been friends for a long time, he and I. I worry about him. He's not getting any better, you know. When he leaves his room these days, people hear him talking to himself—arguing, some say. Cursing. Sometimes pleading. He mentions you often, going back to this encounter that he says you had with Caldane's agent, hinting at all sorts of vile things. Sometimes . . . he sounds half deranged."

Kindrie heard the shudder in her voice. After the loss of honor, what most Highborn feared most was madness, knowing that it would come for many of them if they lived long enough.

"Dunfause isn't that old," he protested, longing to take her in his arms, to reassure her.

Even if he were, he wanted to say, *we are still young.*

She paused, looking at him. "Kindrie. Love. These horrid accusations. . . . Won't you defend yourself? Please. Tell me the truth."

He wanted to, but he was afraid. That, he told himself, was stupid; the agent had only made an unwelcome, no, a preposterous proposal. The mere thought of it, however, froze his tongue. Kirien read the fear in his eyes, and in exasperation let the scroll roll up in her hands. It was old. Its edge crumbled.

"Now look what you've made me do. Oh Kindrie, I didn't mean that. At least tell Dunfause, tell the world, that you are legitimate."

"I . . . can't. Not yet. You don't understand."

"True. I don't. Explain it to me."

He began to pace back and forth before her desk, hating himself, almost hating her for making him face this. "You don't know what it feels like to be weak, to be at everyone's mercy. My first memories are of the Priests' College at Wilden. I told you what Lady Rawneth did to me there, once she realized that I could heal myself of virtually any injury. I was her living doll, her pet, sometimes pampered, sometimes tortured, always used. The priests took their lead from her. They would have destroyed my mind, if not my body, if I hadn't taken refuge in my soul-image."

"Which was based on the Moon Garden at Gothregor, where you were born. Yes, you told me that too."

Was that sympathy in her voice? He hoped so, yet blamed himself for so desperately wanting it.

"Don't you see? I had to hide in order to survive. I've done that all of my life. Some might say that I'm doing it here, now. You and the Jaran protect me. When have I ever stood up for myself?"

"You stepped forward to save Torisen at Kithorn when you first met him, and several times since. You have shown courage. I saw it for myself when you brought those Shanir boys, Timtom and Tomtim, here to sanctuary, although Rawneth's people were close behind you."

Kindrie almost laughed. "The twins defended themselves quite handily on their own, by giving their pursuers explosive diarrhea. Then Ashe arrived with reinforcements from Mount Alban. I was called on to do very little."

"You don't give yourself enough credit. You never have. Stop feeling sorry for yourself."

She knew him too well, or not well enough.

"You are a strong person," he said. "So are my cousins. I am not. Don't I deserve some credit, though, for having survived? Do I have to change myself to be worthy of you?"

She sighed. "The question begs the answer. No. You

need to be worthy of yourself. You say you may be becoming That-Which-Preserves. Destruction and Creation are active forces, yes, but must preservation always be passive? How can it, if it is to survive?"

Someone knocked on the door and opened it in haste, without waiting for an answer. The sparrow-like singer peered in. "Lady—oh, and lord—come quick! Scrollsman Dunfause has tried to take the White Knife!"

"Tried?" said Kindrie, aghast.

"And failed. He can't seem to die."

Kirien had turned pale. "There must be some mistake. Kindrie, help him!"

"If I can," said Kindrie, but his mouth had gone dry.

They found an anxious knot of scholars and singers outside Dunfause's apartment. Inside was Director Taur, bent over a huddled figure in a chair, holding shut his slit wrists with big, blunt hands. The room stank with the hot copper tang of blood.

Kindrie hesitated on the threshold. "What if this is what he truly wants?"

Kirien shoved him inside. "Why would he? You are a healer. Heal!"

Kindrie reluctantly took the blind Director's place. He felt the older scrollsman's life flutter against his palms. The wrists, wet with blood, slid under his fingertips.

His craft lay in reaching his patient's soul-image. Sometimes it was easy, but this was hard. Dunfause hid beneath layers of memories, in each of which Kirien played a part. Here she was a wide-eyed child listening to his stories. He had found her amusing then. She had grown into a handsome girl with a tentative smile and an eager mind that challenged his own, then into a young woman, sharper still, ever more beautiful.

"Oh, Dunfause, tell me more."

When had he lost her? Her image receded into maturity. He aged.

"My dear old friend. . . ."

Not old. Never that.

Kindrie moved through layers of time, now going back. A room took shape around him, sparse, elegant. Tables held a scholar's tools—quills, shining ink, translucent scrolls. Light poured in through many windows. The furniture glowed. It was the soul-image of a fastidious man, justly proud of his accomplishments. In pride of place, casting radiance where otherwise shadows would have fallen, was the central statue of a young girl, frozen in innocence. Kirien again. How she smiled at her hands, across which balanced a blank roll of parchment. Who would write on it?

But the room quivered around the edges. A sound struck up a muted vibration there, changing from gibberish into the wheedling voice that Kindrie had only half heard before.

Dunfause, my faithful servant. Tell me.

"You . . . you gave me strong wine to drink. My head spins. To tell you, yes, but I am also a senior member of the college. I owe it, I owe. . . ."

Nothing compared to what you owe to me, to your house. Besides, they have betrayed your trust. You should have been the next director, not that blind cretin Taur. Your rank, your Highborn blood, my favor. . . . Come. Think better of yourself, as I do. Tell me.

The edges of the room darkened. Someone stood in the shadows behind the kneeling scholar with a smug smile, sure of righteous triumph. Cracks skittered across the pristine walls, across the polished floor.

My honor is yours, and yours is mine. I am your lord. What are you without me? Nothing. Only I matter. Trust me.

The cracks spread. Through them seeped sluggish darkness and the stink of blood. The tide lapped about the child's statue.

You think that she is so innocent, so pure. Even now, another courts her, has won her. Should he become my new favorite and not you? Listen, then, and obey. Tell me.

The scrollsman bent over wrists across which slits had opened.

"I will tell, I will tell...."

And he did.

Ah, breathed the shadows. *You were right to do so. This foolish clause in our contract, that was supposed to protect our troops, the other eight that you have guessed, what leverage this will give us with the Seven Kings! Our house will be greater than ever. I will be greater.*

His presence withdrew, turning away, leaving Dunfause crouched over his bleeding wrists. The room around him had dimmed to dirty clothes, dirty dishes, dirty furniture.

"Oh, sweet Trinity," he moaned, "I can't have said that. It can't be my fault. Kindrie...somehow, he is to blame for everything. I will say that, over and over, until everyone believes it. Until Kirien believes it. Until I do."

He had been holding the veins in his wrists shut. Now he let them go. His life sank into squalor.

"Oh, why can't I die?"

Kindrie released him and stepped back. The last throb of blood ebbed, then stopped. At the door, Kirien cried out, hands over her face.

"I didn't tell you," he said, turning to her in supplication. "I will now. Caldane's agent—he brought a message from his lord. Lord Caineron is in poor health. He wants me to become his personal healer. At Restormir."

She stared at him, as if not quite taking in his words.

"What? Oh, go away. Just go away." Then she fled.

Others spoke to him, among them the Director and Ashe. He didn't listen. Once Torisen had driven him out and he had gone. Now he felt that it had happened again. What was there here for him except Kirien? What was there anywhere?

"Visit me at Tagmeth," his cousin had said.

Very well. He would.

⊰⊱ Chapter III ⊰⊱
Summer Solstice
The Village: Summer 65–67

I

EARLY ON A GRAY MORNING, clouds rolled in billowing waves over the escarpment, over Tagmeth on its island fastness, on down the river valley. Above, snatches of mist tangled in overhanging trees so that boughs dripped and cobwebs netted pearls of moisture. Below, stone walls and cliff faces trickled as if with tears. It was cool in the pre-dawn light, but with a louring sense of the day's heat to come.

Within the mirk of the keep, the kitchen was preparing for breakfast. Benches and tables had already been moved away from the walls and the bakers were pulling fresh bread from the ovens. Jame stepped out into the courtyard, straightening her jacket with one hand, chewing on the heel of a warm, crusty loaf held in the other.

Voices within called after her: "Safe journey, commandant, safe journey."

She acknowledged with a wave.

Horse-mistress Cheva waited for her at the door to the subterranean stable, holding her saddle wrapped in its pad against the damp.

"You checked Bel?" Jame asked.

"Of course. She's sound. This will be a nice, quiet expedition, correct?"

"Only up into the hills for the solstice."

Cheva already knew that. It would be a long time, though, before Jame lived down her nightmare ride to Gothregor on Summer's Day.

She took the saddle, crossed the wards, and entered the island's lower meadow with Jorin, the blind ounce, padding catlike at her side. Horses grazed there, dark shapes in the pre-dawn twilight. The Whinno-hir Bel-tairi ghosted out of the gloom. Jame stroked her silken neck, unmuffled the saddle, and slung it over her back on top of its pad. Like Death's-head, Bel accepted no bit. Those few who rode her only did so with her consent.

Jame was pleased to be getting away without hindrance. Jorin might cling to her, but maybe her people finally trusted her enough to let her go off on her own again. So she thought at least until, with a chink of tack, Rue emerged from the keep leading her new favorite mount, the ugly little post pony that she had named Stubben.

"Take me with you," she said.

It began to drizzle.

"Rue, that might not be a good idea."

"Why not? I followed you to Tai-tastigon."

"Yes, you did. I remember how you spoke about the

natives near Min-drear, though. You might not like what you find in the hills."

Rue blinked rain out of her eyes. "I wondered about your past in Tai-tastigon. A thief? A tavern dancer? Then I met your friends, and they were good people. Before, I wondered what it would be like to be bound to you. Afterward . . . lady, what happened outside Gothregor? You really scared me, falling into the water like that. I thought you had dropped dead. And then . . . then you nearly bound me. I would have welcomed it. Why didn't you?"

Rue had begun to cry without realizing it. Her tears melted into the rain.

Jame felt helpless. Tori wanted to do away with all bindings, forever. Had either of them adequately considered how the Kendar would feel about that? But Rue didn't understand the danger in which she had stood.

"I nearly hurt you," Jame said to her, as close to the truth as she could bear to get. "Worse than you can imagine. That terrified me."

"All Kendar, always, want to be bound. What are we alone? What am I?"

"I wouldn't have you be anything less than what you are, and I value that."

Rue wiped her face. "You do? I . . . I thought that, somehow, I had let you down. I wasn't worthy. What was I supposed to think? You've hardly spoken to me since then."

Jame realized with chagrin that this was true. They hadn't even discussed what had happened by the creek. Every time she had looked at the girl, she had felt paralyzed with guilt. Had the other Kendar sensed her withdrawal? Was that why Brier had ignored Rue in the apartment the other day?

"I didn't want to take advantage of you," she said. "It never occurred to me that you might feel rejected. I'm an idiot."

Rue blinked. "It wasn't my fault? I didn't presume?"

"Not at all. After Marc, I would have chosen you, but when Tori heard what I had nearly done, he forbade me to bind any more Kendar. I agreed. Maybe no one should associate with me anymore. Maybe I'm becoming too dangerous."

Rue sniffled and snorted. "You've always been that. What, did you think none of us noticed?"

Jame smiled. "Marc did. He told me so. We need to start over again, you and I. Yes, come with me if you want. You might find other good people in the hills."

II

THE DESULTORY RAIN lasted into mid-morning, to Jorin's disgust, before the sun burned off the clouds. By then, they were well above the cataracts, riding under a canopy of dripping leaves. It was becoming hot. Jame lashed her jacket behind her saddle. So did Rue behind her own. Her pony gathered himself as if to kick, but Bel snorted him into sullen acquiescence.

Behave.

As Jame had promised Cheva, they were taking it by easy stages, as much to save Jorin's paws as Bel's legs. The tough little post pony, on the other hand, could have trotted the whole way in half the time. It was some twenty miles to Kithorn by the River Road and another one or two to the Merikit village. At a sedate walk, they passed Kithorn in the late afternoon.

Through the gatehouse, up the road, the keep's courtyard stood open. Within milled a crowd of men in costume, rehearsing for the next day's rites. There went the Falling Man bedecked in feathers; there, the Eaten One in a shimmering fish-skin cloak. The Merikit's Earth Wife squatted in a corner, oh, so much less impressive than Mother Ragga herself. Where was Chingetai, who usually represented the Burnt Man? To one side of the inner gate, talking to a stranger in a pale robe.

The latter glanced toward the gate as Jame and Rue passed. His face in the shadow of his hood shifted from an obsequious smile to a smirk then back again, as quick as a lizard's flickering tongue, as he returned his attention to the Merikit chieftain.

Jame rode on, disquieted. She knew most of the villagers. That man wasn't one of them, and yet she almost thought that she knew him.

Dusk had settled when they came within sight of the Merikit village on top of its hill. The Silver rushed past to the east, joined at the hill's foot by a stream descending from the northwest. Above was an earthen bulwark topped with a wooden palisade. Fire light shone between the trunks of the latter. Voices rang out within. Here, beyond the bridge across the Silver, was the gate and guards who stepped forward to take their mounts. These were war maids, Jame noted. The next day's rites were divided between male and female participants, the latter obviously in charge of the village proper tonight.

Inside, the wooden walk echoed under their boots as it wound back and forth between sunken lodges crowned with paddocks and gardens. Light showed at the bottom of steps. Smoke drifted up through many vent holes along with the savory smell of cooking.

Rue looked curiously about as they went. She had met the Merikit when they had visited Tagmeth after the yackcarn hunt the previous autumn but had never before seen them at home or, for that matter, as anything except interlopers.

Near the top of the hill, just beyond the thatched roof of the communal hall, was the subterranean lodge of the Merikit queen, Gran Cyd. Torches lit the open space before it. Gold and silver gleamed in swirling patterns around its doorposts and lintel.

"Hello?" Jame called, descending the steps.

Women clad in bright woolens bustled up to her, laughing, all talking at once:

"Favorite!" "Come back to us at last!" "Welcome, welcome!"

Jame led Rue up to the golden chair where Gran Cyd sat, a smile on her generous lips and in her smoky green eyes. Rue gawked at her. When they had last met, the Merikit queen had worn a rough doe-skin shift, amber beads, and boots soiled from the hunt. Moreover, she had intruded on an injured Jame who, to Rue's mind, should better have been left alone to rest. Her dress now was of purple wool shot with gold thread, her long red hair ornately braided. She extended a round, white arm and a be-ringed hand in gracious greeting.

Jame returned her salute. "May I present Rue? You have met before but not, I think, been properly introduced."

Gran Cyd smiled at the Kendar. "My beloved's friends are always welcome here."

Jame had spoken in Merikit, the queen in Kens.

Rue blushed.

Gran Cyd turned, gesturing behind her. "Here is our daughter, Tirresian."

The child tottered forward, grinning. She had an unruly mop of hair the color of pale smoke and Jame's silver-gray eyes. The intelligence in the latter was startling in one so young. Rue had seen her before too, but had not realized who or what she was.

"Daughter?"

Jame gave a lop-sided smile, as if herself not quite sure what to think of this. "It's complicated. When I first met the Merikit, they granted me male status, or rather their chief Chingetai did. He was trying to save face at the time. He has since regretted it, I think. But the Merikit women decided to play along. They get to decide who the fathers of their children are, you see. On one particular night, all of them credited me. This child was conceived then, and six others."

"Your . . . daughters?"

"So they say."

"Does the Highlord know?"

"About his . . . er . . . nieces? I haven't yet dared to tell him."

Rue looked down. Tirresian had toddled up to her and was holding up pudgy arms. "Me, me, me...."

Without thinking, Rue picked her up. Tirresian pulled her nose and chortled.

"This is a girl?"

"We aren't sure. Her name means 'between.' Such children are considered lucky, but Chingetai sees her as unnatural. That's a problem."

Women ran in and out, bearing dishes.

"The main feast is tomorrow, after the ceremonies," said Gran Cyd. "Tonight, the men fend for themselves."

One of the dish-bearers giggled as she lay a plate of smoked salmon at her mistress's feet. "Chingetai claims that only women cook. Not all men agree. Let them forage for themselves and see."

"And sleep in the rough!" another added.

A girl wandered in, looking disconsolate.

"Prid!" said Jame, going to meet her. "Rue, this is my lodge-wyf."

"Your . . . what?"

"Well, that came rather as a surprise to me too. Somehow, I found myself linked to her as her housebond. The wyves own the lodges, also all property, also the children. We housebonds are only there by permission. I did mention that I was considered male, didn't I? Anyway, I have sleeping privileges in Prid's lodge. Prid, what's wrong?"

The girl blinked and brushed tawny hair out of her eyes.

"Hatch," she said, stifling a sob. "He's going to Kithorn with the others where he's supposed to defend his title as the Earth Wife's Favorite again, but I don't want him to. I don't! He belongs to me."

Rue took a guess, based on hill tribes she had known at home. "The Favorite's virility is shared by the village at large, isn't it?"

Prid gulped. "So everyone says, but he is mine!"

Jame patted her shoulder. "There, there. Maybe this time it will be different."

The girl smiled though tears. "So he says. So let it be."

They settled at Gran Cyd's feet and ate. While dishes were presented to the queen first, she waved them on to her guests. Jorin flopped down beside Jame and begged for treats by tapping the back of her hand with a paw. The lodge filled with chattering, laughing women.

"How is it between you and Chingetai?" Jame asked under cover of the clatter. "At the autumnal equinox, there was some tension."

Gran Cyd was holding Tirresian in her arms. She popped a morsel of fish into the child's mouth and wiped her own long, white fingers on a clean cloth. A cloud seemed to flit across her face.

"We quarrel," she said in a low voice. "It does not help that a shaman from his home tribe has come to visit him. The Noyat, as you know, have different ideas about a woman's place in life."

"Would this be a thin fellow in a pale robe?"

"Yes. You have seen him?"

"At Kithorn, talking to your consort."

The memory made Jame frown. The Noyat not only considered men superior to women, but they also lived to the north, on the western shore of the Silverhead, under the shadow of the Barrier and Perimal Darkling. Her experiences with them had not been pleasant.

I know that man, she thought. *But where from, and how?*

That night she and Rue slept in Prid's lodge, or tried to. For one thing, the Merikit men caroused outside the village walls with leaping bonfires, shouts, and hearty mugs of fermented fish piss. Also, Prid cried most of the night until Jame left her couch to comfort her. Jorin came, grumbling, to Rue and settled beside her with a huff. Fondling his tufted ears, Rue listened to the low voices across the room in the dark. Eventually, she slept.

In the morning, Jame took her around the village to introduce her to its inhabitants. All welcomed them. Many shared tidbits from their cooking for the evening's feast. Others teased Jame about her role as a former Favorite— too good a joke, apparently, to let go.

"Nice people," Rue admitted, grudgingly. "Those I knew at the High Keep were less friendly."

"Noyat?"

"A different tribe, but with some of the same customs. We clashed with them, now and then, especially when they raided our cattle. These are really the folk who slaughtered Kithorn's garrison?"

"Their fathers or grandfathers did, anyway, but it all turned out to be a misunderstanding."

Rue snorted. "Some mistake, an entire Knorth cadet branch destroyed. That was Marc's home. Well, if he can forgive them . . ."

"He did, when he met Gran Cyd at Tagmeth."

"Oh," said Rue, impressed.

The women waited for their men's departure. This came in the late afternoon, to the beat of drums outside the palisade.

Boom, wah, wah, boom. . . .

Was it imagination that made the pulse seem more irregular than usual? How much had the men drunk the night before? Was the Noyat shaman still whispering in Chingetai's ear?

Women gathered around their queen's lodge as daylight faded and the full moon rose. Their own music rose in a skirl of pipes and tapped drums under flaring torches. To the left a bonfire ignited. Before it sat a skeletal form.

"Who is that?" asked Rue, staring.

"Granny Sits-by-the-fire. She's a story-teller, older even than the Earth Wife. Every hearth is her home."

The woman's grinning jaws opened on fires within, showing red between her few remaining teeth.

"Hah'rum! Heed me, my children, for I tell truth even if I must lie to do so. In a village much like this one, long, long ago, there was an old woman who lived in a lodge . . ."

"Ah, that story," said Prid, settling beside Jame, Rue, and Jorin as they sat on a neighboring lodge-top.

Gran Cyd held up a sack. Out of it she took rag dolls and threw them at random into the audience, who snatched them out of the air and hurried down into the open space to take their parts in the ceremony.

"She took a housebond older even than herself but, oh, so distinguished that she humored him."

One of the women brandished an obviously male doll.
With it in the crook of her arm, she strutted back and forth
before her queen, nose in the air. Her friends bowed to
her, but snickered behind their hands.

"... thinks he's so special ..." "... a mighty warrior, yes,
but one who chooses his foes carefully ..." "... if he were
only better in bed ..."

Granny smirked. "For, you see, he was not only old
but ..."

Horns and drums sounded, approaching: *Wah, wah,
boomph* ...

"Are they coming back so soon?" asked Rue, glancing
over her shoulder.

"Strange," said Jame. "What could have happened?"

The gates opened. Torches came down the walkways,
many of them sputtering. Chingetai emerged on the
plaza.

"You have cursed us!" he bellowed.

Jorin flinched. He didn't like loud voices.

Gran Cyd stood forth. "Housebond," she said. "These
are our rites. You intrude."

"No, you do! How else to explain this?"

He reached behind him and jerked out a tattered
figure. It was Hatch, the red clothes of the Favorite in
rags, his face swelling with bruises. Prid stifled a shriek
half of horror, half of joy.

"Oh, you gave up the Favorite's position! Now at last
we can be together!"

Chingetai snarled at her. "You welcome that? He is
disgraced!"

"I would say, rather, that he is freed," said Gran Cyd.

"You don't understand. He won. The Challenger ceded. But Hatch wouldn't accept his victory."

"He just fell down!" Hatch protested. "You told him to, or that creature at your elbow did."

The Noyat shaman stood there, close enough to rub against the chieftain's side. At this attack, he drew back. In the shadow of his hood, his thin lips twitched as if with amusement to see such children's play.

"I do what my honor dictates," said Hatch. He looked torn between pride and tears. "And it was Chingetai who beat me, not my rival."

The women's drums still beat, soft but persistent, marking time.

Tap, tap, tap. . . .

"What story are you telling?" demanded Chingetai. "What secrets are here? F'ah, women's mysteries, dark and dirty."

The audience murmured, the women in protest, some of the men in agreement. Others among the latter looked uneasy, including the Merikit shaman Tungit, smeared white with ash, hung with goat udders, who had come up on Chingetai's other side.

"Housebond," said Gran Cyd, drawing herself up nearly as tall as her consort. "You forget yourself."

"No, I have remembered. Women in my mother's village knew their place."

"Then why did your mother take refuge here? We welcomed her, and you, and your little sister."

"Your filthy rites killed my sister! 'The fish is caught'— oh, I remember that well. Then you fed her to that monstrous catfish."

"She was chosen as the Ice Maiden on the vernal equinox, but that was a long time ago. It was also an honor. That 'monster' is one of our gods, the Eaten One."

"It is still a monster!"

For a moment he looked near tears, then anger swelled again and he stomped like a bull about to charge. The Burnt Man's charcoal, smeared over his bare, tattooed skin, rose in a murky cloud. Those nearest him coughed. He saw the male doll and snatched it out of its bearer's arms.

"You mock us! Tell me this poppet's role. I will play it myself and then we will see who wins your foolish contest."

Gran Cyd sighed. "Must we play to win or lose? These are sacred stories. Would you have welcomed me at Kithorn?"

He glowered. "I didn't welcome you at Tagmeth, but there you were."

She stifled a giggle. "Yes, and your britches caught fire. Mother Ragga is late again. Granny . . . ?"

The eldritch figure by the bonfire grinned and bobbed her scarecrow's head in assent.

"Then listen, beloved. You are my housebond, a famous warrior, but in this story, you are old. . . ."

"Never too old." He made as if to seize her but she slipped through his grasp.

"*Hah'rum!*" said Granny. "Old we say, old you are. And so jealous that your lodge-wyf must slip out to find one younger."

"Never!"

The queen dodged him again. He turned, but dropped

the doll and grabbed his back in pain as it locked on him. "Witch! What are you doing to me?"

Granny cackled. "Only what the poppet represents, as the story retells. Was it not her right to choose a second housebond, or a third, or a fourth? The lodge was only yours on sufferance, after all."

Women tossed ragdolls back to Gran Cyd and retreated to the sidelines. She returned them to fresh, eager hands for the next round. Jame found herself clutching the male poppet. Prid laughed.

"Oh well," said Jame to Rue, and went down into the arena.

"Dance with me," said Gran Cyd, and began to sway to the beat of the drum. The pipes picked up the rhythm, adding flourishes that set flight to her eloquent hands. Jame followed her lead. It was like a wind-blowing kantir, weightless except when feet hit the ground.

Stomp, stomp, stomp. . . .

The audience started to clap, men and women both. Chingetai lurched after them, grimacing, more shrunken and decrepit by the moment, raging against his state. Then a fourth dancer floundered into their midst in a swirl of multicolored skirts.

"Am I late?" panted the Earth Wife. "Wheee!"

The lodge door slammed shut.

"Housebond!" the queen cried, and beat on it. "Come out, or let me in!"

"I won't," came Chingetai's muffled voice from inside. While he no doubt meant to sound masterful, petulance was more his note. "By right of male dominance, this lodge is mine, mine, mine!"

"Oh, what a child. Housebond!" She dropped her tone to a play-actor's wheedle. "Beloved, let me in. Our neighbors will see how you disrespect me. They will laugh at me, and that I cannot bear."

The other players converged, brandishing their dolls at her. "Boo, boo! What, you can't manage one mere man?"

Mother Ragga stepped forward with a wink. "D'you hear them?" she called, dropping her voice to a good approximation of Gran Cyd's own. "There is a well nearby. Open, housebond, or I will drown myself in it."

Gran Cyd raised her eyebrows at this. There was indeed a public well to the west of the lodge's front. The Earth Wife tiptoed up to it with elaborate caution, picked up the bucket, and dropped it in.

"Ohhhh!" she squealed, artfully dropping her voice to indicate rapid descent.

Splash.

Chingetai scrabbled at the door, threw it open, and stumbled out. He looked ancient, his wispy hair white, his flesh shriveled beneath a sagging screen of tattoos.

"No, no!" he cried.

Cyd went to him. Her white arms cradled his spare bones and the flesh on them began to return at her touch.

Tap, tap, TAP! went the drums, then fell silent.

Granny disappeared in a bloom of fire.

The ceremony was over.

"I was old," Chingetai sobbed, hands over his face. "I was weak. What happened to me?"

Gran Cyd held him. "Age before your time, beloved. I

am sorry, but you must learn: It is dangerous to mock women's rites."

He thrust her away and stumbled to his feet, wiping his streaming nose, smearing soot and snot. "Bitch! Oh, you will suffer for this, and you too." His attention had turned to Jame, and to the poppet in her arms.

"Don't!" she cried as he snatched for it. "What would you do, tear it apart? Think!"

She threw the doll to Gran Cyd, who thrust it along with the other dolls back into her sack, which Mother Ragga took in charge.

"Think," the latter echoed in a rumble that made the dust at her feet shiver.

Chingetai looked wildly about, but the Noyat shaman had disappeared and many of his followers would not meet his eyes.

"I will be avenged!" he howled, and stormed off.

Gran Cyd sighed. "Always, these scenes. Come. Shall we feast?"

Most of the village withdrew to the subterranean banquet hall where the women produced great platters of food and ale mugs began to pass freely. Rue noted some men who looked less than happy, and others who didn't appear at all, including Chingetai. His act of rebellion, apparently, hadn't entirely fallen flat. There was unfinished business here.

Prid and Hatch sat to one side, quietly talking. Long before the end, they rose and left together.

"Lady," said Jame to Gran Cyd, "may we beg the hospitality of your lodge tonight? I think, under Prid's roof, that we would only be in the way."

The queen smiled at her. "One thing, then, at least, has come right. I wish my granddaughter joy, and you welcome."

III

JAME, RUE, AND JORIN left the next morning, to a round of female good wishes and a few covert male glares. They rode south through a bright summer's day with Jorin bouncing ahead after every butterfly that Jame saw.

"You were right," said Rue abruptly. "I like your friends—some more than others, agreed. Gran Cyd is . . . remarkable, the women likewise. Tirresian, Prid, your other family, I like them too. Ancestors know what your brother will think, though. When d'you mean to tell him?"

"Ah. How d'you think he will take it?"

Rue considered, frowning. "I don't know the Highlord well," she said. "I only knew a few Highborn before you, and you aren't exactly typical, are you?"

Jame laughed. "Hardly."

"Well, then, your brother isn't either. You both think more like Kendar until . . . well, until you don't. You both have enemies, and those have to be considered too. Also, responsibilities to the rest of us. What do I know? The Highlord might be more upset if you don't tell him than if he finds out on his own, but how likely is that?"

"Not very. Why should he ever go above Tagmeth, or certainly above Kithorn? About not having bound you, though. . . ."

Jame paused to think.

"I was afraid that I would rob you of your will. Now, I wonder if I could. You're as stubborn as ever. Remember, though, I'm not used to servants. Just stop following me everywhere. It gets on my nerves."

IV

THEY REACHED TAGMETH at dusk on the 67th of Summer. Forewarned, Brier greeted them at the gate.

"There's an urgent message from your brother," she said.

Jame ran up to her quarters. There it was, a scrap of parchment on her desk, screwed up in Torisen's usual impatient style.

"Come to Gothregor," it read. "Now."

Chapter IV
Dinner at Omiroth
The Riverland: Summer 68–71

I

THE NEXT MORNING, a mounted ten-command formed in Tagmeth's lower meadow, along with several pack-ponies.

"The postscript did say that you should bring an escort," said Brier, noting Jame's expression.

"What, I might get lost?"

"I think, on Summer's Day, that you scared him."

Jame thought that she probably had, showing up in such a state. Torisen still hadn't gotten used to her return to the Kencyrath. To lose her again, when they had come so far, would have been hard. For her too, to lose him. Just the same, they still found ways to irk each other.

"He could at least have told me what was wrong."

If nothing else, that lack of information had made choosing the ten more of a challenge. For what, after all, were they being chosen? An escort wasn't a war guard. A guard wasn't a diplomatic mission. A mission wasn't a pleasure excursion, not that Tori was apt to summon her so peremptorily on one of those, if ever.

She had decided that Brier should stay at Tagmeth, considering that it was only days since she had dismissed Rush. His one-hundred command had been reassigned to Farmer Fen and seemed content to be so, but what if Rush had followers who would rise if she, Jame, also departed? Tagmeth might yet need a firm hand.

Damson's ten-command remained intact although both she and her five-commander Quill had graduated to officer rank. There simply weren't enough Kendar at Tagmeth to give them the enlarged commands that they deserved nor, like Dar and Mint, had they yet asked for reassignment. Let them come, then. Anyway, Jame wanted to keep an eye on Damson a while longer given that Kendar's odd, potentially lethal nature. The Shanir's power, as near as she could understand it, lay in manipulating other's bodies. At least two people had stumbled to their deaths after crossing her. Worse, she had no innate moral sense. Instead, she had turned for guidance to Jame, who herself was none too sure of her own moral compass.

Then there was Rue, holding back as if to stay as much out of sight as possible.

"Stop following me everywhere," Jame had said, but that was before she had acquired an entire entourage.

And there was Jorin, plumped down in the midst of everything, busily washing his face with the back of a paw.

Cheva, again, handed Jame a saddle, this one a heavy affair with raised pommel and cantle. "No sign of him yet?"

"No sign."

At the head of her troop, on foot, with the saddle slung awkwardly over her shoulder, Jame left Tagmeth.

And walked. And walked.

Horses clopped after her. Tack clinked. Past Tagmeth island, past the water meadows on the west bank, past the steep slope on the east that had been intended for winter wheat and since had been abandoned for fields anew. The wooden saddle tree chaffed her shoulder. The stirrups banged against her thigh. Her legs began to ache under their combined weight.

"This is ridiculous," said Damson behind her. "At least give me the saddle."

"Quiet," said Jame, not looking back. "The more uncomfortable I am, the more he is too. I hope."

They had gone perhaps a mile when Death's-head came thundering up behind them. The escorts' horses shied, eyes rolling, nostrils flaring as they caught the rathorn's reek of outrage. He came up behind Jame and snorted fiercely down the back of her neck.

"All right," she said, stopping, turning. "You don't want to go. I understand that. But I may need you. Choose."

He snarled. His ivory horns carved the air inches from her face, daring her to flinch within their strike. Then, with a grumble of disgust and a shake of his tangled mane, he submitted to the saddle with an ill grace.

Off they set again, Jame this time riding. The other horses kept a wary distance behind them. Perhaps with more trust than good sense, Jorin trotted just ahead of the rathorn's hooves.

Jame had expected Death's-head to leave the River

Road to guide them through the folds in the land;
however, he remained grumpy and disobliging. At this
rate, it would take them a good three days to reach
Gothregor. She had thought that it would serve Tori
right if she didn't travel at the break-neck pace that had
last brought her to his doorstep. Now, though, she had
too much time to wonder why he had summoned her
at all.

By early afternoon, still on the River Road, they crested
a rise to find Restormir spread out before them on the
other side of the river. The Caineron fortress might have
been a fair-sized city with its eight walled compounds and
its bustling streets. Scarlet flags flew, each figured with a
golden serpent devouring its young. The water of marble
fountains flashed in a dozen public squares. Over all
loomed the tower. Its shaft was capped by the family
quarters known as the Crown, and that in turn was topped
by a garden. Half hidden by fruit trees was the stone
cottage where the Matriarch Cattila had dwelt. Jame
wondered who lived there now, if anyone, since the death
of that redoubtable old woman.

Behind her, the Knorth ten-command shifted into
formation. Travel on the River Road or its counterpart on
the west bank was supposed to be protected, but one
never knew what to expect from M'lord Caldane. Indeed,
as they approached, a body of riders spilled out of the
main gate-house and galloped across the bridge to
intercept them. It was at least a one-hundred command,
ten times their number. Tiggeri led it.

Death's-head snorted and his horned head came up,
balancing its lethal array of ivory armor and horns.

Whatever his mood, he was always ready for a fight. The ten-command stopped. The one-hundred slowed. Tiggeri urged his reluctant mount forward. The rathorn stepped to meet him, red eyes glaring down his long, armor-plated nose.

"Permission to pass?" asked Jame.

Tiggeri blinked, then grinned. "What, you don't mean to attack us?"

"Why would we do that?"

There was something wrong here, Jame thought. She and Tiggeri were enemies, no doubt, but surely no fight between them would be this random. Besides, what sort of a fool did he think she was, to bring so few warriors to an open assault?

"In that case," he said, his grin broadening, "why don't you come in? I've breakfasted at your keep and dined at your brother's. Time, perhaps, to return the hospitality. Besides, there is someone here whom you might like to see."

Lyra Lack-wit came immediately to mind. Jame worried about the girl, pitched back into the same mess she had been subjected to when barely a child. But she must long since have been sent south to Karkinor. Jame was tempted to go in to see for herself, but she didn't trust either Tiggeri's smile or his air of presenting, however obliquely, a hidden trap.

"Some other time," she said, and nudged a reluctant Death's-head past him.

The Caineron command parted to let her pass, or perhaps their mounts gave them no choice in the matter. Few equines could stand up to a rathorn, whose very scent could drive them mad. Death's-head stalked between their ranks, turning to hiss contemptuously in faces as he passed.

Huh, he seemed to say. *No fun here.*

Jame's ten followed.

They reached Mount Alban around dinnertime, and Kirien came down the long wooden stair to meet them. The young scrollswoman was usually so cool and poised. She still wore that mask, but as if it were something brittle, about to crack. Kindrie didn't appear at all, then or at supper. Jame had the impression that he and Kirien had disagreed. That put her at a loss. On one hand, she was eaten by curiosity. On the other, she didn't want to pry. What, after all, did she know about lovers' quarrels? What if something she said only made matters worse?

"I apologize if I seem distracted," said Kirien, stirring the acorn stew of which she had eaten none. "A dear friend died recently. He took the White Knife."

"Who?" asked Jame, before she could stop herself.

"Dunfause."

"Oh."

Of course, she remembered the man. He hadn't seemed happy at the Jedrak's dinner, and Kindrie even less so.

"Er . . . do you know why?"

Kirien played with her spoon, not raising her eyes. "No one does, nor why Kindrie didn't try to save him."

So that was the problem.

"My cousin is a dedicated healer. He must have had a reason."

"What could that have possibly been? He said that

Dunfause might have wanted death, but why? Oh, I knew that Kindrie was jealous, but I never dreamed...."

She stood up suddenly, upsetting her bowl so that its turgid contents spilled across the table.

"Oh," she said again, staring down at the mess. Her face had gone white. "So clumsy. I—I have a headache. We will meet again at breakfast." And she fled.

But she didn't come down the next morning, sending only an apology: "Sorry."

Kindrie sent nothing, not even himself. Jame was a bit miffed at that, but she supposed that he was off in some corner of the college nursing a similar sore head and heart.

That night her ten stopped at Shadow Rock, where Cousin Holly appeared to have his own problems.

"It's not as if m'lady Rawneth has done anything recently," he said, fingering a mug of cider, regarding his young son as the boy rushed back and forth in the hall shouting "Kitty!" while a harassed Jorin slunk from cover to cover. "I would almost feel better if she did. This quiet is...unsettling. Like a bated breath."

"Have you sent your troops off to Lower Bashti?"

"Yes. Not many of them, mind, but we feel their absence here keenly."

The Danior numbered only about one thousand at the best of times, the Randir eight or nine times more.

"Caldane's opinion lingers," Holly said, as if reading her mind. "Not one lord from each house as equals on the High Council but the houses in command by order of size. That would be the Caineron, the Ardeth, the Randir, and the Brandan."

"Tori would never agree."

Holly laughed without mirth. "That's if he maintains his rank as Highlord. Remember, cousin, your house is only twice the size of mine."

With his words still ringing in her ears, Jame reached Gothregor the next day.

II

"I ADMIT," said Torisen, a bit sheepishly, "that I panicked. This is the letter that Harn sent."

Jame took it and read.

It was late afternoon on the 70th of Summer. The sun had recently set behind the western Snowthorns and cool shadow flooded the river valley below. Sparrows, homing, rustled the ivy outside the window with sundry scuffles and chirps. How much more peaceful this was than the last time she had been here, yet tension still filled the air.

"I see what you mean about local politics," she said, glancing up. "There's a lot here about the Bashti royal family, especially about Crown Prince Jurik, who is either promising, or a problem, or both. The references to his mother Queen Vestula puzzle me too. Harn sounds afraid of her. The king of Bashti is currently using our troops to parade about his country, I presume to his greater glory. He's also negotiating a trial match between them and Duke Pugnanos of the Transweald, also against Karkinor. What does that mean?"

Torisen began restlessly to pace his study which, being

in a narrow drum tower of the old keep, was only a few strides in each direction. He looked better than the last time she had seen him, but new lines furrowed his fine-drawn face. Were there more silver strands in his black hair than before? He was Shanir, after all, and might eventually go pure white like Kindrie even without added stress. So, for that matter, might she. She at least had understood that beforehand.

"Since Caldane withdrew his offer," he said, "Duke Pugnanos has employed a company of Brandan. As I understand it, in the past the Kings set their Kencyr troops against each other in arranged fights, almost like competitions. Political or territorial stakes were decided in advance. Bets too. The randon guaranteed a fair outcome and, because no one dared to accuse a Kencyr of lying, they were believed."

"I can see that working, up to a point."

"You have to understand that the Central Lands were barbaric when we first encountered them. No rules. No mercy. No honor. Harn used to say that, in a sense, we civilized them. However, it never became instinctual. Every generation had to learn the rules anew."

"This time, it's thirty years later and the rules have changed."

"Apparently. No one has yet tested that, as far as I know. Some older rulers are still in power—Prince Uthecon of Karkinor for one, King Mordaunt of Bashti for another. Rothurst of Mirkmir. Ort of Ordor. And there are younger Kings: Pugnanos of the Transweald; Ostrepi of the Midlands; Harward of Hathir. The east and west bank, Hathir and Bashti, might still be at war if Vestula, a

Hathiri princess, hadn't been contracted to Mordaunt, the king of High Bashti."

"I still don't understand what upset you so much."

"Read on."

Several scrawled pages later, she looked up again. "He offers to resign his commission. Then he says that he can't leave. It isn't clear what he wants, or what he will do, or why."

"Now read this." He handed her another scroll.

Jame regarded the broken seal. "From the Commandant? But he's stationed with the Caineron at Karkinaroth across the river."

"Read."

Jame did, frowning. "Sheth Sharp-tongue is oblique, as always. He says that Harn appears to be giving Prince Jurik randon training. That's unusual, although not actually forbidden."

"What follows is worse."

"I see that. Sheth hints, oh, so subtly, that Harn might compromise the Transweald or Karkinor games to favor this prince. That, he says, would be unfortunate. I should think so."

Torisen turned on his heel to face her. "So do I. The betrayal of the clauses has cut the ground out from under us. On what can we still depend, except our honor?"

"You hinted that you saw something in the contract to our advantage."

"Potentially, at least. The bad news is that it now states explicitly that we have to follow all orders, up to and including mutual slaughter. Then there's a piece of old news. I've compared notes with Mount Alban. The scrollsmen tell me that the contracts have always had a clause that if either party violates its terms, the agreement is void. That's in there too."

"Isn't that our answer? If the Kings order us to do the unthinkable, we refuse and walk away."

"There's more: according to this clause, if we break the contract, we forfeit all pay, past, present, and future. So far, Mordaunt hasn't paid us anything at all."

"Oh," said Jame. She understood that Gothregor had to survive the coming winter, hoping that the gates would support it in the coming year. "But if he doesn't pay us, isn't he in violation of the contract himself?"

"For that he isn't penalized, except by losing our service. That was their hidden clause, which we didn't discover until after we signed. The table turned, as it were. It never occurred to me that he simply wouldn't pay. He may yet, of course. Just the same," he added, returning to his current worry, "how can I question Harn Grip-hard about his honor?"

Harn had been his commander, then his subordinate, then his war-leader. He would never have risen without Harn's support, nor Harn without his. If Ganth and Adric had failed him as fathers, the burly randon had come close. Now, however, Tori found himself in the role of protector. Jame understood that, as she did the worth of the man. She had also depended on Harn during her year at Tentir, and had needed several times to protect him from himself. He was a Shanir berserker, after all, who had once dismembered a fellow Kencyr in his mad rage. Even the Commandant, it seemed, felt protective toward him.

"Agreed," she said, answering an unspoken question. "This is the other side of the bond. He needs us. Either you or I have to go to him."

Torisen gave a helpless shrug. "It can't be me. If I were to leave the Riverland now. . . ."

"I've talked to Holly. I understand. I'll go."

He gave her a crooked smile. "Yes. I thought that you would. We can keep company at least as far as Omiroth. Don't look so surprised. You said, when we last met, 'Ask questions.' Well, I've been getting messages from both Dari and Lady Distan about the Ardeth succession—this, while Adric is still alive. They both want my blessing without, necessarily, wanting me."

"So you mean to descend on them."

"How else can I judge the case?"

"This," said Jame, "should be interesting."

III

THE NEXT MORNING Jame and her ten again took the road south, this time accompanied by her brother, the Wolver Grimly, and a hundred-command honor guard.

"I forgot to tell you," said Torisen as they rode along, his black war-horse Storm keeping a wary eye on the white rathorn by his side who in turn regarded him with what seemed like amusement. "Farmer Rush turned up at Gothregor several days ago, much wroth. He accused you of quite a few things, which mostly boiled down to his claim that you were mismanaging a valuable asset, namely the gates."

"I wondered what he would say. Did he tell you that he tried to drive me out of Tagmeth?"

Torisen's smile quirked. "He didn't mention that. My impression, though, was that he thought he could do a better job of running the keep than either you or Brier."

"He wrongs Brier, at least."

"And that you were ignoring a wealth of gold and silver."

"Only obtainable if we want to invade Skyrr. Against Arribek sen Tenzi, though, I wouldn't recommend it."

"Ah, well."

"What will Rush do now?"

"A good question. He left for Tagmeth to great fanfare with a large command. Now he has returned alone, his pride gravely wounded. You, apparently, told him that he didn't belong in our house. Perhaps he will go elsewhere."

At this, Jame shifted uneasily in her saddle. "He knows about the gates now. He could compromise them, and us."

"Let's worry about that later," Torisen said, and his face settled back into lines of preoccupation. Was it Harn he worried about, or Adric, or both?

Word had gone ahead of them, so Omiroth was prepared for their arrival if not necessarily glad of it.

Before the great hall lay a courtyard lush with banks of flowers, filled with winding paths and miniature fruit trees. Here was a marble-rimmed fish pond, glinting with silvery scales. Jame wondered if this was where the cherished carp of Timmon's half-brother Drie had swum, before their father Pereden had make him catch and eat it.

"I never realized the horror of that before I met you and the Falconeers," Timmon had said, speaking of the

cadets at Tentir who were bound to various animals as
Jame was to Jorin, as Drie had been to his carp. "Now, the
whole thing seems abominable. And Father laughed."

With a shriek, a white peacock shook out its fantastical
tail at them. Feathers shimmered.

Such grace. Such remembered cruelty.

Dari and Lady Distan waited for them at the top of the
marble steps that led up to the great hall.

Dari was somberly dressed, as usual, and his mouth, as
usual, was tightly pursed. Allergic to his own rotting teeth,
he wouldn't show them if he could help it. Unfortunately,
their state also affected his disposition.

Lady Distan stood beside him, a vision in layers of pink
chiffon under a pale green damask robe, rather like a
middle-aged rose bud that refused to unfurl. Behind her
was her son Timmon. He might have matched her
splendor in a guard's coat of sky blue with silver lace trim,
but he also looked uncomfortable.

"Hello," said Jame to him, as her brother and the
Ardeth traded stilted greetings. "Nice jacket."

Timmon grimaced. "Don't tease me. It was Mother's
idea."

"Still playing dress up for her, are you?"

"You, on the other hand, appear set for an expedition.
I envy you. By the way, do you know where Lyra is? I sent
her a message at Restormir but never received an answer."

"For one thing, I doubt if any Highborn girl would be
allowed to correspond with anyone outside her family. For
another, she may not know how to read, much less how to
write. For a third, I think that she's been sent south to
Karkinaroth to Prince Uthecon."

Timmon looked aghast. "Her father has contracted her to that old man?"

He was used to getting what he wanted from women. At Tagmeth, however, Lyra had thwarted him with her sheer innocence—or was that ignorance? That he still thought about her at all surprised Jame.

The Wolver Grimly skirted the reception committee and joined them, looking ill at ease.

"So much finery," he said. "Too much."

"What happens to your clothes when you change into a wolf?" asked Jame.

Grimly considered this. "I never thought about that before. They just go away, and later come back."

"Maybe your clothing and fur are the same thing, in different forms."

"Maybe. At least I don't remember ever being naked."

"We have been invited to dinner," said Torisen, approaching them. Given that it was late afternoon and they were guests who had travelled all day to get there, this seemed reasonable.

"Oh," said Distan, behind him, "perhaps your . . . er . . . pet would feel more comfortable in the stable."

Jame looked around for Jorin, who was discovered dabbing at a bee head down in the throat of a lily. It buzzed angrily. He retreated, looking nervous.

"I think," said Torisen, "that she means Grimly. My . . . er . . . friend goes where I do, lady. Or we can reverse that, if you wish."

"Now, now, now," said Dari, screwing up his mouth, making a sour face. "Let's not quarrel. Omiroth can feed more than we few."

They were given guest quarters in which to refresh themselves and, later, in which to sleep. Not knowing what to expect, Rue had packed Jame's crazy-quilt court coat. Now she tried to press the creases out of its rich, heavy fabric.

"I'll sleep with this under my mattress tonight," she said, giving it a shake. "Tomorrow...."

"Or the next day, or the next, it will be wrinkled again."

Rue harrumphed.

Once dressed, Jame left Jorin curled up for a nap on her bed and went down the hall to her brother's room. Grimly was there, crouching in a corner.

"You don't have to eat with us if you don't want to," Torisen was saying to him.

"It's not just that Lady Distan was rude." The Wolver gave a shaky laugh. "After all, to many people we of the Holt or the Weald are only filthy vermin." Then he shivered and rubbed his arms as if against a chill. Was that rough cloth on them or prickling fur? "Worse, there's a bad feeling here, a bad smell, and no, it isn't just m'lord's unfortunate teeth, although they don't help."

Torisen regarded him with concern. "What do you fear?"

"I don't know! Nothing good."

"Where are your guards?" Jame asked Torisen, aside.

He gave her a disbelieving look. "You can't possibly believe ... in the mess-hall, I suppose."

"Humor me. Take your sword."

It was a keen-edged, businesslike weapon, she noted as he buckled it on over his black dress coat whose fit it distorted. However, it wasn't Kin-slayer. For the most part, he had put aside that dire blade. Perhaps in his recent illness he had feared he would go after either her or Kindrie with it. This one would have to do. Also, they had Rue. Also, Grimly, who went down with them slinking at Torisen's heels.

Dinner was served in the great hall, in the midst of which a table had been set. The Ardeth sat on one side of it, the Knorth on the other. Grimly slunk to cover behind Torisen's chair. Rue self-consciously took the seat to Torisen's right, there being none beside Jame. They were to be a small party, it seemed. Presumably the keep had another, less formal dining room for its other Highborn residents.

He doesn't want witnesses, thought Jame, glancing across the table at Dari.

A harpist began to play in a screened off alcove. Servers offered basins of hot water in which the diners might wash their hands, then departed. The first course was brought in: frumenty with almonds and venison, cheese tart, and sorrel soup. Evening light fell dimly on the tiled floor from high, stained glass windows. The table was lit by a many branched chandelier.

"Where is Adric?" asked Torisen, taking up a spoon to address his soup.

Distan fluttered a pink gloved hand. "Oh, he often eats in his room. So much more discreet. His table manners . . ."

Dari glared at her. "Quiet." He too was drinking soup, or trying to. His teeth, thus revealed, were a distressing series of gaps, rotten stumps, and fresh white nubs. Obviously, not all of them fell out at once; rather, the cycle of decay and regeneration never seemed to end. "Lord Ardeth is well enough, considering."

Distan pouted. "Well enough to have chosen my son as his heir, at least."

"Well enough to rule himself, if he so chooses. D'you think I want to supplant him?"

"Of course you do. Do you think that I am unaware of the messages you have sent our dear Highlord, asking to be made lordan regent?"

Dari looked disgusted. "He only has to pull himself together."

"It doesn't work that way! He is old, old, old, and so are you. This house belongs to the young."

"You and I, lady, are much the same age."

She looked flustered, a rose bud about to erupt. "I meant my son, and well you know it."

The second course was brought in, to a sudden silence at the table. Trenchers of bread were cut at a sideboard and placed before them. Silver platters were set on the table, laden with roast capon, dilled veal balls, humble pie, and swan neck pudding. The diners helped themselves sparingly. By now, only Rue still had an appetite, and the parade of food showed no sign of ending anytime soon. It also occurred to Jame that the courses were coming rather fast, as if to forestall disaster.

"A morsel of meat, my lord?" said Distan, graciously offering Torisen a slice of capon. "I find that it goes very well with lemon wine sauce."

"Thank you," said Torisen, and cut the smallest possible bite.

The attendants left.

"Really," said Dari to the lady, "I find your reasoning difficult to follow. You hold that Adric is competent to choose his lordan, but not to rule himself."

"That was then. This is now."

Timmon put down his knife with a clatter. "Would anyone care to ask me if I want to be the next lord of this house?"

"No!" Dari and Distan snapped at him simultaneously.

"Mother knows best, dear," the latter added, patting his hand. "Be quiet."

Jame stirred. "Surely he's entitled to an opinion."

Distan blinked wide eyes at her from behind her froth of a mask. "Of course he isn't. Neither are you. But do have a veal ball. They are excellent. I . . . we have the finest cook in the Riverland, if sometimes somewhat distracted. Of course, Pereden should have been Adric's heir, and was until his heroic death against the Waster Horde. Dari, your reasoning puzzles me too. You say that Adric could govern if he put his mind to it, and yet you plot to steal both his power and that of his designated heir."

"This is now. That was then."

"Oh, now you're just being snide."

Dari had been dissecting a morsel of humble pie, smaller and smaller, as if to fit it between the gaps in his teeth.

"Would you like a servant to cut up your food?" Distan asked sweetly.

Dari snarled at her. "It always comes back to Pereden, doesn't it? Your perfect courtier. Your perfect mate. Adric adored him, more than life, as well I know. I'm sure you did too," he added, turning to jeer at Timmon. "Who could ask for a more noble father, eh?"

Timmon had gone white. "You don't know anything," he sputtered. "You don't know what he was, or how he died."

Jame reached across the table and tugged his sleeve. "Timmon, think."

He turned on her, looking stricken. "Can you imagine that I haven't? Many a night, many a day . . . here, in this house, I am the shadow of a lie."

The servers trotted in with the third course, this time fish: smoked pike in pastry, roast salmon, baked lamprey, gingered carp. These platters jostled with the meat course before, threatening to spill off the table.

"Oh, clear, clear first!" Distan implored, and some dishes were.

"Get out!" shouted Dari, rising and stomping a foot. "Out, out, out! You, cousin, what do you mean?"

The hall emptied of scared servitors. The harp had fallen silent with a discordant fumbling of fingers. Timmon was left leaning on the table, panting.

"I have to say this," he said to Jame. "My soul isn't my own until I do. Mother, I saw him in the soulscape, in the Gray Lands, a wretched thing woven of dry grass and dead twigs.

"'I . . . I . . . I was my father's favorite,' he said. 'I . . . I deserved to be. I deserved everything.'

"And then he told me he thought he could turn the Waster Horde, but he couldn't. 'Everyone fails me,' he said. 'Poor me.' The Wasters told him that if he joined them he could take Torisen's place. He joined. That was

Pereden at the Cataracts, calling on our troops to surrender. That was Pereden fighting you, Highlord, in the Heart of the Woods, but you already know that.

"'I will have my revenge,' he said. 'I will tell my father what I have done, and why.'

"'It will kill him,' you said. 'And I promised to protect his interests. I keep my promises, Peri.'

"And you broke his neck. To protect Adric. To protect us all. I honor you for that."

"Well!" said Dari, sitting back down. "I thought there was more to the story, but this . . . !"

"I don't believe it," said Distan. Her mouth had fallen open. Within her mask, she looked almost as hollow as her consort had in the Gray Lands. "This is delusion. Madness. Son. My child. You can't mean it."

"Trust me. I do."

Dari started to laugh, in the process spitting defunct teeth tipped with blood on the snowy tablecloth. "Oh," he said, wiping his mouth, "this is delicious. Highlord, if you fail to confirm me as lordan regent now, what a tale I will have to tell Adric!"

"If you do," said Torisen, "it will kill him."

A servant appeared in the doorway. "Lord Ardeth," he announced.

Adric came into the hall, smiling. His white hair hung in straggly locks. His face was as creased as old leather. Food stains disfigured the front of his ivory lace court coat.

"Ganth!" he said, opening his arms to Torisen. "And Pereden, my dear son." This, to Timmon, whom he also embraced.

Timmon took his fine-boned hands and led him to the

table. Rue quickly gave up her seat and went to stand behind Jame. "Grandfather. Come. Sit. Eat."

"Adric," said Torisen. "How are you?"

"Fine, fine, fine, now that all of my loved ones are here. And you too, Distan? Tell me: have your outgrown your spots yet?"

"That," said the lady with a tight smile, "was long, long ago. Here is your grandson, Timmon."

"I remember when you were freckled like a trout. Or a lamprey. Of course, a matron's mask may cover many sins."

Servitors rushed in carrying platters of sweet tarts and pastries—tansy cake with peppermint cream, shortbread, elderberry funnel cake, and butternut. These they piled on top of the fish course, which no one had had time to taste.

"Oh, go away!" shrieked Distan.

Adric sat down and picked up a tansy tart. "My favorite," he said, taking a bite. "Ganth, pray try one."

Torisen resumed his seat as did the rest except for Grimly, now cowering flat to the floor in his complete furs, trying unsuccessfully not to whimper.

"Speaking of sins," said Adric to Distan, "tell me: do you still maintain your supposedly secret correspondence with the Randir?"

Distan looked momentarily discomposed, but rallied. "Our dear Lady Rawneth as good as rules a major house," she said. "I find her interesting."

"Has she also interested you in the scheme of her ally, Lord Caineron, that the largest houses should rule the Kencyrath?"

The lady nervously played with the frilled neck of her mantle. "Well, it only makes sense, does it not? The bigger the house, the more powerful the lord. After all," she added with a simper, "here you are."

"Here, also, at our table, is one who rules over us all by sacred tradition and blood right. Would you care to explain your views to him?"

Distan gave a light, brittle laugh. "Now, would that be gracious? He is, after all, our guest."

"Ganth, would you care to comment?"

"By no means, sir," said Torisen politely. "Continue."

Adric turned to Dari. "And where does your allegiance lie, grandson?"

"Grandfather, you know that I am loyal to you."

"And yet you aspire to the position of lordan regent that should, in the fullness of time, be your nephew's."

Dari looked confused. "Who? Pereden's? You must mean Timmon's."

Jame wondered: *Had the old lord overheard at least part of the previous conversation? If so, sweet Trinity, how much?*

"You never liked Pereden, did you?" Adric said to Dari. "Is it because he is all the things that you are not? Brave, faithful, charming . . . what are you compared to that?"

He spoke genially, but Jame noted that his hand shook. The hair rose, quivering, on the back of her neck. There was power here, barely contained, deeply flawed.

"And you question my wisdom in making my grandson Timmon my heir. Surely it is my right to do so."

The room seemed to tilt, past and present shifting.

Madness is contagious, thought Jame, and saw Dari sway where he sat under this assault.

Distan drew away from him.

Timmon looked confused.

"We were a great people, once," said Adric gently. Crumbles spilled down his cuff from a pastry too tightly held. "We kept our god's faith. We maintained our honor. Now what have we come to, that creatures like you crawl among us? Have I lived to see such dishonor?"

"Grandfather . . ."

"Be still!"

The whiplash of his will threw plates from the table and the chairs lurched back a step. The Wolver yelped.

Attempting to distract him, Distan offered Adric a plate. "Another of your favorites?"

Adric looked down. "Carp for dessert? How eccentric."

"I . . . I . . . I do not deserve this," Dari stuttered, rallying. "I said you could still rule, if you would just try. I only want what is good for our house. Don't you?"

"Traitor!"

Dari gagged. He had inhaled one of his own loose teeth and was choking on it.

Torisen thrust back his chair to rise. Its back legs caught on Grimly, who crouched behind it. The chair tipped. As Torisen went over backward, clutching the chair's arms, Adric reached across him and gripped the hilt of his sword, which slid smoothly out of its well-oiled sheath. Torisen rolled over his shoulder, back onto his feet.

Too late.

Adric had lunged across the table and driven the point

of the sword into Dari's throat. Dari tumbled sideways out of his chair into Distan's lap. Distan jumped up, screaming, and spilled him onto the floor.

Jame and Timmon both scrambled to help, but it was a hideous wound. In a tide of blood, looking incredulous, Dari choked out the errant tooth and collapsed. Eyes, mouth, and throat all gaped.

"I think he's gone," said Timmon, as if hardly believing it.

"I know he is," Jame said, and closed his eyes.

Adric dropped the sword on the table and swayed where he stood, one hand pressed against his heart. Torisen caught him as he fell.

He smiled up into Torisen's face.

"My son," he said, and died.

Servants ran in, stared aghast, and ran out. The keep's alarm began to sound.

❦ Chapter V ❦
Bound South
The Silver: Summer 72–99

I

"IT WASN'T YOUR FAULT," said Jame.

"It was my sword."

"Which I asked you to bring, and I apparently am becoming That-Which-Destroys. Am I to blame, then?"

"Of course not."

"The thing is, if you start taking responsibility for everything, it never ends. Believe me, I know."

They were sitting on a bench in the court garden by the fish pond, stalked by haughty peacocks but otherwise left alone. It was the next day. Few in Omiroth had slept the night before, nor probably would until both Adric and the unfortunate Dari had been given to the pyre on the morrow. The new Lord Ardeth went where he was told and did as he was bid, all in a state of shocked disbelief. His mother seldom left his side. It was anyone's guess, though, how many of her whispered admonitions he actually heard.

"Who will rule at Omiroth?" Torisen asked, as if reading her thoughts.

"The Ardeth have chosen Timmon and you confirmed him last night."

"I'm only the Highlord. Lady Distan will still be here when I go, after the pyres. You should leave for Bashti as soon as possible, though. There's still Harn."

On to the next problem, thought Jame. How like her practical brother. Only time would tell how Timmon faced up to his new, unwelcome responsibilities. In the meantime, Tori would have to confront his own, as would she.

"I still think you were right to come," she said. "This was a festering situation. It needed to be lanced."

He looked sharply at her. "At such a cost? Pardon me if I am less free with the life of my oldest friend. No. That was unfair." He clapped his hands on his knees, frustrated. "You see, I meant to go on to Kestrie and Kraggen to see what I could do about the Edirr and the Coman. Now I wonder if I might cause harm there too."

"Someone told me once—an Arrin-ken, I think—that a potential Tyr-ridan will be potent across all three aspects of our god until each of us settles into our own. While I often destroy, I have also preserved and created, if not quite as competently, or do I mean 'completely'? If I had stopped to think too much, though, might I have done nothing at all, for good or ill? I wish you would go on asking questions. The answers could save us all."

He gave her a wry smile. "You've thought about this, haven't you?"

"Well, I came to it younger than you did. That's some

revenge for the ten-year gap in our ages, twin. And, as you say, you're still Highlord."

"Ah. Just the same, Kraggen and Kestrie look like squabbling children compared to Omiroth. I find that I don't have much patience with the Edirr and the Coman. As soon as I can, I will return to Gothregor. Will I try this experiment again? That remains to be seen."

II

AS IT HAPPENED, Jame didn't leave until after the pyres either. To have done so earlier would have seemed disrespectful, and she didn't want the Ardeth any more upset than they already were. Besides, she wanted to talk to Timmon.

"I wish I were going with you," he said when they could finally snatch a moment alone together. "If Grandfather hadn't died, I would have, despite Mother. She says that I have duties here now. She's probably right. You'll ask about Lyra there?"

"As soon as I get a chance. I hear that the Knorth have games scheduled in Karkinaroth after the ones in Transweald. If I can, I will go. But see here, Timmon, what do you mean by that girl?"

He laughed ruefully. "Be damned if I know. She's a pest and sometimes a twerp, but I've never met anyone like her—except, perhaps, for you."

That surprised Jame. "I'm also a twerp and a pest?"

"You have no artifice, as far as I can tell. I wouldn't call you innocent, exactly, but you don't play silly games."

"You have no idea what I've seen or done."

"Someday," he said with, a touch of his old, charming smile, "you will have to tell me."

Then the Lady Distan found them and they had to part.

III

THE FUNERAL was held at dusk that night in the garden, a large swatch of which had by then been cleared to make way for it. All day, retainers and family visited the court bringing tokens of respect as well as spices and precious oils hoarded for just such an occasion. The two pyres rose side by side, one low, the other increasingly high with stepped sides built of rare, fragrant wood, garnished with all the flowers of the despoiled garden and several peacocks, their tails displayed, their necks wrung.

A gibbous moon rose. Under it gathered Adric's household and as many of his Kendar as could fit in the surrounding arcade. This would be a strictly traditional ceremony, Jame supposed; Adric had, after all, been a very traditional Kencyr. That he had put up with her at all she still found amazing, but then Tori had never been conventional either and the old lord had supported him faithfully, despite their differences and Adric's need to manipulate.

She noted three women standing at the foot of the larger pyre. Judging by their fine clothing and masks, two of them were elderly Highborn, one supporting the other who silently wept. The third woman was younger and more plainly dressed, a Kendar with broad shoulders, strong arms, and a nervous air. At least, her hands kept opening and closing. A black robed priest stood by them.

"Who are they?" Jame asked her brother.

"Adric's oldest women-kin and his last attendant. That must be a position of particular honor."

The biers emerged from the house, surrounded by torches, and were carried down the steps by the old lord's remaining immediate family. Timmon walked foremost among these, looking as pale as his grandfather. Lady Distan followed in dignified silence, no longer a bud but now in her crimson robes a full-blown, regal rose.

This is a queen, her proud stance seemed to assert. *Make way for her.*

The bearers raised each bier to the top of its mound. Dari was covered with a plain cloak, to signify his dutiful if reluctant humility. Adric's shroud was richer, cream velvet beaded with pearls, scattered with luminous moonstones. Wealth would go to the fire with him, to his house's honor as much as to his own.

The priest gave the three women each a cup. They drank. Then they mounted the pyre, the Kendar helping her older companions. All three lay down on its steps beside the peacocks and folded hands across their chests.

Jame realized that there would be no blood spots on cloth here, no surrogate sacrifices. This was the real thing.

"I didn't know that Adric was a blood-binder," she said, feeling breathless.

"Neither did I," Torisen replied through tight lips.

The priest took a flaring torch and offered it to him. "Lord, honor your patron," he said. "Light the fire."

Torisen looked at those still figures. "No," he said.

The crowd murmured. This was an insult.

The priest leaned closer. "Take it," he said. "They are already dead."

Timmon seized the torch from the priest's hand, but then he hesitated, looking ghastly.

"Go on," mouthed his mother.

"Not the boy," said Torisen, glancing at him.

Jame grabbed the priest. "If they are all dead as you say, prove it. Say the pyric rune."

He glared at her, then took a deep breath. The rune scorched its way out of his throat, making those who heard it flinch back as if from searing heat. It struck the bodies on the pyre so that they too seemed perforce to inhale.

Ahhh, hahhh . . .

Chests rose, chests fell, exhaling smoke. More seeped out from under robes, from under masks. Tongues of flame licked outward, blackening cloth, blacking faces. Deep within the pyres, oil-soaked kindling caught. Torisen watched as the man who would feign have been his father crumbled into charred ruins.

Jame was about to look away when her breath caught and she grabbed Torisen's arm.

"What?"

The principal pyre folded inward, as it was designed to do, dropping its occupant into its incandescent heart. Flames leaped upward. Sparks flew against the moon. Onlookers sighed.

The priest choked on a seared, constricted throat. He was

trying not to laugh. "Highlord, you have proved yourself false to your oldest friend. Who will trust you now?"

"Oh, shut up," said Jame.

IV

LATER, she told herself that it was only heat that had made the young Kendar's fingers clutch each other so desperately. She couldn't still have been alive in that inferno . . . could she?

Then, it had all collapsed.

What came to mind was Bear on his pyre in the White Hills, how his brother Sheth had seen him move in the fire and had pulled him out. Life had been a torment for Bear for a long time after that, in so many ways. Here, once the pyre had fallen, surely there had been no more hope, no more fear.

But the memory haunted her.

Could Tori put an end to such practices? How would traditional Kencyr respond if he tried to do so?

"Who will trust you now?" the priest had asked.

V

THE NEXT DAY, early, Torisen left for Gothregor and Jame for the Central Lands. Grimly went with her. Events at Omiroth had so badly shaken him that he too only wanted to go home. Jame also had Damson's ten-command, and was glad of it. Apparently, this was what

Torisen had had in mind when he had ordered her to bring an escort—Kendar she knew to accompany her into a strange new land.

He had been thinking about more than that, as it turned out. Before they parted, he had turned to her and said, "One more thing: in Bashti you should be able to make judgments based on what you see and hear, without waiting weeks for my approval by post rider. I authorize you to act for me."

The memory of that still stunned her. How far they both had come in matters of trust, and what a weight to place on her shoulders.

That first day, they passed between Kraggen on the west bank and Kestrie on the east.

"Greetings," said Essiar, Lord Edirr—or was it his twin brother Essien?—tumbling down a bank to the road on the back of a bright chestnut mare, his hunting party behind him. The horses below jumped. Death's-head hissed through his fangs. Jame clouted him on the ear.

"Quiet," she said. Then, to the newcomer, "You don't mean to poach again, do you?"

Essien—or was it Essiar?—grinned. "What if we do? Daring Edirr, stodgy Coman. The game goes to the most skillful, whichever bank it is on. Why else maintain a bridge between us, eh?"

There was, indeed, a bridge. The Silver had many such crossings between keeps, although they had to be rigorously maintained and often rebuilt, given the writhing of the River Snake down whose length the Silver ran.

"Won't the Coman be watching their end?"

"Oh, they did at first and may be doing so now, but with so many of their troops stationed in Mirkmir they have few to spare. We Edirr, likewise, are short-handed."

"Cousin Holly at Shadow Rock says much the same. It strikes me that the smallest keeps suffer the most from the current situation."

"And you don't?"

Jame considered that. "Torisen hasn't complained about it, but it did occur to me that our barracks at Gothregor rang a little hollow. Then too, we all miss Harn. By the way, your raids are making my brother nervous."

His smile broadened. "So?"

"He needs your support, and you need his. Think about it."

Essiar thought, and grinned again. "Essien sends his greetings. You and Torisen are also twins, yes?"

This was far from general knowledge. Some like Adiraina might have guessed it, but there was still that ten years' difference between their ages.

"Why would you say so?" she asked.

"An instinct. Don't you also finish each other's thoughts?"

That, at least, was true.

"Ride wary," Jame said to him.

"Ha!" he said, and spurred away.

VI

THAT NIGHT they camped ten miles south of the keeps, where the Riverland ended.

From here, the Northern Host had taken nineteen days to reach the Cataracts when Torisen had led it down to face the Waster Horde. However, that had been largely a forced march at seventy miles or more a day with *dwar* sleep at night. The Kendar on foot had done better than the horses.

"The fastest way would be to travel by post," Torisen had said, with a sidelong glance at Harn's letter. "There are stations roughly every twenty-five miles. Eleven or twelve days from here to Bashti..."

But those stations were set up mostly for messengers, with a limited number of remounts each. Even a party as small as Jame's would have over-taxed if not crippled that vital service. Besides, she didn't want to arrive alone.

"Harn has survived this long," she had said. "He can wait a few days longer."

So here she was, looking south down the slide of the Silver, with her command making camp behind her. Had she been right about Harn? How would she feel if she arrived too late, whatever that meant?

Damson spoke at her shoulder:

"One of our horses may be pulling up lame. Already. Permission to swap it out for a pack pony?"

"Yes, of course. The next station may have an available replacement. Let's hope there aren't more drop-outs."

"Forty-five miles a day from now on. You hope to keep that up?"

"Weather and terrain permitting. We can but try."

The next day they came to the first station, which did have a mount to spare although it cut their tiny herd by a third and Jame got some sour looks.

Rue's Stubben tried an experimental limp of his own, but gave it up when strenuously urged.

Death's-head snorted with disgust at a pace that must have seemed painfully slow to him. He showed no sign of leading them off into the folds in the land, however, assuming they even existed here. At least, Jame had never seen any signs of them. As the day's heat settled on the rathorn, he seemed to go to sleep on his feet while still shambling forward. The rest of the company loped after him. That night and each thereafter, he shook himself awake and disappeared to hunt, with Jorin and Grimly trotting hopefully on his heels. All three were carnivores if not, on the rathorn's part, omnivores.

On the fourth day from Omiroth, they passed the way that turned off to the Grindark keep at Wyrden, but had no reason to visit it. This was where Torisen had nearly gotten his throat cut, Jame remembered. It was also where they had found the lost mail pouch with news in it of the Southern Host's disastrous encounter with the Horde in the Wastes. Here Torisen's mad dash to the Cataracts had really begun.

Beyond that, the Oseen Hills opened out on the eastern bank and rolled on for three more days, parched and singing under the late summer sun. The wells at post stations supplied water. Dried rations came out of packs.

On the 81st they reached the Ever-Quick as it rushed down from the Ebonbane and the Anarchies between the Oseen and Ordor, northernmost of the Central Lands.

"A third of the way to Bashti," said Grimly, coming up beside Death's-head although maintaining a respectful distance from him. The Wolver rose and shook off the road's dust. Fur flew. In the heat, he was shedding. "Halfway to my home, the Grimly Holt."

"How are your paws?"

"Sore."

"You could ride one of the ponies."

"Better you should ask your cat."

Jorin had plumped down to chew noisily on spread, tufted toes. He sneezed, stood up, and jumped onto Death's-head's back behind the saddle. The rathorn jerked awake and bolted. The saddle's high cantle kept Jame from shooting off over his tail. Jorin dug in his claws and wailed. Sometime later, they juddered to a stop, whereupon Death's-head put his hooves together and bucked them both off.

"That could have gone better," said Jame, picking herself up, ruefully regarding a rip in the knee of her pants. Nothing was broken, however, and Jorin, catlike, had landed on his feet.

Damson pulled up beside them on a sweating horse. "This is no time," she said, "to show off."

"Somewhere in the luggage is my armor, also a crupper. Find it, will you?"

While Damson did this, Jame had words with a truculent Death's-head. "You don't like having your rump attacked. I understand that. This should help, though."

The Kendar brought back barding in the form of a heavily quilted cape that fit over the rathorn's otherwise unprotected hind-quarters.

Jame secured it to the saddle, then wrestled up Death's-head's tail, which he was inclined to clench between his haunches. "Quit it," she said, slapping him on the flank and buckling the crupper's strap when he flinched. "What?"

This, to Rue, who had also flinched. "Nothing."

"Now, let's try this again. Jorin, up."

The ounce looked dubious. However, obedient, he crouched and sprang. The rathorn shied under his weight but steadied, still glaring.

"Better," said Jame. "I do prefer it when my children don't quarrel."

Their bolt had brought them up to a bridge. For some reason, at this point the River Road shifted from the east to the west bank, although Jame could see that a minor road continued on the way they had been going. A scout went ahead to make sure the span was sound—always a risk over the Silver. This was the cadet Wort, Jame noted. She had been aware of the girl on the ride south but hadn't known quite what to say to her. Wort had declared her loyalty to Jame by growing long hair and elaborately braiding it, in contrast to the usual randon short cut. During his invasion of Tagmeth, Gerridon had made her hack it off. That might seem trivial, but it wasn't.

The way having been proven safe, they crossed over and camped on the western bank, lest something untoward happen in the night.

For the next two days they rode around the White Hills. While the company had talked and sung before, here they were quiet in the shadow of that ominous land. No one would ever forget how Ganth Gray Lord had descended on the Kings' Host of assembled Kencyr mercenaries. It was said that Ganth's hands were still red with the blood of his slaughtered womenfolk and that his madness had infected those who rode after him. That the Bashtiri Shadow Guild had slain them, there was no doubt, but who had paid for the contract? Ganth blamed the Seven Kings. His own people stood in the way of his vengeance. He struck them down until through sheer numbers rather than force of arms they overwhelmed him. Exile had followed, and thirty years of darkness for the Kencyrath. Before that, the hills had earned a new name, white as they then were with the ashes of the Kencyr dead.

They still had a bleached quality and were often overhung with dust, or mist, or the ghost of smoke. Birds had skimmed the Oseen Hills, crying. None flew here unless so high that they were mere silent dots against a stricken sky.

"Torisen cut across those," Jame said to Wort, peering into the twilight beyond their campfire. "He was in a hurry, of course, but oh so rash."

"What did he find there, lady?"

"It seems that the hills have gone soft. When two parts of Rathillien are somehow alike, they may overlap. Tori wandered out of the Central Lands altogether and into the Haunted Lands. Haunts followed him back."

"Like the ones that came through Tagmeth's gates last Winter's Eve?"

"Yes, very like. They are the returned dead, you know. Nothing where I grew up was entirely dead or alive except for us, and sometimes we weren't sure. It was all very unpleasant."

"I saw them then," said Wort with a shudder. "Can they look anything like that?"

She pointed.

Jame blinked the firelight out of her eyes. A tall figure stood motionless between the initial swelling of the dark hills. Wisps of luminous mist wreathed its unseen feet and swirled up its pale robes. It appeared to be watching the camp through what might have been a smiling waxen mask. Then, between one blink and the next, it was gone.

Jame shivered. "I don't know what that was," she said, "but I don't like it. Damson?"

"Here." The ten-commander materialized out of the night so suddenly that she must have been standing nearby, also watching.

"From now on, set extra guards."

Damson grunted in assent and stumped off to do so.

Again, Jame wondered where she had seen that face before. A similar tremor had run along her nerves at Kithorn with the Noyat shaman. Where else?

Wort nervously cleared her throat with the air of one determined to change the topic. "What are you making, lady?"

Jame held up the tangled work, noting that in doing so her hands shook. Trinity, that specter in the hills really had rattled her. With improvised needles, she had been attempting to knit something using long, white strands pulled from Death's-head's curry brush and woolen threads teased from a spare blanket. The result was not unlike an untidy bird's nest, made worse by the stitches she had just dropped.

"It may not amount to anything," she said. "I thought, though, that I would try to make you a hat. I'm sorry about your braids."

"Oh!" Wort involuntarily touched the dandelion ruff of her cropped hair. "Something with rathorn in it? That would be . . . wonderful!"

On the 84th they left the hills, glad enough to see them fall behind. By now, the country of Mirkmir was on their side of the river and ancient Hathir opposite them, the respective temporary homes of Coman and Ardeth forces.

Of course, Jame had travelled this way before, going to and coming from Kothifir. Then, however, her attention had been fixed on the immediate route. Now she noticed more. The Silver remained largely empty, no surprise given its treacherous nature. There were more bridges than she remembered, though, and more relics of those that had been abandoned. These latter often corresponded to the ruins of cities set back from the River Road, often no more than a few easily overlooked stones in a field. The capital of Mirkmir was an exception, although even it seemed to have turned its back on the Silver. At least, the company passed the moldering remains of extensive wharfs, only a few of which still welcomed small, scared-looking boats, some with chunks bitten out of their gunwales, others sunken and moldering in their slips with breached hulls.

That night Jame dreamed that the Master spoke to her out of the dark.

"Poor little girl," he said, and she could hear the smug smile in his laughing voice. "Do you really think yourself a match for me? Your brother and cousin are even more pitiful. I have bargained with Perimal Darkling itself and gained my wish. Who are you, to contest that?"

No one, she wanted to say. *I was a fool ever to think that I could.*

And with that she woke, shivering. His voice had taunted her before, since she had last heard it wail off into the desolation of his soul-image. She had freed the souls which her mother, the Dream-weaver, his sister, had reaped for him. What would he do now? How could she counter him?

I'm not ready, she thought. *Will I ever be?*

There was no more sleep that night.

A day later, on the 88th, they came to the edge of the great forest known as the Weald.

"Nearly home," Jame said to the Wolver Grimly. "Are you excited?"

He grinned. At the same time, though, he looked nervous. "It will be good to see my pack again, of course, but will they be glad to see me?"

"Why not?"

"Before I went north to the Riverland, I was in the Deep Weald with Yce for over a year. We Holt dwellers tend to look down on the Weald wolvers as primitive. Yes, that makes us snobs. Poetic ones at that, and again yes, I still think of myself as a poet. Where do I belong now?"

"Will you go back to her?"

"I don't know," he said, helplessly. "If I value my soul, I shouldn't, but I just don't know."

The Weald enclosed them with maple and birch and green, green shadows, so welcome after days in the hot glare of the hills. This easternmost corner of the vast forest was known as the Holt, a refuge for Grimly's folk. All day the company was aware that they were being followed although the watchers broke no branch nor snapped any twig. Fur brushed leaf, however, and wary eyes gleamed in the shadows. A murmur of speculation seemed to surround the riders:

Who are these people? Why is our prince with them? What prince?

"Hoy!" Grimly shouted at the trees. "This is me and these are my friends. Make us welcome, damn you!"

Near dusk, they came to the wolvers' lair, the shell of a keep in the heart of the Holt, to find a company of Jaran already ensconced as guests.

"We've always gotten along well with the forest-folk," their commander explained. "Sharp," she said her name was—a squat Kendar, once a randon, now a scrollswoman. The college at Mount Alban accepted many such people as they aged, although some became singers rather than historians or scholars. "Story and poetry create a mighty bond."

"Where are you bound?"

"To Mirkmir. There's a festival there soon to commemorate the breaking of the Elder Empires. Huh. Trust the Mirkmirians to make a celebration of something that only isolated them further. In the old days, they were part of Bashti. They still are, I suppose, but the Weald and the Silver have cut them off from the rest of the Central Lands. Perforce, they make a virtue out of that, and maintain more ties to the forest than anyone else does, for all that that pipsqueak Pugnanos calls his country the Transweald."

Wolvers moved among them in half-furs, shy but bright-eyed and prick-eared with curiosity, bringing cups of mead and skewers wrapped with strips of roast rabbit.

Out in the dusk, others of their number yipped and crooned softly, a chorus tuning to the night.

"How is your approach to the contracts working out?" Jame asked.

"Well enough so far. The Jedrak was right: people here love history. On the other hand, they howl if we present anything that conflicts with what they think they know, and stories vary from country to country. We nearly had a riot in Transweald."

"I've wondered as we rode: why has no one spoken of the Central Lands before this summer? I've travelled through them several times by the River Road, hardly knowing what I passed. They could have been blanks on Marc's stained-glass map, for all I knew."

Sharp grunted. "You are young, my lady. So are your Kendar. We randon elders, we remember too much. The White Hills were a horror beyond imagining. No one cared to remember, much less to reminisce, and so we turned our backs on the Central Lands, hoping never to return. You'll find Commander Harn much more knowledgeable than I am. After all, he was deeply involved with the Bashti court before Ganth's fall, but he may not care to talk about it, even now."

Jame stirred uneasily. She didn't like to be ignorant. Neither, like her brother, did she care to interrogate Harn Grip-hard. Graykin had sent her some reports, but he still seemed to be finding his way through a complex situation. Maybe he could answer more questions when they met.

"What will you perform in Mirkmir?" she asked, to change the subject.

"As usual, a mix of song and story. Would you like to hear?"

"Oh, yes," breathed the nearest wolver, putting down her ewer, to an eager, muted chorus from the others. They pressed close and crouched to listen. Jame's command also gathered around, Quill foremost. A mighty bond indeed.

"Well, then." Sharp settled back. Other Kendar sat down behind her, attentive, as if at a rehearsal. "Harrumph. First, some history:

"Long, long ago, Perimal Darkling, ancient of enemies, invaded that series of connected worlds known as the Chain of Creation, of which Rathillien is part. The Three-faced God bound together the Three People—Highborn, Kendar, and Arrin-ken—as the Kencyrath to fight it. Then our god abandoned us. We have fought a long retreat down the Chain ever since.

"When we came to this world over three thousand years ago, at first we concentrated on establishing border keeps. Yes, the shadows had followed us to the very rim of Rathillien and there we stopped them, but not at the cost that we expected. Instead of immediate war, years of mounting guard followed.

"In the meantime, we had to maintain our outposts. Those of us not on frontier duty contracted as mercenaries to the Central Lands, to the Seven Kings, to support our kinsmen where we expected the battle to break. Here, we became the kings' champions, settling their quarrels by force of arms, Kencyr against Kencyr, for the blood of Empires was too precious—they said—to spill. Years passed. A thousand of them. The waiting . . . it was hard."

The wolvers made plaintive sounds. The Kendar swayed to them.

Sharp slapped her knee, making everyone start.

"Then came the great weirdingstrom, of which I am sure you have all heard tell."

A singer behind her leaned forward and took over in a husky whisper. "Picture it: Night in the Central Lands, oh, so many, many years ago. All the dogs begin to howl . . ."

The surrounding forest swelled with low ululations. In the shadow of leaf and bark, eyes caught the firelight and glowed back. The audience had grown.

". . . and the wolves too, I suppose. They make so much noise that orders are given to strangle them all."

The howls died to a one last, plaintive yelp.

"That accomplished, a silence falls, but not for long. The earth begins to growl."

"Grr . . ." said the wolvers, tasting the sound with relish.

"A red mist comes down the Silver. It kindles lights in the air, on the water, and under it, as if whole weed beds have caught fire."

"Catfish jump out of the river and then head for the hills," another singer exclaimed. "Then the water boils and leaps up like a fountain. Whoosh!"

"It swallows islands," chanted a third, "jumping its banks, flooding the shore. Forests lance down from high banks like so many cast spears. Some lands sink. Others rise into new islands, new earth. Imagine!"

"Whole populations disappeared that night," Sharp added, in the historians' past tense. "Drowned, the survivors thought, but no bodies were ever found. On land, the ground rolled like waves, higher and higher until their crests burst."

"Cities fall," said the first singer in a hushed voice. "They have not been rebuilt to this day."

Another picked up the story, and another, and another, passing it from mouth to mouth behind Sharp, who seemed to be brooding between past and present.

"Then comes a great silence," a voice in the chorus cried. "Then comes the weirdingstrom itself."

"It smokes. It glows. A river of mist rises above the Silver's ravaged bed."

"Aroo!" breathed the wolvers.

"Some call it the Serpent's Breath," called one of their voices out of the dusk.

Another, excited, answered: "Yes, yes! Others say that this world rests on the back of the great Chaos Serpent. Its offspring run like veins under the earth, under the water, yes, even under the Silver."

"The Breath woke the River Snake," said Sharp, with a sudden drop to the matter-of-fact tone of a historian, "nor does it yet sleep. You ask why the Silver devours those who travel on it? Here, some would say, is your answer, and that led to the fall of the Elder Empires, which did not survive its emergence."

The audience, wolver and Kencyr, breathed again.

"Do you believe that, about the River Snake?" Jame asked as the keep returned to its hum and a light dusting of nervous laughter.

"I have heard it said." The Kendar accepted another mug of mead. "Do I believe it? Well, let's say that history is seen though many eyes. Sometimes, I don't know what

I believe. But we scrollsmen can at least fall back on that useful artifice, the Lawful Lie."

"You as well as the singers? I didn't realize that. Sorry. I don't mean to tease you. Actually, I first heard that part of your story from the Caineron Matriarch, Cattila, who told it to me as fact, with the Earth Wife sitting at her elbow. Then, later, I saw the River Snake's scales on the bed of the Silver, also his mouth under the well at Kithorn when I nearly fell in."

Sharp stared at her. "Truly? I was told that you had had unusual experiences."

Jame laughed. "Oh, believe me: this world is stranger than you can imagine."

The wolvers had resumed singing, their voices lacing in and out of the night air. Those within the keep sang in counterpoint to those who still haunted the shadows without, one inviting the other into the light, the other praising the dark. It was a warm, harmonious song evoking the night, and community, and love.

When they paused, a new voice arose. With growls and snarls and coughs, it traced a different side of life. Here the hunter chased the prey, and killed, and fed.

Red meat, its undertone said. *Fat on the bone. Who is to deny me those, and love beside?*

The Holt wolvers fell silent. Was this too raw for their poetic taste if not for their nature?

Grimly lowered his muzzle and waited.

The keep's murmur began again, but he was outside it.

"It made my hair crawl," said Jame to him, aside. "But it spoke a truth."

Later that night Jame woke suddenly, aware that

someone had moved. She saw Grimly rise and leave the keep. Beyond its shattered walls, a white wolf waited. Grimly went out to her and they padded off together, he a pace to the rear.

The next day the Knorth party emerged from the Holt, diminished by one. Had Grimly been right to go back into the Deep Weald with Yce? Jame didn't know. More and more, love struck her as a peculiar obsession, but since when had she thought about it at all?

Kindrie and Kirien, Grimly and Yce . . . would she ever have what they did? Did she even want it? Then there was Ganth and the Dreamweaver, also Gerridon with his honeyed promises to her in the dark. Ugh.

The next day, the 90th of summer, they began to pass between the west bank Transweald and the Midlands to the east. From now on, in the heart of the Central Lands, the River Road showed more traffic—merchants coming and going; herds of cattle being driven; wandering entertainers; priests and soldiers including a Brandan troop whose leader saluted Jame as they passed. There were also bold-eyed nobles who stared and laughed. Carts moved in nearby fields, following the late summer harvesters of rye, barley, and wheat. Smoke smudges in the distance marked towns, manors, and forts set well back from the ill-fated river. There were more bridges and more ruins, but only a few timid boats.

They passed the borders of Karkinor. A company of Caineron rode parallel to them for a day on the eastern road, watching their progress. Jame noted that none of them smiled. She wondered to what extent events here would reflect those in the Riverland.

On the 93rd, her company crossed a tributary's bridge into northern Bashti, or so Quill gleefully informed her:

"See? Here we are!"

Not quite.

Had she really paid so little attention to such details the last time she had come this way? Then again, she had been travelling with a broken collarbone, which did tend to distract one.

Two days later they turned westward off the River Road. This, she was informed, was Thyme Street, an ancient way leading back along the River Thyme all the way to High Bashti and beyond. From here, the rich plain with its fields of grain extended back for league on league. A low, rough horizon marked the Snowthorns on Bashti's western border. These grew in size, almost (it seemed) stealthily over the next few days. The land began to roll. Soon it turned to hilly pastures and orchards, dotted with groves of tall trees. The Oseen and the White Hills had seemed to be molded into swells that only varied according to size. Here the knuckled toe bones of mountains began to burst through the earth and goats clung to them like so many clumps of hairy lichen.

Meanwhile, traffic on the road increased—pedestrians, horse carts bearing families, ox wagons bound for the capital laden with fruits and vegetables or rumbling back empty, herds of swine and complaining cattle.

The number of roadside villages also increased. As they passed, children ran out to offer water for sale in leather cups or roast dormice on sticks. Many of them gathered, themselves like clamorous mice, to see the rathorn pass.

In turn, they were delighted to be snarled at. Death's-head didn't like civilization.

"Why don't you show off?" Jame asked him. "Prance a little."

He did for half a street, half-heartedly, then subsided with a grumble.

The hills grew more precipitous, the mountains ahead higher. They were following the river Thyme now along its north bank, where it cut through the hills on into its valley. Unlike the Silver, it was open to travel. Shallow-draft, broad-beamed barges slid past near the southern bank, going downstream. Others were rowed or dragged westward against the current by teams of oxen along tow paths.

On the 99th, the travelers began to pass plaques set in the surrounding sandstone bluffs, more and more of them. The cliff-face appeared to be practically hollowed out.

"What do you suppose . . ." Rue wondered.

Jame peered upward. "Names, dates, praise. At a guess, those are burial slots."

Where the bluffs receded, first into rocky canyons, then, grudgingly, into open land, there were more monuments. Some of these were simple tombstones. Others were guarded by elaborate statues: husbands and wives seated side by side, immortalized in stone; mythological beasts; geometric shapes. Others amounted to small marble houses, or not so small, set back from the road. A few mausoleums there could have comfortably housed a deceased family of forty and as many living guests. Perhaps, on occasion, they did. Many were beautifully maintained with guards lounging about their portals.

The largest of these, however, appeared to have been viciously ransacked. Three stories' worth of stained-glass windows had been smashed, opening into cavernous space. Doors hung ajar. Statuary lay in fragments across its facade, so many shattered marble limbs, so many truncated feet. Carrion birds squabbled on its threshold. A dog slunk out of a broken portal, something red in its jaws that looked like a severed human tongue. This despoliation must have happened recently.

The bluffs pinched in again, then spread out to ring a broad river valley full of cultivated fields. At the valley's heart stood High Bashti.

"Big," remarked Damson, reining in beside Jame.

This was an understatement. The city loomed out of the haze of smoke—cooking, incense, votive lamps—that hung over it. Two walls surrounded it. The outer circled the valley, to the south facing a secondary road that ran beside the river, to the east and north skirting the cliffs that were precursors to the mountains beyond. The inner wall was nearly embedded in the surrounding city, as if the latter had outgrown and was busily consuming it. Within both rose at least ten prominent hills topped with white marble structures. Oh, so much stone piled on top of stone.

"All right," said Jame. "I'm impressed."

Her small company rode down to the eastern gate, in the midst of a crowd, and were engulfed by it.

≈≈≈ Chapter VI ≈≈≈
High Bashti

High Bashti: Summer 99–100

I

"I DON'T KNOW why you're here," said Harn Griphard, fidgeting with a boot as if unsure how to put it on. "Everything is just fine."

Jame regarded him skeptically, then turned her attention to his lodgings, always a good measure of his true state of mind. While the room in which they stood was spacious and elegantly appointed, most of its sparse furniture was festooned with Harn's clothing and other possessions—pants in need of darning here, a dirty undershirt there; a pile of dismembered armor in one corner, the remains of supper on a tray in another. Harn's disorder had always kept a step ahead of him. Now it seemed to have progressed two or three paces beyond that. Without thinking, she picked up a crumpled jerkin and began to smooth it.

"Huh," said a disapproving voice.

There behind the door stood a sour-looking individual whom Jame recognized as Harn's servant Secur, a former randon excused from active service after an axe had taken off his right foot in a training exercise. Now he walked on a solid wooden shoe that clacked in counterpoint to the squeak of its leather ankle hinge.

That is my job, his expression said.

Feeling self-conscious, Jame dropped the jacket back into the general mess.

Light flooded into the room through its arcade of western-facing windows. The sun had nearly set behind the nearest hill, glaring through the white columns that crowned it. Jame's small command had taken hours to find its way here, across a broad, empty forum, through twisting roads, up and down slopes, between hovels and markets and the walled gardens of mansions. They might not have found it at all without the help of a gap-toothed urchin who, strangely, claimed to live here.

"Call me Snaggles," he had said, with a wide grin. "I watch out for the likes of you Kennies, I do."

Campus Kencyrath itself had also come as a surprise. It stood in a vale between hills near the center of town, a two-story ovoid of barracks surrounding a long, broad training field. During the Kencyrath's absence, a four-story wall had been built around it, with stepped benches perched on top of the original structure. Games had been waged below, Snaggles claimed, and religious rites that had outgrown their local temples. There were also sometimes inventive public executions, of which he spoke with great enthusiasm.

The field faced north and south along its long axis. On it, sargents could be heard shouting orders. A formation of Kendar charged up the green sward.

"Right face!"

As one, the column pivoted eastward as if about to storm their commander's quarters. Sunlight caught the tips of their raised spears.

"Right again. Wait for it, wait for it ... hut!"

Step, turn, and back they went southward, keeping cadence. *Thud, thud, thud* went feet. *Clash, clash* went armor. Someone nearby burst out clapping.

"Battlefield maneuvers," said Harn, absent-mindedly noting them. "There wasn't room for that at Tentir except in miniature around the keep. King Mordaunt is still negotiating a contest between our troops and those of the Brandan in Transweald. Duke Pugnanos keeps pushing for more autonomy from High Bashti. In particular, he wants the freedom to invade the Weald."

"Where the wolvers live."

"Yes. They aren't a country according to Bashti, nor in turn do they recognize Bashti as an overlord. They've always been free, and hold their borders accordingly. This irks Transweald. Well, you can tell that by its name."

"So that's what we would fight against, the Transweald's right to attack."

"And for their conquest to be acknowledged by Mordaunt."

"Who doesn't want to. Given that, why would he permit a contest at all?"

"Well, there's the prestige of the thing. Games are popular. Then too, the rumor is that Pugnanos is bribing him. Mordaunt wants money to build that fancy temple of his. If we win, he gets to keep the bribe and lose nothing."

"Oh, that's a pretty mess to step into."

Harn grunted. "Tell me about it. It will be around the Autumn Equinox, what the Central Lands call Wolf's Day. We need to be ready."

"Have you been in touch with the Brandan host? How do they feel about a clash between our houses, now that the contracts allow for bloodshed?"

"They always did, within reason."

"This time it could be beyond that."

"We'll have to see. Secur! Where's my other boot?"

"On the table, Commander."

There indeed was the boot, filled with over-blown roses, leaking water at the seams. Harn dumped it out on the marble floor with a snarl. "Has that damned woman finally wrangled her way in here?"

"Lady Anthea would not be so presumptuous."

They stared at each other, mirrors of male outrage undercut by uncertainty.

"You don't think . . ." said one.

"Not the Queen, surely," said the other. "The roses, yes, but in something as uncouth as a boot?"

"Maybe, if she wanted to get your attention," said Secur. "That damned urchin Snaggles was in here the other day, messing around. I chased him out."

Jame remembered Harn's cryptic references to Queen Vestula in his letters to Tori. Who, though, was Lady Anthea?

Both Harn and his servant looked unnerved. Neither, however, evidently was prepared to tell her what was going on. She would have to find that out for herself, or admit that she and Tori had been wrong to sense danger here. It wouldn't be the first time she had been made to look foolish.

"Have you arranged for our lodging?" she asked Harn.

He stared at her. "Why?"

"Never mind."

Saluting both randon, she withdrew.

She had barely gone a dozen paces down the hall when a neighboring door was flung open at her elbow. Framed in the entrance was a thin, elderly woman in a purple robe. Skin hung in crepe folds from her bare arms and wattles from her skinny neck. Her eyes, however, were sharp.

"Well?" she demanded. "Have you brought my boys back?"

"Err . . ." said Jame.

"The city leagues, of course. That darling Prince Jurik and his dear friends. Commander Harn said they would return when they were ready, whatever that means. It seems an age since they last competed here."

The room behind her had the same dimensions as Harn's, which it must abut; however, it was much more richly furnished. Moreover, it opened onto a luxurious balcony overlooking the field, where grapes and a pitcher of iced white wine waited beside a couch. The lady, it seemed, had been reclining at her leisure to view the troops as they practiced below, and applauding them.

Voices piped down the hall to the slap of bare feet.

"Auntie! Auntie!"

The lady jammed fists on bony hips. "Well, what now?"

A flock of scruffy children skidded to a stop before her, elbowing Jame out of the way. Among them she recognized their previous guide Snaggles, his ill-spaced teeth in wide display. Perhaps he really did live here.

"Treats, treats!" they clamored.

"You little wretches. Does not Mordaunt feed you rations of grain every day? Porridge and bread fill your little bellies, do they not? What else does the king owe you? Where are your parents, to do better by you?"

"Gone," said a little girl, with a dolorous frown.

"Drunk," said another child.

"Dead," said a third.

"T'cha. Here, then."

She drew candied orange slices out of a pouch suspended from her belt and disbursed them. The throng fled, crowing. The door slammed in Jame's face.

Damson approached down the hall. "There you are."

Jame indicated the closed door. "Who was that?"

"The widow Anthea. Snaggles told me about her. She and her husband loved the games so much that they bought an apartment here and augmented the stadium for the enjoyment of others. He died. She remains."

"And these children?"

"Thirty years ago, we Kencyr left and the street orphans moved in. These are their great-grand-children. Trespassers, the lot of them. Commander Harn didn't think to provide rooms for us. Surely he knew that we were coming."

"My brother wrote to him. Harn seems...distracted, though."

"Huh. I was about to drive out a shoal of squatters, but Quill said you wouldn't approve. Why?"

Damson was a dangerous Shanir not least because she

had only a rudimentary sense of right and wrong. She was well aware of this, however, as if it were a form of moral tone-deafness, and had turned grudgingly to Jame for advice. After years of looking to Kendar such as Marc for just such guidance against her own Shanir nature, Jame was bemused by the situation.

"What accommodations are there?" she now asked.

"There used to be a lot more of us here before the White Hills, when the Knorth was a bigger house. Now, maybe two-thirds of the apartments are empty."

"So there's room for both us and them."

"Yes. I suppose."

"Then let them stay. First rule: don't hurt if you can help."

Damson nodded, not really understanding this, much less agreeing, but dutifully taking it in.

The sun set. Jame's stomach grumbled.

"They will at least feed us, won't they?"

"Oh," said Damson, showing her teeth, "I made sure of that."

II

THE ROOMS that Damson had found for her ten-command lay between the Kencyr and (as Damson would say) the squatters, halfway down the western side of the barracks. When Jame emerged the next morning, she nearly trod on a tangle of leggy wildflowers. Doors stealthily closed down the hall. Children behind them giggled.

"We seem to have inherited a family," Jame said to Damson.

The Kendar snorted.

As they had learned the previous night, the mess-hall was close to the barracks' southern end, near Harn's apartment. The garrison looked up from their breakfast as the newcomers entered, some who knew Jame from Tentir waving to her.

Jame's former cadet Mint rose to greet them. At supper, it had been Dar. Jointly, they were in charge of King Mordaunt's personal guard, she by day, he by night.

"Our schedule doesn't give us much time together," Dar had commented ruefully the evening before, "and it involves a lot of standing around. Still, it's an honor. I suppose."

"You can always transfer back to Tagmeth," Quill had said wistfully. Everyone knew that he fancied Mint, just as they did that he had no chance of winning her away from Dar. Quill knew as much himself, but was of an optimistic disposition.

"Oh, we still enjoy it here too much," Dar had said, cheering up. "Later, maybe."

Now it was morning, and breakfast finished.

"As the Highlord's emissary, I should pay my respects to the king," said Jame, rising. "Do I need to make an appointment or, worse, dress up?"

Mint cast a critical eye over her lady, who in honor of the occasion was wearing a clean jacket and polished boots but, to Rue's chagrin, pants with patched knees due to the mishap with Death's-head on the way south.

"Citizens tend to wear the finest clothes they have,"

said Mint judiciously. "They can look pretty pretentious, not to say silly. Patricians make less of an effort as a matter of pride. Regals—that is, members of Mordaunt's own family—dress however they choose. You may be the Highlord's sister, but you're also a randon officer. What you have on suits you, knees and all. As for an appointment, I think I can slip you in."

Jame paused on the way out to check on Death's-head. The northern end of the training field had been set aside as pasture for the garrison's horses. These currently stood in a wary clump as far from the ivory-clad newcomer as possible while the rathorn glumly grazed apart. He could, of course, eat anything up to and including small rocks, but preferred roast chicken. She would have to arrange that with the kitchen, Jame thought. How long, though, would he put up with such cramped quarters? If they were here long, she would have to think of something else.

Snaggles waited outside a side door. "Heard you were going to the palace," he said, jumping off the back of one of the two stone lions that bracketed the stairs leading down to the street. "Come to show you the way, didn't I?"

Mint smiled at him. "You take good care of us, don't you, Snaggles?"

"Awww . . ."

South of the barracks, still in the valley between hills, was a large, covered market. Arcades lined its walls, two levels high, with the more elegant shops above. A double row of columns marched down its interior, supporting a vaulted roof under which pigeons fluttered and shat indiscriminatingly. Beneath, between the arches, between the columns, was a wilderness of booths selling everything from silver thimbles to silk tents, from spiced fish to cursing parrots. People wandered from stall to stall, pointing, exclaiming, bargaining. Many appeared to be common citizens shopping for mere necessities. Others were elegantly garbed patricians, men and women, out for a morning's indolent stroll among the lower classes. One group dressed in white robes, wearing featureless wax masks, paced among the throng.

"Renounce death!" their leader cried, echoed in chorus by his followers. "Join the Deathless!"

Some shoppers bowed to them as they passed. Most turned away.

Colors, smells, humanity. The noise was tremendous. Jame was glad that she had left Jorin back exploring the barracks; he hated such uproars, much more so people stepping on his toes, which always seemed to happen.

"Can I have this?" Snaggles kept asking. "Can I have that?" And each time Mint rapped him on the head to shut him up.

Jame fingered the coins in her pocket and wondered about Graykin who had taken a bag of them south with him. If he was in High Bashti, it would be a test of his skills how soon he learned of her presence here and sought her out. The city was obviously a complex place. She already felt atwitch for more intimate news of it. She and Graykin, perhaps, had more in common than she liked to admit.

In the meantime, thanks to her allowance from Aerulan's dowry, she still had funds. Here, indeed, was an arax from Kothifir, ollins from Karkinaroth, and bools from Hurlen.

How was she to learn what each was really worth? As for Bashti currency...ah, some copper pence, a clutch of silver fungit, and even a golden regal imprinted on one side with a narrow face not unlike that of a ferret, on the other with another visage, whose smiling, handsome features were vaguely familiar.

Jame stopped short. As she fumbled the coin, shoppers ran into her, cursing, hardly noticed. This was the face she had seen in the White Hills, if not quite that from Kithorn, but who was it?

Composing herself, she stepped out of traffic, returned the gold coin to her pocket, drew out a copper pence, and presented it to Snaggles.

"What will this buy?"

He took it, grinning hugely. "Food!"

"You'll spoil him," said Mint as the urchin scampered off. "Then again, we all do."

Several times, they had passed booths decked with white bunting, sporting row upon row of miniature plaster busts. A card hung around each neck with numbers scrawled on it. Attendants changed these incessantly while their masters argued with clients. Around some booths angry crowds had gathered.

"What's going on?" Jame asked Mint.

"Oh," said the Kendar, "they bet on the strangest things here. Those busts may represent politicians, sports figures, or their illustrious ancestors who have become their gods, if you will."

Snaggles wriggled through the on-lookers, munching on a roast dormouse on a stick.

"'Course they're our gods," he said indistinctly, and

spat out a wad of tiny bones. "Deified Suwaeton, Sanctified Herbata, Honored Timbuk ... I'm a descendant of old Timmy m'self, or so my mother told me, and Lady Anthea agrees. Proud of it, I am."

Jame reflected that she had spent most of her life trying to figure out what constituted a god. For most Kencyr like Mint, that question never arose. The Three-Faced God had chosen them to fight Perimal Darkling. What could be more straightforward than that? Well, yes, he (or she, or it) had then abandoned them, which in turn had led to a millennia-long retreat down the Chain of Creation with the Shadows and that arch-traitor Gerridon snapping at their heels.

Here on Rathillien, things had gotten even more complicated.

All along, it seemed, each world had had native forces upon which the Kencyr temples had preyed, fatally weakening them against the Shadows' onslaught. Not so here where, by some glitch, the Kencyrath had fed the local powers, thereby creating the New Pantheon and the Four. Jame had seen other strange twists as well. Was High Bashti about to provide yet another that would finally make sense of everything? Or was she foolish to hope that all answers would suddenly be laid bare to her? Enough, she wanted to say. How much could one person comprehend? But then she had nearly given up the problem as solved after Tai-tastigon. What a mistake that would have been.

"Tell me about your gods," she said to Snaggles.

The boy puffed out his chest, proud of his heritage. "First, there were the ten founders of the city. Their

wooden images still sit in their halls on top of the ten main
hills. We haul 'em out for the occasional parade. At some
point, though—oh, long ago, now—we started to worship
more recent ancestors until we had a whole pantheon of
'em. King, queen, warrior, artist, and so on, one for each
of the founding families. Some have been around for ages.
Well, I mean to say all of them have been, of course, but
sometimes they change."

Mint looked confused. "What do you mean, 'they
change'?"

The boy fidgeted. He wanted to sound knowledgeable,
but this was a complicated subject. "I mean, for example,
there's always a king, like in the old plays, the ones that
run forever during the festivals, but the actor who plays
him changes over time. I know what I'm talking about! Go
to the theater whenever I can sneak in, don't I? A religious
duty, isn't it? Didn't believe it at first, but either they
changed actors or one king shrank half a foot between
shows. Fact! What's more—and, mind you, this hasn't
happened in my lifetime—they say that the images of the
gods outside their temples in the Forum have replaceable
heads. Sometimes, those change too."

"I think you mean that the role is permanent, but just
as the actors sometimes change, so do the gods," said
Jame. "Perhaps you should start over."

He gave an exasperated sigh at her dimness. "See,
when a regal or a patrician dies, the Council decides if it
wants to put him or her up for godhood. Roles usually run
in families—the king in the Floten, the queen in the
Tigganis, the judge in the Lexion, and so on. Then, if their
house can get enough people to worship them, they

ascend and the old god falls. The king is dead. Long live the king. Or queen. Or whatever."

Jame began to see a familiar pattern. "Faith creates reality. The candidate with the most followers wins, and takes over the role."

"Mind you, some have lasted just about forever. General Suwaeton has been king for thirty years, ever since he died. That's Mordaunt's dear old granddad, of course."

"'Of course,'" Mint echoed him, rolling her eyes.

They passed another white booth full of little busts, some presumably of the late general, just as a fight broke out.

"Passionate about it, aren't they?" remarked Mint, raising a hand to hold Jame back as two combatants lurched past them into the opposite booth, which collapsed. City guards came running to separate the disputants. "What's set them off this time?"

"Desecration," said Snaggles darkly. "See, Lord Prestic of the Tigganis just died. Each member of the Council— that is, the current lords or ladies of the ten patrician families—claims that his (or her) own ancestor and not Mordaunt's founded this city, which means that they should be the true regals. Been going on forever, hasn't it? Old Prestic, he wanted to be king. Now. To replace Mordaunt. Who is not popular. But Prestic died first. Poisoned, they say. Funny, how often that happens. So m'lord's family wanted something even better for him, namely that he should have a chance to replace Mordaunt's grandpa Suwaeton as king of the gods."

"You said that the Tigganis usually provide the queen."

"Now, be reasonable. How could anyone worship Prestic as a woman? The fact is, most members of any given house aren't a good fit for godhood. Have to choose them carefully, don't they?"

"Still, you seem to be talking about an entire house choosing a particular role. King, queen, judge, and so on. Does everyone fit?"

"Of course not! See, young nobles decide in which house they want to be—judge, artist, merchant, whatever—and then they petition for adoption there. It's up to the Council and the families who goes where."

"All right," said Jame. "That makes a certain amount of sense. We Kencyr sometimes change houses too, but not that often, and usually with bad results."

"Sometime," said Snaggles, with the air of regaining control of the conversation, "houses may try to skip a rank like with Prestic from queen to king. It could have worked, too. Suwaeton is popular, but so was Prestic. Very. And if the divine king changes, then so might the mortal one. Then too, Mordaunt is down to one legitimate heir. A failing house, that. But he bullied the Council into putting Prestic up for sainthood instead of for deification."

Eek, thought Jame. Too many levels of power. And she had thought that the Kencyrath was complicated.

They emerged from the market. Beyond, multileveled dwellings reared up on either side of the road, creating a canyon leaning inward toward to top, full of voices as children chased each other though the shadows. A grated drain ran down the middle of the street, gurgling, stinking. More discreet gutters trickled slyly down side alleys to join the general effluvium. Despite that, there was the fragrant smell of cooking and a certain cool, green scent from terraced gardens and willows leaning out from breached walls.

"D'you understand all of this god talk?" Mint asked Jame under her breath, over the boy's head.

Jame stepped around a particularly fetid puddle. "Not entirely. I'll sort it out sooner or later, though, if we're here long enough. Er, Snaggles . . . to sanctify rather than to deify . . . what's the difference?"

"Listen! You Kennies are supposed to be smart, aren't you? To be a saint isn't as important as to be a god, is it? True, you get to stay with your family as long as they remember you, but you're a servant to the gods forever, or at least until your family forgets you and your body begins to rot."

Another link. Kencyr death banners only survived as long as their names were remembered, hence their recitation on Autumn's Eve. Then too, the blood that bound souls to warp and weft only lasted as long as memory, if that.

"The thing here," said Snaggles, "is that would-be gods and saints have a trial period—you know, to see if they stay fresh or start to stink. Gods spend it in a temple, in a rock crystal coffin, guarded by priests. The bodies of potential saints get sent out of the city into the Necropolis, to their families' crypts. No corpses within the city, thank you very much, unless they're either gods or would-be. Common citizens get burned in common pits. Oh yes, there are guards in the gentries' Necropolis too, but they might be bribed to run away. Two nights ago, the Tigganis guards did. When they're caught," he added with relish, "they'll be impaled alive, maybe on our own campus."

"Not if I can help it," said Jame. "What then?"

"They destroyed Prestic's corpse, didn't they? Hacked it apart, I hear tell."

Here, perhaps, was another common thread linked to the Kencyrath. "If the body is destroyed, so is the soul, although that usually involves complete destruction, as with cremation."

"That's right! So, no godhood for old Prestic, nor even sainthood. No kingship divine or mortal, either. No nothing, except as an abomination. That's what no house will accept, if they can prove who did it. The bookmakers claim Prestic's fate was a divine act. All bets off. The gamblers cry foul. You tell me."

"I think we saw that tomb yesterday, on the way into the city," Jame said, and shivered at the memory despite herself. "It was a savage act."

At the mouth of the next road was a simple shrine.

"These, for the cults of the Honored," said Snaggles, dropping a pebble on it as he passed. "Just citizens, most of them. They only get to keep their ashes, no souls attached, but we don't let their memories die." For a moment, he looked almost fierce. "Not Regal, not Patrician, not Ennobled. They belong to us."

"Like your ancestor Timbuk."

"Yes. Like him. Mind you," he added, as if wishing to be fair, "there are other cults as well. The Founders, now. That was over three thousand years ago. What's left of them now? Wooden statues, if that."

That was when the Kencyr temples had come to life

and the Four awoke, thought Jame. The Four, once mere humans, emerged as forces of nature, of Rathillien itself. The gods of this land rose from mortal to immortal status, at least until their influence waned. Certain divine rules came into play at that point: the faith of worshippers created reality; bodies were linked to souls; wooden effigies gave way to new, more popular gods.

"What of Princess Amalfia?" she asked.

"Oh," said Snaggles, "she died ages ago, but her images are still plastered all over the city, so you tell me how to judge immortality. Then," he added, "there's the Deathless. They're different, much more recent, but still a cult. We passed a cohort of them in the market."

"They reminded me of Karnid street prophets," said Jame. "'Death itself will die,' they claimed."

Snaggles glowered. "Don't know about that. The Deathless, though, they speak about immortality for all classes, even street rats like me. Wish my mum had known about them."

The road cut between buildings and tilted upward, climbing the shoulder of a hill. Now they were passing high walls, some with gates standing open to the street. Within were flowers and walks and trees. Among groves of the latter in some gardens stood small marble houses.

"Cenotaphs, most of them," said Snaggles, his pride in knowing such a big word overcoming his scowl, although that crept back. "These folk are the Ennobled. They were just citizens, but wealth raised them, especially those connected to the Floten. They think that they're better than us, their dead worthier than ours. If their families choose them and the Council agrees, their bodies lie in mausoleums outside the city awaiting sanctification."

"Psht," said a voice beside one gate, out of the shrubbery. "Help Mother come home? A pinch of incense? A prayer? She may even talk to you. That would count as a miracle."

They walked on, urged by Snaggles.

"For a gift?" the voice keened after them. "For a bribe?"

"They get desperate," said Snaggles. "Twice a year, on her death-day and during the Festival of the Dead, papa will check. If she's still fresh, the prayers worked and momma can come home to be with her family forever. That's sanctification. It doesn't work that way for the rest of us, though. Gone is gone, unless the high and mighty say that you're honored."

"Did you lose your mother, Snaggles?" asked Mint.

The boy wiped his nose on his sleeve, then scowled. "Went away, didn't she, and she's not coming back. I reckon that she lost me."

The Builder Chirpentundrum had chided the Kencyrath for cremating their dead and scattering their ashes on the wind.

"To destroy the soul forever," he had said. "What an abomination."

What a waste, Jame had since thought, if souls were what held the Chain of Creation together. The Bashtiri, it seemed, valued at least some souls, and connected their continued existence to the preservation of their bodies. What the Kencyrath considered a curse, these people blessed.

They rounded the hill top. From here, the city spread

out before them on all sides, dotted with more hills and valleys, the former crowned with gleaming marble, the latter holding more apartment buildings and occasional green spaces. Deeper still were foundries, factories, and abattoirs, their low-hanging murk dotted with the flicker of a million candles even this early in the day. A muted clamor arose from them, and a great stink. How big High Bashti was, how ancient, how packed with life. By comparison, Tai-tastigon seemed almost quaint.

The highest prominence of all rose to the south, its foot connected to the height on which they now stood by a saddle of land. Its sides were nearly perpendicular, clothed in trees below, topped by a high wall. Tiled roofs showed over the latter. A stepped ramp led up to a colonnaded portico on the east side that contained its front gate. This loomed as one approached, cast bronze with figures in high relief, row upon row of naked horsemen with the spoils of war strewn under their feet.

The gate was shut.

The Kencyr guarding it came to attention as Mint approached.

"Captain," said one, saluting her. "My lady. Password?"

"Sweet Trinity," muttered Mint. "I haven't seen Dar yet, have I? How would I know?"

A smaller door opened within the larger frame and Dar emerged, yawning. "There you are," he said to Mint with a smile, adding to the guards, "The watch word is 'Vigilance.' He's really on edge today, Mint, and insisting on all of the forms. Be careful."

Mint made a face. "If not us, whom can he trust?"

Dar shrugged. "How should I know? He still hasn't

paid our wages. Perhaps that makes him feel nervous, or guilty."

Leaving Dar to seek breakfast and bed, they entered the hilltop compound, Snaggles left to fret outside. The ground within had been leveled off, allowing for a complex of buildings. A grassy square fronted the gate, surrounded by more colonnades. At its heart was an elaborate fountain of river nymphs spouting water from every orifice. The basin, Jame noted, was green with algae.

"No pay?" she asked Mint.

"So far, not a pence. Mordaunt spends everything on that precious temple of his or on that mob of thugs he subsidizes with a private dole. And he taxes both the patricians and the citizens for all they're worth. You heard that he sent us out to parade around the countryside? That turned out to be an attempt to make the provinces pay a higher tax. We were supposed to enforce that—what, us?"

"What did you do?"

"Mostly, stood aside and looked impressive. Sometimes, we stepped in when his collectors got too enthusiastic. King Mordaunt was not pleased with us. We were supposed to support his interests above all else, he said. Well! Meanwhile, merchants here have extended us credit in gratitude, but that can't go on forever. Some of us are already badly in debt. It's a city rotten with diversions. Even Dar . . . well, never mind."

Jame thought back to the terms of the contract. It seemed to her that Mordaunt was walking a fine line. He didn't want to pay his troops, but he wanted as much service out of them as he could get. That might prevent him from making outrageous demands at least for a while. As it was, they were putting up with slow attrition.

They passed through lofty buildings with leaves scuttling in the corners. A few minor patricians and servants passed, looking preoccupied. Guards paced here and there, some Kencyr from the city, others in straggling, strutting bands that suggested Mint's "mob of thugs." These latter wore scraps of silk, bullion fringe, and tatters of lace, held together with strips of gaudy cotton, gilt thread and panels of cheap sequins. The largest of them led, wearing the most glitter, taking up the most space with great, waddling self-importance. He could easily have made three of his followers. Scruffy citizens trotted along after him and his cohorts. These latter wore yellow scarves that might have been intended to signify gold. It occurred to Jame that if Mordaunt paid the ruffians, they might in turn let the stray coin trickle down to buy the loyalty of lesser citizens. Mordaunt had to get his "popular" support from somewhere.

"Huh," said Mint, looking around. "No soldiers. High Bashti has a sort of standing army made up of troops drawn from all of the western bank lands. It's unclear, though, if the king or the Council commands them. The latter pays, so usually they obey it unless Mordaunt can make a case for an emergency. The same holds true with the city guard."

"What about wars?" asked Jame.

Mint grinned. "Over the millennia, Bashti got used to settling those with Kencyr, one country's mercenaries against another's. The army and patricians usually went along as support, but mostly to see the fun. We haven't

had much action since we got here. There are stirrings,
though. On the east bank Hathir and the Midlands have
been testing each other, gingerly. The Ardeth versus the
Randir, you know. More seriously, the Midlands and
Karkinor are scrabbling over the gold-rich Forks, which
has no Kencyr troops and no desire to belong to either
neighbor. That's the Randir and the Caineron, but we hear
rumors that Lord Caldane and Lady Rawneth are courting
each other, politically, so things have gone easy. Then too,
the Forks have probably been bribing both of their
neighbors forever. Here in Bashti, Mordaunt isn't eager—
wars cost money—but our precious Prince Jurik would
dearly love to command a battle."

More courtyards. More buildings faced with marble,
elaborately decorated, empty.

"In Suwaeton's day, his people inhabited this entire
complex," said Mint, "or so I've heard, they and his patron
kin. Now most of the latter live on nearby estates,
Mordaunt not trusting any of them and vice versa. Here,
there's just the king, his son Jurik, and his wife Vestula.
Also servants. Also Mordaunt's concubines, his illegitimate
children, and Jurik's friends. Those last two categories
tend to overlap. No one asks any of them for passwords."

"Complicated," Jame remarked. "Is Mordaunt really so
short on money?"

"Yes. Now see why."

They had left a banqueting hall and passed into yet
another courtyard. To the right was a three-story building
covered with low relief depictions of warriors and maidens
swooning in each other's arms. Below that was a religious
procession. Below that were rank upon rank of wild

animals in sedate procession. Paws draped over doorways. Hands twined around windows. Feet padded on lintels.

Beside this, to the left, was the beating heart of the compound. While the rest had been nearly deserted, here workmen swarmed. The base of a building had already been laid out, some three hundred feet long by maybe half that wide. Ponderous cranes swung six-foot-wide cross-sections of columns into place. Rows of them already towered, complete, in colonnades down three sides of the foundation. Nearby, masons were unloading marble blocks from wagons to construct the architrave and the inner walls.

In a wooden structure to one side serving as a workshop, Jame glimpsed relief panels being carved, full of cavorting horses and leering monsters. In pride of place, at the center of the room, loomed a huge statue, nearly finished. It sat on a marble throne, impressive in its muscular legs, torso, and arms but, so far, without a head.

What had Snaggles said? "Sometimes, those change too."

"When the temple is done," said Mint, "it will be the largest in private hands in the city, just for the king of the gods and the regals, his mortal family. All of the other major temples are public, clustered around the Grand Forum."

"So that's Mordaunt's grandfather, Suwaeton," said Jame, staring at the truncated statue.

"The Thunderer, they call him, for the staff he carries and smashes on the ground whenever he's angry, which is often. There are a lot of lightning strikes in High Bashti.

Also earthquakes. Also fires. Those apartment buildings are mostly wood and can go up like tinder. Meanwhile, Mordaunt keeps raising taxes to pay for this pet project of his, which is odd because otherwise he doesn't seem to have liked his grandpa much. Next, they say, he may end the dole. That will be asking for trouble, but he doesn't seem to care."

A Kencyr guard hurried up to her.

"Trouble at the gate, Captain. There's a new shipment of stone and the driver is drunk. He insists on yesterday's password."

Mint tsk'd. "I need to see to this, lady. Please wait."

She and the guard left. Jame regarded the busy scene before her until a workman shouted at her to get out of the way. She stepped aside as people rushed past to steady one of the cranes whose load had shifted, threatening to crash into the nearest column. Would they all fall down, one after the other? It seemed not, but the workers gave her dirty looks as if the near catastrophe had been her fault.

"No women on site," a man snarled at her in passing, and spat at her feet.

They hadn't done so to Mint. Mint, however, was uncommonly pretty. Oh well.

Where to go, though? There stood what she assumed to be the royal residence, her destination in any event. Two Kendar guarded the door, both male. They looked at her askance, but stood aside as she approached.

Inside was a vaulted passageway, then an atrium. Light lanced down from a hole in the ceiling onto a shallow basin of rain water beneath. Pigeons whirred up toward the roof, white wings flashing, as Jame entered. The floor was a mosaic of tiles, presumably depicting figures of mythology, given their exaggerated features. Around them rose three stories of open hallways. In front of them ran a balustrade; behind, a row of closed doors. This must be where Mordaunt's family lived. However, the space was dim and echoed hollowly. Somewhere, someone laughed. Other muted voices sounded, but no one appeared.

Across the atrium was another passage, leading to another courtyard. Here too was a pond, in the midst of which sat the stiff wooden statue of a man. Moss grew on his bearded cheeks and on the flat slabs of his chest. He looked, however, immemorial, impervious to rot. It was hard to imagine any other than that rough head on those square shoulders, staring out of those sunken eyes. Could this be an image of Floten, the ruling family's cult figure? How much more real he seemed than the headless statue waiting outside in the workshop.

Beyond, yet again, was a third passageway. From this a voice reached Jame as she approached, strident, high pitched, like a small dog yelping:

"You didn't . . . you did . . . where . . . why . . . how . . ."

Jame approached. The yapping went on.

A scrawny figure paced back and forth across the third courtyard, gesticulating wildly. He wore what appeared to be a tattered dressing gown. His slipper-clad feet slapped the tiled floor.

"I tell you," he cried, brandishing knobby fists, "the gods are against me! What? No, of course I don't deserve it!"

He seemed to be speaking to someone. The atrium,

however, appeared to be empty except for him. A voice murmured. Was that here or elsewhere?

"You say you destroyed his body, but where are the limbs, the gods-be-damned head? Not burned. Just gone. Who took them, eh?"

Something caught the corner of Jame's eye, there, up on the third floor leaning against the balustrade. It was gone when she stepped forward for a better look, but the impression remained of a white figure with a gently smiling waxen visage.

Her movement caught the pacer's attention and he whirled, glaring, to face her.

"Who are you? What are you doing here?"

"I came to see King Mordaunt. Please, don't be alarmed."

"Why shouldn't I be? Everyone is against me. Guards, guards!"

His shrill voice set up echoes. Someone shouted in answer and feet ran down stairs. First, however, the Kencyr guards from the outer door arrived, swift and deadly, swords drawn. Then they drew up short, looked at Jame, and hesitated.

A tall young man burst onto the room on their heels. He wore a purple, fur-trimmed jerkin, also a golden band around his brow.

The guards sheathed their blades.

"Your Highness . . ." said one.

"Ha!" said the newcomer, and attacked them.

More young men spilled across the threshold, far outnumbering those already there, and threw themselves into the brawl. The Kencyr retreated, using defensive water-flowing moves. Meanwhile the thin man, whom Jame now supposed must be the king, flailed at anyone who came within reach with his slipper.

"This is ridiculous," she said, and attempted to step between the combatants.

The tall man turned on her with a grin. He was older than she had thought, at least in his late twenties, but the eager gleam in his eyes made him look like a boy. She jumped back barely in time to avoid a fire-leaping kick. He went after her, towering, pressing the attack. That he should be using the Senethar momentarily threw her off-balance, so that he managed to catch her a glancing blow on the cheekbone. Then they were at it in earnest, lunge and counter, fire against wind, earth against water.

But Jame kept tripping. This puzzled and annoyed her, besides bringing her closer than was comfortable to the other's big hands. Besides, there was nothing to trip over except the low rim of this atrium's pond, the third she had encountered here so far.

"Stop ducking!" complained the man as she stumbled yet again, nearly into his grasp.

"It isn't deliberate!"

Something, someone, breathed in her ear.

"Ahhh . . ."

Exasperated, she unleashed a blow at what appeared to be empty air. Her fist connected. The unseen stumbled back, gasped as it caught a foot in the pond's rim, and tumbled into the water. Dimples appeared in its surface, some reaching down to the bottom. Then they lifted.

"What . . . ?" said her opponent, staring.

Something floundered out, spraying water that partially

defined its outline. So, not *mere* tattooed skin but dyed cloth, with a sleeve torn to reveal a pale left shoulder. However, no arm hung from it. Wet footprints appeared on the floor and ran to the door, just as Harn Grip-hard stepped in through it. There was a collision. The big Kendar swatted by reflex, whereupon something yelped and rebounded against the doorframe, leaving a wet mark. Then it scuttled away.

Ignoring it, Harn glowered at the chaos within. The look he darted at Jame's opponent, however, verged first on panic, then on apoplexy. Afraid that he was about to suffer a berserker flare, Jame stepped up to him and put her hands on his chest, as if to soothe an overwrought stallion. His massive hands flexed over her head. He was breathing hard.

This is dangerous, she thought, trying not to flinch.

Harn looked down at her, gulped, and, with an effort, regained control of himself.

"Stop it!" he bellowed at the room in general.

The attackers withdrew, looking sheepish, but their leader stepped forward, still with a grin.

"You said we had to prove ourselves, commander, to continue our training." He grabbed Jame and presented her for inspection. Her cheek throbbed. Already it must be swelling. "See? I landed a blow!"

"Well, good for you, boy," the big randon said gruffly. "May I present the sister and lordan of the Kencyr Highlord, your father's ally? This, my lady, is King Mordaunt's son and heir, Prince Jurik. Now both of you, behave."

Chapter VII
Night at Falkirr
The Riverland: Summer 110–111

I

SUMMER WAS ALMOST OVER. The Riverland's Minor Harvest had come and gone, and with it the Knorth cadets from Tentir who had helped to bring in the hay. It had been a good crop, all the more so because no one had come down with the dreaded hay cough.

Then the rains had stopped.

Torisen Blacklord stood on the cracked clay of the water meadow amid rows of stunted oat, rye, and wheat. Morosely, he scuffed up dust with the heel of his boot. The upcoming Major Harvest at summer's end looked all but doomed even if now, at last, it should rain.

At this season, as usual, last year's provisions were running low. Bread was down to dense, dark loaves made of buckwheat. The cows, usually bred in the fall, had run dry. So had the last wheels of cheese before they cracked from dehydration. Last year's field vegetables, down to wizened relics, were only good after long soaking, the same for such left-over pulses as beans and peas. The garrison was growing heartily sick of soup. How many cows, pigs, and sheep must be slaughtered in the fall, for meat and to preserve the fodder? Some even spoke of the horses.

On the other hand, there were still some ripening vegetables in the inner ward's garden, painfully watered by hand, also bushels of fruit. Apples in particular had been plentiful to feed man, beast, and the busy cider press.

"Two more weeks for the first batch to ferment," said the harvest-master at Torisen's elbow, as if reading his mind. Then again, he might have been considering the jug hanging at his waist, which he had just emptied.

"Well, that's something."

"And those mysterious supplies keep coming from your sister's keep, in season and out. I know, I know: we aren't supposed to talk about that. Rush might have told us more, if only to boast, but he's gone."

"Where?"

"No one is quite sure. He took a post horse. I hear that he turned right on the River Road at the Silver and rode north. There isn't enough from Tagmeth, anyway, to see us through the winter. When can we expect shipments from Bashti?"

"Soon, I hope."

"Huh."

All of the contracts had specified that the first delivery be made by Autumn's Day. Wagons full of provisions from the other Central Lands had already begun to pass Gothregor on the way to the northern keeps. Presumably others had stopped in the south.

Autumn's Eve was near.

Torisen didn't feel that he could complain until that was past, in the meantime hoping for the best. Was his instinct that Mordaunt meant to shirk his duty as paymaster true? Torisen had thought himself worldly-wise after dealing with Kothifir as the Host's commander, but had he really been? It came hard to think of anyone foreswearing his word. After all, besides the question of honor, what lasting good would it do Mordaunt? What other factors might be involved, and did the king even think along such lines? Torisen was experienced enough to recognize a congenital manipulator. The main thing was that pertinent shipments should arrive before winter closed the Riverland's roads.

Time enough, he thought, but with a twinge of unease.

Was Harn keeping all of this in mind? Torisen had received a post letter from Jame announcing her arrival in High Bashti, but about Harn she had only written that he continued to be preoccupied. Also, the Bashtiri garrison hadn't yet been paid. That was to have been according to the half season, with the first payment due on the arrival of the troops, back-dated to midsummer in consideration of the time spent getting there. It wasn't like Harn to let such a thing slip. What sort of trouble was he in?

What, for that matter, about Jame? Knowing his sister's knack for mischief, by now there had to be something.

"Ask questions," she had said.

Trudging back to the keep through dry grass singing with crickets, he considered this. More and more, he found himself restless, his own attention divided. Was this what it meant, to become That-Which-Creates? If so, it made him profoundly uncomfortable. Since when, though, had his comfort been important? He was responsible for his people, for the entire Kencyrath. Now it required something of him, but what?

When he started to open the door to his drum tower study, Burr's voice spoke within:

"Careful."

Books slid out, like a paper tongue extending to envelop him. The room beyond was awash with them, and with scrolls piled on every flat surface. Stiff, dry, and musty, their odor likewise rolled out. Burr stood up to his shins in chaos, glowering.

"More arrived today," he said. "You can't read all of these." Himself a traditional Kendar, he couldn't read at all, but it seemed to be primarily the disorder that offended him.

Torisen stepped in cautiously, groping for the floor.

"Sorry. I got carried away."

His servant snorted.

The Highlord slung his coat over the stack on his chair, which consequently took on the appearance of a headless, hunched figure with flaccid arms. That was much how he currently felt.

"The scrollsmen claim that they have the answer to everything, if one only asks the right question."

"Let them sort out tomorrow's dinner, then," said Burr.

"We aren't that desperate yet. Questions, though— those are hard."

He waded gingerly to the window, perched on the

ledge, and bent to pick up a book. Its pages were vellum, crisply inscribed with elegant text. Tiny, vivid figures danced up the margins. Here a hunter scrambled after a hare that jeered back at him over its shoulder; there stood a cook white up to the elbows with flour in the midst of energetically making a pie. They seemed almost to move. He blinked, then closed the book carefully.

"I'm a fool," he said. "These are treasures, not to be scattered underfoot. I thought, though, that the more I had, the more I would know. Well, I do know more— about hares, about pies—but it's the wrong knowledge."

Burr grunted. "This I can tell you: more books won't help."

Torisen wished that Harn were there. Admittedly, as a boy he had listened more to the big randon than talked, but he had learned much.

Then he had become Highlord and, to his regret, his relationship with all Kendar had changed.

Then the Riverland had become a closed book to him during the year during which he had been so deathly ill.

His sense was that each house, likewise, had shut up within itself to face a changing world. Divided . . . weakened?

To whom would he talk now, if he could? The Kendar would help him and often did, but they didn't share the same burdens. Among the Highborn Brant, Lord Brandan, was his closest neighbor, a steady, honorable man with a deep regard for the welfare of those dependent upon him. From the beginning, he had been a Knorth ally. He was also old enough to be Torisen's father.

That gave Torisen pause. Would consulting him now be like seeking a father's approval? The thought made him cringe. Both Ganth and Adric had called him "son," but they had tried mostly to use him. He would have turned to neither of them now. Brant was unrelated and was therefore (Ancestors, please) different.

Absentmindedly, he reopened the book, on the same page that he had closed it. The hare had scampered off. The pie had been baked and eaten, its cook grinning widely, replete. Torisen returned the volume to the floor, which rustled to receive it.

"Pack up," he said to Burr, rising, his mind already on new details. "We're going to pay Falkirr a visit."

Burr looked dubious. "That last trip to Omiroth didn't work out so well."

"My sister was with us then."

But Jame had suggested that the Tyr-ridden might manifest themselves across all three faces of their god before the end. Dari slain by Torisen's own sword, Adric on his pyre . . .

"Oh, cheer up," he said, bracing himself.

"If I had stopped to think too much," his sister had said, with that rueful, lop-sided smile of hers, *"might I have done nothing at all, for good or ill?"*

There was an urgency in her that pushed him, as it always had. Did he resent it? Yes. But that didn't mean that she was wrong.

Across the room, on the chair, his empty coat shivered as if with anticipation, but could not raise its arms.

"Brant is my oldest friend, now that Adric is dead," he said to Burr. "What could go wrong?"

II

BY EARLY AFTERNOON they were on the road with a small, armed escort, the latter at Burr's insistence. Torisen wondered what he feared, then dismissed the thought. Surely things hadn't become as dire as that, on the common road. He hadn't wanted to stand on any ceremony whatsoever, even declining to send a messenger ahead to warn Lord Brandan of his approach. He wasn't nervous, he told himself. There was simply no need to put undue stress on this visit. In the meantime, it was pleasant to escape Gothregor's gray walls for a while. Here the swaying gait of the horses was soothing, the air crisp, and the hillsides painted all the shades of impending fall.

That reminded him: it was only days until Autumn's Eve when he was honor bound to recite all the names of the death banners in the old keep's lowermost hall. The family dead must be remembered or they would crumble, not that some already weren't as tapestries decayed and the dried blood that held soul to weave flaked away. He hadn't been aware of the latter connection until Jame had learned of it and given many banners to the torch to free the souls trapped within them. The ones that remained, presumably, wanted to stay, or at least he hoped so. To them, at least, he owed a duty.

How had he gotten through that task last year with his mind addled by illness? Harn, Burr, and Rowan must have helped. Again, he was reminded of that lost year. While

Jame had been proving herself at Tentir, he feared that he had lost ground in the Riverland as a whole.

The sun had set beyond the western Snowthorns by the time they reached Falkirr. Brant's steward said that his lord was still in the fields but would be summoned at once. Then he showed Torisen into a reception room and left him there with a bottle of wine. Torisen wondered if his stiff manner indicated disapproval. Perhaps it hadn't been such a good idea after all to arrive unannounced.

He had poured himself a glass of wine and was sipping it by the window when the Brandan Matriarch Brenwyr burst into the room. At the sight of him, she stopped so suddenly that her heavy skirts rushed past her, then rustled back into place. She was wearing the divided riding skirt that so offended her fellow matriarchs, also boots, also a boxy, shabby jacket, also the customary mask of a Highborn lady. Her eyes glared through the latter, brown tinged with red. With an effort, Torisen refrained from falling back a step, which would have tumbled him over the low window sill into the garden beyond.

"My lady," he said, bowing.

Now he remembered at least one reason why a visit to Falkirr could be dangerous. Brenwyr was a Shanir maledight, whose curses could kill. She had cursed his sister.

"'Rootless and roofless,'" Jame had said, with a shaky laugh. "'Curséd be and cast out.' That hasn't happened yet, thanks to Tagmeth, but who knows?"

Dying, his father Ganth had said much the same thing to him: "Curséd be and cast out. Blood and bone, you are no son of mine." But he had called him son again, before the end, when he had begged to be set free from the sterile wasteland of Torisen's soul-image where his own self-hate had trapped him.

"So," said Brenwyr now. She tried to speak calmly, but sounded half strangled. "You have come at last."

"Er . . ."

"Did my brother summon you? He worries about me, you know. He should not. While I have her, I am safe." Her thin lips jerked up at the corners. "Wine?"

"Of course." He poured her a glass which she took, but made no move to drink.

She paced before him, skirts swishing, wine sloshing over her gloved hand. "Imagine! He even keeps servants out of my rooms and does their tasks himself, as if I would harm them, as if I would not notice. You know what they call me."

"The Iron Matriarch, lady, for your self-control."

"Also, the Maledight. I killed my own mother. Did they tell you that? She railed at me because I chose to wear boys' clothing and she took them away. I cursed her. She tangled in their threads, storming down the stair, and broke her neck. 'Breathe!' I told her, but she could not. Ah! Cross me and I will curse you too." She clutched the bulky coat tight to her spare form. "Aerulan is mine, I say, and always will be!"

Brant entered abruptly and pulled up sharp. He wore a tunic dusty from the fields. His face was as brown as a Southron's from the sun, creased before its time with care.

"Sister, you should rest."

"But Aerulan . . ."

"Let her rest with you."

Brenwyr smiled at him and went out, hunched, hugging herself.

Lord Brandan poured himself a cup of wine and gulped it down.

"I'm sorry I didn't tell you that I was coming," said Torisen.

"It doesn't signify, although I might have kept her out of your way."

"About Aerulan . . ."

"She thinks that you mean to reclaim her, never mind the dowry that we continue to pay for her perpetual contract."

It was indeed a prodigious sum which might, with caution, sustain Gothregor over at least the fall, if Jame didn't draw too heavily on her portion of it.

"I appreciate that."

Brant gave him a crooked smile. "I would guess that you do. King Mordaunt is slow in his payments, is he not?"

"You expected this?"

"Not so, exactly, but Mordaunt has always been peculiar and parsimonious. I should have warned you."

He well might have, thought Torisen. Then again, that was the sort of information he should have learned on his own.

Ask questions.

"In what way is he peculiar?"

"There are stories. Ever since he was a boy, people say that he has been obsessed with death and immortality. Then too, he grew up in the shadow of his grandfather, General Suwaeton, whom he feared and hated. Mordaunt didn't much like his father, either, for not standing up to the old man. Suwaeton died, and was popular enough to be deified—as king of their gods, no less. Not so his son, who died soon after. That left Mordaunt as mortal king. The timing of both deaths was thought to be suspicious."

"And this, somehow, leads to Mordaunt not paying his bills?"

"Presumably he has other expenses that he considers more pressing. Myself, I don't understand Bashtiri politics, much less their religion."

They ate later, figs stuffed with cinnamon eggs, a beef roast garnished with leeks, a damson tart. None of these were soup, Torisen was glad to note. Brenwyr dined in her own apartment, also to his relief.

Brant poured more wine.

"I've been meaning to talk to you," he said. "Has Lord Caineron sent you any messengers?"

"Not one."

"He has to me, repeatedly. Once, even, he sent his uncle and chief advisor, Lord Corrudin, who wanted to know where I stood on the issue that larger Kencyr houses should have more power than smaller ones."

The Brandan was the fourth largest house, the Knorth seventh or eighth, depending on who counted. Torisen had thought that matter settled. Apparently not.

"How is Lord Corrudin?"

"He still prefers enclosed spaces as I found, after meeting him in the reception room where I met you. Did your sister really . . ."

"Yes. He gave her an obscene order regarding a Kendar. She told him to back off and he did, out a second story window."

Lord Brandan smiled. "He's still doing it, if on the ground floor this time. That didn't help his dignity, or his nephew's case. I wonder, though..."

"What?"

Brant fiddled with the tart. "Does it really work, that smaller houses should rule larger ones? In the beginning, the Knorth was the most powerful. Did that determine its rank? A Highlord was chosen from among its ranks, in any event, and so served for millennia. Then came Master Gerridon's Fall, then Ganth Graylord's retreat after the White Hills. Whom were we supposed to follow after that?"

"You chose Ganth's son."

"Yes, I did."

Torisen regarded his cup. He was used to cider. This potent vintage threatened to go to his head.

"If the biggest house was to rule," he said, listening to his words, glad to hear that they didn't slur, "that means the Caineron. Would you prefer Caldane as Highlord to me?"

Brant made a face. "That's the sticking point, isn't it? No. For one thing, you are by far the better man. How not? The Kendar and the randon raised you, wherever you came from before that."

He paused, regarding his guest over the lip of his cup, one eyebrow raised. Torisen didn't reply. His sister might have secrets, but so did he.

"For another," Brant continued, "our god chose the Knorth to lead us. I'm traditional that way, whatever I think of our subsequent fate. The Arrin-ken might depose you, but not that clown Caldane. There's something wrong with that man, and it's getting worse. I won't soon forget the trick he played with the hidden clauses in the contracts or the way he reneged on his word to the Transweald and the Midlands. He smiles and smiles, but what he says doesn't always make sense. His latest message hinted that he believes you to have failed and that 'the divine mandate,' as he calls it, has passed to him. How could it be otherwise? He trusts I have the wisdom to see that, for the sake of my house."

"Threats?"

"Veiled, but there. Behind him in order of size stand the Ardeth. What do you think of their new boy lord?"

Torisen shrugged. "I hardly know. My sister trained with Timmon at Tentir. She had mixed feelings, the last time we spoke. He's spoiled and raised to be trivial, but there's something there. Jame considers him potentially worth saving, in her words, if he ever manages to escape his mother."

"Then there are the Randir, and another mother. Distan is silly, Ancestors know, but Rawneth is poisonous and powerful. I also fear that she pulls Caldane's strings."

"How?"

"By flattery. By hinting that she knows deep secrets. This is the Witch of Wilden, after all, who has ambitions of her own. Now they say that she also has a new councilor who whispers to her that one need never die. Deathless. I know that because my sister has received honeyed letters from her, referring to Aerulan."

"You permit that?"

Brant gave him a level look. "Brenwyr is her own mistress. Yes, I protect her when I can, but I also respect her. You, I think, have not always done the same with Jameth."

Torisen shifted uneasily in his chair. "True. She is ... so much younger than I am and, I thought, so different. I didn't trust her at first." No, nor any Shanir. That was their father's work. "She still scares me. But I made her my heir, and sent her to Tentir, and to Tagmeth, and, now, to the Central Lands as my emissary, with my mandate. Yes, I respect her that much. All the time, though, I have never known what she will do next."

They talked more, into the night, then parted. Torisen was shown to a guest apartment where Burr waited by candlelight to relieve him of his court coat and boots. Wine and fatigue made his head spin. So did the realization that the Riverland had indeed been talking, but not to him. It had been good, however, to discuss matters with someone so much older and, presumably, wiser than himself, although in many ways Brant's life seemed simple compared to his own.

Shanir, whispered the memory of his father in his mind. *See what you get for embracing the Old Blood*.

"What choice did I have? She is my sister."

You are yourself.

"And your son. You were a Shanir blood-binder too, and tried to bind me."

Ah, ha-ha-ha. How do you know that it didn't work?

Torisen sat bolt upright in bed. "It didn't," he muttered to himself, dashing sweat from his brow. "I know that it didn't."

Burr snored on a pallet at his feet.

The fire had burned low on the hearth, leaving the chill

of stone walls like those of a cave despite the late summer heat outside.

Someone had cried out, a familiar voice in distress, but whose? Let the Brandan deal with it? This, after all, was their house. However, such inarticulate pain required an immediate response. Somebody needed something of him. Rising, he went out into the hall.

"Hello? Is anyone there?"

Silence answered, then a sound like a distant hoarse sob. The voice spoke again, angry now, still indistinct but in a tone that pricked his nerves with warning. He turned left, toward it, into a portion of Falkirr unfamiliar to him.

Graded candles lit the walls at intervals, burning down the hours of the night. Doors, closed. Then one that stood partly open.

Click, click, click went heels inside, pacing.

Torisen entered warily. Within was a spacious room. It would have been luxurious, but most of its furniture had collapsed into piles of rubble on the floor. Brenwyr trod between them, hunched over, clutching herself or rather the frayed ruins of her coat.

"You took her from me," she railed. That was the angry voice he had heard, half choked with grief. "You slit her throat. I cursed you. 'Shadow, by a shadow be exposed.' And so it was. Then that little Knorth bitch summoned the dark Kencyr and he opened up the seams of your being, cut by cut, until your guts spilled out on the floor. Was that enough? No. Someone paid the price for her death, and Kinzi's, and all of the rest. The Knorth Massacre, they call it. But I only care about her. Oh, Aerulan!"

Torisen understood some of this, but not all. By flickers he saw someone pressed against Brenwyr's back, arms around her waist. No, not arms: rather, tattered cords like the warp threads of a death banner.

"Where is her blood price?" Brenwyr cried, beating her breast. Flakes of dried blood rattled down on the floor. Fragile weft strands of fabric disintegrated. The warp threads tried to restrain her, but could not.

Brenwyr stumbled blindly against one of the remaining tables.

"Rot you!" she cried.

The table groaned and slumped. Its top cracked. Its legs crumbled into dust, dumping it onto the floor.

"Don't!" Torisen protested, stepping forward.

He was pushed out of the way by Lord Brandan, who threw his arms around his sister and hugged her, to a further cascade of flakes.

"Don't you see?" said Torisen. "The tighter you cling, the more the tapestry disintegrates. Can life embrace death? This is the destruction that you both fear."

Brenwyr glared at him. "Damn you . . ." she began, but her brother clamped a hand over her mouth. She fought him. Blood trickled down from between his fingers. In her savage grief, she had bitten either them, her own lips, or both.

"Get out," Brant said to Torisen over Brenwyr's shoulder. He might have spoken in anger or impotent despair. "Just go."

Torisen backed out, then returned to his room.

"Wake up," he said to Burr, shaking him. "We're leaving."

Burr blinked at him. "What, in the middle of the night?"

"Yes. Now. I think that I was just almost cursed by a maledight."

⟨⟨⟨ Chapter VIII ⟩⟩⟩
Autumn's Eve
High Bashti: Summer 120–Autumn 1

I

"NORMALLY, he's quite fastidious," Jame remarked to Graykin who, that morning, had finally presented himself at Campus Kencyrath.

Although the sun shone now, it had rained hard during the night and the part of the training field set aside for pasture was sodden, where grass didn't actually float under water. Hooves had churned some of these shallow ponds into deep, boot-sucking mud. Death's-head had found one such puddle and rolled in it. Jame regarded his besmirched form with chagrin. He, in turn, curled his lip at her, over sharp fangs, in a sneer. Like any creature with a white coat, he was attracted to dirt, but usually he also had access to a river or stream in which to bathe.

"Then too," she added, thumping the rathorn on his shoulder, raising a shower of drying mud chips, "right now he's bored out of his tiny, little mind."

Graykin smirked. He himself looked almost dapper,

clad in the style of a Bashtiri dandy with an ersatz dab of elegance.

"Sorry I didn't come to see you earlier," he said. "I was out of town."

"What, High Bashti bores you already?"

He made a face. "This city will take years to master—not, mind you, that I haven't made progress—but it also has relationships with the rest of the Central Lands, on both banks of the Silver. I was in Karkinor."

"Ah."

She continued to curry the rathorn's back and sides, down to where the ivory began, loosening the dirt. He shifted under her touch. There had, of course, been no question of tying him up. A grinning campus urchin scattered fragments of roast chicken before him when his attention wandered and these he snuffled up, bones and all. Jame began to scrape the ivory along the upper edges of its bands.

"What news from the Karkinoran capitol? I promised Timmon that I would ask about Lyra."

Graykin looked even more sour. He had previously been Lyra's servant in Karkinaroth and they shared Lord Caineron as a sire. Graykin was a bastard, however, his mother a Karkinoran chambermaid. Lyra never let him forget that.

"She landed on her feet, as usual." *The spoiled brat*, said his tone. "Old Prince Uthecon treats her more like a favorite granddaughter than a bride. He's been unwell, though, and his would-be heirs are starting to swarm. She'll make a fine prize for one of them, and a validation of his claim to the kingdom."

Jame paused. "Caldane would do that, just transfer her contract from one Karkinoran princeling to another?"

Of course he would. To him, Highborn women were only bargaining chips and Lyra was the most dispensable of them all, now that her great-great gran Cattila was dead. Once again she would be dangled before one lord after another as she had before Uthecon's ill-fated predecessor, Prince Odalian. Lyra was probably even less valuable now, having been contracted twice to Karkinor although never bedded, as far as Jame knew.

The rathorn rubbed impatiently against her hand. He wanted to be scratched, there, below the upper edge of the ivory where, day by day, it continued to grow. She had wedged the diamantine panel from the white city in the Anarchies into a tree trunk for him to whet his horns against and he had done so. Rathorns were potentially immortal, their own ivory their ultimate enemy. Hopefully, neither horn would ever grow around to pierce his skull from behind. What did one do about the chest and belly armor, though, which someday might encase him, living, in an ivory tomb? All she could think of was to extend a nail and scratch gingerly along the growth line, trying not to draw blood.

"Who told you that about Lyra?" she asked Graykin.

He shuffled, not meeting her eyes.

"I was in the new palace in Karkinaroth—yes, they've rebuilt since your last visit, and a proper mess you left of it, what with our temple imploding."

"That wasn't my fault."

"Somehow, nothing ever is. Anyway, Commandant Sharp-tongue passed me and paused. I was in deep shadow. I swear he didn't see me. But he told me, more or less, what I've just told you. 'Inform Jamethiel,' he said, and walked on, smiling. That man terrifies me. What is he, a Shanir?"

Jame laughed. "Perhaps. He is, at least, always extraordinary. I'm glad that he's keeping an eye on Lyra. Returning to the subject of High Bashti, what do you make of this?"

She fished the golden regal coin out of her pocket and flipped it to him. He caught it, barely not fumbling.

"Valuable," he said, examining it. "This is the first one I've actually seen, but I hear that the king has melted down as many gold coins as he can get his hands on to gild that new temple of his."

"I meant, the face on the obverse side, or do I mean the reverse? One, of course, is a young Mordaunt. I would recognize those rodential features anywhere."

"I'll have to ask about the other. It must be someone important to the king, from—when? Thirty-some years back? That's the date, anyway, inscribed on it. Why this interest in ancient history?"

"I swear that I've seen that face before. Once at Kithorn. Once on the edge of the White Hills. Once watching me from a balcony in Mordaunt's palace."

She didn't mention that she had also glimpsed that pale figure in dreams out of the corner of her eye, smiling at her, gone when she turned to face him. If he had spoken, she thought she would have known his voice, and what an unnerving thought that was.

She nodded to Snaggles, who in turn gestured to his cohorts. Urchins staggered out into the pasture, a brigade lugging buckets of sun-warmed water. Jame had been combing out the rathorn's mane and tail with her claws. Now she sloshed him with water and scrubbed.

He moved away. More chicken fragments distracted him. "Huh," he snorted, munching, then shook himself.

Jame wiped stinging soap out of her eyes.

"There's this too," she said over her shoulder. "When I visited Mordaunt, I also met a man who wasn't there. That is, someone kept tripping me and breathing in my ear, but I couldn't see who it was until I got annoyed and knocked him backward into an ornamental pond. Even then, he only made a dent in the water before scuttling off."

"It sounds as if you ran into an assassin of the Bashtiri Shadow Guild."

"I think so too. It wouldn't be the first time, either."

"For most people, it would be both the first and last time. Those folk are scary. There are rumors that Mordaunt uses them for spies, no hard task for people who can use *mere* tattoos and dye to render themselves invisible, never mind that it tends to drive them insane. There are also cracks in the Guild between traditional members and those aligned with the Deathless, or so I hear."

The urchins presented more buckets of water. Jame emptied them over the rathorn's back and scraped off the excess with the edge of her hand. By now her braids hung down in damp loops and her shirt clung to her in wet folds.

"Kinzi, Telarien, Aerulan ... so many other Knorth ladies. The Shadow Guild slaughtered them all. Then the assassins came back for me, or rather one in particular did—he who killed Aerulan, whom Brenwyr cursed, now a guild master. I ran away."

"There, you surprise me."

"But, you see, you were in trouble at Restormir. I knew that because of the bond between us. It drew me."

"Oh," said Graykin blankly, for a moment forgetting to be snide. Could it be that he hadn't heard this story before? Parts of it, perhaps not.

"He caught up with me at Mount Alban. I hadn't come under the terms of the original contract, he said. That was determined by the number to be killed, although once I thought otherwise. But he missed one: my cousin Tieri." Who, later, had become Kindrie's mother, sired by Gerridon. However, Jame didn't mention that. Let Kindrie keep his own secrets. "Now it was his turn to choose a target. He chose me. To make a clean sweep of the Knorth ladies, he said, although I think he was also being blackmailed by Ishtier. Yes, I know: It was a confusing situation."

Graykin shook his head. This was more information than Jame had previously given him, and less than he felt he deserved. "That leaves it up in the air, doesn't it? The Shadow Guild is or isn't after you now. I would say not, because their agent didn't try, seriously, to kill you in the palace."

"It seemed pretty deliberate to me."

"Still . . ."

Jame sighed. "Yes, I should have thought about all of this before I came south. 'Ancient history' is no such thing, is it?"

Snaggles tugged her sleeve. "Here comes His Highness."

"Scamper," she told him. "You too." This, to Graykin. "We'll talk later."

Prince Jurik sauntered across the practice field, the sun catching his golden brow band. He was trailed by a clump of his half-brothers, friends, and other assorted hangers-on. Since that day at the palace, Harn had let them return for training at the campus. They were, most of them, able young men, but their ideas of discipline and honor seemed lacking. The randon looked at them askance. Senethar technique, they felt, was not enough. Jame agreed. What was Harn thinking?

"Hello," said Jurik, leaning on the rail. "Don't you have servants to do work like that?"

Death's-head shook himself again and wandered off. Jame was acutely aware of the damp shirt clinging to her slight breasts and of Jurik giving them a dismissive leer.

The rathorn found another mud puddle, sank to his knees in it, and rolled, groaning.

Jame sighed. "I give up."

"I would say that you spoil that beast, but it's obviously too late to complain. Still, I want to ride him."

"Ask his permission first."

"Seriously? He lets you. How hard can it be?"

The rathorn continued to roll, his hooves flailing the air. Then he lurched to his feet and shook himself again, spraying fresh mud.

"Hard enough, potentially, to be fatal."

On a higher, dryer patch of the field, two randon ten-commands had begun to practice the kantirs of Senetha earth-moving. One command was Knorth, the other Danior from Nether Bashti. Training had begun for the Transweald games, at which only the best twenty of these two combined houses would compete, against twenty seasoned Brandan. Down came a score of right feet as one. The left swept back for balance. Arms traced patterns in the air. They were moving slowly, ritualistically, which was more of a challenge than the speed of combat Senethar. Jame admired their grace.

Jurik and his cohort wandered over to join their ranks, edging in to make space between them. The Bashtiri had obviously learned the basics, but they were slightly out of step, as if the deliberate pace fretted them. One stumbled, lost patience, and hooked the leg out from under the Kendar beside him. Caught off guard, the man fell, rolled, and neatly regained his feet. The Bashtiri laughed.

"What," said Jurik, "you can't deal with surprise?"

It only seemed to occur to him then that both commands had swung to surround his people, poised to attack. His face flushed with anger. For a moment, he reminded Jame of Harn.

"It was only a joke!" he sputtered.

Harn Grip-hard had come out onto his balcony to watch. So had the Lady Anthea on her adjacent porch. He shook his shaggy head and went back inside. She remained, glowering. Perhaps these were no longer her darling boys, now that the professionals had returned.

II

THAT WAS MORNING on the last day of summer. Autumn's Eve would arrive later that night. Jame had heard that the Bashtiri took this holiday seriously, hence she and Rue went out that afternoon to see the sights, Jorin padding along beside them.

The air buzzed with excitement. Skulls wreathed with evergreen boughs decorated every house. More swags of that greenery stretched across the streets from upper window to window—to signify death and immortality, Jame supposed. She noted, however, that these crania were never actually human skulls. Rather, the poorer dwellings made do with clay or white-washed wood representations while the wealthy favored porcelain or polished stone. Here and there, someone had substituted the skull of a horse or a cow or a swine, but these were rare, even more so those adorned with cosmetics. The idea, apparently, was to laugh at death rather than to fear it.

Children from the apartment blocks were also abroad wearing rags and cheap masks constructed of wood pulp or, in some cases, with mere soot smeared across their features.

"A fig for the feast!" they cried outside the doors of their more affluent neighbors.

Apples, nuts, and, yes, figs were thrown out to them. These they popped into sacks. Rather than eat them, they munched on walnut-sized skulls molded from flavored ice.

"Those come down from the mountains wrapped in straw," said Rue wisely. It seemed that she had been talking to Snaggles, who was a fount of such information. "Everyone fasts until midnight when the dead are invited in, but before that they're allowed to drink."

Proof of this came wobbling down the road—Dar,

taking a holiday rather than spending his off-shift from the palace asleep.

"Hello!" he cried, throwing an arm around each of them.

All right, thought Jame. *Very drunk*. She didn't have the heart, however, to shake him off.

Crowds rushed past them. They came to Thyme Street and Thyme Side, the district that ran beside it with docks to the south and warehouses to the north, the latter dotted with residential mazes. The thoroughfare was already lined with throngs of people leaning out into the road, peering west toward where bands could be heard approaching.

Bang, bang went the drums. *Wha, wha* went the horns, *whee!* the pipes.

The musicians came into sight, dressed in gold and purple livery. Acrobats tumbled before them. Guards marched on either side. Following them was a huge wagon, three stories high, drawn by ten paired oxen. The first level encompassed the cart's bed, which was at least six feet deep. On top of that was a stage. Over all, on a platform to the rear, loomed an effigy. Jame recognized it from the palace—bearded, wooden, moss-encrusted. She had guessed then that this was Floten, who had established Mordaunt's lineage and his claim to kingship. This, therefore, must be Mordaunt's wagon.

A trap door opened with a thud and nine actors climbed up from the wagon bed onto the stage, greeted with a blat of trumpets and a cheer from the onlookers. All were elaborately costumed in a rainbow of colors and wore wooden masks. The carven faces struck Jame as

caricatures, none too kindly drawn. The actors paced back
and forth with their noses in the air, then began to
pantomime squabbling. Some pushed. Some pulled.
Others made insulting gestures or surreptitiously tripped
their fellows. Alliances were made and broken. Duels
were fought. Lovers met, betrayed each other, and parted.
What ancient stories these skits must represent. The
slapstick elements were hard to follow for anyone who
didn't know the history of their relationships, but the
audience greeted each jest, broad or cruel, with
uproarious laughter.

A tenth actor ascended to the stage. Unlike the others,
he was modestly dressed and wore a dignified mask to
match that of the effigy looming above him. The others
tried to engage him in their petty disputes, but his
attention was fixed on the small model of a plow which he
had brought with him and continued to carve.

Stagehands dressed in black began to move as if
invisible among the quarreling actors. They stripped the
finery off one after another, down to the rags which each
wore underneath. This, Jame thought, no doubt signified
the poverty that had fallen on them unnoticed. At last all
were nearly naked and shivering. They held out their
hands in appeal to the tenth of their number who must
surely represent Floten. He rose and began to mime
plowing a circuit around the stage, presumably to signify
the founding of the city's outer wall. As he went, the
others resumed their finery and, prosperity restored,
bowed to him. Then all saluted their audience and
descended to cheers.

The musicians and acrobats limbered up. The white

oxen bellowed under the whip and lurched forward. The guards marched off. Another wagon took their place.

Each troop from then on presented its own version of the origin story, with its own hero, its own comic touches, its own family colors. Sometimes Floten was honored. Sometimes he was presented in muddy purple robes without the touch of gold, as a simple-minded bumpkin.

Then, last in line, came something different.

The other wagons had approached with a joyful skirl of pipes. This one also beat its way down the road, but with the measured throb only of drums.

Boom, doom, they went, over and over. *Doom, boom*.

The oxen who pulled this cart were black. So was the vehicle itself, as if touched with flame. The effigy also was charred and aflutter with flakes of ash. A chorus of mourners paced around its stage, gray clad, beating their breasts and wailing. Their grief seemed too deep for pantomime.

"Don't tell me," said Jame. "This one belongs to the Tigganis. Who is the girl?"

A stocky young woman stood at the feet of the statue, dressed in black. She also wore a veil, but this had been thrust back from a defiant, miserable face. Fine eyes under heavy bows swept the audience, seeming to challenge it.

"That's Pensa, Prestic's favorite daughter," said Dar. "She was his brains, some say. She hasn't taken his death at all well."

The crowd had fallen quiet. Some looked offended by this breach in decorum. Others appeared to be sympathetic. After all, Prestic had been well-loved and his death suspicious.

The wagon passed without slowing, trailing after the rest of the procession like a dismal period. The street filled with people in its wake.

"Come on," said Dar. "After that, I need a drink."

He took them to a tavern in the Thyme Side warehouse district and ordered a round of beers. Jame would have preferred cider. She also wondered about his ability to pay, given Mint's hint that he was already deeply in debt. Then too, how much drunker did he intend to get? Life in High Bashti was not an unqualified blessing.

Jorin tapped her knee with a paw, begging, but the fast applied here too. Still . . .

"A bowl of milk," she told their waiter, who gave the ounce a wary look. High Bashti wasn't used to wild animals prowling its precincts, assuming that that applied to well-behaved Jorin. More than one child had rushed up to him in the street to throw arms around his plush neck, crying, "Kitty-boo! Kitty-boo!"

"I heard about Jurik turning up at the campus this morning," said Dar, after drinking deep. "I almost feel sorry for him."

"Why?"

"He's the crown prince, isn't he? Mordaunt's only legitimate heir. Otherwise, it's a bit of a joke here that the king only sires bastards. But Mordaunt won't give his son any real responsibility. Here, fathers decide when their children come of age. That's usually in their early twenties, if not before, especially for girls. Jurik is much older than that. He's on a generous allowance from his mother, but otherwise at a loose end. His followers are too. Y'see, they can't come of age before he does, unless they want to leave his service. One did recently, and he's been in a foul mood ever since."

"I suppose," said Jame, "that's why he's so avid right now to ride the rathorn."

Dar blinked at her owlishly. "I suppose so. But then you did, both literally with Death's-head and figuratively at Tentir. Jurik would give anything to be a true randon, like you. Like us. If we did, why can't he?"

"'How hard can it be?'" Rue quoted with a snort. "That's what Jurik thinks, anyway." She, apparently, also had heard about the encounter that morning and relished it. No doubt the entire campus did. Pompous Jurik was not popular.

"Huh. Then too, he wants to be a big noise in the Princess cult, like his mother who's its high priestess. But Jurik can't do anything until he's recognized as an adult. That must grate on him too."

Snaggles had mentioned that cult. Jame knew little more about it, except that the girl's image appeared all over the city. They were currently drinking in "Amalfia's Arms."

"Tell me about her."

"Oh, that was a long time ago, thousands of years at least. There are lots of stories, some very different, depending on who tells them. Most agree, though, that she was a princess of Hathir, sent to Bashti to marry its crown prince, Bastolov, and seal an alliance between the two banks, just as Vestula was sent to Mordaunt much later. Some say that Bastolov was so enflamed by Amalfia's beauty that he forced himself on her, and she died of shame. She was so beautiful, though, and so beloved that her admirers couldn't bear to let her go, so they spirited away her body. To this day, they claim that that their devotion has kept it from decay. If she had been Bashtiri, she would have been nominated as a goddess or a saint. Instead, she became a cult figure. Only her initiates have ever seen her, though, so who knows? My guess is that she's just another artificially preserved corpse or a wax effigy. Every family has rumors of such shams in the past. A big part of Autumn's Eve is proving to the people that the gods they worship are real."

"Er . . ." Rue said.

"Yes," said Jame. "We've seen beings that claim to be gods elsewhere. You did, Dar, in Kothifir, although you may not have recognized them as such. Rue and I also did in Tai-tastigon. Whatever they were, wherever, they were evident. What to believe about these, here?"

"Listen," said Dar, his words becoming increasingly slurred. "Today High Bashti honors its ancestors. Well, you just saw that. Later, there's Autumn's Eve itself for the recently dead. Who survives as a god, who as a saint, and who goes to the pyre, eh? The current pantheon will also be displayed in their temples. Said they had to prove themselves, didn't I? I've placed a sure bet that Suwaeton will survive. I mean, who's to challenge him with Prestic gone? But tomorrow are the temple plays, where some of the gods deign to speak through their priests. We have the God-voice. Why shouldn't their gods speak too? Let you in on a secret, though: Suwaeton only speaks through his favorite actor in a god farce, if he speaks at all, and the king has forbidden those performances. Sacrilege, he calls them. Also, his grandfather loved 'em, so Mordaunt hates 'em. But they still take place, in secret, at a different location each year. I've just heard where Suwaeton's favorite is acting tomorrow. D'you want to see him perform?"

"Yes," said Jame, "if you promise to go back to the barracks now and sleep until then."

He pouted. "Well, I'm on duty from dusk to dawn in charge of King Mordaunt's security, but except for that ..."

"Good. Then go."

III

THE AFTERNOON PASSED. Children began to disappear from the streets while more elaborately costumed adults appeared, many already very drunk. At dusk torches flared and fireworks crackled, dropping multicolored lights on the city. The tantalizing smell of cooking arose, but so far no one ate.

"Ah!" exclaimed Rue as golden stars burst overhead.

Blind Jorin blinked uncertainly at the light reflected in Jame's eyes and flinched at the bang.

Neither Tai-tastigon nor Kothifir had put on such a show, although Jame remembered the night when the former had nearly been set alight during the Thieves' Guild election in the middle of a drought. It was perhaps fortunate that it had rained so hard here the night before. Now, thunder rumbled above the city in the mountains like an enormous clearing of throats following a nervous stutter of lightning.

People began to stream eastward down the streets of the city. In contrast to their drunken peers above, most of these men went in solemn procession, wearing white robes as well as scarves dyed the colors of their respective houses. Some had also donned waxen death masks, presumably of their ancestors given how individual each was. Some women also went with them, in silence, wearing black, as if to appear invisible.

Drawn by curiosity, Jame allowed herself to be carried along with the crowd, followed warily by Rue and Jorin. Although some eyes slid sideways to observe them, no one commented on their presence. Here and there were other strangers, perhaps visiting from other Central Lands. The reputation of such a massive annual festival would have spread far and wide.

Here between the Sanctor, the Tigganis, and the easternmost Artifax hills lay the valley set aside for the Grand Forum, which Jame recognized from her arrival in the city, although then it had been nearly empty. At its center was a large paved expanse with a raised dais at its heart. Surrounding this and edging backward up the adjacent slopes, like so many craggy cliffs, were the major temples of High Bashti's Pantheon as well as many smaller chapels dedicated to their lesser divinities and to other past dignitaries. More fireworks exploded overhead. Their flash reflected off marble and gilt facades, off the huge stone statues that sat before each structure, painted to look life-like and, in the sudden glare, rather surprised.

The open space was already filling, with more left to come. One hundred thousand? Two? A vast babble of voices arose, mostly cheerful but with an underlying nervous tension. Tonight, after all, this multitude would see for themselves if their patron gods still survived or had failed over the past year. Some would pray for the former, some for the latter.

Boom, went a drum by a temple door, and again: *Boom*.

A common wooden coffin was carried down the steps, accompanied by mourners and the stench of decay. There, either a god had succumbed or his mortal challenger as nominated by the Council. The betting stalls had favored the latter in regard to the house of the Merchant. The crowd held silent while the coffin passed, then cheered the survivor, whichever he was. Would the worshippers know before they entered? Ah. Here came workmen to remove the head of the sentinel statue, later to replace it. An old god had fallen.

Blatt! sounded a horn, blown from the dais. *Harrooo, blatt*!

House standards and colors rose above the crowd. People began to sort themselves into alignment with much jostling.

In the swirl, Jame glimpsed a familiar waxen face. It looked at her and its eyes lit with gleeful malice, made all the more disconcerting by the sweet curve of its pale lips. It inclined its head in a mocking bow, then turned and melted into the press.

Jame darted after it. She heard Rue cry out for her to wait, but in her haste she left her servant behind. Jorin pressed against her leg, nearly between her feet, shivering. The crowd swirled around them. Other white faces bobbed up here and there, some individual death masks, others the featureless blobs of the Deathless. The latter circled her.

"Renounce death," they crooned in her ear. "Join us and never die."

"Oh, shut up."

Someone ran into her, hard.

"Watch where you're going," an angry voice snarled at her. "Oh. It's you."

Jame found herself clinging to Graykin, as he did to her, both off-balance. He peered around.

"Damn. I've lost him."

"Who?"

"Your mystery man on the coin."

Someone had climbed onto the dais. He, too, wore a waxen mask, but not the one that they had been chasing. His scarf was purple and gold, his face square, blunt, and bearded, with a heavy brow. Below that, his coat of gold brocade hung on him like boxy armor hollow at the core. He raised an ebony staff.

Thud, thud, thud, it went against the floor of the dais, echoing across the suddenly hushed forum.

Then people began to sing. The language was archaic but somehow it spoke to the immortal glory of the gods, to the faith of their people.

What is, will be, it said. *We are the heart of this world. Our ways endure.*

The standards came to the fore, each followed by its adherents, winding up the steps of their respective family god. Jame followed the Floten gold and purple. Indeed, she could hardly help but do so, given how tightly the crowd was packed. Graykin pressed against her shoulder.

A distressed Jorin trod on her toes when she wasn't actually lifted off her feet. Where was Rue?

The procession mounted the stair of the biggest temple on the western side of the plaza. Jame remembered its counterpart currently being built by Mordaunt for his private use. How could it compare? This was a place of public worship, sanctified by many offerings, some humble, others breath-taking. Its floors were polished stone, its columns enormous, supporting a high roof. Rich tapestries hung against the walls depicting scenes from Suwaeton's life. Candles burned everywhere.

Jame picked up Jorin and draped him over her shoulder, no light burden. He trembled in her arms.

"What did you mean, my 'mystery man'?" she asked Graykin, raising her voice to be heard over the uproar.

"Set me to find him, didn't you?" *What*, his affronted tone said, *you expected me to fail*? "Actually, it wasn't hard to find out who he was . . . or rather, is . . . assuming you ask someone old enough. Thirty years ago, when Mordaunt was still just a prince, he met a stranger who promised him eternal life. The Prophet, people called him. The Deathless cult gathered around him. Then came the White Hills, the death of Suwaeton, the prince's rise to kingship, and the Prophet's disappearance. Not before Mordaunt honored him on a specially minted regal coin like yours, though."

"And now he's come back?"

"You saw him, or it, or whatever that waxy thing is, and the cult has risen again. Suddenly, everyone wants to be immortal."

Jorin sneezed in Jame's ear. She had been aware of

someone pressing up behind her, breathing hard. Now through the ounce's senses, to a lesser degree through her own, she caught a whiff of burnt wood. In the press, however, she couldn't turn to look. Besides, they had finally come to the temple's inner room.

On the altar lay a rock crystal sarcophagus, its lid open, its contents from this angle invisible except for a long, shapeless blur seen through a clouded side panel.

Behind the altar stood the king. He had removed his waxen death mask and given it to the priest beside him who held it up as if on display. Mordaunt's hair was plastered to his skull with sweat—a wonder that the mask hadn't melted in place. More sweat ran down into the folds of his heavy robe. He looked thoroughly uncomfortable, his sharp face drawn into sour lines. While he had cast off his grandfather's mask, he clutched Suwaeton's black staff with its silver knob in both hands in a choke grip, and glowered over it as if to say, *Who dares challenge me?*

Dar stood to one side, in full armor, looking more or less alert after his day of debauchery. Well, he had said that he was responsible for Mordaunt's safety tonight and here he was, representing Kencyr honor.

The king's eyes darted around the hall, trusting no one.

Worshippers inched into the hall, past the coffin, back out. Jame approached it. She saw the legs first, then the chest, then the face. Overall, General Suwaeton wore golden armor, which fit him as it should a soldier. His face was familiar from his death mask, but ruddy above his hoary beard, above close-set lips and a furrowed brow. He radiated power. Moreover, the smell that rose from the sarcophagus was not so much sweet as fresh, with a tang of masculine sweat. One would have thought that he only slept, except that he did not breathe. This, Jame thought, was no ordinary corpse.

Mordaunt glared at her over the casket.

"You," he said.

Then his gaze shifted behind her and his eyes widened.

Someone pushed Jame aside. She staggered, pulled off-balance by Jorin's weight, even more so when he twisted in her grasp and, rather than fall to the floor, launched himself on top of the altar. The stone there was highly polished. His claws scrabbled on it as he tried to stop, but he still collided with the coffin which slid backward off the altar with a crash.

"Oh!" wailed the crowd.

The black-clad woman behind Jame lunged with a knife. However, Mordaunt had already scrambled back out of reach. Dar leaped to his defense, but collided with the priest. By the time he had disentangled himself, the would-be assassin had disappeared into the growing chaos of the hall.

Thud, thud, thud.

Everyone froze.

There lay Suwaeton on the altar, without his coffin but with his ebony staff back firmly in his hands. Mordaunt goggled at him, horrified.

"You're dead!" he cried. "Dead, I tell you! Stop coming back!"

With that, he fled, Dar trailing after him trying to apologize.

"All right," Jame said to Graykin when at last they made

their way out of the temple. Being among the closest to the altar, they were practically the last to leave, and lucky at that not to be detained by a thoroughly rattled city guard. "More is going on here than I realized."

IV

BY NOW, it was midnight. Doors opened as Jame passed, a shaken Jorin trotting at her heels. Within, families laid out the long-promised feast and welcomed their ancestors to partake. Did wisps pass in the street and enter? It seemed so to Jame, but she felt particularly suggestible after the night so far.

The day had been warm. Now autumn's chill crept into the air. Breath smoked on the air. Thunder rumbled closer. Was it about to rain again, or sleet, or snow?

Here at last was the Campus Kencyrath, with horses held by squires outside its door, the breath of both steaming on the chill air. Surely that flashy black belonged to Jurik, and what about that litter drawn up next to it, draped in purple and gold? Regal visitors, this late?

Jame passed Lady Anthea's door on the way to her own quarters. The widow looked out. "Do something!" she hissed. "That harpy is going to ruin him!"

Beyond was Harn's apartment. A sharp voice spoke within.

"Is that all you can do for him? Paltry lessons in your oh-so-special fighting arts? I thought better of you."

Harn muttered in reply. Jame could imagine him, hunched to one side, turning his shoulder, but against whom? "Has to prove himself, doesn't he? The bloodline isn't enough."

"It should be!"

The door to his apartment opened. A woman stood on the threshold, small, shapely, fierce. She wore a purple mantle trimmed with gilded fur. "I gave you roses to remember me by, oh faithless one," she spat. "After what you did, you owe me!" Then she turned and left. Jame ducked out of her way.

That, surely, had been Queen Vestula, but what was she doing here, much less addressing the Commander in such terms?

Rue waited for Jame in her quarters, with a simple dinner of bread, cheese, and date-stuffed figs laid out by the fire.

"I thought that you might want me here," she said. "Also, that you might be hungry."

"I am," said Jame. "Ravenous."

As she ate, Rue sorted her meager wardrobe for the morrow when High Bashti's current gods were supposed to manifest themselves through their priests.

"You need more clothes," she said.

"For your benefit or for mine? Sorry, Rue. I just don't care what I wear as long as it's clean, decent, and convenient, with a few court coats for special occasions. What does it matter what I look like, beyond that?"

"It does to your people."

"Then my people must take me as they find me, or go elsewhere."

"Ha."

Yet Jame wondered. She hadn't bound Rue, as much

as the young Kendar deserved that distinction. Did Rue still see it that way? So far, she seemed loyal despite what she had first felt as an undeserved slight. A new world was coming. Tori felt that too. How would they all fit into it?

Anyway, what did one wear for a divine manifestation, assuming Dar was still available to escort her to the performance of Suwaeton's god farce? Whatever that was. Assuming that Suwaeton appeared.

Rue had been too far back in the press to see what had happened at the altar. Jame told her, omitting only Graykin's report. She had given the latter much thought, though. It wasn't the first time she had heard someone call himself a prophet and declare that "Death itself will die."

After all, what had Gerridon's entire life been but an increasingly desperate quest for immortality?

As the old song put it, "Gerridon Highlord, Master of Knorth, a proud man was he. The Three People held he in his hand. Wealth and power had he, and knowledge deeper than the Sea of Stars.

"But he feared death.

"'Dread lord,' he said to the Shadow that Crawls, even to Perimal Darkling, ancient of enemies, 'my god regards me not. If I serve thee, wilt thou preserve me, even to the end of time?'

"Night bowed over him. Words they spoke.

"Then he went to his sister-consort, Jamethiel Dream-weaver.

"'Dance out the souls of the faithful,' he said, 'that darkness may enter in.'

"And she danced."

Two-thirds of the Kencyrath had fallen that night, the rest fleeing down through the rooms of the House from link to link of the Chain of Creation into a new world, Rathillien, where it now found itself.

And where did Gerridon find himself?

As far as Jame knew, he had dwelt in the back rooms of the House for eons, where time moved more slowly than it did here, hence the ten-odd years that her brother had gained on her during her sojourn there. So much longer must have been dull for the Master as he had slowly eaten through the souls that the Dream-weaver had reaped for him.

Then he had started to meddle on Rathillien, apparently with Bashti and a young Mordaunt first, only to disappear abruptly during the massacre in the White Hills. When a young Torisen had encountered him in Kothifir some fifteen years later, he had moved on to become the Karnids' Dark Prophet, preaching his message of triumph over death. Now, with the fall of Urakarn, was she to believe that he was back in High Bashti? Why?

She had never supposed that he seriously wanted to conquer death for everyone. That was just the hook with which he baited his cult. Only his own immortality really mattered to him. Perhaps, though, once having been Highlord of the Kencyrath, he wanted followers with whom to play. Then too, maybe he wanted to use them in other ways. In Kothifir, the Karnid horde had tried to defeat the Southern Host while his priests had preached his message in the city. He had done that twice—when Tori had been there and later when Jame was. Gerridon was a creature of habit. He did the same thing over and over, each time expecting a different outcome. There had to be a word for that. Oh, yes: madness. What was he trying to accomplish here, now, when the stakes for him had grown so dire? Was the wax-faced man even Gerridon at all? Trinity, she hoped not.

Too many questions. Too few answers.

An unfamiliar shiver ran up her spine, jolting her hand, causing the cider mug which it gripped to spill.

Rue stared. "What is it?"

"Death's-head is having fun."

She leaped up and ran out of the apartment, followed by Rue's plaintive cry:

"D'you really want to interrupt him?"

Here was the grassy heart of the barracks. At its far end, a dozen or so people lined the pasture's fence. More were within, apparently chasing the remount herd. Horses swerved back and forth like a flock of birds, kicking up muddy spray. Then Death's-head charged through their ranks, scattering them left and right. The human invaders fled before him and scrambled out between the bars of the enclosure. The rathorn swerved, snorting with derision, his tail held high. Nothing had amused him more in many a long, dull day.

Jame recognized Jurik and his friends. So he hadn't left with his mother, assuming she had indeed gone home. What the prince was up to now was all too clear.

Two of his followers remained in the pasture. Now they were trying to sneak up on the rathorn. Death's-head charged one. The other used the distraction to snake a rope around his foreleg. Tangled, he fell, plowing into the mud on his shoulder. A second rope snared another of his flailing hooves.

Jurik straightened, climbed over the fence, and sauntered toward the prone beast, a bridle with a cruel, spiked bit dangling from his hand. He might even have laughed, as if it had been so easy after all.

As he approached, Death's-head glared at him through a besmirched mask, panting. The prince was within feet when the rathorn hooked his nasal tusk under the ropes and ripped them off.

Jurik stopped.

Death's-head regained his feet. Head low, horns poised, he moved toward the prince. Stalking. One slow step, then another. Oh, never offend a rathorn's dignity.

Jurik dropped the bridle, turned, and ran.

Jame was running too, toward the enclosure, toward the watching, horrified Bashtiri. She slipped between them, between the bars, between the prince and his would-be prey, just as the latter charged.

Jurik scrambled to safety behind her.

The rathorn sat on his haunches, forelegs braced, trying to stop, but he skidded on slick mud and crashed into Jame, throwing her backward against a post. For a moment, dazed, she couldn't breathe. A mottled wall of equine flesh loomed over her with horns and red eyes. She grabbed blindly for the flying mane, caught it, and swung up onto his back.

Jurik was shouting for spears, arrows, rocks... anything!

Death's-head stopped short, gathered himself like a cat, and sprang over the fence.

He could have done that anytime he wanted to, Jame thought, hanging on for dear life. Bored as he had been, his supposed imprisonment here had only been a game. Then he came down again and she was jolted face foremost into his rising neck. For a moment, she wondered if she had broken her nose. Then they were galloping across the training field toward the gate. From there one way led into the beast pens, currently used as stables, while the other opened below the outer stair onto the road.

A white face watched them pass—Queen Vestula, waiting after all to see her darling son's conquest.

Out on the street were the horses of Jurik's entourage. When Death's-head charged through their midst, they scattered in panic, pursued by their attendants, dragging the regal litter after them until it smashed turning a corner. Good. Hopefully Jurik wouldn't be able to follow her, and his precious mother could damn well walk home.

Meanwhile the rathorn's hooves skidded on slick cobblestones. *It must have rained again,* Jame thought, clinging to his slippery back. *Oh, for stirrups.* The thunder seemed closer, if that wasn't just the echo of hooves against close-set walls. Where were they going? Oh, for reins or a bit with which to steer, not that Death's-head had ever accepted the latter. Instead, this was a run-away, pure and simple. She must either cling or risk breaking bone on stone. No other way offered itself.

People were still abroad, going from door to door for the Autumn's Eve feast, perhaps also hoping to greet old, long-lost friends. They shouted at her as she tore past, nearly trampling them. Mired as Death's-head was, no one seemed to realize what they had just seen.

It occurred to her that they were following the route through the city that they had taken on their arrival, except in reverse. Here was the Thyme Side district, then the now deserted Grand Forum except for workmen busily replacing the head of defunct Merchant god. Beyond was the eastward-facing main gate through which they had entered, which now stood open as did all gates on this night. Beyond that again was the farm land of the river valley.

Jame didn't know where the rathorn was taking her. His mind seethed, incandescent with rage. "Beasts of madness," some called his kind. Perhaps that had touched her too, to have taken such a ride, but then what had been the alternative? Fall. Break.

When he had galloped out his fury, however, he dropped to a canter and began to consider. At least, she felt that he did. His moods had always been more apparent to her than his thoughts—with Jorin too, for that matter. Bonding had its limits.

Fields of cabbage and carrots spread to either side, then of lettuce and lentils as they passed eastward through the cultivated fields of the Thyme River Valley. Potatoes. Onions. Parsnips. On and on and on, grown for the maw of the city.

The road swerved. Here was the gate in the outer curtain wall, beyond which the main road joined Thyme Street with the river running beside it. Beyond that, bluffs rose. At their feet lay the western edge of the Necropolis. Monuments and mausoleums lined both banks of the rushing river—rows of miniature houses, obelisks, statuary, stretching in the gloom back to the cliffs.

Thunder rumbled in the throat of the hills. Another wave of storms was coming.

They began to pass citizens returning from the ancestral feast—early, Jame thought, and looking distraught. Cart after cart passed, carrying mostly women and children driven by servants. Some looked shocked. Others were crying. More than a few cast glares in her direction, as if they longed to blame someone for whatever grief had befallen them.

Death's-head eyed them askance, slowing to a wary trot.

The bluffs pinched in at the foot of the valley, then drew back in scalloped cliffs slotted with crypts. Flickers of lightning glinted off plaques, gold and silver and bronze, proclaiming the virtues of the dead, begging mercy from death. Angry voices and wails sounded ahead. Something burned in a low-hanging haze of charnel smoke.

They came to flooded strips of road. Earlier, it must have rained furiously in the mountains. More than one stream had burst its banks and was now rushing down to join the Thyme.

The rathorn stopped, snorting, before one such overflow. Would he refuse to cross? Instead, delicately, he stepped into the current, turned left, and waded northward into the overhanging trees. Jame had no idea where he was taking her. Farther and farther back into the undergrowth they went, away from the noise and the stench, through leaves, between trailing vines, around fallen trees. Underfoot, underwater, ran a path paved with smooth stones. The way opened here and there into gardens of sculpture, into ranks of statuary, into squares of small houses grouped as if in communities. The farther they went, the more weathered their surroundings became. This city of the dead appeared to have been built from the back out, tending toward the river. This region, at least, was nowhere near as well kept as that closer to the Thyme. Also, the dates on the tombs were much older, going back centuries when they still stood at all. Everything was overgrown and untended. Foxes barked. Owls hooted. Undergrowth rustled with nocturnal life unaccustomed to human incursion.

At length they came to the nearest edge of the bluffs, where water cascaded down into a spreading pond. Jame swung down off Death's-head's back as he waded in among the tombstones. The water splashed on his head, and back, and flanks. Mud washed off. White glimmered in the dark among the monuments, a marble statue come to life. He snorted and shook himself. Here at last, he was clean.

Jame watched him for a while. So. This was the refuge that he had chosen. She had seen at Tentir how he could disappear even in closer quarters to the college than this. Given how he could manipulate his smell, no hunting dog could follow him here. As for his tracks . . . well, he had taken care of that.

Reassured, she turned and traced their path backward along the margin of the submerged path. Her boots, at least, were new and more or less waterproof, although they soon began to squelch.

They must have come a mile or more off the main road. What a vast city of the dead this was, and so far she had only experienced one bank of it. Indeed, High Bashti was a very old city with a ban against burying an ordinary corpse within its walls. Most of its dead were cremated. Their ashes might come here, but so did the rest of the bodies, with a few exceptions for the deified and the sanctified. Odd, how municipal reverence for death mingled with repulsion, largely on the basis of class. Snaggles was right to be outraged. No wonder the cult of the Deathless had attracted so many followers.

Here again was Thyme Street, which ran all the way across Bashti down to the Silver. The river Thyme coursed along beside it, dividing the Necropolis in half, north from south.

The disturbance before had come from nearby, farther eastward. The noise had subsided, except for a low, moaning chant. Who sang? Why did the night air still reek of charred flesh?

Curiosity edged Jame forward against her better judgment.

Ahead, flames licked out the windows of a majestic three-story mausoleum. That ravaged exterior with its shattered statuary looked familiar. Could it belong to the Tigganis, Prestic's family, much as she had seen it on her way into the city? The main door had been broken down. No dogs or carrion birds haunted it now, just a roaring wind tipped with orange against the night. Within, piled furniture blazed and wooden rafters sagged, eaten by embers. Were those figures reclining on stone couches? If so, they too burned with an oily smoke that roiled out of the shattered door.

People with torches watched. Firelight glimmered on

their tears—of grief, of rage. Men sang a deep-throated dirge to their departed kin, to vengeance:

"Our blood rises, as did yours.
Father, mother, brother, sister, aunt, uncle.
Ah, dear grandparents. Who will avenge you?
We, the living.
And so we swear."

Some women beat their breasts and wailed. Children? There were a few with wide, disbelieving eyes, and if it was wise to retain them as witnesses, who could say? Vengeance could run for generations.

Jame didn't know what she was seeing, but the raw emotion of it drove her back, one step, then another, until she found herself in a clearing between tombs, sheltered by their walls. Or perhaps not. More thunder. The rain had held off, but now it began to slice down in icy, hissing veils.

Lightning flashed. Around her stood hollow cavities in the air, given shape by shells of streaming rain. Darkness fell again, but by torchlight she could see their breath hanging before them like so many ghosts.

"No," she said, backing away, into something.

"Yes," said a voice in her ear, behind her.

Hands closed on her arms, twisted them. The feverish heat and steam of invisible flesh closed in—that, and the light of yellow, bloodshot eyes.

In a sudden rush, something large and dark burst into the clearing, scattering the assassins of the Shadow Guild. One gave a thin scream. A body thrashed in the grip of the newcomer, defined now not by rain but by blood as it was ripped limb from limb. One arm here, the other there. When the head tore off, the scream suddenly cut short. His fellows had already crashed away through the undergrowth.

Jame had backed up against the side wall of the mausoleum without being aware that she had moved. The fire still raging within warmed the stones. Another flare of lightning illuminated her . . . rescuer? She stared. He panted, glaring. Mismatched hands flexed. Stitches tore flesh. Then night fell again and he was gone.

Trinity.

On the road, wagons were limbering up and leaving. Jame perched on the tailgate step of one, below the occupants' line of sight. She hoped that they would talk about what had just happened, but no one spoke. The ride back to the city was long, cold, and miserable, even after the deluge spattered to an end. At the eastern gate she dismounted, stumbling a bit with cramped legs, and made her way back to the Campus Kencyrath. Autumn's Day dawned as she arrived.

⋙ Chapter IX ⋘
The God Farce

High Bashti: Autumn 1

I

OUTSIDE THE GARRISON MESS-HALL, Jame ran into Dar, just come off night duty at the palace.

"Hello!" he said, cheerfully munching on a hot biscuit. "I've been looking all over for you. Ready for the god farce?"

"Dar. I'm cold, wet, and exhausted. Yesterday was long, followed by a night not without adventures of its own."

He looked chagrined. "But this may be the most important performance of the year! And you promised."

All Jame really wanted was to rest and to think about what she had just seen, which so far made no sense to her whatsoever.

"I'm surprised that King Mordaunt still employs you," she said, to stall for time. "Yesterday, at the temple, he wasn't best pleased."

"Oh," said Dar, with a nonchalant wave of his breakfast, scattering crumbs, "he knows that we Kencyr are the best he can get, whatever our momentary failings. Clearly, he doesn't trust his own people. Even his son he keeps at a distance. And no one trusts that Hathiri queen of his. Now, about the farce . . ."

As tired as she was, it was hard to disappoint her former cadet who now reminded her more than ever of a bumbling, eager Molocar pup.

And he might have a point about the event's importance.

"All right," she said with a sigh. "It's too early to go to bed—or maybe too late. First, though, I have to change into dry clothes, if Rue can find any."

II

SOON AFTERWARD, the city awoke. Shops opened. People disgorged from doorways, yawning, into the street where neighbor met neighbor. A buzz of gossip arose, mostly distressed.

Snaggles skipped along between Jame and Dar—not, it seemed, to be shaken off.

"Suwaeton to perform?" he said, over and over, his gap-toothed grin spread from ear to ear. "Just try to stop me!"

"It may only be the General's favorite actor, old Trepsis, speaking for him," Dar warned both the boy and Jame. Now that he had more or less coerced his commandant's attendance, he seemed to be having second thoughts.

Jame, on the other hand, was getting her second wind. After all, what was a single sleepless night when she had spent five of them consecutively in Tai-tastigon? That had proved interesting, when not purely terrifying. This might yet too, on both counts.

They passed through the covered market, setting up

for the day. The betting booths, however, had already been smashed, fragments of white plaster busts strewn across the street, the agents nowhere in sight.

"Damn," said Dar. "I bet on Suwaeton to survive and so he did. Where's my pay-off now?"

Snaggles, on the other hand, looked almost gleeful as he eyed the more agitated of the citizenry. "Now they know what it's like to lose someone they love, forever."

"What do you mean?" asked Jame.

"You didn't hear?" said Dar. "An entire year's worth of saints were violated and went to the pyre last night in the Necropolis, already beginning to stink. The gamblers were not pleased, nor the faithful among the populace."

"Help Mother come home?"

So that desperate voice had pleaded from the shrubbery on the edge of a palatial estate.

"For a gift? For a bribe?"

Now Mother would never come home again.

"Oh," said Jame, taking this in. "It was unexpected?"

"Totally. Of course, families check the dearly departed before the Eve to be sure that all is well. No one wants a nasty surprise. On one hand, it's embarrassing for a revered ancestor to go soft, but such things happen. On the other hand, think how terrible it would be to arrive for a festival meant to welcome them back only to find a feast for crows. To make it worse, the longer they've been dead, the faster they decay. Not so bad after a week. Awful after a month or more. I hear that some families just about went mad. I mean, to set a pyre in someone else's crypt in the middle of the night to dispose of the evidence . . ."

"You think that was why they did it?"

He grimaced. "Well, maybe not that exactly, but there's something obscene about a rotting corpse. Would we tolerate it?"

"No. Then too, this pyre was in Prestic's mausoleum. Could they still be protesting his death?"

"That might be part of it. I hear that it was his daughter Pensa who tried to assassinate Mordaunt last night in Suwaeton's temple. I shouldn't say this, perhaps, but many people wish that she had succeeded."

"Not popular," Jame mused. "I wonder how he will shape up in death against his revered grandfather."

Dar laughed.

"What will happen to Pensa now?"

"A council trial, presumably, with Mordaunt's thumb heavy on the scales and his followers baying for blood. First, though, they have to catch her. Some families may hide her for her father's sake. Her own certainly will. There are even rumors that they might propose her for her father's place both as head of the Tigganis and as a rival to Mordaunt. Yes, a mortal queen instead of a mortal king. People really don't like Mordaunt. For that matter, she was once engaged to Jurik and, some say, was in love with him. Maybe she still is. There's no accounting for taste. I've heard that he snubbed her once in public as being too plain for his regal appetite. How's that for a mess?"

III

THE SITE OF THAT YEAR'S GOD FARCE turned out to be south of the Palace Mount, tucked into a bend of the River Thyme, in the first of a trio of apartment buildings largely patronized by the city's theatrical community. They entered by the block's northern door, into a corridor redolent with cooking, sweat, incense, and sewage, echoing with excited voices. A stream of people arrived with them, of all classes mixed indiscriminately, cheerfully jostling each other. If this place was supposed to be a secret, many shared it.

The central courtyard of the first building presented itself, a hundred-foot square.

On the western side was a wooden stage backed with second story apartments curtained off with blankets.

Rough-hewn ramps lifted benches against the other three walls, higher and higher. Most were already full.

Above, the courtyard opened into a shaft reaching up seven stories toward the morning sky. Windows lined it, also improvised balconies, also wash-lines extending from side to side, now festooned with bright scraps of cloth like so many ragged banners. The windows were full of eager faces, the balconies of bodies, leaning out over the groaning rails as struts creaked beneath them.

"Occupants rent them out to the upper class," said Dar, following Jame's apprehensive upward gaze. "A good box balcony can equal a year's income."

With difficulty and not a little shoving, he found them three seats together in the eastern stands, mid-way up, crammed together. Several tiers below were rows of somber figures, each with a wax tablet balanced on his knee.

"Look there," said Dar, pointing. "Those are Suwaeton's priests and some others. It must grate on them that they have to come to a lower town apartment to hear whatever their high god has to say. Most elder priests stay away altogether. These are the young sparks, avid for fresh words."

"What happens today at Suwaeton's own temple in the Forum?"

"Oh, solemn recitations of his previous pronouncements, always at least a year out of date, sometimes twitched by the actors to suit current events. I don't know what the other temples do. Sometimes their god appears. Mostly, they improvise."

"How long do we have to wait?"

"For the main show here? Until after the prelude, which will go on until the actors are ready."

By "the prelude," he apparently meant a troop of bedraggled children who trotted out onto the stage and began to sing. Belatedly, instruments joined them from an upper balcony.

> "Welcome, our king!
> In life, in death, welcome!
> We, your people, greet you!"

On they went, praising Suwaeton, lauding the current pantheon. Snaggles might scorn the latter for favoring the upper class, but here people cheered the gods, if with some not so subtle jibes. It seemed to Jame that while many Bashtiri took their pantheon without subtlety, without humor, those did not attend anything as frivolous as a farce. These, here, enjoyed themselves—yes, even the novice priests, who put down their styluses to applaud when the song ended.

Out came a fox-faced comic. His sharp jokes appeared to be based on his neighbors, who responded with more groans than laughter and with flung, over-ripe fruit.

"The host—that is, in this case, the apartment block—supplies the entertainment," said Dar, aside. "Also the chorus. There they are now."

Six figures edged self-consciously out from behind the blankets. They seemed to be wearing the finest robes they could assemble, even if several of these were merely dyed bed sheets. Some looked eager. Others were so stage-shy that it hurt to watch them. They began to sing in cracked voices:

"Our gods, our royal houses.
Whom do you praise?
We praise all!"

An actor emerged from the back-stage behind the blankets. By its stylized wooden mask and ornate gown, it was meant to be a middle-aged woman with pretentions of youth.

"Oh, woe," she quavered, through a voice sufficiently magnified by the mask to project to the farthest rows. Jame thought that she sounded younger than indicated by the painted mask that she wore. "I have lost it!"

"Imagine us in a rich hall," said the chorus in unison, aside. "The walls are draped with golden tapestries. The windows"—here, with a gesture to the audience above—"open on gardens full of the choicest flowers. Oh, Queen Tigganis, what have you lost?"

She beat her breasts, cruelly hard. Here was passion indeed. "If I knew, I could find it."

"Hush," said the chorus. "Here comes Lord Schola. Surely he will know."

A second actor entered, wearing an old, peevish face. "Lady, what would you ask?"

"I have lost that which I fear most to lose. What would that be for you?"

Pursed lips worked within the mask. "Knowledge, of course. Dithos claims that the fourth stanza of the Ithica refers to Livacious when obviously the poet means Sedulous. How can we endure such ignorance?"

"Well, well," said the chorus as Schola retreated, mumbling, beyond the curtain. "To each, his own. Here comes Lord Sanctor. What has our priest god to say?"

Out came a figure in hieratic robes. If there were only two actors, one of them was very quick at his trade.

"Orthodoxy!" he bellowed. "What is worse than to question the gods themselves? Our faith sustains them, does it not? If we fail to support them, though, what becomes of us?"

"What indeed?" murmured the audience, and Suwaeton's priests assiduously took notes.

The judge Lexion came next, a-quake in linen robes embroidered with the words of legal briefs. "Must I depend on my own views alone? Oh no, oh no. Preserve to me the authority of the law!"

"Perish forbid," intoned the chorus, "that you should have to think for yourself."

"War!" proclaimed the next actor, nearly running the previous one over. Three performers on the stage now?

The newcomer wore armor and stomped forward on wide-spread feet, belligerent. His mask was painted red. Behind it, blood-shot eyes bulged. Then he jumped.

"Eek! A mouse!"

"Courage," murmured the chorus. "Or perhaps reputation. Ah, Belacose, what is a warrior without both?"

The courtesan Delectica emerged in her gilded wig and grotesquely padded bust to bewail the loss of her beauty; then the craftsman Artifax, of his skill; then the actor Thespar, of his inspiration.

. . . six, seven, eight . . .

Out shambled a fat man, his stuffed bulk in contrast to the actor's skinny shanks revealed beneath a short robe. "Where am I? Who are you all?"

"Your gods," roared Sanctor, who couldn't seem to speak below that register. "New to our ranks, are you not? Well, learn your place and play our game."

"I am . . . I was Lokus."

"Now you are Mercanty, god of merchants. Get used to it. Tell us: what do you fear?"

It seemed to Jame that multiple gods now milled about the stage. They wore different caricature masks and were diversely dressed. When revealed, however, their spindly legs and knobby knees were all the same and each one appeared to be lame. Of them all, only Queen Tigganis remained herself, wringing her hands.

"What do you fear?" she echoed.

"To lose a deal, of course," the merchant snarled, as if insulted by her ignorance. Some of the audience hissed at his disrespect.

"Profit, knowledge, religion, courage . . . but what

have I lost?" wailed the queen, tearing straw out of her flaxen wig.

Someone came down the ramp from the east, and people rose in a wave to greet him. Jame also stood, trying to see over their heads. Gray hair, a furrowed brow, a ruddy face above a hoary beard, white touched with red ... was that a real face or a particularly well-defined mask? Whichever, she recognized it from Suwaeton's crystalline coffin and, less distinctly, from Floten's wooden effigy.

Dar cheered. Snaggles jumped up and down. A blizzard of flowers rained from the balconies above, some enthusiastically thrown still in their pots which exploded on the boards.

Suwaeton mounted the stage, brushing petals off his simple white robe. *Tap, tap, tap* went his ebony staff on the steps. A breath of fresh air entered the courtyard with him. All the rest had been a prelude, Jame realized. This had now truly become sacred space where anything might happen.

Ahhh ... breathed the audience, settling back.

The chorus held out their hands to the newcomer.

"Oh, our king, our arbiter, to our confusion bring judgment: What do *you* fear most to lose?"

He paused and stroked his beard. Its white tips snapped as if with muted lightning. "Well, I value honesty, and loyalty, and common-sense ..."

The gods booed. They wore the same faces as before and had the same knobby knees, but now their features moved, as if the newcomer had brought a fresh level of reality to their improvised performance. If anything, though, by contrast with him they were all mere caricatures of themselves. Glaring warrior, pursed scholar, fearful judge, sanctimonious priest . . .

Again, Queen Tigganis remained the exception, wooden-masked but rendered human by her distress and her eloquent hands.

"All right," said Suwaeton—or was it the actor Trepsis? Features shifted subtly, as if one personality over-lay another. This, at least, was no mask. "My queen, what ails you?"

"I . . . I . . ."

The curtains behind her bulged and flailed as a figure fought its way through them. Tattered dressing robe, flopping slippers, yapping voice—a buck-toothed boy, bare-faced except for smudged streaks of make-up, playing Mordaunt.

"Where am I? What sordid, stinking place is this? Who are these pathetic people?"

The audience jeered.

Suwaeton feigned surprise. "Did I hear something? It sounded like the whine of a pup."

The actor playing Mordaunt drew himself up and wrapped his robe around himself, baring skinny shanks. "Who are you, old man?"

"Don't you recognize me, boy? Oh, but I forgot: you may build that gaudy temple of yours, but you never pray to your gods."

Mordaunt sneered. "Why should I? Who are these so-called gods but preserved corpses, that I should bow to them?"

"And who are these people, that you should serve them? Then again, if you do not, who are you?"

The crowd booed. The priests among them frantically took notes.

Dar nudged Jame. "This is why Mordaunt bans these plays. Where else can the gods speak their minds?"

Mordaunt sneered. "You, old man, to challenge me? I am twice the man that you ever were."

He loosened his belt. Down from it tumbled a tube of sawdust to dangle between his scrawny knees.

"Huh," said Suwaeton. His own sausage, twice as thick, thumped against the floor. "Don't challenge your granddad to a pissing match, boy."

A disturbance erupted by the door as men forced their way in, bedizened with fringe and silk scraps and cheap sequins. Jame recognized them from the palace. These were Mordaunt's hired ruffians with citizen toadies huddled behind them wearing yellow scarves, nervously clutching torches.

"Well, well, well," said the broadest of the thugs, filling the doorway with his bulk and sheer gaudy splendor. "What sedition have we here?"

Sacred space ruptured like a burst bubble.

Wooden visages and empty robes tumbled onto the stage, tenantless. Left behind were a boy with scarred, knobby knees, a masked woman, and a white-bearded old man.

"Who are you, to threaten my people?" quavered the latter, brandishing his black staff, which looked more like a lightning-struck tree branch than ebony and about as sturdy.

"Not so impressive now, are you?" the brigand leader said, chuckling. "Shall we see what your king makes of you?"

When he stepped into the square, however, the audience rose up against him with a roar. People threw themselves out of the bleachers and some off of the balconies. Suwaeton's priests clung to the arms and legs of the broad ruffian who nonetheless continued to trudge forward, bellowing, dragging them with him. Over-ripe fruit rained down, also half-empty wine bottles, also more flower pots. The three actors cowered back against the blanket curtains, forgotten.

"We have to get them out of here," Jame said to Dar, raising her voice to be heard over the tumult, "but where can we take them?"

Snaggles tugged her sleeve. "Trepsis knows. Let him show us."

They fought their way onto the stage where the old man waved his branch in their faces.

"No closer!" he wailed.

"Fire!" someone shouted.

One of the yellow-scarved citizens had started a conflagration under the benches and smoke rolled out around the steps, licked by tongues of flame. Fire-traps, Mint had called these wooden apartment buildings. Few things could have terrified their inhabitants more. People fled in all directions, their cries spreading:

"Get the mats, get the vinegar, get the fire watch!"

Sparks smoldered in the folds of the back-stage curtains. Jame and Dar ripped them down before the spreading flames could cut off their retreat. Behind was an apartment turned into a theatrical dressing room, currently empty and in disarray. A back door opened on an internal corridor. Several turns later and down a flight of stairs, they emerged onto a street clear below but laced overhead with skeins of smoke. Behind them, bells, whistles, and pounding hooves announced the arrival of the watch, hopefully in time to save the building. Neighbors rushed past to help, dragging vinegar-soaked blankets and clay vessels containing acetic acid to fling as retardants into the blaze. Everyone knew that a fire in these close quarters could doom an entire district.

Unprompted, the elderly actor tottered off, followed by Jame. Behind her, Dar and the masked woman supported the young man whose legs seemed about to give out under him. Snaggles trailed hindmost, watching their back.

High Bashti was a maze of neighborhoods, crossed by major thoroughfares. Jame hadn't been in this area before. They passed several looming structures that, by their ornate facades and dramatic statuary, suggested theaters. Yes, she had heard of at least half a dozen public play houses here, where the wealthy supported performances to honor their gods and to advance their own political pretentions.

Side streets twisted around them, some devoted to costumes or wigs or masks, others to huge sets on rollers stationed in yards—a temple here, a palace there, a hanging garden, a battlefield complete with dummy corpses. Off from these branched tangles of lesser streets with lodgings and a few private houses for the more successful actors.

Over all loomed the Thespar Hill, itself like a particularly sumptuous back-drop, misty with morning.

Trepsis led them to a quiet, close-set courtyard lined with shut doors.

"He lives here, sometimes," Snaggles explained as the old man fumbled at the lock with shaking hands. "His friends open their houses to him when they're on tour in the provinces. He moves around a lot."

"And you know about this . . . how?"

He grinned at her. "I hang around theaters. I like mysteries. I listen."

The door creaked open. They entered.

IV

THE QUARTERS WITHIN were modest. Three small, clean rooms, Jame reckoned—an entry way, a living space, and a bedroom. Food, presumably, was acquired from street vendors. Sanitary facilities must be held in common with the rest of the neighborhood. Furniture was sparse. The only ornaments were a frieze of dramatic masks painted around the upper edges of the rooms and, below that, alcoves which held what presumably were shrines interspersed with awards.

"I can offer you wine as thanks for our rescue," the old actor said, rummaging about in a cabinet, looking embarrassed, "but it isn't very good."

"No matter," said Jame, who didn't much like wine anyway. "Excuse me. I thought that such loyal service to your god would have brought you greater rewards."

He laughed ruefully. "Say, rather, that I am rich in friends. To gain other wealth, one must pander to the mighty. I could be rich, if I pretended to speak in my god's name as the temple wants me to. Could I speak at all, though, if my lord god didn't inspire me? He doesn't like priests, even his own. Politics, always politics, even more so since Mordaunt became king." He leaned toward her as if to share a secret. "Suwaeton hates his grandson."

"I got that impression, and vice versa. Still, Mordaunt seems to be building his grandfather a magnificent temple."

"We don't understand that either. Much, over the last thirty years, has been a mystery."

"Including Suwaeton's death?"

The actor brushed his beard with nervous fingers, took a cup from an alcove, and poured himself some of the maligned wine. "We don't talk about that at all," he said, gulping down a mouthful. "Wasn't what happened terrible enough as it was?"

"What did happen?"

"The general just dropped dead. Roaring fit one minute, slamming his staff on the floor, flat on his back the next. No one knows why. Some priests claimed that it was punishment for mortal hubris. Then, of course, he became the king of the gods, so what do they know?"

Snaggles and the masked woman had entered behind them, between them supporting the gangly young man.

"Did you see me? Did you see?" panted the latter. He looked both exhilarated and terrified, with wide, pale eyes and a mouth that drooped at one corner. Then he began to cough up blood. His companions helped him into the bedroom. Jame gestured Dar back to the outer door to keep watch on the courtyard. This didn't strike her as a particularly safe haven.

"Oh," said Trepsis in admiration. "That boy has such

talent, enough to animate an entire stage-worth of characters at once, and mock gods at that. The effort is likely to kill him, though."

"Can't you make him stop?"

"And interfere with such genius? The gods will have their due."

"Even in a farce?"

"Well, that's a question, isn't it? When do they speak and when do we? Sometimes I hear a true voice and repeat accordingly, as today. Often, we improvise."

"Even you?"

He chuckled and drank some more. Rank and red, it stained his white beard like blood about the lips. "Not when I can help it. Understand, when I speak for myself, I do so with as much justice as I can muster, until I am possessed. Then he says what he will."

He drank again, more deeply. Some of the tension eased from his taut shoulders and the lines of his face settled into resigned contours. Once, he must have been a handsome boy. In repose, he was still dignified.

"Really," he said with a sigh, "I never wanted to be a farceur. I even changed my house and name to become a serious artist. I was born a Lexion."

With that, he drew himself up and puffed out his cheeks.

"Can you see me as a judge?"

For a moment, he looked as pompous as one, truly an actor. Then his breath puffed out again in a sigh and he seemed to deflate.

"Or more likely as a clerk. I had no taste for the legal life, although my father tried to convince me that it had its dramatic side. The court was his stage. Oh, you should have seen him plead the case of the rankest criminal, so long as he was high enough born. Hypocrisy, I called it, and sneered. Was I a fool? Perhaps. But I was also idealistic and desperate. The Thespar adopted and trained me in the classical arts. Ah, those early days! So much hope. Such potential glory."

He fingered the cup in his hands.

"I won an award like this in my junior year, playing Sedulous against Livacious. Controversial, that interpretation. But the judges chose me, and the General saw me act. He had just begun writing farces, on the sly. Like a fool, I played to please him, and succeeded all too well. He took me on in the farceur company that he secretly sponsored. That seemed like a blessing at first. I was young, my future and infinite possibilities ahead of me, or so I thought. After his death, though, he spoke only through me. I couldn't gain any other role and be taken seriously, not even when I applied under a false name with a false nose."

He sighed and filled his cup again. The bottle was nearly empty.

"I say all of this, but would I have ever really succeeded as a classical artist? Perhaps, rather, I have found my true calling. How many actors, after all, can claim a god as their patron? And the General is a great man, alive or dead, whatever one chooses to call him."

A stocky young woman emerged from the back bedroom, dark-visaged with a heavy brow overhanging haunted eyes. It was Prestic's daughter Pensa, stripped of her theatrical trappings, down to a white under shift. Jame was surprised to see her. She had wondered if the Lexion and the Thespar still supported their hapless son, in whatever meager form. Perhaps they did. Perhaps, so did the Tigganis. Was Trepsis now, in turn, sheltering their daughter?

"He sleeps," Pensa said. "If he does this again, I think it will kill him."

Trepsis spread his hands. "I know that, but what can I do?"

The girl sagged into a chair and covered her face. "What power have any of us, now? Mordaunt rules—over the Council, over all things. And I, what horror have I committed?"

"Err," said Jame, not knowing what else to say.

Trepsis had turned his back. It seemed to broaden and the ebony staff again grew stout in his firm hand. Fresh air flooded the close room. The masks painted on the wall breathed deep.

"Answer your own question," said Suwaeton, resonant, through the actor's mouth. "What most do you fear to lose?"

She burst into tears. "You know, you know!"

He turned a kindlier regard on her than before. "You have lost much, have you not, all of your life, starting with a mother when you were only a child."

She gave a cracked laugh. "Not so much lost as misplaced by death. She is queen of the gods now, reigning from her holy crypt—your queen, although you don't seem especially fond of her. Nonetheless, she has gladly forgotten what it ever meant to be mortal."

"Or how to be your mother, assuming that she ever

knew. When that degree of abstraction happens to gods, we truly become caricatures of ourselves. Should I love such a painted, vacant face that appears so much younger than what lies beneath? Her mask is now permanent. Her power and godhood will fade as worshippers begin to sense the void at her core. Then you lost your beloved Prince Jurik when you were a girl, although I still say good riddance there."

Pensa snuffled. "I told you about that, didn't I?"

"Yes. I listen to such prayers."

"I-I was going to a party at the palace where our betrothal was to be announced," she said, perhaps to Jame, perhaps to herself, picking at the scab of memory. "Mordaunt had agreed, if only for political reasons. It was set. I wore the best clothes I had, stitched by all of my aunts, and felt oh, so happy. I had loved Jurik since I was a child. He seemed so noble, so romantic. If his courtship was perfunctory, I forgave him. He was an important man; he had much to do. That night I should have been conducted to his family hall. Instead, Jurik brought me into his personal quarters. All of his friends were there, snickering. He showed me Amalfia's portrait. She was beautiful."

"'How can you compare to that?' he said, and laughed. He was very drunk. 'Dark, squat, ugly. Why should I settle for less than I deserve?'

"What did he mean? I still don't know.

"Then his followers shoved me back and forth from hand to hand, tearing at my clothes, laughing. I fled. No one followed. The party roared on, so loud that it drowned my tears. I would have refused to talk of it afterward, but my father heard, of course, and was enraged that I had been so humiliated. That was why he pressed his claim to the kingdom. Now he is dead."

"Thus you lost your father. Should you blame yourself for that? I see that you do. You should not. But all of this goes deeper. I ask again: what do you fear most to lose?"

"I . . . I . . . fear that I have lost my mind."

"Humph. What you did next was extreme if . . . I suppose . . . understandable. I must ask, though: child, was it wise?"

She wrung her hands. "I don't know! He lay in state in his mausoleum dressed in his finest robes. I visited him every day to set fresh flowers at his feet and he remained incorruptible. Vindictive Mordaunt had pressed the Council to nominate him as a saint instead of as a god. He could overcome that, I thought. Unconquered in life, unconquered in death. Then came the day when I found the chapel in ruins, his remains strewn about the floor, carrion fowl at the door."

Jame began to understand. "Someone hacked your father's body apart, denying him his immortality. You did . . . what?"

"Sewed him back together!" she wailed. "Each stitch was a curse against those who killed him, whomever they might be!"

"All right," said Jame, considering this. "That's potent."

Suwaeton shot her a look over his shoulder. "Would you have had the courage to do as much?"

"Probably not, but then my relations with my own father weren't that close and I never was much good with a needle. Lady, I think that I met your father last night in the Necropolis. At least, his clothes were stitched to his flesh and his hands were sewn on backwards."

The girl stared at her, aghast. "Did I do even that wrong?"

Jame shrugged. "He didn't speak, but he moved and seemed aware of what he did. He also saved me from the Shadow Guild."

Suwaeton swung around on her. She had to brace herself against his concentrated attention. In sympathy, several tribute dishes fell off the wall and shattered. His hosts would not be pleased.

"Those filthy assassins, those eaters of carrion? What were they doing there?"

"That," said Jame, "is a very good question."

They had been outside the mausoleum where the Blessed had been laid on the pyre. Were they responsible for the mutilation of the would-be saints? If so, why? Prestic, also, had been torn apart. Was their hand in that too? If so, again, why?

Some of this she said to Suwaeton, thinking out-loud.

"What was the Guild to you?" she asked him. They had begun to pace back and forth before Pensa, who with admirable if quivering strength had pulled herself together to listen.

"Spies," he growled, turning, pacing. "Invisible, they can go anywhere. Did I trust them? Not entirely. Most have been driven mad with their damn *mere* drug. But they hear things that no one else does except—heh—for me."

"You mean . . . ?"

"I'm the king of the gods, dammit. My people pray to

me. What better intelligence agents could there be than that? You do, Pensa, don't you? How else would I know about your plight? But few of the Guild pray. Most take a vow, I think, not to. No one is supposed to supersede their grand master, gibbering madman that he has become. Do I trust them now? No."

Jame thought about this. "When I first met Mordaunt in the palace, a Guild member was there too. Mordaunt was upset because Prestic's remains hadn't been destroyed, especially his head."

"That would be the seat of intelligence," muttered the god, still pacing. "You Kencyr have it right: fire is the only cure for mortality. Listen, girl: you know things, I know things. Will you pray to me?"

"You ask me, a Kencyr monotheist, for that?"

"All right. Will you report to me as an agent?"

"I might at that," said Jame, considering. "If you share information in return. Neither of us have cause to love the Guild."

"Done!" said Suwaeton.

The actor swayed, seeming to shrink. Pensa jumped up to steady him. As Jame, Dar, and Snaggles left, they heard Trepsis say, plaintively, "My sausage has lost its stuffing."

❦ **Chapter X** ❦
Among the Ladies
Gothregor: Autumn 20

CRICKETS SANG in the dry grass and jumped before Torisen's boots. The major grain harvest was over. Ploughing had begun for the winter crops, not that seed preserved from the recent harvest looked very good. Still, the husbandry-men would try. In the meanwhile, thrashing had begun.

Torisen walked up the broad outer steps, through the shadow of the massive main gate flanked by drum towers, into Gothregor's sunlit inner ward, turned into a sprawling vegetable garden.

This latter at least flourished, thanks to laborious watering by hand during the drought from the keep's deep wells. Tomatoes and green beans were already being picked, cauliflower, broccoli, and peppers likewise. Most of the root vegetables—beets, carrots, potatoes, parsnips, and onions—were still in the ground and would remain so until the first light frost. Then most would go into the root cellars, if they weren't pickled or dried like the fruit already there. Turnips had been harvested and reseeded for an early winter crop. Meanwhile, the garrison enjoyed a second summer's table stocked with any damaged produce that couldn't survive storage.

Would there be enough left to last the winter, though? Torisen hoped so, but doubted it.

No supplies had yet arrived from High Bashti, nor any word from King Mordaunt.

Torisen had hesitated to comment on this state of affairs before Autumn's Eve. He hated to write letters anyway, even to his sister. Now he must. To Mordaunt. To Harn. Jame had informed him by post rider of the chaos on Autumn's Eve and Day. Mordaunt appeared to have problems of his own. She had also mentioned the upcoming games between the Knorth and the Brandan in the Transweald and the stakes involved there. Torisen could threaten to withdraw his troops if they weren't paid. That would get Harn out of whatever fix the Commandant had foreseen and would also give Mordaunt a well-deserved black eye. If the king forfeited the contest, though, would that give Pugnanos permission to invade the Weald? Grimly, Yce, and the other wolvers came to mind, as formidable as they were. Certainly, it would cut off Gothregor's chance of supplies.

"Mordaunt and I seem to have each other by the throat," he muttered.

A flash of yellow among the tomatoes caught his eye. At the nub where ripe fruit had been picked, new flowers bloomed. That was odd, so late in the season. So was the size of many tomatoes still growing on the vine, and a rich crop of greenlings close behind them. He had heard rumors of such things—feathery carrot tops six feet tall, hinting at massive taproots below; ponderous, dappled melons; a cucumber as long as a man's arm and twice as thick. . . .

For the first time, Torisen wondered if his own creative powers had finally begun to play a constructive role, assuming nothing untoward lurked within these glossy skins. Jame had told him about her misadventure with raising bread in Tai-tastigon, laughing at it but also grimacing, as well she might. The Tyr-ridan's gifts often came with a twist, as he had already learned for himself, such as thistles erupting from a privy. As for the garden, there were rumors that some over-ripe vegetables had become carnivorous and gone rogue. No one walked there at night if they could help it.

The horn at the north gate sounded. Someone of note was entering—a friend, by the lilting note. Torisen followed the northern walk between beet leaves, green veined with ruby red, to see who it was.

A horse guard rode into the upper end of the ward, escorting a masked lady on a gray palfrey. By her erect carriage, Torisen recognized her as Dianthe, the Danior Matriarch, thus his distant cousin. Other members of the Women's World had begun to drift back over the past few weeks, as if draw from their homes to this communal hearth. Maybe the randon felt similarly about Tagmeth, or priests about their dank college at Wilden, each a little world of its own within the greater whole. Karidia and Yolindra, matriarchs of the Coman and the Edirr, were also here, plaguing him whenever they could catch him about their houses' quarrels, of which he had become increasingly tired. Adiraina of the Ardeth had also arrived, although Torisen hadn't yet sought her out. What she had to say to him in the wake of Adric's death he didn't want to hear. She, likewise, hadn't acknowledged him.

To his regret, Trishien hadn't yet returned. He missed her advice.

In general, he didn't know how the Women's World now regarded him after their previous unceremonious exodus. The game, he felt, had changed, but exactly how?

He reached the visitors in time to offer his hand to Dianthe as she slid down from her mount. Given her traditional tight underskirt, she perforce rode side-saddle.

"My lady, welcome back."

"My lord cousin," she said, holding his hand, then self-consciously releasing it.

He smiled at her. He and the Danior, in general, dealt well with each other.

"To what do we owe the honor of your return?"

"I heard that my dear Adiraina was in residence, and so I see that she is. Here she comes now."

The Ardeth Matriarch had appeared in the gateway that led beside the old keep back into those halls claimed by the Highborn ladies as the Women's World. Clad in a pearl-gray gown with a full, rippling skirt and a tight under-shift that reduced her steps to a mincing glide, she was as neat and trim as Torisen remembered although, it seemed, smaller. He was reminded, with a pang, that she was nearly as old as her kinsman Adric had been. If that needle-sharp mind also ended in dementia, what a tragedy.

She and Dianthe clasped hands. Their finger-tips moved delicately against each other's wrists—another more intimate form of communication, perhaps? He understood that they had been friends for a long time.

Over-burdened, Dianthe burst out in speech: "And when Rawneth said that, of course, I had to leave. My dear, what advice can you give me?"

The horse guards were listening, although they turned their eyes away.

Torisen stepped in.

"Perhaps you will both join me for refreshments in the Council Chamber," he said to them. "My own quarters, alas, are too small to host such distinguished visitors. Nutley has baked strawberry tarts this morning, that crop being ripe. They should just be out of the oven."

Adiraina bridled. Her eyes, embroidered in silk and jewels on her blind mask, seemed to flash.

"We would be honored," said Dianthe quickly, to douse that flame. Of course. She was bone-kin, of a house that had always supported the Knorth. She couldn't be pleased that it was currently at odds with the Ardeth.

He bowed to them, crossed the death banner hall, and ran up the northwest spiral stairs, first to Marc's studio with its piles of raw materials awaiting his return, then up to the Council Chamber with its soaring stained-glass windows. Three sides, north, west, and south, were graced with the crests of the nine houses. The east displayed Marc's incomplete map of Rathillien, the original having been shattered by Jame the night that the Shadow Guide had come to kill her.

Burr met him at the foot of the tower stair leading to his study.

"Tell Nutley to bring up tarts and tea," he told his

servant. "Quick. Use the southwest stair or you'll run into our guests."

Burr gave him a blank look, then hustled away.

When he turned to face the room, memory presented it to him askew, as fever had left it to him. At the last Council meeting, the chairs around the ebony table had been thrust back by the lords who had sat at them when he had challenged Caldane. Glasses had shattered spontaneously. Wine had spilled. Caldane had wanted the biggest houses to have the most power, his own first among them. Torisen had charged Caldane's son Tiggeri with attacking Tagmeth, which he had. Hiccoughs had sent a startled Caldane floating out the window. Then Torisen had started to cough up blood from lung-rot and Brant had hustled the others out of the room. It had been, at the least, an eventful meeting.

Torisen remembered the ebon surface of the table tacky with drying wine and gore, strewn with shattered glass, and the chairs scattered. He had almost died.

Since then someone, probably Burr, had cleaned up. The table top was not only clean but dusted, the chairs in place.

Except for one.

This latter faced the map window, its back to the room. When Torisen approached to straighten it, however, he found that it was occupied.

"Oh," he said, falling back a step. "I didn't know that you were here."

"Ha," grumbled a fusty, subterranean voice from the depths of the chair. "About to have a party, are you? D'you mean to throw me out?"

"I wouldn't dare."

"Smart boy."

Breathless voices sounded in the northwestern stair well. It occurred to Torisen as he returned to the table that he had just asked two elderly women in tight under-skirts to climb two flights of stone steps. How were they managing? By raising their hems? By hopping? Dianthe, at least, was helping her old friend, as became obvious as they emerged into the chamber. Adiraina was breathing hard. Her mouth, ajar, downturned, looked grim.

"Ah," said Dianthe, glancing around, panting. "This room always takes my breath away. What a pity that the east window was shattered."

"You don't approve of the repairs so far, lady?"

"They are . . . baffling."

In a way, Torisen agreed. The original glass had depicted Rathillien in recognizable shapes and colors, if not always in its proper proportions. Marc was rebuilding it with materials taken from each geological area where he could obtain them. Different minerals gave the glass different colors: carbon and sulfur for amber, cobalt for deep blue, gold and copper for red, cranberry, and pink, iron oxide for red-brown, and so on. A scrollsman intimate with the geology of this world could have read them at a glance. Anyone else would have seen an abstract sprawl of colors, mingled in streaks at the rivers. Still, what an intriguing experiment.

Nutley arrived with a tray of tea and tarts. Out of respect, he had pulled up his bodice, but his generous bosom still threatened to spill out of it. Dianthe glanced at him, then hastily away. Torisen signaled his appreciation and the bake-master gratefully withdrew.

The Danior and the Ardeth had clearly been talking, both below and, intermittently, on the stair.

"Well," demanded the former again, "what do you advise?"

Adiraina sipped tea, thin fingers cradling the warm cup, her nose over the fragrant steam. The leaves came from the south, a rare delicacy this far north. Torisen knew of the matriarch's taste for the beverage and hoped that she appreciated his courtesy in offering it out of his small store.

"You say that Rawneth has come to you," she replied to Dianthe. "She brought her daughter-in-law Kallystine with her, who does not seem best pleased with her pregnancy. How could she? Thanks to her father Caldane, that was not a courtship but a rape, with an uncertain issue. And Rawneth said . . . what?"

Dianthe curled a lip. "It wasn't so much what she said as how she said it. She looks forward to the High Council meeting on the 100th of Winter. There the Highlord—you, my dear," with a glance toward Torisen, "will be called on to uphold his role as our leader against more powerful lords such as Caldane, my brother, and your grandson, Timmon. Can tradition stand against such pressure? She hinted that we Danior must follow her lead or fall under her heel."

"She, and not her son Lord Randir?"

Dianthe snorted. "He may think so. We both know, however, who rules Wilden—or do we? M'lady Rawneth has a new councilor upon whom she dotes. I have glimpsed him standing on the walls of Wilden, gazing across the valley at us. He casts a pallid light."

"What more?"

Dianthe slapped her hand against the table top, nearly overturning her cup. "Oh, the impudence! Rawneth proposed all of this, but still she smiled and smiled, oh so condescendingly. We aren't worth her time, you see. The Danior are too small. We will go the way of all weaklings, deservedly so."

"You are one of the founding houses. Never so."

They seemed to have forgotten Torisen. Perhaps, he thought, having proven himself bashful as breeding stock, in future all Highborn ladies would treat him as a servant or as a pet.

Dianthe sighed. "That explains my presence, at least. Why are you here, Adiraina?"

The Ardeth Matriarch sipped her tea as if to collect herself. "My story is similar to yours. Lady Distan drove me out. Her attitude is like Rawneth's, with whom she corresponds, and she seeks to bend the new lord, her son, to her will."

"How strong is Timmon?"

"I would have said not very. He was spoiled by his mother as a child, taught to think that everything he desired was by right his. Granted, the Randon college seems to have changed him. So has Jameth. I cannot like that girl—so difficult, so disruptive—but she may be the first female who ever told him 'no' and meant it. What's more, she challenged him. Now there's a core of iron, if I am any judge, and a moral code to stub the toe of any brat. Still, how long can he stand up to his mother? The habit of obedience, of self-indulgence, is strong. She is confident of her success, enough to tell me that I should tend to my knitting and leave affairs of state to her."

Dianthe laughed. "As if you could ever knit."

"Well, so I could, when I was a girl, before I went blind. Then it became too frustrating. I miss the calm it used to bring me."

"But you still knot stitch, given your letters to me."

"Yes. That I can do by touch."

Torisen considered the High Council meeting on the coming 100th of Winter. The Caineron and the Randir would stand together. That was twenty thousand or more, if one went by the number of bound Kencyr. He, on the other hand, could count on the Knorth, Danior, Jaran, and Brandan. Fifteen thousand. Who knew where the Edirr and Coman would fall? Of the major houses, that left the Ardeth at nearly ten thousand as the linchpin in any vote, if he should be driven to such an extreme.

But must he be? The millennia-long history of the Kencyrath stood on his side. Before Caldane and Rawneth, no one would have questioned it.

Am I so weak? he asked himself.

Yes, came the first answer, *by your own failings*.

It wasn't just that he had been ill for a year with lung-rot, although that hadn't helped. For longer than that, he hadn't faced himself in regard to the Shanir. His father. His sister. His cousin. Himself.

And—as a second thought—his ideas were different now too. He hadn't talked to anyone but Jame about his reluctance to bind more Kendar. How would that work out, most of all with the Kendar themselves? Creation worked in him like a seething stew, still too hot to taste. To feed or to burn?

"Someone told me once," Jame had said, "that a potential Tyr-ridan will be potent across all three aspects of our god until each of us settles into our own."

If so, he could still wrack ruin. Was this what it felt like, to be his sister?

Adiraina put down her cup—the tart she had never touched—and rose. "What good does it do to talk? The power is out of our hands."

Torisen roused himself. "What would Adric say?"

She glowered at him with stitched, unblinking eyes. "How should we know? Your patron, your oldest friend, is dead. He should not be, if only you had had the sense to keep him calm."

She turned, outer skirt swirling, and glided out of the room. Dianthe cast Torisen a worried look and followed.

"Well," said the rough voice in the chair. "What d'you make of that?"

"Nothing that pleases me."

He poured a new cup of tea, took a strawberry tart, and presented them to the Earth Wife.

"Thank ye," she said, gulping down the former, taking a prodigious bite of the latter. "I thought you would never ask."

She herself looked rather like a slumped dumpling, seated in the regal chair with her knobby feet dangling. Her clothes, as usual, seemed to be slapped on in layers pasted together with mud and bird droppings. Pastry flakes spilled out of the toothless corners of her mouth.

"Don't like you very much, do they?"

"Dianthe does, well enough. I don't know about Adiraina, and she's the one who counts. Perhaps she's right that I should have prevented Adric's heart attack by keeping him quiet."

"Could you have?"

Torisen sighed. "Probably not. Jame called that situation a festering sore, all the worse because Dari only did what he thought was right and Adric wasn't fit to listen to reason."

"Heh. What else did your sister say?"

"That it wasn't my fault."

"She has some sense, that girl, although a lot else that makes me very uneasy."

Torisen smiled. "You too?"

"She plays with my world—not maliciously, true, but with a power that we Four do not understand nor, I think, does she. You too, Highlord. Do you know what you are doing?"

"I'm trying to learn. Give me time."

"How much do we have of that?"

"Little, according to my sister. Things are coming to a head, and she seems to be the forefront of that."

Ragga gave him a shrewd look. "D'you resent her?"

Torisen considered. "A bit. I am, after all, the Highlord. While she was gone, doing what I still hardly know, I held the Kencyrath together, or thought I did. Recent events make me wonder."

The Earth Wife snorted. "Honest, at least."

They regarded the map. Torisen reflected that the Earth Wife had once coveted it as a scrying glass, to complement the earth map to which she had listened.

How much of that had gone into Marc's store of materials, waiting below to be worked into the map above?

"D'you think he will ever finish it?" asked Mother Ragga.

Contingent glass had melted together in places where region met region. The wonder was that they had joined in upright panes. Beyond that was leading, then patches temporarily filled with cullet from the original smashed window and from common glass tinted green with iron. Rathillien was speckled with such neutral areas, especially in the Riverland, which had always defied cartographers. Most of the keeps were recognizable but not all, if they hadn't supplied materials. Wilden, for example. And Restormir.

"See that glowing fleck of red?" said the Earth Wife.

Torisen peered. "It seems to be around where I would place Gothregor. By accident, I nicked my hand and let a drop of blood fall there, into the melt. Do you suppose . . ."

"That it represents where you are? Could be. Look, here's another fleck in the Central Lands, even brighter than yours. Your sister, maybe. After all, she's also of your blood."

They scanned the map, looking for more, seeing none.

"It could only be the two of us," Torisen agreed, but he thought, *Shouldn't there be three*?

As quiet as Kindrie was, Torisen and Jame had agreed that he would be safest at Mount Alban in the care of the Jaran lordan and of the randon scrollsmen who, though retired, were fiercely protective of any within their walls. No one else besides Kirien knew that their cousin was legitimate, much less Gerridon's son, and therefore a candidate for the Tyr-ridan. All others scorned him as a bastard and considered him worthless beyond his skills as a healer. It had been best, they had thought, to keep him out of sight, his identity secret, until he stepped into his role. After all, neither one of them was ready either. It would be dangerous to call attention to Kindrie prematurely.

As to the blood flecks, Marc's abstract map was hard to read and incomplete. That was all.

⚜ Chapter XI ⚜
A Game of Gen
Restormir: Autumn 25

THE GILDED HALLS were lined with mirrors, reflecting fragments of other mirrors, and then other layers of gold. The effect dazzled and bewildered. The air was close, thick, and heavy with perfume, overlaying a reek of feverish, rank sweat.

Kindrie knew that he was not alone. At first, however, he saw nothing but his own reflection seen from so many fractured angles, looking so scared.

Where am I? How did I come here?

Somewhere out of sight something shuffled and grunted, distorted sounds that seemed to come from all directions at once. Something moved in the mirrors. Even seen piecemeal, it was obese, clad in a golden dressing gown that trailed at its bandaged heel. Oh, the stench that rolled from the latter's folds.

Huh, huh, huh. Oh, I am so great. My very musk enriches the air. Who is not intoxicated by my grandeur?

Kindrie thought he caught the flicker of a reflection,

or was it a real figure? Whichever, it was huge—a statue, he thought, poised in portentous thought, heavy brows furrowed over small eyes. It seemed to feed on the knuckles jammed against its pursed mouth. Munch, munch went its golden teeth, feeding on themselves. In the statue? In the mirrors?

Now, what was I thinking of? the figure seemed to say with ponderous deliberation. *Nothing. Why should I bother to think at all? Image is everything. So am I.*

Reflected in the nearest mirror, the statue seemed heroic, muscular. Up close, it was lumpy. Fat sagged in folds on bones. One thick leg and foot were wrapped with bandages.

Other shapes lumbered to one side, to the other. In the mirrors? In the molten flesh?

One raised a swollen hand to acknowledge unheard cheers.

Yes, I am your savior, breathed the air. *Forget the impotent Highlord, that silly little man. Cleave only to my divine mass.*

Another opened its arms to bless unseen worshippers.

"Cal-DANE, Cal-DANE...!" came the ghostly whisper of an adoring chant. Thousands bowed to him. Millions. The whole world loved him. It was inevitable.

And here in multiple reflections a mighty warrior bestrode the broken forms of his vanquished foes. Their flayed skins wrinkled under his feet, topped with elaborate Merikit braids. Among them, Kindrie barely made out the smashed form of Torisen, face trodden to pulp, limbs shattered. Caldane's feet had left a mere smear of him.

Huh, huh, huh . . .

Jame lay beside her brother, recognizable only by her spill of black, braided hair. Her burst body disgorged organs like so many red and purple fuzzy toys, to be stuffed back into their skin and trampled again every night. Oh, how Caldane enjoyed that. Never think how her defiance had humiliated him. Never. Never. Never.

Whose eyes watched him from the corner, though? That tilted gaze, that dark sardonic smile. Sheth, always Sheth.

Destroy me, the randon murmured, *and you destroy yourself.*

Why? Kindrie asked himself, bewildered. *Commandant, Sharp-tongue, what does your lord fear from you?*

"Aaiieee!"

A figure plummeted from the ceiling, all swirling saffron robes and flailing limbs. Though it continued to fall, it never hit the floor. Rather, it seemed to swim precariously in mid-air, now right side up, now upside down, always with its white braided beard streaming after it. Kindrie felt as if he was falling beside it.

"You have strange dreams, young man," the Tishooo said. "I've visited them before."

Kindrie remembered, although when he woke he always forgot, until the next time.

"Falling Man, why are you here?"

"Why am I anywhere? Curiosity. You and your cousins intrigue us. We don't know what to make of you. Torisen seems like a pleasant chap, but Jamethiel is terrifying. Earth, air, fire, and water, what is this world to make of you?"

"Creation, destruction, preservation. We three to you four, Kencyrath to Rathillien. You should ask Jame. I wouldn't even know who you are if she hadn't told me. I still don't really understand."

The Tishooo pouted. "Then why am I talking to you? But you should get out of this place, young man. It isn't healthy."

Sunlight struck Kindrie's closed eyes, red against purple veins, and he woke with a start.

A dream, he thought, panting, clutching his coverings. *Only a dream, within a dream, within a dream.* But were they his or Caldane's, and what had been that odd flash at the end? The latter faded, except for the memory of a streaming beard and the sensation of falling. Always falling.

The dreamscape was like that.

What he really feared, though, was Lord Caineron's soul-image, which mirrored the gilded reception hall in Restormir's Crown, or so he supposed. He hadn't yet worked up the courage to engage with it directly by touch. Caldane would be strongest there, his will nearly overwhelming. The white flowers in Kindrie's own soul-image, that of the Moon Garden, were already tinged with blight from mere dream contact. If they succumbed, how long could he maintain his precarious health?

The wall before his face bore his nail marks, over seventy straggly scratches to match the crawl of time. Had it really been so many days since he had tried to creep past Restormir on the way to Tagmeth and been captured by Tiggeri's patrol?

"So you've decided to accept my lord's offer after all,"

Tiggeri had said, smiling. In a way, he was handsome, but
with so many large white teeth and with such cold eyes.

"Please, let me go."

"Why should I do that? My father needs a healer. You
swore to him once. You owe him now. And if you fail, who,
pray tell, will miss you?"

He had told Kindrie that his cousin Jame had passed
by Restormir at midsummer without bothering to ask
about him. The implication was that she didn't care.
Kindrie suspected that she hadn't known that he was here.
Still, it hurt.

Why had no one noticed that he was missing? Kirien,
at least, should have, but he hadn't told her where he was
going. Where did she think he was now? Did she care?

Someone gave a perfunctory knock to the door, then
shouldered it open without waiting for a response.

Tiggeri, thought Kindrie, his heart lurching in his chest,
and he struggled out of his nest of blankets. His quarters
in the tower's Crown were luxurious, but he only occupied
a corner of them. To do more would have been to
recognize Lord Caineron's hospitality, such as it was.

Gorbel entered, bearing a tray.

"I met your servant on the threshold," he said. "This
must be your breakfast."

It would be lumpy oatmeal, the same thing, day after
day, with the same results. His stomach clenched at the
thought.

Tiggeri had some pretense to good looks, no doubt due
to his mother. His younger half-brother had none. Rather,
Gorbel's features were small, crowded into the middle of
a round face under a heavy brow and a prematurely

receding hair line. Kindrie's first impression had been that he was brutish and stupid. Then he had learned, to his surprise, that this squat hulk with his scowling continence and perennial gravy stains was not only a newly minted randon officer but also a friend of Jame's.

"I come to do her a favor," he had said that first time he had appeared at Kindrie's door, glaring, resentful of the obligation, "although she may never learn of it, and there's my thanks. Besides, everyone else here is a moron."

Now he looked unusually disheveled, as if he had spent another night up drinking with his would-be cronies. Everyone knew that he was the Caineron lordan, Caldane's heir. Some took him seriously as such while others did not, especially his brother Tiggeri, their father's current favorite. The other older six brothers might have districts of their own at Restormir, but beyond that they hardly counted.

"Let us see which matters more," Tiggeri had said, with a confident smirk. "Their seniority, your rank, or Caldane's love."

Now Gorbel belched and rubbed the small, bloodshot eyes of a massive hangover.

"G'ah, wake me up before I die of boredom. A game of Gen?"

Beside the tray he had brought a board tucked under his arm, a sack of stones, and a pack of hazard cards. Kindrie had only recently learned how to play this game thanks to Gorbel, which he understood to be popular among the randon for the training that it gave in strategy. Gorbel was a master at it. That he put up with such a novice as Kindrie at all surprised the healer. He supposed, however, that Gorbel was starved of occupation here at Restormir. Lordan he might be, but his father didn't trust him with any significant work, and one could only eat so many meals a day.

Gorbel set down the tray and produced the board. When set up, it had forty markers on each side, flat black river pebbles here, white there. On their base, concealed, was the worth of each one: a commandant at thirty points; three ten-commanders at ten points each; three five-commanders at five; twenty-four common cadets at two; four hunters at one. In addition, there were four hazards and one flag. These latter didn't move. The idea was to capture an opponent's flag or, failing that, to have the highest score of surviving pieces when the game ended. The trick was that each player not only had to remember where all of his own markers were but also to guess the location of his opponent's, especially of the flag.

Gorbel chose black; Kindrie, perforce, chose white.

"It goes with your hair," the lordan had said. Kindrie still wasn't sure if that was a sneer or an acknowledgment of his Shanir nature.

Gorbel advanced a pebble from his front rank. Was it a mere cadet or an officer? Both moved only one square at a time, vertically, horizontally, or diagonally. It could even be a hunter, whose progress in a straight line was unlimited.

Kindrie moved a five-commander.

Soon the board was busy with sliding pebbles and players intent on their game.

Gorbel attacked one of Kindrie's pieces by moving into its square. "Ten," he said, indicating his ten-commander.

"Two," said Kindrie. A cadet, now forfeit.

"Ten takes two."

He lost several more cadets in rapid succession, then two five-commanders, then a ten to Gorbel's commandant. At least now he knew where that crucial piece was, but where was Gorbel's flag? His own huddled in a corner behind his commandant and a shield of tens.

Timid, he thought, ruefully. Kirien had implied as much about his conduct in general, in remarks that still stung.

You say you may be becoming That-Which-Preserves. Destruction and Creation are active forces, yes, but must preservation always be passive? How can it, if it is to survive?

So far, here at Restormir, he was playing merely on the defensive, and where had that gotten him?

A straight path opened across the board. Recklessly, he sent a hunter down it against an immovable black pebble.

"Hazard," said Gorbel, putting a thick finger on it.

He drew out his deck of cards, each lovingly illustrated and very personal. These he spread face down before Kindrie. Kindrie drew one. Golden vestments, a bored smiling face remarkably like his son Tiggeri's . . .

Kindrie stared at it.

"Lord Caineron," he said. "You too?"

He knew at once that he had broken a cardinal rule of the game: hazard cards were secret until drawn, and now he had betrayed one in his own deck.

Gorbel grunted and took back the card. "Forget that you saw that."

He picked a breadstick from the tray and bit off one

end. When he started, absentmindedly, to scoop up porridge with the other, Kindrie stopped him.

"Why?"

"It's treated with autumn crocus. Your father has a savage case of gout."

"So?"

"His herbalist tends to overdose, not least because he's jealous of me. There are side effects. Nausea, for one, and loss of appetite. Also diarrhea." At the thought of which, his bowels stirred. "Luckily, I can control those. Most of the time. But I can't get your father to stop eating rich meat or drinking wine to excess."

Gorbel slapped the table, sending pebbles flying. "When my father gets drunk, he passes his hangover on to his followers. I've seen it. That's led to many recent suicides. Likewise, are you expected to suffer while he gains the benefits? You've lost weight, haven't you?" He caught both of Kindrie's wrists in one fist. His strength made the healer wince. "Otherwise, does it work?"

"Not that way," said Kindrie with a crooked smile. "Next, though, he may decide to smash my feet."

Gorbel rose and paced.

Kindrie shrank back in his seat. Gorbel had considerable power of his own, although he didn't often express it. Caldane might respect him more if he did. What would it take for him to break free?

What, for that matter, would it take for Kindrie to do the same?

"The sins of an honorable man should be his own, likewise the cost," Gorbel snarled over his shoulder. "Have we learned nothing from Gerridon? He thought everyone should pay except for him. That was the heart of his bargain with Perimal Darkling, wasn't it?"

No argument there.

"Are you equating your father with the Master?"

Gorbel turned on him. "Did I say that? Do I mean it? I don't know. You tell me."

Kindrie might have. He, after all, was Gerridon's true son, although few knew it and he was hardly proud of the fact. Here, he thought, was his spiritual half-brother, in doubt, in pain.

"So," he said, "what do we do about such a hazard to continue the game?"

Gorbel threw up his hands in disgust. "Trinity be damned if I know. I think...I think that sometimes he lies. That should be the death of honor. But we ask ourselves: what did he mean? Did he believe what he said? Who heard him? Who repeated it and how accurately?"

"You could oppose him." Kindrie leaned forward. "I say that he is insane, and getting worse. You know it."

"Huh. He is a powerful Shanir. What he says, others perforce believe. It only makes him and his grip on our house stronger. And that you know."

True.

"But you still won't help me escape from Restormir."

Gorbel's shoulder's slumped. "Caldane is my father and my lord," he said. "Where is honor due, if not to him? And yet...and yet...he strains the bond."

~ Chapter XII ~
Trials and Tribulations
Bashti and Transweald: Autumn 15–30

I

THE CHANT was getting closer.

"Keep the dole!" cried the poor, advancing to the slap of bare feet and of sandals, to the beat of pots and rusty pans. "You patricians, you ennobled, are we not citizens too? Don't let us starve!" They sounded angry, defiant, and afraid.

Some merchants in the market hastily closed their stalls. Others stood defiantly before them, clutching whatever weapons lay to hand. City guards kept pace with the disorderly mob down parallel aisles, not so far interfering with it but alert to incipient trouble. A clash, after all, might bring an open, spreading conflict.

"I didn't know that the dole was at risk," said Jame, watching.

Snaggles, at her side, wiped his nose on his sleeve, torn between excitement at the uproar and apprehension at its cause. "That'd be because King Mordaunt says he'll pocket its funding if the Council doesn't raise taxes again to build that damn temple of his. But if the tax does go up, bet you fungits to fennigs he pockets that too."

"Mordaunt seems to be getting desperate. Why?"

"You tell me," said Mint, "and we'll both know."

Jame had been walking part way to the palace in company with her former cadet, whose day shift there was about to begin. She had been aware of things changing in High Bashti but what with training for the Transweald games she had yet to catch up on local events.

The mob passed, trailing wary guards.

Jame found herself outside one of the white-draped betting booths and idly glanced over the miniature plaster busts on display. One caught her eye.

"That's Pensa, Prestic's daughter," she said. "What is she doing here?"

Snaggles beamed at her, glad to pass on news. "You didn't know? Her house voted her its lady with a seat on the Council. That's a rare thing, a lady instead of a lord. But Prestic was popular, his daughter likewise."

"Mordaunt permitted it, after she tried to kill him?"

"Can't tell the other houses who is to lead them, can he? 'Least not without six other votes to back him, and none did. Oh, there was a trial of sorts. They gave her a pass b'cause of her grief and—ahem—righteous anger. Many patricians still blame Mordaunt for Prestic's death, not that they have any proof. Then too, the Council is mad at the king for his tax finagling. If this attack on the dole goes through, they'll have to support their own, the poor without patrons be damned. Ancestors know how they'll take that."

"I suppose," said Jame, "that we at the campus will have to support you, going deeper into debt in the process."

"Oh well," he said, cheering up, "there's always Lady Anthea. D'you think she will let us starve?"

"You, no. The rest of the city, maybe."

Another plaster bust near the back caught her attention. "Who is that?"

Mint laughed. "Granted, it's not a very good likeness, but if you were more familiar with mirrors . . ."

Jame peered. "Sweet Trinity. That's me. What am I doing here?"

Someone tugged her sleeve. She turned to confront Graykin.

"Where have you been?" she demanded. "You should be my eyes in the city, and you've left me blind."

When he flinched, Jame realized that she had used a Shanir command tone on him.

"All right. Sorry. What's going on?"

The spy glanced at Mint, who took the hint: he wanted a private conversation with her lady, and besides she was late for duty. Off she went, dragging a reluctant Snaggles with her.

"Well?" said Jame.

Graykin looked both nervous and obscurely proud of himself. He pulled her aside, away from the regathering crowd. "People are placing bets because the Shadow Guild has been making inquiries about you. That gets noticed."

Jame blinked. When nothing had happened after her encounters with the assassins in the palace or in the

Necropolis on Autumn's Eve, she had stopped thinking of them as a personal threat. Perhaps that had been premature. "Who, for how long, and why?"

"That took some finding out."

He looked even more sly, and apprehensive. Now she understood his expression; here his craft had come into play, but he had tweaked the tiger's tail in the practice of it.

"Your name came up in certain Thyme Side taverns, from certain snitches known to collect information for the Guild. This would have been since Autumn's Day. Someone wanted to know who you were, where you came from, and why you are here. Many a pretty coin of yours I spent, buying drinks, to get a name, but get it I finally did, just last night: Smeak, a junior archivist of the Guild."

"Why such interest in me, though, from someone I've never heard of before?"

He glanced at her askance. "Maybe you should ask him."

"I can?"

"There's an obscure door in a dismal little maze, off Thyme Street, in Thyme Side, that has no hinges, that never opens. But there's a crack in it. People whisper secrets through it to a listening ear within, usually whom they want the Guild to kill and how much they are willing to pay. Sometimes an answer comes back, shoved under the door. Ask there for the junior archivist. You have a name now. Use it."

"You haven't?"

He showed the whites of his teeth, of his eyes. "What I dare, I dare. Not this."

II

THREE HOURS LATER, after much searching, she found the door and whispered a name to it. Within the dark interior, someone sighed. Nothing more.

III

"THERE IS THIS TOO," Graykin had said to her in parting. "Rumor has it that the Shadow Guild is split. Traditional assassins follow the Guild grand master, as mad as he is, although no one has seen him in years since his final set of *mere* tattoos. Heh. How far into any orifice can the needles reach? All that's left of him is a whisper in the dark, gibbering. Still, his followers support King Mordaunt and are his spies. Others ally themselves with the Deathless and their pale Prophet. 'Death itself shall die.' After murdering so many others, my guess is that what they fear most is their own mortality. But it's more confused than that. The king and the prophet support each other in some things, but where do they differ? The difference between them may be the razor's edge."

Jame thought about that as she walked back to the Campus Kencyrath through the teeming streets. There was so much she didn't understand. Moreover, she had just made an approach that she might yet regret. The next move was up to the Guild.

She was scheduled that afternoon to practice with the

scythe-arms, although no one knew if Transweald would ask for a demonstration of such a skill. Duke Pugnanos still hadn't defined the terms of his contests. In the past, Kencyr troops had sometimes fought a pitched battle; in other more civilized times, a rousing game of *kouri*. In general, though, Jame didn't expect to be sent north for the first Knorth trial. After all, other Kencyr were more skilled than she except, perhaps, in the Senethar, the Senetha, and the Sene. Well, maybe also in the clawed Arrin-thar, but who would ask for that?

"The commander wants to see you," said his servant Secur, intercepting her in the corridor outside Harn's apartment, announced by the clap of his wooden foot.

"Of course," she said, wondering if this would delay the practice. Well, they could start without her, small loss to them.

Harn Grip-hard sat at his desk, shuffling papers.

"About the games," he said and stalled. His mouth moved silently.

"What news from the other garrisons of the Host?" Jame asked, hoping to jolt his thoughts. She still found his uncertainties baffling, although he had often hesitated about his berserker nature which, with good reason, he deeply distrusted. "How are they dealing with the lost clause to prevent slaughter?"

"So far, the issue hasn't arisen."

He picked up a paper knife and idly tried its point. Sharp.

"The Kings are using us gingerly," he added, frowning at the drop of blood on his fingertip, then sucking it. "I think the ferocity of the White Hills scared them.

Unleashed, we are a terrifying force, sharper blades in their hands than they ever expected. Well, they've played for us and won. Now what?"

Jame already knew from Mint about the Edirr and the Coman clashing, also about the Randir's and the Caineron's squabbles over the gold-rich Forks. These she mentioned, adding, "The Central Lands may mean to settle old scores through us, but it seems to me that our troops are acting primarily in accord with their lords' politics back in the Riverland. That could be a problem. Do you have any idea yet what Duke Pugnanos wants us to accomplish in the Transweald, besides clearing his way to invade the deep Weald by losing?"

Harn picked up a ball of twine and started to fiddle with it.

"One thing I've heard," he said, wrapping the cord around his fingers. "The Transweald nobles want to see that rathorn of yours fight."

"Sweet Trinity. Against whom?"

"Does it matter?" He paused, glancing up at her under shaggy brows. "Prince Jurik wants to ride him, but that has to be you, doesn't it?"

"I should hope so."

But did she? The last time she had fought Death's-head, at Kothifir, she had fallen off and broken her collarbone. Well, not that exactly. She had thrown herself from the rathorn's back and knocked the Master of Knorth off his haunt mount, but his armor had been empty when the rhi-sar tooth on the shoulder of her armor had gouged into the eye hole of his mask. Then, oh, the crack of bone.

One was never quite felt the same after the first break, Harn had said.

The big randon wasn't meeting her eyes again.

"King Mordaunt wants me to stay here," he said, "in case of trouble. These riots worry him. Prince Jurik and his friends are going. Jurik…" He cleared his throat. "Jurik is to be in charge of the mission. His mother insists."

His hands had become thoroughly entangled in twine. He rose abruptly and stomped out onto the balcony, tugging irritably to get free, only binding himself tighter.

"Don't ask," he said, his back turned. "Just … don't ask."

Jame left, speechless. She was going to Transweald after all, she realized. Under the prince's feckless command.

IV

"HIS HIGHNESS TO GO TOO?" said Graykin when Jame told him later that day. "That surprises me. He'll be missing the Wolver Hunt on Wolf's Day, which is a big occasion for the Princess cult."

"Explain that."

"The cult blames Prince Bastolov for her death, he who became the first wolver. So they hunt his effigy through the city and bring it to her preserved body, in flames. Queen Vestula will undoubtedly play the reborn princess, handing out vengeance—unless she tweaks the myth and presents the king, Bastolov's father, as the true villain. She and Mordaunt aren't on the best of terms these days, after all."

"And Jurik?"

"The word is that he sees himself as the prince destined to wake the princess from her sleep of death. His mother has told him so. Does he believe it? Who knows?"

"But what can he do about it if he's in the Transweald?"

"That," said Graykin, "is a good question."

V

THAT EVENING, Jame found a scrap of parchment on her bed. It seemed at first to be blank. Thinking that it might be written upon with invisible ink, she tried various agents without success. Then it occupied to her that this might be *mere* dye, and so it was; letters floated like holes on the white paper when held against the dark background of her blanket.

Tonight, they read. *Come to the door.*

By then, it was late. Rue snored softly on her pallet at the foot of Jame's bed, tired of watching earlier futile experiments. Should Jame wake her? No. She would only raise objections. Sometimes one was the Knorth lordan and a randon officer. Sometimes one was the Talisman.

She went through the midnight streets, which still seethed with the unrest of the day. Many of the poor were out, but most houses and businesses were closed.

Finally, she arrived at the obscure door of the Shadow Guild.

"I'm here," she breathed into its crack.

"Ha," said a voice at her elbow.

She turned, but saw no one.

"Ha-ha-ha..."

A hood dropped over her head. Its draw-string closed around her throat. Unseen hands grabbed her, jostled her back and forth.

Don't struggle, she told herself, choking down the impulse, tripping over uneven cobblestones. *If they wanted to kill you, they would have already.*

Oh, but what a mistake she had made in telling no one where she was going. If this turned out badly, Rue would never forgive her.

She was being herded somewhere. In Tai-tastigon, she would have known every turn even blindfolded. Here, from the many sharp turns she suspected that she was being hustled farther into the miniature maze, under the shadow of towering warehouses. Another door opened. Hands thrust her inside. She stumbled, then scrabbled off the hood, gasping: the fabric had been thick and the draw-string tight.

A narrow hallway lay before her, lit with candles, lined with niches in which were piled parchment scrolls. Black beetles scurried among them, busily sowing ruin. Moreover, many apertures were so full that the bottom, oldest layer had crumbed into flakes under the weight of those above.

Jame edged out one of these latter and gingerly unrolled it. Like the scroll in her quarters, its surface at first appeared to be blank. As she tilted it against a candle's light, however, words appeared to shine through it although her finger tips could find no holes. That was how *mere* ink worked: while the substance remained, the image disappeared.

"Clever, clever," she murmured.

Well, it would be. This, presumably, was the Shadow
Guild's archive.

...*scratch, scratch, scratch*...

The sound, muffled and as faint as a mouse's claw, came
from down the hall. Jame followed it to another door, this
one opening into a low-ceilinged room whose dimensions
at first were hard to guess. Facing her was another wall of
shelves groaning under their load of documents. Around
the end of that was another over-loaded case, then another
and another, laid out in a labyrinth.

...*scratch, scratch*...

Candlelight flickered on the round mouth of rolls.

...*scratch*...

Jame turned a corner. In an alcove, overtopped with
leaning shelves, was a small desk. At it sat a thin, young
man, quill poised, bent over a parchment on which he was
making the copy of a fragmented scroll. His hair was so
blonde that it shone nearly white, with yellow touches
from the candle light. Jame noted that his left sleeve hung
empty. He only had one arm. He sighed and looked up.
What a haggard face. What distraught eyes.

A shadow bent over him and whispered. Who or what
cast it?

"Heh, heh, heh," it said, snickering.

"It is you after all." The clerk sounded thoroughly
defeated. "What do you want?"

Jame blinked. This was hardly the greeting that she had
expected.

"Some answers, to begin with," she said. "You're
Archivist Smeak, aren't you? Why have you been asking
questions about me?"

He dropped his quill and put a hand briefly over his eyes.

"I recognized you at the palace," he said. "I had to know why you were here, didn't I?"

"You did?" she asked, her wits scrambling. Could this be the Shadow assassin she had met talking with King Mordaunt, the one she had shoved into an ornamental pool? He too had been missing an arm, as a tear in his *mere*-dyed tunic had revealed. Now that she saw his face, it was also vaguely familiar, but from where and when, if he had recognized her on what she would have said was their first meeting?

He half rose, thumped his fist on the desk, and shouted, "Why do you torment me? Again, what do you want?"

Only one thing came to mind. "Well, now that you mention it, I want the contract for the massacre of my kinswomen, the Knorth ladies, thirty years ago."

He looked as if she had punched him in the gut. "You . . . what? Oh, go away, damn you. Let me think. Let me think."

She went—out of the room, the hall, the door, to find herself on a dingy side street in a minor maze.

What was that all about? she wondered.

VI

THE NEXT MORNING Jurik arrived, swaggering, to take over "his" troops. Everywhere he went, a dozen of his cronies went with him as, it seemed, they meant to do on the expedition itself. Chief among them and most assiduous in attendance was his smiling half-brother Cervil. Jame didn't like any of them. It seemed to her that Jurik was more in the way than in charge, but his followers continued to egg him on with fawning praise.

Over the course of the day, the number of people involved in the journey grew. Each of Jurik's friends had two servants; he himself had five. Then there were representatives of the other houses and their host of attendants, "come to see the fun," as Mint had put it earlier, at Jurik's invitation, as his special guests. That didn't even count the contestants themselves—seventeen Danior and Knorth, including Damson, each with a Kendar to act as servant and second, including Rue. The other three challengers were Bashtiri—Jurik and two of his friends. The total result was well over one hundred riders and three times as many horses including pack animals and remounts. It was, in short, a small army, even at this late hour still debating its course of action.

Given authority by Jurik, Cervil wanted to change the line of march.

He met with Harn in the commander's quarters on the evening of the 16th. Unbidden, Jame joined them. She didn't like the way Harn dithered whenever the prince was involved, and here Jurik presumably spoke indirectly.

"But why go by the River Road at all?" Cervil asked with a beguiling smile. "That's some five hundred miles to the Transweald capital of Wealdhold. Cross-country it's more like a hundred leagues." He spread his hands. "Where is the argument?"

Harn grunted. "I know that road. And that terrain. And the storms of autumn."

"How long will it take to get to Wealdhold?" Jame asked.

"By the River Road," said Harn, "travelling at a good pace, fourteen days."

"And we have to be there by the 31st, preferably earlier to receive our orders and to coordinate with the Brandan."

Cervil clapped his hands. "You see? To get there in time, we would have to start tomorrow, and my prince is not yet ready. At thirty miles a day, by the short cut, we can be there in ten."

"Over rough roads, through uncertain terrain, amidst autumnal storms," murmured Jame, as if to herself.

Cervil presented her with a glistening smile. "My prince would like to see more of the country that he will inherit, oh, any day now."

Jame gave a dry cough. "That last will no doubt come as a surprise to his lord father."

Harn looked profoundly uneasy. "His mother did say that his wishes were paramount."

Jame could see him caving. "All right," she said, to forestall the inevitable. "Assuming Jurik can keep up the pace."

VII

THE NEXT DAY was a scramble. More travelers arrived at the Campus Kencyrath, bringing more luggage, tents, and horses. Presumably they also brought their own supplies since the Kencyr had only packed with themselves in mind, not expecting such a host of camp followers or the luxuries that they seemed to find indispensable.

This, thought Jame, did not bode well for an expeditious expedition.

The lot of them departed on the 18th of Autumn, led through the twisting streets by everyone in Mordaunt's court who wasn't going along. Even the king's brigands showed up, the largest of them, familiar from the god farce, bedecked in even more gaudy finery than usual, waving his massive arms to lead a bouncing chant:

Umph pah-pah, umph pah, umph pah-pah-pah!

As for the local crowd, some booed and spat until the city guard rousted them. Jame wondered, passing their raised fists, if Jurik was as popular as he thought he was as the self-styled champion of the poor. With Jurik, she had learned, declaring something meant that it was true. It never seemed to occur to him that work might also be involved.

Their escort stopped at the main gate, cheered them through it, and shut it in their wake. They passed eastward through the fertile valley, between crops ripe for the harvest, down to the gate in the outer wall where their road joined Thyme Street, and from there into the Necropolis.

Bashti was considerably farther south than the Riverland, where leaves would already have fallen and the cold of an evening bit. Here in the Central Lands, foliage was just beginning to turn, red, gold, and orange against the darker evergreens. In the gardens of death, squirrels chittered from tree to tree while foxes slunk in the undergrowth. It was beautiful, thought Jame, looking back from stately tombs into the tangle of wilderness beyond.

Within the latter, she sensed the presence of Death's-head. The rathorn was deep in those green shadows, but he caught from her thoughts the prospect of combat. That was enough to draw him. The pack horses following the main party shied with his approach on their heels, although he kept back far enough not to otherwise be noted.

Ahead, someone in Jurik's party began to sing:

"Oh, we ride forth to glory and fame.
Hurrah, hurrah!
Our cause to win, our might to prove.
Hurrah, again hurrah!"

Wine skins were passed. Laughter rang out.

Here was the Tigganis mausoleum, which was being rebuilt. With Pensa as its new lady, the house could presumably reassert itself to this degree, if not potentially to more. Did that devoted daughter still bring her dead father flowers? What was he now, in her life? For that matter, where was he, and in what shape?

The shadows seemed to rustle, and a chill touched the day like an eclipse of a sun hidden by clouds:

I'm hungry, I'm hungry . . .

At length, they passed the graveyard. The cliffs drew back. The land opened into steep hills. Here at a fork in Thyme Street was a way opening northward. They turned left onto it.

The first five days passed blithely, with more singing, more drinking. Jame began to wonder if Harn had made too much of the route's trials. They were even making good time on a road well-maintained in Suwaeton's time and not much degraded since. She did note, however, that each night Jurik caroused later and slept longer. Her people were ready to travel an hour or more before his were.

Then on the 23rd they came to the river that divided Bashti from the Transweald. The bridge here was broken in the middle by the autumn floods and not yet repaired. Swimming all of the horses across took the better part of a day. In the process, several of them were lost along with their burdens. Beyond, the road twisted and turned on irregular cobbles, between steep hills. It began to rain.

The next four days were miserable.

It seemed to Jame that they were now merely dithering along, slowed by the weather, the rough road, and Jurik's contingent ahead of them. That was agony. If before they had made good time, now they traveled at half that.

On, she thought, plodding at the tail of Jurik's cronies, fighting the impulse to crowd up against their flanks and physically push them forward. Oh, to summon Death's-head to rouse these sluggards. *On*. The Kencyrath was better than this.

Then on the morn of the 28th they stopped moving altogether. Somewhere above the clouds it must be well past dawn. Jame went forward to ask.

"It's too wet," said Cervil, with an apologetic shrug. "My prince decrees that we wait for better weather."

"We only have four days to reach Wealdhold," she said,

trying to curb her frustration. Water dripped off her hood, bedraggling her braids. Behind her the prince's horses snuffled in discontent along the picket line, unattended. "Our honor depends on us arriving in time."

"Ah, you Kencyr and your honor. Surely the Brandan and Duke Pugnanos will wait for us. They can hardly start in our absence, after all."

"They can declare us forfeit," said Jame tartly. "Then the games don't matter. Your king and your prince lose. The Weald is forfeit too, assuming that the duke can take it, which I doubt."

"If so, what does it matter?" said Cervil, spreading his wet gloved hands, smiling. "Patience, patience."

Be damned, thought Jame, splashing back to her people where the Kencyr were breaking up camp.

"Map!" she called to Rue, who spread out Harn's parting gift under the shelter of their tent. "How far would you say to Wealdhold?"

Damson emerged from the drizzle, shaking droplets off her sleeves. She measured distances with her stumpy fingers. "We passed this hamlet yesterday, yes? There was a fortress above it. Then maybe a hundred miles more. Three or four days if we hustle, given the terrain, given the weather. Nothing if we don't."

Jame considered this, but briefly.

"All right," she said. "We hustle. Pass the word. Only take what you need. Food, yes, but leave the tents behind and hope that it stops raining."

Damson nodded and left. The camp began to buzz with new purpose. Even the rain was endurable, as long as they were moving. Soon afterward, the Kencyr contingent mounted and rode. Only when they were underway did Jame consider that she had just taken command at least of the Kencyr contingent, and no one had stopped her.

Most of the expedition had camped on hillsides overlooking the road with ditches dug around canvas walls to deflect the water that cascaded down beside them. The road itself ran like a shallow river. Bashtiri looked out as the Kencyr horses splashed past below them. Prince Jurik's encampment sported the biggest tent, temporary home to his numerous followers. He came to the front flap as the riders approached. Cervil emerged and appeared to speak to his half-brother. When he received no answer, he turned and plunged down the slope, his jacket pulled over his head against the deluge.

"Where are you going?" he demanded of Jame, grabbing her horse's bridle.

"To Wealdhold."

"But—but you can't! My prince leads this expedition and he forbids it."

Damson rode up beside Jame.

"He hasn't led us anywhere," she said, scowling, "except to near disaster."

"But—but—but you need him and two of his friends in order to compete."

"We can replace them with three of our own backups," said Jame. "If Jurik reaches Wealdhold in time, he can still play his part."

Jurik was coming down the hillside in what appeared to be his sleeping attire, without anything over or under it.

Cervil looked terrified. "Please," he begged. "Don't

anger him." With that, he backed away, wringing his hands.

"Go back to your campsite," Jurik growled. His face was screwed up with fury. Rain plastered straggly locks to his skull and dripped from his furrowed brow. One could see, more clearly than ever, that he was going prematurely bald.

Jame's first thought was that he was drunk, then that he was massively hungover, but something beyond that made the hair on the back of her neck bristle and rise.

"We have to go," she said, wary now, attempting to sound reasonable. "We are under contract to do your father's will. Surely you want that too."

He grabbed her arm and yanked her out of the saddle. She was too surprised to do more than make sure that she fell cleanly, feet free of the stirrups, which was fortunate because her horse bolted. *Splash* she went into the flood. He loomed over her.

"Go back to your campsite," he said again, and reached for her.

She let him pick her up, then stuck at the nerve center in his arm. He bellowed, letting go, and swung at her. She channeled his force aside with water-flowing Senethar, which seemed appropriate under the circumstances. He stumbled on the uneven cobblestones, fell and rose. They faced each other, both dripping wet. There was madness in his eyes. Jame wondered what was in hers.

"My command," he panted. "Damn you, obey!"

She was on the edge of losing her temper too. This was ridiculous. "Not to you, spoiled boy. Not ever."

Damson had caught her horse. Jame was aware of her former cadet behind her.

Jurik gasped and fell. Struggling to rise, he fell again, face down in the flood.

Jame realized what was happening. "Let him go," she said to Damson. "Dammit, woman, don't kill him."

"He would have killed you," said Damson, holding her horse as she remounted.

As they rode on, Jurik's people surged down the slope to pick him up. His legs didn't seem to work properly.

"What was that all about?" Damson asked Jame as they left the rest of the party behind. "Was he drunk?"

"I thought so at first," said Jame, shivering. Only now did she feel the full impact of his emotions, and of her own. "But no. That was a genuine berserker flare."

VIII

THE NEXT THREE DAYS were unpleasant, although the rain did stop. On the 28th, Damson called an early halt because Jame was still sopping wet and turning blue with the cold. They at least had a dry night and enough dry wood for a rousing fire.

Jurik didn't catch up with them on subsequent days, which was a relief. Jame wondered if he was still recovering from Damson, who had apparently cut the legs out from under him. How long did the Shanir's influence last? Most people stumbled to their deaths quickly thereafter—the cadets Vont and Killy came to mind. Maybe he would have the sense to stay still until the curse passed off but, oh, he would be furious.

She thought about that, and also about the fact that he

was a berserker. Other people beside her own could manifest unmanageable rage, though. Also, Damson had demonstrated that she could affect non-Kencyr when she had broken the leg of a driver fool enough to grab her in the Southern Wastes. Still, it all gave Jame pause furiously to think.

Other less kempt roads joined theirs, and more travelers, all bound northward toward Wealdhold. Many appeared to be small farmers, whole families of them in mule drawn, two-wheeled carts. The children cheered and waved as the Kencyr troop passed. The adults looked curious but wary. Several carts tried to keep up on their heels, to benefit from an impromptu armed escort, but soon fell behind. Other travelers, more well-to-do, kept pace on horses. Judging by the general chatter, all were going to the games.

⋞⊠⊠ Chapter XIII ⊠⊠⋟
The City and the Forest
Transweald: Autumn 31–50

I

THE KENCYR ARRIVED at Wealdhold on the 31st of Autumn in the late afternoon. The city first presented itself as a wooden citadel behind a wooden palisade on a bare plain. A bustling tent city huddled against its southern wall to welcome visitors. To the east were the playing fields. To the north rose the forest wall of the Weald, cut off as cleanly as if by a knife from the city's pasturage where, mostly, horses, sheep and cattle grazed. But not under the shadow of the trees. There, the line of demarcation was clear, also the hostility of city against forest.

"We'd almost given up on you," said Garr, the Brandan commander, a dark Kendar with a good-natured but badly scarred face. Here was a man who took nothing seriously except the essentials. "Sharp and her troop of Jaran singers arrived days ago. They will compete too, but mostly, I suppose, it will be you against us."

"Doing what?"

"Pugnanos hasn't told us yet. I hear that he longs for a pitched battle, but his nobles fear another White Hills. Anyway, there aren't enough of us to do the job properly nor, I suspect, do you want to shed our blood any more than we do yours. Oh, you've walked into a proper hornets' nest. Our duke is quarreling with his nobles and with his people. He supports the Princess cult. Most of them don't. And they know how dangerous it is to meddle with the Weald. This country wasn't even called Transweald until Pugnanos's great-grandfather changed it—another small man with grandiose ambitions."

That evening the duke set a feast of sorts for his most recent visitors. Jame found him short, bad-tempered, and inclined to talk past her to the males in her party. He had been expecting Jurik, judging by all the images of Princess Amalfia scattered about his hall, in silhouette, in high-relief, in statuary, all wooden, all mottled with moss or lichen. There were also demonic figures representing Prince Bastolov, almost in equal measure, the wood here charred as if each image had gone through the fire as had its original. It clearly irked the duke that Jurik had not yet appeared, also that he had gotten Jame instead.

In this atmosphere, he rose to salute his current guests.

"I give you strong herbs, and sour dough, and raw fish. Also mast pastries, if you last that long."

"He could have served us raw oats or mangelwurzel and be done with it," said Garr aside to Jame with a scar-twisted grin. "Horse-fodder for the unexpected."

"I have on occasion been made to feel more welcome. We could use lodgings, though. Our tents got left behind."

Garr gave her a shrewd look. "Something to do with your missing prince, perhaps. Yes, we've heard rumors about King Mordaunt's heir. In the meantime, we can accommodate you within doors, if you don't mind moss on the walls."

One of the Transweald nobles rose, saluting the duke. "Your grace, we have yet to learn the terms of this contest. Would you care to enlighten us?"

They didn't know either, thought Jame. Pugnanos really was at odds with his court.

The duke scowled and chewed on his mustache. "Very well," he said crossly, spitting out wet hairs. "You keep saying that after thirty years on our own we don't need the Kencyr to decide our quarrels for us. Let us see. For the first three days of the games the Kencyr of all three houses will compete against our own people and they against each other."

"And on the fourth day?" said the noble, pushing.

"Maybe Brandan against Knorth, for possession of the Weald. Maybe something else. Wait and see."

"And that," said Garr as he afterward showed the Knorth and the Danior to their quarters, "is his grace in a nutshell. He hates to be pinned down. Also, he likes to keep his people off-balance, guessing. Maybe, though, he just can't make up his mind. The games that he spoke of take place every four years, so I haven't seen one before. I hear that they tend to focus on native sports and military competitions, not all of which we hold in common. There will be a scramble tomorrow sorting out our contestants according to prowess."

"Not so with them?" asked Damson.

"Oh, they've been competing against each other for a quarter year already, to determine that."

The lodgings, as Garr had warned, were damp, which seemed to be true of the entire citadel, perhaps of the entire city. The largest halls, such as the one in which the Kencyr found themselves quartered, had their own cloud banks wreathing the high rafters, dispensing dew by dawn. The bedding, however, was of honest wool and quite warm against the chill even if beaded by moisture. Jame woke blinking droplets off her eye-lashes, staring up into a sketchy fog. If Pugnanos hated the forest, he could hardly escape it in his own home. Maybe that was why he hated it.

Breakfast was bread, butter, and a curious, crunchy preserve made from hazelnuts, akin to the mast-filled pastries of the previous night.

Everyone, Kencyr and Transwealdian, assembled in the main courtyard for the opening ceremony. Even some of the wax-faced Deathless were there, but pushed to the rear. The duke emerged in a green robe trimmed with spiky lace, wearing a gilded crown that looked like either a bird's nest or a pile of kindling, and dedicated the contests to the princess. This was met with murmurs from the crowd. When athletes, trainers, and judges stepped forward to swear to behave honorably, they spoke to a charred statue shoved off to one side, on which the duke turned his back. No one demanded that the Kencyr bow to either figure. Their honor, Jame noted, was still trusted to themselves, and well it should be if the last day of these ceremonies was to have official weight.

She met with Garr after these preliminaries, while the Transwealdian crowd went to honor their ancestral gods, to visit camp to camp, or to view the moldy wonders of the duke's palace. Meanwhile, the blare of trumpets sounded from the inner courtyard where trumpeters competed to announce the winners.

"As I understand it," said the Brandan, "today we have the poets, the historians, and the scholars trying to put this whole farce into context. All right. I'm a snob. But what is their history compared to ours? How can they begin to understand who we are or where we come from?"

Jame bit her tongue. Kencyr in general were ignorant about Rathillien's history. She hardly knew if she understood it herself although she was still trying mightily. What the Kencyrath didn't understand could still damn them.

"Tomorrow," Garr continued, "there are equestrian events in the morning. Bare-back races. Chariots. Trotting mares. Squealing foals. We brought horses, of course, but not ones trained to such sports. An endurance event, maybe, but that's not on the schedule."

"They still want to see Death's-head fight, don't they?"

"Oh, yes. That will come on the third day, when the combat sports are featured and there, I imagine, we will be expected to compete. In the afternoon of the second day, running and jumping. I ask you. We can run seventy miles in twenty-four hours, for days on end with intervals of *dwar* sleep, but not all at once in a sprint. How far can we jump? That depends on what we have to do. As for strength, there's wrestling, boxing, and their version of the Senethar, which involves all of their combat skills. Third day stuff. These, I remind you, do not necessarily correspond to our own disciplines."

"How do we sort this out?"

"Pick our strengths and adapt our techniques to theirs where we can. Not all of us will compete each time."

They spent the rest of the morning sorting out who among the Brandan, the Knorth, and the Danior fitted best in the schedule. Jame found herself passed over again and again, not that she minded. Riding the rathorn in battle (again, against whom or what?) struck her as challenge enough.

That afternoon, she and Rue went from tent to pavilion to tent, listening to poets and scholars expound on the mysteries of the Princess and the Prince cults. Anyone wishing to curry favor with the duke praised the former, with his guards monitoring to be sure that it was so. Most of it Jame had heard before from Dar. The princess and the king were victims, in this version, the prince an inhuman villain. What could be worse, after all, than regicide paired with parricide?

The tents praising the princess, however, were mostly empty. Others, praising the prince, were full.

Walking down the line of pavilions, Jame heard familiar voices. Here was a packed tent in which the Jaran spoke. Sharp was conducting a dissertation on the prince.

"He was crown prince of his land," she said, spreading her hands to encompass all. "The princess of Hathor was offered to him to end the long conflict between the right and left banks of the Silver. This was before the great weirdingstrom that sundered them forever."

"Long, long ago," murmured the Jaran singers who backed her up. "We Kencyr had not yet come to this world. Its sorrows were not yet counted among our own."

"She was beautiful," Sharp continued, as if speaking to

friends who had asked for enlightenment. "He loved her at first sight and she, him. Two young people, fated. Why not? But his father the king also saw her and lusted after her. He assaulted her. She killed herself out of shame. His son killed him and so became a parricide, that deadly sin."

The audience muttered, some in protest, others in comprehension. Like Jame, they apparently hadn't heard this twist before, that Bastolov had killed his father to avenge his love. Jame had thought that murder strange when she first had heard about it, the work, surely, of a madman. This interpretation changed the balance of sympathy, if not necessarily of guilt.

"But what then," said Sharp, "of the prince?"

A new voice rose, and this Jame also knew by its rough edges, by its croon. A shaggy young man shuffled forward, shy but defiant. The Wolver Grimly nervously began to keen his song, translating it from Rendish as he went:

"Came he to the green Weald,
Heart sore, in search of refuge.
Wolves greeted him.
One sought him out and loved him.
Pups they had, the first wolvers,
A balm to his wounded heart.
But foes hunted him, his own brothers.
That any kin should be so unkind!
They sought to burn him alive.
The heart of the Weald embraced him.
Charred, he lives on.
Never will we forget his pain."

It struck Jame suddenly that she was listening to the story of the Burnt Man.

Voices jarred at the threshold, the duke's guards demanding entry.

"Filthy wolver," one cried. "To spread such lies! And you, to listen to them!"

Sharp thrust Grimly into Jame's arms. "Get him away from here," she hissed.

They escaped out the back of the tent as guards boiled into it from the front. At first the churning audience baffled them. Then it cleared and they were met by a more formidable wall of Jaran randon.

"You would have to stick your neck out," Jame chided the wolver as they cut between tents into the clear of the eastern playing fields. From the sound behind, the clash was spreading with enthusiasm on both sides, within the tent and beyond.

Grimly giggled nervously. "I should pass up a chance to perform, and with such a subject?"

"You might, if you valued your skin."

"Rather, I value my people and our beliefs."

"I beg your pardon. I forgot that the wolvers claim the Burnt Man as their sire."

He cast down his eyes. The Holt wolvers, as a rule, were not confrontational.

"Sorry," he muttered. "Why should you know how engrained some of these issues are? Truly, though, all of us in the Weald fear the autumnal equinox, Wolf's Day. That's the 36th of Autumn. This is the 32nd. The duke is planning something. We all sense it. Will you help us?"

"If you need it. If I can see how."

II

ON THE SECOND DAY the equestrian sports were held. Dawn saw the start of preparations in the eastern fields where a whole cavalry of horses was assembled. Thirty four-horse chariots were to compete. Enthusiasts and gamblers thronged the sidelines. Some had been up at dawn to scent the horses' droppings for omens— enough grain? Too much? Others whispered to trainers and charioteers, who pretended not to hear. The results, everyone knew, lay in the laps of ancestral gods, and the shrines of these too had their share of early morning supplicants.

Trumpets sounded. The horses pranced forth with glossy hides and flashing eyes, with silver-inlaid harnesses and gilded rigs. The crowd roared. The horses charged around the course, down a six hundred yard straightaway to the sharp turn at the end. Chariots crashed. Charioteers flew over their rigging and were dragged under pounding hooves. Horses fell with shattered legs. Attendants ran out to clear the wreckage. Twenty-three turns to each race. Fifteen minutes to cover six miles, which seemed to last forever.

"Ugh," said Damson, watching a pileup on the fifteenth turn. "We should subject our horses to that?"

It was the first time Jame had heard her express empathy for anything. Was she finally learning what that meant, at least for animals?

Trumpets blared again. The carnage was over, until

naked, bare-back riders took their place, then trotting mares, then skittering foals.

At noon, the hurlers took the field with a ram's head gripped by its horns. The rest of this unfortunate beast had been sacrificed at dawn, its blood poured over an obscure white stone. Much importance was given not only to the length of this throw but also to the style of its delivery—one spin or two, then the release, then how far the blood splattered.

The winner of the ram-throw stepped up to the mark with a javelin. This weapon was a lance about the height of a man and perhaps a thumb's width in thickness. It had a sharp point, also a leather throwing thong attached halfway down the shaft. The contestant hooked two fingers in thong's loop, ran forward with the javelin drawn back, and launched it. It hissed through the air, spinning, farther than seemed possible, toward the distant target of a melon on a pole. The crowd held its breath. The lance missed.

"Ahhh . . ." said the onlookers, disappointed.

Nine more competitors tried, some falling short, others overshooting. The tenth split the melon.

This athlete went on to the broad jump, where he landed off-balance and fell over backward. Someone else won.

"Aren't you Kennies going to compete in anything?" demanded a young Transwealdian noble, draping himself over the shoulders of Jame and Garr, who had come up during the latter competition. "Come on. Be good sports."

He appeared to be very drunk. Jame wondered about that, having last seen him whispering into the duke's ear and laughing at whatever answer he got. The glance he had shot at the Kencyr visitors had been distinctly mocking.

"What comes next?" she asked Garr.

"A foot race through the city from gate to gate."

"Shall we?"

Garr shrugged. "We might as well stretch our legs."

A team was hastily assembled of those Kencyr who were closest, including Jame and Damson, ten in all, half of them women. It wasn't clear to Jame if this was a group sport or rather an individual contest. What had she gotten her people into? A dozen of their opponents waited for them at the southern gate next to the camp grounds and jeered at them as they came up.

"Come to see the fun?" one called; and another: "We've been waiting for you!"

The wooden gate ground open onto a jagged maze of streets. The Transwealdians poured in and took off at a sprint. The Kencyr followed, running in cadence as they were trained to do. It quickly became obvious that their opponents had the advantage stemming from knowledge of a tortuous street plan. Wooden planks boomed under foot. Painted walls rushed past. Where were they going? Generally north, but dead ends threatened to delay them.

"This is ridiculous," Jame said to Damson.

Here was a gutter reaching from street to roof. Jame grabbed it and climbed. The wooden walls were slick with moisture, the pipe scaly with rust, but she made it up and over the eaves onto an expanse of slimy shingles. Wealdhold's roof-scape was trickier than Tai-tastigon's if only because it was more slippery. Otherwise, Jame felt almost at home. She paced the runners below her, scrambling up inclines to see ahead, noting where the way twisted and turned.

"The next street to the right!" she called down to Damson. "Then past two and left."

The Transwealdians lurked, waiting for them, at the mouth of a blind alley.

"Ambush, right!"

The Kencyr pivoted and charged. Their formation crashed into their opponents, bowling them over.

"Not fair, not fair!" came the plaintive cry from below as the Kencyr turned away.

"Straight on."

There was the northern gate, standing open. Those who waited to greet the victors looked startled.

Oh well, thought Jame, clambering down to the street to rejoin her troop. At least the Kencyr had at last made an impression.

III

THE THIRD DAY, as Garr had said, was devoted to combat sports, and here the Kencyrath was expected to shine. Or not.

On the way to the contest field that morning, Jame stopped to watch the Transwealdians practice. They were big men, for the most part, and formidably aggressive.

Nearby, two wrestlers grappled with each other, their backs creaking under the strain, their bodies striped with torrents of sweat. Barrel-chested, ox-necked, bulging with muscles, each strained against the other as if striving to uproot the world. One shifted his feet, hoisted his opponent over his shoulder, and slammed him down on the ground.

Boxers jabbed at each other's heads with fists wrapped in leather thongs, some with iron weights bound to the knuckles. Although this sparring was only practice, blood and sweat streaked their faces. One forehead had already been laid bare to the bone. The unlucky participant staggered away, blinded, pursued by his opponent who continued to pound him unmercifully on the back of his head until a judge separated them.

Most violent of all, however, was a third set of competitors who used a mix of the other two disciplines, apparently with no rules whatsoever. They wrestled and punched and gouged and tripped and kicked and bit and, often, tried to strangle each other. Moreover, they didn't stop until one of them had collapsed in a bloody heap. More than one would not go on to the general contest.

Jame watched this carnage for a while; then, thoughtfully, she went on her way.

The Kencyr had gathered in a tent on the edge of the playing field to prepare for the morning's contests. Jame heard voices as she approached, but all fell silent as she entered. Most looked at her, except for a few who deliberately didn't. She cleared her throat to break the tension.

"I've been watching the Transwealdians train," she said, going to a side-table, pouring herself a cup of watered wine, and sipping it. "It occurs to me that the wrestlers can be countered by earth-moving and water-flowing

Senethar. I saw one use a basic earth-shifts move, throwing his opponent. Not very good form, but it worked. With the boxers, fire-leaping strikes and especially wind-blowing evasions. With that last group, a bit of everything. I don't say that it will be easy."

"You're right," said Garr, finally speaking. "Just the same, it's probably a good thing that you won't be competing."

"What?"

"The combat Transwealdians say they won't be called child-killers."

"You think that I'm a child?"

"No. You are a randon officer and have proved yourself again and again, if in some unusual ways. We of the collar appreciate that. Our strength lies in diverse talents. There is this too, though: Duke Pugnanos has banned you from participating this morning. It seems that he heard about your part in the foot race yesterday and disapproved. He doesn't think much of women in general, except for the princess."

"That's true," said one of the nine Knorth women, looking sour. "Don't take it personally, lady. We are banned too. The number will be made up of our male seconds."

"Couldn't Pugnanos have said something about this before now?"

"You may have noticed," said Garr wryly, "that all of the duke's Brandan are men. We wondered about that, but it seemed like an accident. After all, Lady Brenwyr is our patron too and our war-leader is a woman. We don't tend to think along such lines."

"Does Pugnanos also not want me to fight Death's-head this afternoon?"

"He didn't say that. My impression is that he wants to see you dead, in the most humiliating way possible."

"Oh."

Garr looked apologetic. "Myself, I wouldn't care to go up against you. Sweet Trinity, you tackled Bear as the Monster in the Maze!"

Yes, thought Jame, walking away, but Bear had stopped when he realized that, like him, she also had claws. He had become her Senethari, her teacher. She honored him, as she did Harn. Her luck with big men—like Bear, like Harn—had mostly been based on a common Shanir link. With others—for example, Bortis and Jurik—that luck had come from them underestimating her. Would the Transwealdians have done the same? Strength to strength, she wasn't their match. Skill to skill, who knew? Perhaps it was just as well that that had not come to such a test, nor had she really expected it to. Randon she might be, but the Kendar were instinctively protective of the more fragile Highborn. She was sorry, though, to have cost other women their chance to compete.

That left Death's-head and the duke's champion, by whom he hoped to see her defeated.

She crossed the field, drawn to the southeast by her link to the rathorn. Here the plain began to roll, with sparse undergrowth in the hollows and a stream running through it. She followed the marshy bank until she came to a pond. There was Death's-head, pawing at the mire, a thorough mess. She had brought brushes and combs, expecting this, and set to work on his coat. Bit by bit, the white emerged. He snorted as she combed his mane and scratched under the ivory plates of his armor to pry out dried mud. It was too long since she had tended to his needs, not that he recognized them as such.

This task took her longer than she had expected. The morning was passing. Her allies would be proving themselves against their opponents, the Senethar against whatever they called their martial arts, all to demonstrate that the Kencyrath were still masters of the battlefield and worthy of employment.

With the sun nearly overhead, she finished scraping the rathorn's coat clean and swung onto him bareback.

Part way back to the city, she met Rue riding her post pony, leading a pack-horse laden with arms, armor, and Death-head's heavy tack.

"Thought you might have forgotten," said the Kendar, scowling. "Half of your audience has already turned up, although when I left most of them were busy eating lunch. Bloodshed and a hearty appetite seem to go together."

Jame herself didn't feel remotely hungry, which was good because her servant hadn't brought anything to eat. A welcome water bottle would do, as the day was turning hot.

"How did our people do in the contests this morning?" she asked.

"Very well, with only a few injuries on our part. You were right about the Senethar's advantage over brute strength. The duke is said to be furious."

They saddled and bridled the rathorn, who pawed the ground but otherwise stood still for this procedure which he had come to welcome as the prelude to battle. His natural armor protected him from the head, down the throat, across the chest, over the barrel and the groin. Rue had brought his crupper, previously Jorin's perch, to shield his flanks, also a new addition: a segmented crinet to fit over the crest of muscles on his neck. Jame noted, however, that his shoulders were bare. How had she come to overlook that?

Then there was her own armor. When had she last donned that, much less practiced in it on Death's-head? Too long ago.

I'm a fool, she thought, *worse, an ill-prepared one.*

Most of it was rhi-sar leather, hardened, shaped like plate armor and just as strong, but much lighter. Master artificer Gaudaric of Kothifir had made it for her out of the hide of a giant white rhi-sar lizard that she had helped to slay in the Southern Wastes. Then there was the vest of rathorn ivory scales—high at the collar, long enough to protect the upper thighs, divided for riding, worth a small province.

"Please accept this," Gaudaric had written, *"as a gift from my family and a grateful city."*

Lordan of Ivory, Timmon had called her in jest. Or perhaps not.

It clinked softly as she raised it, like wind chimes, and Rue said, as she had before, "It's beautiful. But this is all defensive. What weapons d'you want? Here's a sword. Here's a dagger."

"When could I ever hang on to any blade throughout an entire battle? What do they say?

"Swords are flying, better duck.

"Lady Jameth's run amuck.

"Besides, the Commandant told me that Death's-head was my primary weapon."

"At least take the shield."

This, also, Gaudaric had made out of the braided hides of lesser rhi-sar laced back and forth over a round ironwood frame.

"All right," said Jame, grudgingly accepting it. Why such hesitation? The whole thing seemed silly although, of course, it wasn't.

"And don't forget to wear your helmet."

She had the last time.

They rode back to the city.

The crowd there had grown. Usually, the combat sports drew the largest audience, but this was a unique event. The duke's champion sat his black warhorse on the western end of the field. Both shimmered in silver, the horse with scale armor, the rider in chain mail. The latter also carried a long lance, more like a young tree than a spear. Jame hadn't expected that. Perhaps, after the javelin contest, she should have. It occurred to her, not for the first time, that this really wasn't her kind of a fight.

Death's-head, though, clearly enjoyed himself as he circled the field, prancing. The audience stood up on the surrounding grassy embarkment and cheered. Rathorns were rare in the Central Lands except for the Anarchies. Most people here had only heard about them in stories, and many had taken them for myths. The rider in chain mail pivoted his mount to face them as they passed until once again they confronted each other down the east-west axis of the field.

Boom, went a drum. Rattles hissed under its echo in anticipation. *Boom*.

Duke Pugnanos rode onto the field on a tall dun draped in green and gold barding. He stopped between the two contestants, and a trumpet sounded its clarion note:

Hear, oh hear.

"Good people," he shouted. Was it his fault that he sounded so shrill after the horn's sweet call? His horse curvetted at the noise, rocking him in the saddle. "I give you the champions of Transweald and of the Kencyrath. Let their combat decide the fate of our common enemy, the Weald!"

What? thought Jame, aghast.

Was the other rider Brandan? If so, why hadn't Garr told her? If not, who was he? She had believed that this was a novelty match, of interest but not of much importance. How had such a responsibility suddenly fallen on her shoulders?

The challenger's black horse rocked back on his hocks, then launched himself into a charge. He was huge. The ground shook. Down came the point of the lance.

The duke scrambled out of his way.

All right, thought Jame, setting her heels to Death's-head's sides, and the rathorn plunged forward. This was all happening too fast. Think. Think. The distance between them closed, with a rush at the end and the lance head aimed directly at the rhi-sar tusks that guarded her face. Almost as an after-thought, she jerked up her shield to meet it and legged the rathorn aside. The steel point on the lance glanced off the rhi-sar leather with a snarling rasp. The impact drove her back against the saddle's high cantle and ripped the shield out of her grasp. Everything to her left roared—the black stallion's breath, his jaw jammed agape by a cruel bit, the silver of armor, the rush of legs, the eyes glimpsed through the rider's helm slits.

Those eyes. Whoever the warrior was, he was enjoying this. It was personal.

Death's-head surged on, snorting. As the lance had dipped, it had scored his bare left shoulder. Blood ran down over muscle and ivory, crimson stark over white. His pace, however, was unhindered, and his temper roused.

They swerved back to the right. The other rider was having trouble turning to meet them. While his charge had been thunderous, he maneuvered badly as the ponderous lance dragged him off course.

Death's-head cut in and rammed the war-horse broadside. A twist of his horns raked scale armor and tore mail. It gouged both, drawing blood, but only ripped off a few plates, a few links. More compromised was the girth, which the nasal horn had snagged in passing.

Jame pulled back so that she rode neck to the other's crupper, still at a gallop. Her opponent tried to turn his head to see where she was, but his helmet permitted little sideways movement. Now that they were pacing each other, she heard more: a great clatter as if of a careening cook wagon. Sword, hammer, mace, axe—the black's rider was festooned with more side arms than she had ever seen before attached to one horse. Reaching out, she detached the mace from a hook on his saddle and let it fall, unheeded.

The crowd roared its approval.

They were turning again, he trying to cut across her path. She reined back and fell farther behind. The warhorse's scale skirts flared against his flanks, under a flying tail. The rathorn leveled his lesser horn. The horse squealed and bolted.

"Naughty," Jame told the rathorn. She could sense if not smell her mount's scent. His kind had been known to drive enemies mad with fear at their mere smell. His opponent, however, was a seasoned beast of battle. It would take more than that and a poke from behind to rattle him.

She surged up again on the horse's left and plucked off first an axe, then a hammer. Did the rider notice? The lance still swung in search of a target, the black horse roaring with effort and, perhaps, with frustration. Its rider flailed with spurs, at the same time sawing on the bit to regain control.

Jame swerved away. If she and the rathorn were becoming partners, not just weapon and wielder, that would indeed be something.

The war-horse plunged to a halt, nearly throwing his rider.

Jame swung around to face him. He huffed and blew and pawed the torn earth. His rider's lance dipped, then rose again.

"Ha!"

He charged.

So did Jame. The rathorn battle-cry rose, tearing in her throat and in that of her mount. On came the lance, aimed this time at the rathorn's eyes behind their ivory mask, but it shivered and swerved as the horse shied at that terrible sound. Death's-head's horns caught the weapon's pole between them. With their leverage and a twist of his powerful neck, he snapped off the lance head and shattered its shaft.

The black skidded to a halt, throwing his rider forward on his neck. The frayed girth snapped. The saddle slid sideways and the rider toppled slowly with it. On impact with the ground, his sword slipped out of its sheath. He scrambled after it, but Jame dismounted and grabbed it first.

"Better duck," she said, breathing hard. "Lady Jameth's run amuck."

How odd to feel the blade's hilt in her hands, as if for the first time. At last. Rue would be pleased.

The other rider tore off his helmet and dropped it, revealing a sweat-streaked, familiar face.

"You little bitch," panted Jurik, glaring up at her.

His breath came harder and harder as laughter from the crowd brought home to him the full scope of his humiliation. His eyes bulged, the whites turning red. He was about to flare again.

"You stinking, rotten, little cheat!" he said thickly, and lunged at her.

Jame had been presenting the sword's point to his throat. Was he about to impale himself on it? Bracing herself, she fought the impulse to draw back.

Then he tripped over his own helmet and fell sprawling at her feet.

The audience roared.

Jurik beat the ground with frustration, his berserker fury spent.

Jame lowered the sword.

"Well," she said, feeling shaken. "So nice of you to join us."

IV

ONLY LATER did she find out what was going on.

Rue brought her part of the puzzle after talking to one of the duke's pages, who found the story too good to keep secret and was busy spreading it all over the citadel.

Jurik and his people had arrived the previous night, when everyone else had gone to bed. After that, he and the duke had sat up even later, drinking.

Both belonged to the Princess cult, so they had that in common.

The page himself—made of sterner stuff, he proclaimed—followed Prince Bastolov.

As the night had dragged on, he had longed for bed and become increasingly disgusted at the drunken delay although of course not saying anything about it, which would have been several steps above his station.

The duke and Jurik, he reported, were also united by their hatred of Jame. Somehow, she had gotten under both of their thin skins, beyond sense, beyond reason. A nice enough lady, he had told Rue, with a touch of condescension. Why, she had even met his eyes when speaking to him, and had smiled. A pity about that scar that tweaked her lip. Otherwise, she would almost be handsome.

Oh, and the Deathless had come to the door, but had been turned away. They only wanted to cause trouble between the duke and his Brandan, said the page. His grace had trouble enough as it was.

Anyway, Jurik had been excited by the prospect of riding a prime war-horse in full armor against Jame and that freak beast of hers, neither one of which could possibly be trained for such a match. He had presented himself as an expert horseman and warrior. He, at least, had had no doubt that he could make mincemeat of both opponents. The duke seemed to agree. He proposed that Jurik be his champion—in the princess's name, of course—instead of the noble, Stennen, who had promoted the foot race and considered that he had been made a fool of by Jame's rooftop stunt. Now that was another person with a grudge against the lordan.

"But," Jame said, "that would set Jurik up as an opponent to King Mordaunt, whose cause he came here to support."

Rue reverently folded the rathorn scale armor back into its lambskin pouch.

"I don't think Jurik considered that," she said. "He's used to getting what he wants, and he thinks a lot of himself."

Jame touched the rhi-sar shield, which had been recovered from the battlefield and would need repairs to its torn grip. How close that lance had come to slicing off her face. "Even if the duke doesn't believe in Jurik's prowess, this gives him a ridiculous story to use against his overlord. What is it about Jurik that makes him everyone's fool?"

"Stupidity," said Rue.

That night Duke Pugnanos held a banquet in Wealdhold's great hall. All the champions of the contests were there, each to receive his laurels, to acclaim and much quaffing of wine. The Transwealdians had done well, when not confronted by the Kencyr. Much was made in particular of the horsemen and the charioteers—with good reason. Their performance had been bloody, but magnificent.

Less was said about the combat sports. Jame wished she could have seen them. Some contestants had been reduced to the status of ground meat—teeth smashed, noses squashed, ribs, eye sockets, and jaws broken—but at least none had been killed, which seemed to be a record. Thank Kendar restraint for that. The Kencyr winners received no wreaths. The general idea was that they were professionals, playing for pay, and with that they would have to be content. Luckily, that was all they expected.

If anything, though, this equanimity further inflamed the duke's sense of grievance, which otherwise seemed to be focused on Jame. He, Jurik, and Stennen exchanged snide remarks and glanced often in her direction. Pugnanos's features turned redder and redder, the more he drank, and his laugh became a shrill whinny.

The feast neared its end with tansy cakes, almond-cardamom pastries, and sweet wines—quite a difference from the parched fare of only days ago. If the Duke could have excluded the Kencyr altogether, Jame suspected, he would have. As it was, most of them had stopped drinking some time ago.

Not so Pugnanos, who now rose with a brimming goblet in his hand.

"To our contestants and to our honored guests!" he cried to the hall at large, to an answering cheer. "Such feats we have seen, such skill and courage! What a pity that it should end in such shame."

This last met with an uncertain mutter except from the Kencyr, who put down their cups and listened intently.

"You are all good men," Pugnanos continued, almost pleading. "Honorable men. What do you know of female duplicity?"

He gestured toward Jame, sloshing red wine over his white cuff. "This woman was forbidden to compete. When have women ever done so in our sacred sports? Did that stop her? No. She brought her mountebank horse to the field. By trickery and deceit, she bested our sworn ally, Prince Jurik. How else could she have won? She defied me. She betrayed you. What judgment shall we pronounce?"

He paused as if waiting for an answer, his arms outspread. The hall murmured in confusion, each to each, until Garr stood up.

"Your grace," he said stiffly. "You gave me to understand that you wanted the Knorth lordan to meet your champion. You announced as much to your own people, this afternoon in the field."

The duke stuttered. "I-I didn't recognize her in such armor. Why should anyone? And that beast she rode ... does anyone believe it was really a rathorn? More tricks and deception!"

Some of his court shouted, "Hear, hear! Was what we saw real?"

"What *did* we see?" others cried, sounding confused. "Who to believe?"

Jame rose, and the hall seemed to subside around her. "Prince Jurik, did you recognize me? Did you recognize my mount? If I say that we both were there, with your knowledge, do you accuse me of lying?"

Everyone looked at Jurik. He in turn regarded his wine glass, then drained it. "I am Mordaunt's heir," he said, sounding stifled. "I am the next king of Bashti. What I say is true."

"What *do* you say?"

He gulped and glared. "That you are a bitch and a cheat. Unnatural. Treacherous. And that *is* true, because I say so."

Jame sagged slightly. "Jurik, you've just called me a liar in front of witnesses. Think of your father."

"Who are you, to suggest that I don't?"

The Kencyr rose as one and turned away from him. Transwealdian guards stopped them at the door. For a moment, carnage seemed imminent.

"I have further orders for you," said Pugnanos, leaning on the table, panting. "I declare the last contest void. We won. *I* won. Tomorrow is the day before the Autumnal Equinox, Wolf's Day. We will enter the Weald. We will kill every wolver we find there. Yes, all of them! Brandan, no clause protects you from this order. What I say, do. Jurik?"

The prince looked sick but determined. "Yes. You Knorth must also go, and so will my friends. I am in charge of this expedition, in my father's name. You are sworn to serve him."

"Sweet Trinity," said Jame under her breath to Garr as they left the hall. "What now?"

He gave her a crooked smile. "What else? We follow orders."

V

BEFORE DAWN THE NEXT MORNING, Jame borrowed a pot of ointment from the Brandan stable and went in search of Death's-head.

She found him in the same sunken waterway where he had been the previous day, again slathered with mud. When she brushed the dirty crust away from his shoulder, there was the mark of Jurik's lance, hot to the touch and pink around the edges, as she had expected it might be. He grumbled, but allowed her to clean the wound and rub the salve into it.

"We keep a watch on this," she told him. "No work for you today."

Back in the erstwhile playing field, a host of hunters was gathering. The Knorth and the Brandan were already there, the latter outnumbering the former ten to one. Then again, this was almost their entire Wealdhold garrison, against a token Knorth presence from High Bashti. The Jaran had also turned out—in search, perhaps, of a new song. The Danior contestants barely made a dimple in this mass.

Jame reclaimed the horse that she had ridden here, a

sensible bay gelding. "So many people," she said to Garr, coming up on him as he checked his tack and tightened his mount's girth.

"Yes. Here comes His Grace."

Duke Pugnanos rode out of the eastern gate. By his side rode Jurik. Their partisans—oh, so many of them—followed.

Trestle tables had been set up and breakfast conveyed to them: wine, plates of spiced eggs, butter bread, braised bacon, and brie cheese with honey among many other dishes. The courtiers of both courts gathered around these offerings, chattering, avid. The outer ranks of the host had no such access. Not expecting it, knowing Pugnanos, they had eaten earlier in barracks. Jame wished that she had.

"What says my master of the hunt?" the duke cried.

A weathered Transwealdian stood forth, looking sour.

"Lord, I have had little time to inspect the ground, much yet to prepare it. You asked for carrion to be deployed, a quartered carcass in each stand of trees, but that only draws wolves. Have you ever hunted wolver before?"

The duke sputtered. "What difference does that make? Both eat the dead. Both are only animals, unless they are demonically possessed."

"He really doesn't understand, does he?" said Jame to Garr.

The Brandan shrugged. "Pugnanos is an avid hunter, at least around the forest's margin. When wolves slink out of the trees to steal sheep (yes, we do have mere wolves) or children wander off, you should hear him rant. He sees himself as the champion of wood-cutters, until the wood strikes back. His ventures into the Deep Weald have been disasters. His Grace claims that he believes in only what he sees, but he is also grossly superstitious. To echo his followers last night, what is real and what isn't? Myself, I think this entire exercise is his attempt to tame the Weald and to turn it into his private hunting preserve—also, by the way, to thumb his nose at his overlord, Mordaunt."

"How many wolvers does he expect to find?"

"A few dozen at most. They are rarely seen outside the wood."

"I think he may be in for a surprise."

The party at the table argued back and forth. Everyone had an opinion: should they single out one wolver to track and if so, which? Should they set loose all of the hounds or establish lines to drive their prey? Should they track one bitch to her lair and so destroy an entire generation of vermin? But nothing had been prepared. Pugnanos, however, clearly felt that this was the hour to strike.

The assembly broke up to the sound of horns. The guides and the hunters with their hounds had already entered the wood. Pugnanos and Jurik followed them, their courts and friends behind, joined by minstrels playing cheerful tunes. After them came the Brandan, then the Knorth, then the servants with their pack-horses. There must have been four hundred in all, Jame thought, settled in more for a picnic than a hunt, and certainly not for a battle.

The wood at first presented a fringe of cut saplings, rotting on the ground.

"When a child disappears into the shadows," said Garr to Jame, "Neighbors cut down trees, hoping this will force the Weald to give him or her back."

"Does that work?"

"Sometimes. Usually not. I don't think these people understand how these things work. For that matter, thanks to Grimly, you probably know more about the wolvers than anyone else here. Even then, Grimly belongs to the Holt, not to the Weald."

"I wonder," said Jame.

They crossed meadows of wild flowers which, surely, would have tempted children. Jame could almost see them, laughing, plucking blossoms, running into the fields beyond. Then the company passed into groves of trees— aspen, sumac, birch. The land rolled. The trees grew. Here were the deeper shades of maple, ash, hickory, and oak under a spreading canopy. The ground became littered with pits and mounds, also with fallen, decaying timber. Only game trails wound through the debris, and the horses perforce went single file. The Kencyr were repeatedly forced to stop while those ahead trickled between increasingly massive trunks, with the pack train bunched up behind them. How long was the line of march? Miles by now, Jame thought.

Here and there, a standing dead tree pierced the canopy allowing shafts of sunlight to reach the forest floor through the skeleton of its upper branches. By midday, though, the sky was overcast. All sense of direction disappeared. At first, hunting horns sounded at intervals ahead and behind, but these drew farther and farther away, as if the line was breaking up. How easy it would be to wander off these faint tracks. Which way was forward, which back, or had they started to go in circles?

Bark made faces at them out of the gathering gloom of late afternoon. Shadows moved.

"How quiet it is," said Damson to Jame.

True, they hadn't heard a bird or so much as the rustle of a leaf unless stirred by a hoof in the past hour.

Dusk fell. The pack train crowded up on their heels, or at least some of it did. The rest seemed to have either turned back or gotten lost.

"Good luck to them," said Rue, bringing rations forward to her company.

"Cut no live wood," Jame ordered, remembering her experiences in the Anarchies. "This forest has known fire. It hasn't forgotten."

They ate and tried to sleep. The night hooted from tree to tree, a quivering, eerie sound. Call and response, near and far, call and response. Jame walked the margins of the camp, listening.

"Friend," she whispered to the encircling darkness. "Friend."

The dawn of Wolf's Day came with tendrils of mist creeping along the ground, stretching overhead from branch to branch. The sky, glimpsed through leaves, was opaque.

"Forward or back?" asked Damson.

"Which is which? Anyway, we have our orders. That way."

She chose at random.

Sometime later, they came across a trail torn through the undergrowth, mired with many hoof-prints. It took them all day to catch up with the main body of the hunt, which seemed to have taken off at a dead run in the middle of the night.

So, at last, they came to the clearing that was the heart of the wood. Its rim was surrounded by tangled deadfalls with few ways in or out. At its center was an inner circle of charred oaks, most now mere stumps or trunks lying on the ground in decay, under a dome of mist. Withered ferns curled in their hollows. Spongy moss felted the ground. The duke's host huddled in the midst of all this, horses nose to tail, shivering, riders clustered nearly as close.

Jame sought out Garr. "What happened?"

He gave her his lopsided smile, with a twitch at the corner, and his eyes more than a bit wild.

"I hardly know. The hounds belled the scent and gave chase. The duke and his court followed, likewise Prince Jurik. They all rode break-neck, as if possessed. So, perhaps, they were. When we finally caught up near dusk, it was in a glen slathered with blood. Neither hounds nor wolvers did we see at first, but the trees dripped. We looked up. Dogs and hunters both were splayed there on a scaffold of limbs as white as bone. Their entrails dangling. Off in the woods, the wolves howled, and howled, and howled."

"They're quiet now," said Jame.

"Is that better? Anyway, the duke panicked and fled. Both courts followed him and we Brandan, his guards, followed them."

Dusk came, the darkening of the equinox.

The duke's people gathered a mighty bonfire within the

circle of oaks. Deadfalls added to it, but also fresh limbs and more than one entire tree, hewed down in a frenzy against the encroaching dark.

"That isn't wise," said Jame. In the rush to collect wood, no one listened, even if it was too green to burn. "Take the horses to the outer ring," she told Damson. "Picket them and stand watch."

Jurik came up to her with a rictus grin. "We thought that you had run away," he said.

She smiled back at him, showing her teeth. "On the contrary, you out-ran us. How does command feel now, Prince? Do you wish yourself safely home?"

His expression turned into a snarl. "Bitch. Cheat. You will see."

She laughed in his face. "Shall I indeed? So will you."

That, she thought as he stomped away, had not been wise. Never taunt the weak; they tend to snap in unexpected ways, at the worst possible moment.

Night fell, just as the few dry leaves within the bonfire finally ignited. Tongues of flame licked at the kindling. Fern fronds flared and died. As the flickering light grew, it was reflected by hundreds of watching eyes in the darkness of the surrounding wood.

A shaggy boy stepped forth and grinned at them. His teeth were white and sharp.

"Let me go, let me go!" cried a Transwealdian noble to the friends who tried to restrain him. "That's my son, lost so many years ago!"

He fought free and ran into the shadows, which closed after him. They heard him scream, and then the sound of feeding.

"His own son," said Pugnanos hoarsely.

"No," said Jame. "A pup learns to shape-shift with adolescence. Wolvers are born, not made. I can't answer for their diet."

Sparks rose from the flames to trace the shape of the long-gone trees—trunk, bough, and branch. Like fireflies, they nested in the phantom folds of bark. Like glowworms, they followed the network of roots under the ground. A spectral grove rose around the huddled hunters. Their horses, panicked by the fire, fled to the outer ring where they circled looking for a way out. The picket line of Kencyr mounts swayed, but Damson and her command went among them with soothing words. In the outer gloom, the wolvers began to croon their invocation:

"Came he to the green Weald.
Wolves greeted him.
One sought him out and loved him.
Pups they had, the first wolvers.
But foes sought to burn him alive.
The heart of the Weald embraced him.
Charred, he lives on.
Never will we forget his pain."

That was the essence of Grimly's lay from the campsite at Wealdhold. Here his voice sounded among many others, in human speech, in lupine song.

The bonfire shattered, then rose on a glowing skeleton of trunks and boughs as a figure climbed limb by limb out of the ruins until it stood as tall as the ghostly trees.

Embers nested in its hair, in the folds of its charred clothing. Its bones smoldered. The Burnt Man stood swaying above all, looking down in bemusement at the rout at his feet.

The Kencyr drew into defensive formation. Everyone else fled except for Duke Pugnanos, who fell to his knees before this unearthly specter.

Jame stood behind him.

She was terrified. In the past, under the influence of the Dark Judge, this Rathillien elemental had tried repeatedly to kill her. If he touched her now, she would burn. She cleared a dry throat and spoke:

"Lord, we are sorry for this intrusion. His Grace, the duke, promises never to do it again. You do, don't you?" she added aside to the crouching noble.

"I-I believe in what I see," the duke stammered. "Prince Bastolov, I see you and beg your forgiveness."

"In return," she said, aware that she was pushing matters, "will you allow his people to leave the Weald unharmed?"

A gray wolver and a white one had come up behind her. She felt their presence like a wall against which she hoped she could lean.

The Burnt Man inclined his head. He trudged past them, out of the circle, trailing sparks, and tore up a section of deadfall. Horses streamed through it. Men ran after them.

Jame sighed with relief. That, she thought, was the first civil encounter she had ever had with the fire elemental.

"Thank you," she said to him. "Grimly, you asked for

my help. Instead I need it from you. Can you guide these people out of the forest? Most of their horses seem to have bolted."

The wolver grinned. "Horses are good meat. Yes, we can accommodate them. First, though, see this."

He led her to the edge of the clearing, into the undergrowth. Yce padded after them, wary, jealous. Here was a burrow and in it four pups, two gray, two white. They tumbled out when they scented their parents, stopped when they saw Jame. She knelt and offered them her finger tips. They sniffed, then licked, then rolled at her feet.

"Oh, Yce. Oh, Grimly. They're beautiful."

"Tell Torisen that I have finally found my heart."

"Yes. Of course. Bring them to the Riverland when they're old enough to travel. Tori will be so pleased."

VI

IT TOOK THREE DAYS to escape the forest, picking up stragglers along the way, driven into the body of the march by the wolvers. Some had recaptured their horses. Both riders and mounts were very quiet and thoroughly spooked. Jame suspected that they would never again be quite the same. Others, however, were loud and given to hysteria when darkness fell.

Pugnanos rode among the former, Jurik among the latter.

Half of the prince's followers and friends had been lost. Those who remained accompanied him warily except for

Cervil, who clung to his heels and tried to quiet him. Everything was someone else's fault, he shouted. How could he be held to blame?

But he must have known that High Bashti would not be pleased nor would its king. After all, not only had he gotten the favorite sons of other houses killed but he had also embarked on this expedition against Mordaunt's express interests.

"Listen to him," said Damson on the second night, referring to Jurik's raging as it echoed over an already unsettled camp. "Can't he control himself?"

"He never has before," Jame said, from an adjacent bedroll. She wondered if Jurik was again losing control. He was a berserker, she now believed, but to what extent? He had abandoned his people's tents on the way to Wealdhold, although not his own. Within it, his shadow stormed back and forth, gesticulating.

"Control is important, isn't it?"

"Yes," said Jame, aware that to this strange Kendar she was setting a precept. "Especially to those with power. Like Jurik. Like you. Like me."

A cry pierced the night. Many rose on an elbow to listen, including Jame and Damson. The shadows within the prince's tent had converged. One fell.

"I think," said Jame, "that he may just have killed Cervil."

"And what do we do about that?"

"What can we? Here? Now? Nothing. Responsibility has limits too, or we would all go mad. But I think, eventually, that someone will have to do something about Jurik, one way or another."

VII

THE NEXT DAY they emerged from the forest, to a valedictory chorus of wolver howls. The city welcomed them back, but in a subdued mood. A third of those who had ridden forth to such acclaim did not come back, nor had their bodies been retrieved. Who knew: they might still wander lost in the forest, on and on and on. At least Grimly had promised to keep searching, although Yce had sneered at his sentimentality. A word from Jame that Torisen would appreciate such an effort might have had an effect.

Once home, Pugnanos retreated into his citadel. It was said that, there, he brought forward all of the monuments to Prince Bastolov and retired those dedicated to the Princess Amalfia. He and Jurik fought over this, loudly enough to be heard in the barracks below by way of the chimney flues.

Jurik damned the Burnt Man as a demon, seeming at times to confuse him with his own father Mordaunt. Vestula, on the other hand, he proclaimed to be the Princess reborn. How dare Pugnanos turn his back on her?

"Easily," the duke snapped. "She's your mother, not mine."

More shouting followed, until Pugnanos sent for his Brandan guard.

"We should leave," Jame said to Garr when he returned, looking shaken. "Soon. Is there any question that we won the contest?"

"I wouldn't say so, if only from the sequel in the forest. Most of the Brandan came back alive, for which I thank you."

Jame shrugged. "They conducted themselves well. That's to your credit, not to mine."

The day after that, on the 40th of Autumn, they left Wealdhold—Knorth, Danior, and Bashtiri. The latter took the lead, as if out of sheer defiance, but all made better progress than on the way there. It didn't rain, and this line of march put Jurik well ahead of Jame. She wasn't sorry for that.

Every morning before they set out, Jame went to check on Death's-head with her pot of ointment. The lance wound healed rapidly, to her relief. Others in the camp also needed tending for cuts, sprains, and a few broken bones. Kindrie would have been useful. Jame wondered what her cousin was doing back in the Riverland. Hopefully he was leading a quieter life than hers had recently been.

Ten days later, without further incident, they reached High Bashti at twilight. Their homecoming, here too, was less warm than their departure had been, but a few people cheered. Jame wondered if Jurik had sent a herald ahead to announce his approach. Certainly, someone should have.

Should that have been me? she wondered, but that hadn't been her job.

Families, patrician and common, clustered on the curb. They could see who had not returned. A groan rose, and then angry voices. Jurik rode on to the royal palace as if he heard none of this. He had done the king's bidding, after all, had he not?

The Kencyr turned off at Campus Kencyrath, where Jame went to the commander's quarter to report on the mission. Here she quickly realized that Jurik had sent Harn no news either this entire time. While she cautiously described what had befallen, he listened, again fiddling with the objects on his desk until he abruptly looked up.

"The prince called you a liar?"

"Yes."

He grunted. "Bad. He should have known better. What next?"

Jame told him about the invasion of the forest, the wolvers, the Burnt Man, and the rout. She didn't mention Cervil. In fact, she said less about Jurik than she could or perhaps should have.

Nonetheless, Harn seemed to listen to the silence between her words. "Bad, bad, bad," he muttered, and shook his shaggy head.

On her way out, Jame paused at the door, turned, and spoke despite herself.

"Commander . . . Jurik is your son, isn't he?"

"Why should you think so?"

"Well, for one thing he resembles you much more than he does the king. For another, Mordaunt is notorious for only siring bastards. Then too, Jurik is a berserker."

Harn sighed. "That too. I didn't know, not until I came back this summer for the first time in thirty years and Queen Vestula told me. She says that I raped her."

"I don't believe that."

"I don't know. That entire night was a blur, or rather a nightmare. The Knorth ladies had just been massacred back in the Riverland and Ganth had run mad. All of us bound to him were touched by that, even before the carnage of the White Hills. I was here in High Bashti. The next day I rode north. After the Hills, we were cut off from the Central Lands for three decades. I returned to find . . . him. What do I do now?"

This, thought Jame, was what had caused the chaos in Harn's letters to her brother, which had led to her being sent here in the first place. Now she had seen and understood, but what could she say?

"This society still considers Jurik a boy," she said slowly. "I think you do too. But he is half Kencyr and, by our standards, a man. Tell him that, if you choose, but hold him responsible for his actions. Good night."

VIII

BACK IN HER QUARTERS, Rue had set out a simple supper and Jorin rolled over on her toes, paws kneading the air, delighted at her return.

"That was on your bed," said Rue, nodding toward a scroll.

Jame picked it up carefully. Although not ancient it was old and fragile, inclined to crack at the edges. She unrolled it, held it against her dark counterpane, and read the words written in *mere* ink that showed through.

"Well?" said Rue, impatient with her silence. "What does it say?"

Jame let the manuscript curl up again under her hand. "What I expected it would."

And there it lay, looking so innocent. At last she had

proof of what had happened thirty years ago at Gothregor, to have caused so much death and disaster in the Kencyrath, to have so warped its future.

That raised two questions, though: What should she do with it now, and why had the Shadow Assassin Smeak delivered it to her in the first place?

❦❧ **Chapter XIV** ❦❧
Into the Den of Monsters
Wilden and Restormir: Autumn 35–39

I

TORISEN HEARD THE HORN at the northern gate signal a visitor to Gothregor—a friend, by its lilt.

Good. He would welcome something to lift his spirits.

He was in his tower study, reading the same report from Harn over and over, getting nothing new out of it. The old problem remained. Mordaunt hadn't yet sent supplies or any explanation as to why not. Torisen's sense was that the Bashtiri king had his own problems and would deal with those of the Kencyrath last, when he finally out-ran his credit there. It was up to Torisen when to say that enough was enough, if it wasn't already too late.

Jame would be in Wealdhold by now, in the midst of Duke Pugnanos's farcical games, fighting Mordaunt's battles. Torisen didn't trust the duke any more than he did the king, but his sister was clever and unpredictable. Those were two of her greatest strengths, on which he would bet against any number of dim-witted Central Land nobles.

He also wondered about Kindrie. Fifteen days ago he had first realized that his cousin had dropped off the stained-glass map, or perhaps he, Torisen, simply didn't know how to read it correctly. The latter could still be true. But he worried. Several days later he had finally sent a message by post to Mount Alban, where he believed Kindrie to be. That was a good hundred miles farther north, but with relays of horses the riders were fast. The missive would have reached his cousin by now. How soon might he receive a reply?

Burr knocked on the door.

"The Jaran lordan," he said, and made way for Kirien.

Torisen rose, startled. Kirien was a very self-possessed young woman. Given that, he was stuck by her haggard aspect.

"Lady." He offered her a chair, but she didn't take it. Instead, she placed a message pouch on his desk.

"You sent this to Kindrie," she said. "He isn't at the college and hasn't been since mid-summer. All of this time, I thought that he was here."

It took some effort to get the story out of her as she paced back and forth, arms wrapped tightly around her chest. Always androgynous, now she was gaunt. Three steps one way, three steps the other, over and over.

She and Kindrie had quarreled. He had left. She knew that he had taken a post horse, but the station attendant had been distracted and couldn't tell her in which direction he had gone, north or south on the River Road. She had assumed that he was bound for Gothregor.

"I waited to hear from him. And waited. And waited. It became a matter of pride, who would apologize first. Oh, I was a fool."

"You were hurt," said Torisen. His relationship with Kallystine had taught him that love could be cruel. Kirien and Kindrie had seemed to have so much more than that. He believed that they still did.

"On the way here, I asked at the east bank keeps if they had seen him. Falkirr hadn't. Wilden just sneered, but then they would out of habit."

"And the west bank New Road?"

"I was in a hurry. I didn't cross the Silver."

Torisen considered this. "There are bridges, of course, if not always reliable. If he had come by the River Road, bound here, I would expect him to have changed mounts at least at the Falkirr station. What reason would he have to go farther south, to Omiroth or Kestrie? No. That leaves Wilden to the east, Shadow Rock, Tentir, and Restormir to the west. To the north, maybe Tagmeth too, although my sister would have left for the Central Lands by mid-summer."

He didn't add that Kindrie, never a good rider, might have fallen off somewhere in between and broken his neck.

He also didn't point out that Kirien's enquiries might well have alerted everyone in the Riverland that Kindrie was more important than the harmless bastard that he appeared to be. She was upset enough as it was.

"I think," he said, "that we need to make a search up one side of the Silver and down the other, starting with Wilden."

She looked at him with a sort of wonder. "You would do this?"

That was too much.

"God's claws! You may love him, but he's also my cousin. Doesn't that count for something?"

II

THEY RODE FOR WILDEN the next day, a journey of some fifty miles with a change of mounts at Falkirr. Burr, again, insisted on the armed escort of a ten-command, and grumbled that it was still too small.

"I don't know what you're doing," said Lord Brandan, meeting Torisen at the Falkirr station, "but be careful. The Randir are on guard. So is the entire Riverland. These are too few retainers to guarantee your safety."

"I should bring an army? Surely it hasn't yet come to war between houses."

"Not quite. My sense is that things won't boil over before the winter High Council meeting, unless something dire happens first. Or maybe not until next spring. Either way, I don't trust Rawneth or Caldane."

Torisen gave a tight smile. "Then I will walk wary."

They arrived at Wilden in the late afternoon, without sending ahead any warning. Torisen wanted to take Rawneth unawares. Apparently, he did.

The horns signaled his arrival with a questioning note. He was almost surprised when the main gate opened for his company. They rode up the steep, jagged road, hearing the roar of the river that cascaded down around either side of the keep into its lower moat. Some Randir came out to watch them pass, but most stayed behind the closed doors of their individual compounds.

Wilden had spent a terrible year during which the spirit of its mistress had been trapped in Torisen's soul-image while, physically, she had wandered from one door after another on Wilden's streets, knocking for release. Where she went, her minions had followed, killing anyone weak enough to open their door to her. That had all been Rawneth's doing, not Torisen's. She was, after all, not only the witch of this keep but, as the saying went, the bitch. Did her ambition and malice surpass her power? In that case, they had.

Meanwhile, shut out of the healing power of his own soul-image, afflicted by lung-rot, Torisen had nearly died.

Still, he hadn't previously considered the price that Wilden had paid. He only knew that a number of its people had been either executed or exiled to Tagmeth where Jame had given them shelter. What the survivors thought was anyone's guess.

The road ended in a high terrace, its flagstones slick with spray from the cataract that plunged down beyond the fortress's back wall. Earth and air shook with the continual roar. The Witch's Tower rose black against the falling sheet of white water.

The ten-command stayed outside with the horses, not without some muttering from Burr.

Rawneth lived in the upper stories of the tower, but as they entered the lower hall she descended the spiral stair, the black train of her white gown trailing behind her. Its sleeves were also black and the mask through which her eyes glittered. She was, in fact, marked like an elegant direhound, down to the white teeth revealed by her smile. Had they previously been filed to sharp points? Otherwise, Torisen had seen her dressed much the same way before.

"Highlord. Lady Kirien. Welcome to Wilden. To what do I owe this honor?"

Torisen decided to be direct.

"Matriarch, I am in search of Kindrie Soul-walker. Has he passed this way?"

"So." She paused on the stair and tweaked her train so that it curled around her feet. One almost expected it to twitch like a tail. "You have misplaced him yet again. I was informed, lordan, that you also inquired after him yesterday. Your interest I understand, although I deplore your taste. But you, Highlord, why such continued concern for a mere bastard?"

She hadn't yet guessed Kindrie's legitimacy, Torisen realized, and was relieved. Perhaps things weren't as bad as he had feared and Lady Rawneth, for all her cunning, was not so smart.

"If you find him," she said with a thin, twisted smile, "you had better leave him to me. I know how to best make use of his kind."

"Oh, really?" said Kirien.

Torisen instinctively drew back from her. Jame had told him that the Jaran lordan had the power to compel the truth when provoked, whatever the consequences, inconvenience, or out-right danger. What had Kirien said at Kithorn, as reported by Jame?

That which can be destroyed by the truth should be.

"And what kind is he?" she now asked.

"I would like to know too," said a voice at the open door. A figure stood there against the sunset, casting a shadow before it across the hall. It advanced, turning into a large, young man with white-tufted hair, wearing a belted jacket and big boots that tracked wet footprints into the hall.

Rawneth stomped on her train, which flinched. "Titmouse, go away."

Torisen regarded the newcomer with interest. "My sister met you in Tai-tastigon, did she not? She said she liked you. What are you doing here?"

"I was recalled to the Priests' College to report after the chaos in the Eastern Lands this past summer. I liked her too."

Jame had also said that she had told this priest more than she probably should have about herself, Torisen, and Kindrie. He, too, could draw forth the truth although not ruthlessly compel it. If so, he apparently hadn't shared it with Rawneth. Torisen smiled at him.

"To repeat, lady," said Titmouse, "what kind of man is Kindrie Soul-walker?"

She looked flustered. "Hardly a man at all. Shanir. Illegitimate. A tool to be used by anyone with the wits to do so. What good are the weak except to serve the strong? The Priests' College too. What fools! They could have bowed to Gerridon as hierophant god. Ishtier would have done so had he lived, but do they? Soon, though, soon!"

Someone descended the stair behind her, clad in a pale robe with a waxen smiling face barely glimpsed in the shadow of his hood. She leaned back into him as if for strength. His arms went around her. The hem of her dress writhed. He murmured in her ear.

"And who is this?" asked Kirien.

Rawneth flinched, more at the power behind this question than at the question itself, and bit her lip, which bled. "I mustn't say, but I . . . I must. The father of my dear son. The rightful Highlord of the Kencyrath. Not you, Knorth upstart! Yours was always a cadet branch, illegitimate, Shanir. Don't think we won't overcome you yet."

"I think you think you will," Torisen said, with a bow, although he was still sorting out what she had just said, finding it nonsense. "Kirien, she didn't directly answer me. Ask her again: does she know where Kindrie is?"

He could feel the Jaran lordan focus her will as if it were a lance couched for battle. The short hair on his arms prickled and rose. Not for anything, at that moment, would he have touched her.

"Matriarch. If you know where Kindrie Soul-walker is, tell me."

Rawneth swayed and would have fallen without the support of her companion. "I . . . I think he is at Restormir. At least Lord Caineron boasted to me of having captured a fine healer, and the description fitted. When I asked that he gift me with this prize, for friendship's sake, he laughed. 'Lady, you had your chance,' he said. 'Now it is my turn to use him as I see fit.' That was last summer."

"Oh," said Kirien faintly, sagging. Torisen caught her. "My poor love. All of this time!"

A door to the lower halls had stood ajar. Now it burst open and Kallystine rushed through it, wearing a loose linen gown that molded unflatteringly against the swollen curves of her body.

"I thought I heard your voice!" she cried to Torisen, shoving Kirien out of the way, almost off her feet, and flinging herself into his arms. "Listen! I want to go home. Tell her that you will take me!"

He held her back, skeptical and at the same time stirred. She made a lush armful. He remembered their nights together when she had been his consort, the hunger she had roused but never could quite slake. Now her breath behind the shroud-like mask stank. He could feel her body move, not in response to his own but to internal pressures. It was like holding a bag full of snakes. He thrust her away. That she was pregnant was evident, but not the site of the baby. Its bulge shifted even as he watched from her abdomen to her chest where it formed a third palpitating breast.

And what was the sound he heard—the ghost of a tiny, mischievous giggle?

"I want to go home!" Kallystine cried again to the figure on the stairs.

Rawneth gathered herself and smiled down at her, or rather again showed her teeth. "You are my son's consort. Your baby must be born here."

"This is too soon! Let me go home first. If that Shanir freak is there, I want to consult him. Please!"

"Kenan was born prematurely. So was the Kendar Shade, for that matter, but we won't speak of her. Your babe, however, is of the direct line to Gerridon. You stay here."

Kallystine stomped her foot, turned, and fled.

Torisen took Kirien's arm to steady her. "We should go too. Matriarch, by your leave."

The pale figure on the stair whispered urgently in Rawneth's ear. She brushed him off and held her head as if it hurt her.

"What, keep the Highlord here? And the lordan? No, no. Send them away, send them all away. Now."

And so they went.

III

"YOU NEED TO THINK ABOUT THIS," said Holly when he heard the whole story.

With night coming on, they had taken shelter at the Danior keep, Shadow Rock, across the Silver from Wilden.

"You can't just march in on the Caineron the way you did on the Randir."

"Why not?" demanded Kirien. Her need to act was palpable after waiting so long for news, but was it practical? Moreover, she was still pale and shaken. Compelling the Witch of Wilden had exhausted her more than Torisen had realized it would.

"You think Caldane will take us hostage?" he asked.

"Lady Rawneth almost did," muttered Burr, refilling his cup. "You could disappear the same way your cousin did."

"Kindrie isn't Highlord. No one expected him to have powerful friends."

Holly sipped his cider, considering his words. "Tonight, just how powerful do you feel?"

It was a good question. Kirien had wanted to ride on to Tentir, although the sun had already set. They would have arrived in the dark, very late. Torisen's instinct, though, had been as soon as possible to let someone not of his party know what had happened and where he was bound next. The lesson of Kindrie's fate had not been lost on him. But what good, really, would that do? Who would come to their rescue if they needed it and even then, what next? Lord Brandan has spoken of some dire event igniting the Riverland. That could be it. Caldane would be a fool to take such a risk, but he was also stupid and unstable.

Still wondering, Torisen rode north the next day on the west bank New Road. Some seventy miles lay between him and Restormir, also the randon college at Tentir, also the Jaran keep Valantir opposite Mount Alban.

Kirien wanted to travel fast and kept edging ahead. Wanting to think, Torisen held back.

If Rawneth considered Caldane a friend, she might already have sent him warning by post rider of Torisen's approach. In that case, he couldn't count on surprise again and speed presumably wasn't an issue. A slower advance might help, if it gave Caldane time to second guess himself or, perhaps, even to come to reason.

In the afternoon they realized that they were being followed. Kallystine galloped up on their heels, riding a lathered horse.

"I said I was going with you," she panted through her mask. Sweat molded it to the ruined contours of her face. In and out it went around her mouth and protruding bones, in and out.

Torisen caught her bridle to stop her. The horse

staggered and nearly fell. "Is this wise? You might miscarry."

"If I do, so much the better. If Kindrie is at Restormir, he will help me. He must!"

Kirien had reined back to ride beside them. "What, to miscarry?"

"Yes! This thing within me is an abomination, not a child."

"I don't think you understand the role of a healer."

"You do know," said Torisen, "that if—no, when—Rawneth hears of this, she is going to be furious with both of us."

"What do I care? I'm tired, though. When can we stop?"

"D'you want the Randir to catch up with us?"

"No! Ride on."

Tentir was several miles ahead of them. They reached it in the late afternoon.

"You do realize, don't you," said Burr to Torisen, "that we're still being followed."

"Yes. I know. One rider keeping his or her distance."

The Coman randon currently in command of the college was not pleased to see them.

"You should have given me advance warning," he said. "Your guest quarters haven't been prepared, nor has anything special for dinner."

"We will take whatever you can offer," said Torisen, dismounting in the hall of Old Tentir, surrounded by the fusty banners of the nine houses, each thick with the stitches of its pledged cadets.

"I need a bed," Kallystine declared, accepting Burr's

hand down from her horse, landing with an ungainly stagger. The fetus jolted downward into her upper thigh where it wriggled under the fabric of her gown. "Bring me a bowl of warm gruel. Now. Good night."

Torisen spread his hands in apology. "What can I say? She's pregnant."

"Humph," said the Coman commandant, and turned away.

Dinner was plain, but acceptable. They ate in the map room of New Tentir, surrounded by the intricate battle plans of a hundred conflicts on Rathillien alone, overlooking the training yard around which the cadet barracks clustered.

The commandant was short with his guests. Finally, his indignation burst out.

"How can we at Tentir expect to inculcate discipline in these cadets when you Highborn persist in fighting?"

Torisen set down his wine glass. "I wasn't aware that I was setting a bad example," he said mildly. "How so?"

"You and Lord Caineron and Lady Rawneth and... and all the rest. Can't you feel it? The Riverland is like jagged glass, catching at every snag. Never mind our divine mandate or whatever it is. Ancestors help me, how am I supposed to know anymore? How are any of us supposed to live here, now, with honor?"

Torisen considered this. "Yes, these are difficult times. Much is coming to a head. You will have to ask yourself, in what do you believe? If honor, what does that mean? Where do you choose to fight? If necessary, where do you choose to die? The days of easy answers are over. As you say, this is here. At long last, after three millennia, this is now."

Voices rose in the training yard. The cadets had come

out of their barracks in the twilight and were singing to the map room's balcony. Torisen went out to listen. The tune was old, fitted to new words:

"You lead us, lord.
If not in you, whom should we trust?
Show us the way. We will follow.
Your sister too, one of us.
Honor her name.
Honor your own."

"And that," said the commandant sourly, "is your answer. Ancestors preserve you both."

IV

WHEN THEY SET OUT the next day, perhaps half the cadets followed them, several hundred in all. The Knorth were there, also the Jaran with their lordan ahead of them. The Brandan and the Danior followed. There were even a few Ardeth, remembering Timmon and, surprisingly, some Caineron, in honor of Sheth Sharp-tongue and Gorbel.

"I don't like this," Torisen said to Kirien, looking back at the train behind them. "We're going to Restormir. That's dangerous."

"On the other hand," said Kirien, "they are witnesses. And their houses will rise up if they are hurt."

"Still, I should shelter behind children?"

She gave him a level look. "We're talking about Caldane here. What realities does he recognize?"

That, thought Torisen, was a good question.

It was another slow ride, thanks to Kallystine's continued complaints. Torisen almost wished that the Randir would catch up with them. Maybe Rawneth, disgusted with her daughter-in-law, hadn't bothered to ask where she was, or no one had dared to tell her.

Next came Valantir, connected to Mount Alban across the river by a much-travelled bridge in a continual state of repair. The Jaran welcomed Kirien with great relief—it seemed that she hadn't told them where she was going or why. The Riverland, thought Torisen, seemed currently full of bolting Highborn. He welcomed the Jedrak's hospitality, though, for both his small party and the considerably larger one following in his wake.

"But we must come too," said Lord Jaran when he heard their story. "Kindrie was our guest. Caldane is our neighbor. Kirien is our lordan. And she looks exhausted. Should we let her venture into that ogre's den alone?"

"Hardly that," murmured Torisen. "I didn't ask for an army, but I seem to be acquiring one."

"Well, then, welcome us too. And the singers. And the scrollsmen. How can I tell any of them to hold back?"

It was therefore a considerable force that descended on a surprised Restormir the next day.

V

TORISEN knew that he was being watched ever since warning horns had sounded the minute the vanguard of his party topped the ridge overlooking the fortress. The size of the latter always amazed him. Caldane had some twelve thousand adherents either bound directly to him or to his seven established sons, each of whom had a compound of his own clustered to the south of his father's original holding. Over all rose the mound on top of which stood the family's tower keep.

The horns kept blowing, sounding ever shriller, as Torisen descended the rise and the number of his followers became evident. Armed riders galloped out of the easternmost compound, enough of them to have surrounded the smaller company that they apparently had expected. Instead, they lined the road on either side and saluted their Highlord as he passed.

The gate stood open, the tail-end of the New Road running through it. Caineron stopped what they were doing to stare at the visitors as they passed. No one cheered. From ahead came the hollow sound of rushing water—a tributary of the Silver tumbling down to join it between close-set walls, under a bridge. On the other side of the bridge was Caldane's much larger compound, and on its western end, across yet another bridge, the tower mound.

Torisen dismounted at the foot of the mound on its river-girt island. Tack clinked and groaned behind him as his attendants also swung down. He didn't look back to see how many of them followed him up the steep stair to the tower on the hill—probably as many as would fit. He felt Kirien close beside him, however, and was again uneasily aware of how much the encounter with Rawneth had cost her.

Kallystine rushed past up the stairs and disappeared

within. A thin, dark randon followed her, perhaps the second rider who had pursued them from Wilden. When they entered the tower, though, they saw no sign of either.

Inside, one could look up the shaft to the apartments of the so-called Crown, Caldane's home, and to the opening into the garden above that where the Matriarch Cattila had once held court. Here on the ground level was a courtyard paved with white marble. At its center was a rimmed well extending down into the dungeons. Surrounding this were tall glass doors that opened into reception halls. In the halls were a host of large, gilded statues striking heroic poses, each with Caldane's smug face but not with his corpulent body.

"Welcome to Restormir," said Tiggeri, stepping forward. His smile, as usual, was wide and full of white teeth, but his eyes were wary. "To what do we owe such a number of uninvited visitors?"

"Rawneth of Wilden informs us that my cousin Kindrie Soul-walker is your . . . er . . . guest," said Torisen. "We have come to escort him home."

Tiggeri's smile twitched at one corner. "Now why would the dear lady suggest any such thing? We never told her that."

Kirien stepped forward. She trembled slightly, like a bow-string just beyond strength's pull. "Nonetheless, she told us that he was here."

"Why should he be?"

"Word has reached us that Lord Caineron is ill. Where would he look, if not to a powerful healer?"

"He has healers of his own. Do you say that ours are insufficient?"

"If your lord is still sick, yes."

"But what good would an outsider do?"

Kirien gulped. "Lord Caineron doesn't know how to deal with any power not absolutely under his control. Even then, whatever he thinks, his control, like his judgment, is limited. How has he used Kindrie Soul-walker?"

Tiggeri grinned, but he had begun to sweat. "I didn't say that the Shanir was here, did I? Even if he was, he owes my father a debt of loyalty for past favors. Should he not pay them?"

"He served Lord Caineron once, perforce, and in recompense was tortured. Don't tell me what he does or doesn't owe this house."

Torisen stepped up behind her. "We Knorth support this view."

"And we Jaran."

"And we Danior."

"And we Brandan."

"You also, Ardeth?" sneered Tiggeri. "And you traitorous Caineron? Oh yes, we note your presence here."

The haunt singer Ashe stepped forth. Torisen hadn't known that she was there.

"All of us ... bear witness," she said in her hoarse, death-halted voice. "Think what our songs ... what history ... will say about you, proud Caineron. Gerridon once stood on such a slope. He fell. Listen and learn."

Tiggeri's grin widened. From one corner of his mouth hung a thread of drool, slickening his teeth, his chin. "Tell that to my father," he said, licking it up. "He comes. He comes now."

VI

KINDRIE COULD HEAR THE MURMUR BELOW, but didn't know what it meant. While the shaft of the tower conducted sound, not much had happened there for a long time. This far within stone and mortar, the outer city was mute.

Someone scrabbled at the door. It had no lock. Kallystine burst in and threw herself at him.

"Now, now!" she panted. "You have to help me!"

He held her off while half supporting her. She had never been his favorite Caineron.

"What do you need?" the healer within him asked, cursing itself even as it spoke. Could he deny no one?

"This child . . . no, this abomination. It will destroy me!"

He could tell by the seething of her body that she was going into labor. Too late to stop that, even if he had been willing.

"Kill it, kill it!" she cried and convulsed under his hands.

Someone, suddenly, was beside him—a dark young randon wearing a Randir neck scarf with what appeared to be a glittering band wrapped around it, except that the band breathed.

"Who are you?"

"Shade. This is Addy, a gilded swamp adder to whom I am bound. That 'abomination' is Lord Randir's son, my half-brother. Please, help him."

This was a lot to absorb all at once. Kindrie had heard

that Kenan, Lord Randir, had taken Lord Caineron's daughter Kallystine as consort for the purpose of siring an heir. He hadn't expected to be presented with the results.

"Help me loosen her clothes," he said to Shade. "What do you know about childbirth?"

"The father, Lord Randir, is a changer. He was my father too, by a Kendar. Changer babies tend to be born prematurely, while their bodies are still in flux. I was one such. My mother hid me, or I would have been killed."

Worse and worse.

Kallystine thrashed. The fetus surged about inside her body, seeking a way out.

"It's a condition called the wandering womb," said Kindrie, trying to track its progress while catching Kallystine's hands as she tore at herself. "It can be deadly to both mother and child."

Someone else entered the room. "Now what?" said Gorbel over Kindrie's shoulder, looking down at his convulsed half-sister. "Is she having a fit, or just a temper tantrum?"

Kallystine wrenched a hand free and hit Kindrie in the nose with it, knocking him over backward. She began to scream.

"Hold her down," he said to Gorbel and Shade, wiping a smear of blood off his face.

Gorbel pinned her flailing arms. Shade steadied her head. Kindrie laid his hands on her heaving body to calm it . . .

. . . and found himself in her soul-image. It resembled a ruined mansion, once luxurious, now fallen into decay and haunted by bad odors. The walls were stained, the floors cracked. Lilies festered in filthy water. Roses dropped bruised petals. No air moved.

But there was sound: small feet pattered from room to room, just out of sight. Someone giggled—a protean innocent, playing hide and seek. But now the walls of flesh were moving, in and out, in and out, pressing ever closer, and the giggle became a frightened cry. Someone, somewhere, was screaming.

Kindrie jerked back his hands.

Kallystine was gasping behind her wet mask. Afraid that she would suffocate, he removed it. Her face was the facade of the ruined house, fallen in around its bony structure yet still desperately alive behind those bulging eyes.

She seemed to be strangling. Her neck swelled.

Sweet Trinity. The baby was coming up her throat.

She choked and gagged. Her jaw gaped wide, wider, until with a crack it unhinged.

"Push, push," he begged her even as she tried desperately to swallow.

The baby shot forth, to be caught by Shade. Kindrie glimpsed its big head and tiny, thrashing limbs before the Randir bore it off to his bed where she snatched up a blanket to dry and swaddle it.

Not "it." Him. She had said that this was her brother, and Lord Kenan's heir. What, then, about Randiroc?

Shade brought the baby to his mother, who threw up her hands in horror against him. She couldn't speak with her damaged jaw, but her rejection was explicit.

"What now?" Kindrie asked.

"I take him to Randiroc," said Shade. "If half of what I

guess is true, it's time he concerned himself with the Randir succession." She chucked the hidden baby under the chin and smiled fondly down at him. Tiny fingers curled around her hand. "Until Randiroc decides or he takes a final form, I will call him Jelly."

"Well," said Gorbel, wiping his hands. "That was disgusting. I came up to tell you that the Highlord is in the lower reception hall, asking for you. You should go down to meet him. Now, will someone please call my sister's ladies to attend to her before this gets even more messy?"

VII

IN THE HALL iron squealed and wood groaned. Caldane, Lord Caineron, emerged from the shadows in an over-sized throne mounted on high, tottering wheels, pushed by his first and sixth sons, Grondin and Higron. Both labored and wheezed. They were middle-aged and grossly fat, but nothing compared to their father, who overflowed the slats on which he sat. His swollen, bandaged foot and leg thrust out before him like an obscene proclamation. His weight bowed both wood and iron.

"Heh, heh, heh," he rasped. "The little so-called Highlord has come to call. To what do I owe this honor?"

Torisen stood forth, slim and needle fine. As usual, in accordance with his nickname, he wore black, which accented the white streaks in his hair. These, only recently, he had come to recognize as Shanir traits. His power might have haloed him, if not for the restraint under which he kept it.

"Everyone keeps asking me that," he said, with a pleasant smile, a rebuff in itself to Caldane's glower. "I am concerned about my cousin. He is here, is he not?"

"I didn't say so," Tiggeri murmured aside to his sire. "Why should he be?"

"Because you plainly need a healer," said Torisen. "How long has your leg been so swollen?"

Caldane smirked. "The more of me, the better. The less of you, better still. Less, and less, and less."

"But you still require a healer."

Caldane pouted. "I need no one. I never have. I never will."

"Then I have no hesitation about reclaiming Kindrie Soul-walker. Clearly, he is wasted here."

Kindrie came into the hall, followed by Shade carrying a bundle.

Caldane pummeled the arms of his chair with pudgy fists. "Everyone betrays me!" he whined. "It isn't fair!"

Kirien walked into Kindrie's arms.

"You're late," he said, smiling down at her.

"I know. I'm sorry."

"I think," said Torisen, "that we should be going."

Caldane scowled. "Not without my permission. I think, Highlord, that you shouldn't leave at all. Why prolong the inevitable? You and your pitiful little house are doomed. You were always a cadet branch of the Knorth. The Arrinken should never have turned their backs on Gerridon. Huh. Cats."

Kindrie gulped as Caldane's renewed will beat against him, febrile, rancid. It seemed about to push everything else out, leaving room only for a vast, infantile *me, me, me*.

The crowd of witnesses swayed, baby Jelly screamed, and even Torisen fell back a step.

Don't flinch! Kindrie silently begged his cousin. *If you can't stand up to this man, how can we?*

But the power to resist lay in everyone here, yes, even in him.

Preserve these people, he thought, embracing Kirien. *Preserve your love and yourself, at long last.*

He put Kirien aside and stepped up to Caldane, who regarded him with dull, malicious eyes.

"M'lord, would you be healed? Take my hand."

Caldane's swollen fingers crawled down the arm of his chair, dragging his hand behind them like the obese body of some wounded spider. Then he lunged to grab the healer's slender wrist.

Kindrie gasped with pain . . .

. . . and fell into Caldane's soul-image.

A golden statue bent over him, smirking. Its grip, oh so tight, made the bones in his arm grate together. More golden figures shuffled in to surround him, all muttering:

Give, give, give, or I will take.

In all the days that he had been a prisoner here, had Kindrie ever touched Caldane even with his fingertips? No. This soul-image terrified him, such of it as he had glimpsed in the dreamscape. So cold, so gross, so overwhelming. If he opened himself to it, might it not consume him utterly? But he must try something.

He dropped his free hand to fumble at the bandages around the other's foot. They were tight, so tight, but here was the end tag of one. He loosened it.

Ah!

Skeins of stiff, gilded wrapping fell. The flesh beneath was red and swollen. Then it cracked open. Yellow fluid seeped out to congeal on the floor in a stinking puddle studded with crystalline acid. The leg above began to drain, then the body.

"No!" cried Caldane, clutching at himself as if to hold on. "Not my divine mass!"

His skin collapsed around him into a tent of crumpled, jaundiced folds. At its heart was a scrawny boy, over whom loomed the golden giant that it had lately been.

"Father!" the child Caldane cried up at it. "Can I help it that I am so small? I eat as much as I can, every day, every meal, more and more and more! Please, don't laugh at me!"

As his grip loosened on Kindrie, Kirien drew the healer back, panting, into the reception hall. His wrist felt fractured and blood squelched in his boot, but an internal glimpse of white flowers told him that his soul-image remained intact. That was a relief.

He hadn't known what to expect when he had interacted with Caldane, only that he must try. This revelation of the Caineron's secret weakness came as a surprise.

Caldane huddled back in his chair, staring blindly, mumbling, "Don't laugh, don't laugh...."

Kindrie gulped. It went against his nature to hurt anyone, but surely it was time to speak the truth.

"Caldane, that tub of lard, but inside a puny man was he."

Catching his tone, Ashe stepped forward to take up the parody of Jamethiel's lament: "The Three People he feign would lead ... drunk with swollen pride."

"Wealth and power had he," said the sonorous voice of Director Taur behind her, "but with less sense than in a thimble full of sand. More than death, he feared ridicule. 'Everyone laughs at me,' he said to the darkness that crawled within him. 'How can I make them stop?'"

Lord Caineron cringed back into his tottering chair, whose front wheels lifted off the floor. His sons leaned forward to prop it up.

"Stop," Caldane cried. "Unfair, unfair! I am greater than that. See? I move. I swell. I conquer."

As he spoke, the gilded images in the hall seemed to turn, creaking, toward his tormentors. Seams split. Molten metal leaked out like sweat. Torisen's supporters fell back another step.

"You are hollow," cried a shrill voice from the back, among the Caineron cadets, "and full of crap! You are a liar! Everyone knows it!"

"False, false, false!"

His accuser, a boy, fell in strong convulsions. He twisted and bent over backward until, with a muffled crunch, his spine snapped. His friends bent over him as his breath faltered and failed. Then they rose, growling.

"We are witnesses," they said, and many of the other houses echoed them. "Keep faith with honor or fall. So say we all."

"You threaten me? *Me*?" Caldane laughed, still shaken but wiping the slabber from his lips and trying to rally. "Know your master, brats, and you too, so-called Highlord."

"You," said Ashe, "are mad. Do not seek to hinder our departure . . . or our scorn will never end."

She laughed, a harsh bark of a sound. Others did too, until the hall filled with derisive mirth.

Caldane's mouth flopped open and shut, open and shut. He looked as if he had been slapped in the face with a rotten fish.

The Knorth and their allies withdrew.

"You spoke up to him," said Kirien to Kindrie in wonder.

"Yes. Finally."

"Now," said Torisen as they left Restormir through the ranks of baffled troops who seemed to mirror their lord's confusion, "where do you want to go?"

Kindrie looked at Kirien and smiled. "Home," he said. "Back to Mount Alban."

And so it was done.

⚜ Chapter XV ⚜
A Paper Inferno
High Bashti: Autumn 55

I

HE SAT AT THE FOOT OF HER BED, smiling sweetly at her out of a waxen mask.

"Child, you have been gone so long. Remember those whom you left behind. Remember, at least, me."

Jame indeed recalled that caressing voice which had haunted the nights of her childhood in the Master's House under shadows' eave. She tried to move, to push off the cold hand which lay possessively on her thigh, but her muscles froze and she could not speak.

"Ah, how soon ungrateful children forget. Would you rather that I had left you with your father? Poor Ganth, driven mad by grief and desire. Yes, if he could not have your mother, he wanted you."

Ganth had slammed her against the wall and pinned her there. She could feel his body shudder against her own, man against child.

"How dare you be so much like her?" he had panted

in her face. "How dare you! And yet, and yet, you are . . .
so like."

And then he had kissed her hard, on the mouth.

The memory made her cringe, and unlocked her voice.

"Go away!" she cried at the night. "He was weak and
wounded. You are worse, who would seduce the world!"

Rue stirred at her feet, muttered, and fell back asleep.

Jame edged herself out of the bed so as not to disturb
either her servant or her ounce, who was curled up at her
side and now rolled into the warm depression left by her
body, his paws curled up on his chest. It was a chilly
morning at Campus Kencyrath, close to what passed here
for winter. Let them sleep. She herself was shaken wide
awake. This was the first time she had heard the pallid
specter speak, although she had guessed before who it
was.

Gerridon, in High Bashti? If so, it wasn't for the first
time. He had been Mordaunt's pet (or vice versa) thirty
years ago when the latter had been a mere princeling.
Ever since, when his attention wasn't elsewhere, he had
led the cult of the Deathless. He always followed the same
patterns. Maybe, this time, his plans would succeed,
whatever they were. After all, since the depletion of his
larder of souls, how many tricks did he have left to play?

Paper crinkled under her hand. What, another note
from the Shadow Guild? Unnerving enough that they had
delivered it while she slept.

No place, they meant to imply, *is safe from us*.

"Come," it said.

She dressed in her black *d'hen*, which somehow
seemed appropriate for such business, and left.

The great city was barely awake. Early laborers, coughing, trudged to their jobs. Cook shops threw open their shutters. Dust men plied the streets, hoping that their gleanings would someday amount to piles of treasure. It had been known to happen.

There were signs, also, of last night's tumult: shattered statues, defaced street signs, ash still on the air from multiple fires, words scrawled on marble walls with pitch.

"Keep the dole!" the latter read, often misspelled. "Down with the Tyrant!"

While she had been absent in Transweald, Mordaunt had not endeared himself to his subjects. Among other things, he had closed all theaters except for the god farce, which remained popular in these days of disorder if with ever shifting venues. Suwaeton spoke there freely through his artist Trepsis, to Mordaunt's fury. Also, the king had closed as many temples as he dared. The idea seemed to be that people should worship at his own nascent sanctuary in the palace complex or not at all. This, too, had not been a popular move. Snaggles had told her as much on her return, grinning. He really didn't like the patricians, among whom he apparently did not count the Kencyrath. Further evidence of discord trotted down the street—the city guards either on patrol or bound back to their barracks after a busy night. It seemed debatable who controlled them, the Council or the king. And there was the west bank army, hovering off to the side. The betting shops must be doing great business. Who would win, and at what cost?

Jame walked on to the house in the maze in Thyme Side. The door, as before, was unlocked. Probably no one came here willingly, much less had anything to do with the Guild unless perforce, and then it would be through the crack in the door by the River Thyme. The inside remained dusty and dark, lit at intervals with solitary, dribbling candles, sharply redolent of mouse droppings. Around one bank of shelves, around another, and there was Smeak's alcove with him in it. He rested his head on the small desk. Near his only hand was a cup half full of strong red wine. Beside him stood a branch of lit candles. Before him lay two scrolls.

"Here," he said without looking up, his voice muffled on the curve of his right arm. "Take them and get out."

Jame paused, perplexed. She hadn't asked for anything except the Knorth contract, which he had already delivered.

A candle-cast shadow rippled across the shelves. Unseen nails clutched at Jame's coat and someone breathed hoarsely in her ear. She turned to grapple with what felt like invisible limbs no thicker than rotten sticks and about as strong. Her assailant tripped and fell.

"Don't hurt him!" Smeak cried, his head jerking up in alarm.

"He? Who? Oh."

She fumbled on the floor, gripped a thin arm, and drew it up. There was a chair. When she maneuvered the other onto it, the cushion dented to receive skinny buttocks and dust puffed up to give them further definition.

"Grandmaster?" she asked, remembering stories of the invisible, insane Guild lord, also the shadow that had bent over the young archivist and snickered the last time she had been here.

"My grandfather," said Smeak. "He should be worshipped. Instead, they hunt him."

"Who? Why?"

"On Autumn's Eve they tried to harvest the souls of the sanctified. That didn't work, did it? More fuel for the pyre."

"Heh, heh, heh."

Jame felt fingertips as light as raindrops tap her arm and seek to draw her down. She bent to listen. A sheen of sweat beaded shriveled lips seeming to hover in mid-air. Crusty yellow eyes blinked at her. Of mouth, tongue, and throat there was no sign.

"How far into any orifice can the needles go?" Graykin had asked. Far enough.

"Want to feed their pale prophet, they do," whispered that thread-bare, avid voice, in a mist of spittle. It didn't sound as if he had any teeth. "Heh, heh, heh. Any willing souls would do, you'd think, if they could find them, but how much better the hallowed dead? Didn't work so well with Prestic or with the would-be saints, though, did it? The Guild can kill but it can't reap. Still, they keep trying. I am shadow, pure soul, or so they think. Fools. I eat, I drink, I piss, and am no grist for such demonic mills!"

"I believe you," said Jame. "Smeak, I had some claim to the Knorth scrolls, but why are you offering me these other contracts? I don't even know whom they involve."

He hit the desk, upsetting the cup of wine. Liquid spread like a blood-stain across the ink-blotched table, threatening parchment. Candles tottered. He was obviously drunk.

"You dare to ask that? What choice did you give me, even from the start?"

"What?"

"Think! I was only a boy, on my first blooding. The Guild Master arranged everything. He said we had to kill every Knorth Highborn female we found, and that was only you. All the rest were long dead, by the contract that you demanded of me. Don't pretend this is about anything else!"

Light dawned, and it dazzled her.

"You were one of a casting of shadow assassins who tried to kill me when I was in the Women's Halls of my brother's keep," she said. "Years ago, when I first reached the Riverland. The blonde apprentice."

"Yes!" He beat the table again. The stump of his left arm twitched as if like a phantom limb it would have followed suit. "You lured us up into that high chamber. The others cast their souls after you. You were as good as dead. Then you said—something."

"A master-rune."

"And a great wind came. It blew out the stained-glass window. It sucked out my companions' souls. They died of shock. I was scared. I ran away."

She remembered him fleeing, the only one to escape. "But we met again, outside Wilden."

"I caught up with you. We fought."

That was putting it generously. He had attacked her, at the same time pleading that she let him kill her. Journeyman thief had stared at apprentice assassin.

"*Please? Please?*" she had cried, outraged. "You want it, you earn it!"

Instead, she had kicked him into a cloud-of-thorns bush where he had floundered until a Molocar bitch had descended like an avalanche upon him. His scream echoed in her memory, cut short by the hound's jaws.

"I thought your skull had been crushed," she said.

He laughed, with an edge of hysteria. "Better that it had been. Instead, the brute only mangled my arm. Only! It had to be amputated. Lady Rawneth helped me. I don't know what I babbled to her in my delirium, but she was pleased enough to send me on the long, painful journey home. Because of my grandfather, the Guild found me work here in the archives. Not as a proper assassin, mind you. They sneer at me in passing, when they notice me at all. Who else, though, would have employed me even here, maimed as I was? But they won't continue to do so if they learn that I ran. Twice. It's all your fault!"

What, that he had come to kill her? That she hadn't let him?

Graykin rushed into the room and grabbed Jame's arm. "You have to get out," he panted. "They're coming!"

"What? Who?"

Scrolls rustled. Jame grabbed the two on the desk, thrust them into her sleeve, and backed away. A wind seemed to blow through the stacks, a rush of bodies seen only in flashes of bare skin, a hand here, half of a face there where neither *mere* tattoos nor dye covered flesh. So many yellow, blood-shot eyes. They must have seized the grandmaster, for his impression lifted from the cushion and the chair itself toppled over backward. He squawked and thrashed. Candles fell over. Scrolls spilled off shelves.

"Your soul, old man," someone hissed. "Give it to us so that we may taste immortality!"

"Fools, fools," he cried. "You and your master both! Haven't you learned yet that murder and dismemberment aren't enough? I do not yield!"

Blood speckled the outlines of a bony, contorted face. Someone had punched him in the nose, which bled freely. Then they drew back, their silhouettes freckled with red.

"Yield, yield, yield . . ."

A bloody line across his collar-bone marked the track of a *mere* knife's blade. Another appeared down the heaving sternum, then across the major pectoral of the right breast, then across the left, jagged as he bucked in their unseen grip. It was the pattern of cuts called kuth, a mark of shame, the precursor to being flayed alive.

Smeak gagged and overthrew the desk. Lit candles, spilled wine, and molten wax flew onto the detritus of tumbled scrolls. Flames kindled.

"You . . . you bastards! Who are you to judge him or me? He is so much better than any of you, while I have never been good enough. But we both serve our king. What do you serve except that false phantom, immortality? Burn, damn you, burn!"

He stumbled over to his grandfather and gathered him up in his one good arm. They clung to each other, the old man's blood painting them both, while all around flames climbed from shelf to shelf with eager flickering fingers. Walls of fire ignited to the left, to the right, then toppled inward in waves of heat.

"Go," said Graykin, grabbing Jame by the scuff of the neck. "Now."

They were swept out of the archives, through the halls, into the street, by a rush of near-invisible bodies—the assassins, panicking. Heat licked after them, and tongues of flame, and screams. Not all, perhaps not even half, had escaped. The door of the archive opened onto an inferno. Then the hungry fire sucked it shut with a slam. Smeak and his grandfather were gone.

Where was the fire watch? Granted, they had been out all night, but still . . . ! Bells, whistles, and hoof-beats echoed in the adjacent streets of warehouses. None, however, came here.

Graykin and Jame huddled against the wall across the street. Already, its bricks were beginning to steam with radiated heat.

"Well . . ." said Gray, panting, one hand pressed to his thin chest, "the Guild has used those contracts for millennia . . . for blackmail. Everyone knows that. It was a major source of their influence . . . and a way of life. Why d'you think your precious archivist crumbled so easily? You may just have . . . broken their back."

"I?"

If so, though, good. They had nearly broken her house. "Damn you," as Smeak had said. How better for That-Which-Destroys to work, even if she hadn't intended it.

But that didn't answer all questions.

"What are you doing here?" she asked Graykin.

He shrugged. "Followed you, didn't I? Did you get the contracts?"

Jame touched them, thrust up her sleeve, crumbling at the edges with heat and age. "Yes, but how did you know?"

"I'm not sure how you did it . . . but you blackmailed that archivist to get the Knorth contract. Didn't you?"

"It seems so, although I didn't realize it at the time."

He looked at her askance. "Strange, strange girl. But you have your mysteries as I have mine. You only choose to tell me so much. I could do more if you fully trusted me."

"I can't trust you with what I don't yet myself understand."

He snorted. "This isn't quite what I expected of you in terms of morals. Still, you aren't stupid. Given Smeak's background of blackmail, what else would he respect, and why else would he give you anything? Much less, why would he cave when I merely hinted that I was your agent? Hence these contracts."

"Yes, but who are they for?"

He smirked. "Look and see. Their choices are logical, when you think of it. You should be pleased."

She held first one contract and then the other up to the morning light and read the letters blazing through.

"Sweet Trinity," she said, letting them roll up again, slipping them back into the full sleeve of her *d'hen*. "Now what?"

II

WALKING BACK TOWARD THE CAMPUS, she thought not only about the fire, and the deaths, and the contracts, but also about the Grandmaster's final, defiant words: "I do not yield!"

She had wondered before if the reaping of a soul worked only with the consent of the victim. Smug Gerridon believed in the power of seduction. Who, after all, could resist him? The Dream-weaver had seduced in order to reap, but only for Gerridon's benefit. As such, had she been an unfallen darkling? Jame wanted to believe so. At the Res aB'tyrr she herself had been tempted to take what her tavern audience freely offered her in that perversion of the Great Dance that the first Jamethiel had performed. The would-be dead saints, by contrast, had no consent to give. Perhaps the already sanctified and deified did. The living could resist, if they were strong enough. It was still a puzzle, but worth thought.

She heard a squad of the city guard come up behind her and stepped aside into a doorway to let them pass. They swerved to surround her.

"You," said the captain. "Where did you come from?"

"Thyme Side," she answered, wondering why they asked.

"Come with us."

They grabbed her arms. Their pace lifted her off her feet and their hob-nailed boots kicked her in the shins. The warehouses around the Guild's archives had burst into flame. Who would have guessed that parchment could burn so fiercely or the fire spread so fast?

"Arsonist," one of her captors snarled. "D'you think you can burn out honest folk?"

"Filthy foreigner," another growled. "The Council wants to see you."

She shouldn't have worn the *d'hen*, Jame realized. They didn't recognize her as an honored guest of the city, nor in this mood would they listen.

They hauled her north, not westward toward the palace

mound as she had thought they would but to the Tigganis hill to the east of it.

The Tigganis compound was smaller and more kempt than King Mordaunt's. Family members walked in the gardens. Children played on the grass. Guards wandered around the edges of the precinct, looking calm but purposeful.

Jame was dragged into an inner chamber with high marble walls, tessellated floors, and alcoves graced with many statues. The guards left her there, somewhat at a loss. What next?

A stocky figure appeared at the head of a flight of stairs, black robed, veiled, descending. Jame recognized that heavy brow, those fine, unhappy eyes.

"Lady Pensa," she said, with a salute, equal to equal.

The other paused, frowning. "Do I know you? I do! Lady Jameth, welcome to my house, and apologies for the manner of your arrival. But what were you doing in Thyme Side when it burst into flames?"

"I had business in the archives of the Shadow Guild."

"Ah, I would like to hear about that."

I deal with politics now, Jame thought, *but also with personalities. Truth or dare? Truth.*

"The fire there arose in part by accident," she said. "There was a conflict between Guild members. A number of them burned alive."

Pensa continued her descent.

"I thought they would fight, sooner or later," she said. "The traditional who support the king against those who follow the Deathless. Now, are you saying that they have killed their own?"

"Yes. A Grandmaster and his grandson. Or if they didn't, the fire did."

"And all of their contracts are gone? Oh." She sat down on the stairs and clasped her hands tightly in her lap. "I hoped that those would prove their guilt in my father's death, also that they would disclose who commissioned it."

Jame considered this. The contracts prickled in her sleeve, lucky not to have been smashed to pieces by the guards' rough treatment. She drew out one, checked that it was right, and handed it to Pensa.

"This belongs to you."

Pensa unrolled it. She caught the knack of reading the *mere* ink faster than Jame had, and stared.

"Oh," she said blankly. "Oh! I guessed that the Guild was responsible, but that Mordaunt commissioned it...." She looked up at Jame. "And you simply give this to me?"

Jame shrugged, feeling awkward. "I don't know what will follow, for good or ill. With my nature, it could go either way. It just seems . . . right."

Yet, in her sleeve, was the other contract. What to do with that?

Pensa cleared her throat. "You do realize," she said, "that the Guild depends on blackmail."

"So I've been told."

"This could shatter it."

"I hope that it will."

"So do I. Let the poison work."

Jame sat down on the step beside her. "I have to ask," she said. "How is your father?"

Pensa laughed, an unhappy sound. "I visit him in the

Necropolis as often as I can, and bring him flowers, and talk to him. He can't reply. I never did find his tongue."

Jame remembered the dog slinking out of the ruined mausoleum, something long and red in its jaws. That had been when she had first ridden into High Bashti. She hadn't told Pensa then. She didn't now.

The girl dragged the back of her hand across her face, smearing tears, and laughed again. "The funny thing is, while he doesn't heal, he also doesn't decay, and he is still dead. Do you think he might become a saint or god after all?"

That was a rather terrible question. Lord Prestic was grossly mutilated, held together by a daughter's love but also by her stitches, each one of which was a curse against his murderers who had not yet been called to account. What kind of afterlife could such a monstrosity expect?

"I don't know," said Jame. "Things work out in this city differently than I would ever have expected."

⟪⟫ Chapter XVI ⟪⟫
Karkinaroth

High Bashti and Karkinaroth:
Autumn 58–Winter 12

I

SOON AFTER THIS came another round of games about which Jame had entirely forgotten. Before the Kencyrath had arrived in High Bashti, King Mordaunt had negotiated with Prince Uthecon for a match between Bashti's Knorth and Karkinor's Caineron. It was meant to be a friendly contest. The prince, elderly, ailing, didn't believe in violence, and his only territorial aims centered on the gold-rich Forks. Those, however, were against the Midlands and their Randir troops, where conflict had come to a stalemate due in part to bribes from the Forkites and to Riverland politics. Most of the prince's Caineron troops had been stationed near the northern borders since the previous summer while the Commandant tried to untangle matters.

High Bashti, of course, was also disturbed and getting worse every day. Jame didn't want to leave it in such a state, but she felt that she must.

"I promised Timmon that I would check on Lyra," she explained to Harn. "Already, I've put that off much too long."

"Karkinor doesn't ask for the rathorn," said Harn, absentmindedly. He was pacing the front line of Kendar practicing the kantirs of fire-leaping Senethar in the campus training field. Exercises such as this had been going on since the Transweald expedition in preparation for the next set.

"Ha!" cried a score of throats as a bristling hedge of fists punched the air.

"However," said Harn, countering the nearest strike, turning to pace back, "the prince has asked for you."

"Oh," Jame said, blankly. She had met young Prince Odalian, the previous ruler of Karkinor and briefly Lyra's consort, but never his uncle and successor, Uthecon. Why would he ask for her now? "Then I suppose I really should go. Not with Jurik, though."

Harn gave a harsh laugh. "His performance in the Transweald did not endear him to the king, or to his mother, or to me. It would be hard to do worse. Also, most of his comrades have left him. I understand that he beat one of them to death and left the body beside the road."

"Cervil," said Jame, sickened. She hadn't liked the simpering Bashtiri, but she also hadn't heard this final detail of his fate.

"That was the name. The last I heard, Jurik was in nominal command of the king's ruffians, bedizened up to the eyebrows."

How did Harn feel about that? Perhaps, at last, he was getting annoyed enough to shake off his officious, ineffectual offspring. It might help that the Kendar were matrilineal. Mothers had primary responsibility for their children, not fathers. Queen Vestula already had much to answer for.

Still, Jame worried about Harn.

"Who leads the expedition this time?" she asked.

Harn caught a flying foot, twisted it, and sent a randon sprawling. Three in the second line, entangled, also fell.

"Watch your balance," he growled. "I lead."

"Pardon, Commander, but you surprise me. Before, Mordaunt wanted you here, to protect him. Now he's in more danger even than before."

"Karkinor is a sideshow for Mordaunt and he doesn't like you for some reason. Or, for that matter, me. He would rather have both of us in Karkinor than here. The queen has been taunting him with tales, some of which he no doubt believes, some of which, regrettably, are true. After all, the man can't seem to sire legitimate heirs, yet he must have one. Jurik came from somewhere. Also, Jurik blames me for his disastrous mission to Transweald."

"But you weren't even there!"

Harn snorted. "Oh, but my troops were, and they, you understand, represent my will. Jurik claims that they never gave him a chance. They hung back, were surly, and defied his orders. That last applies especially to you. Eventually you left him alone, paralyzed by your witch Damson, on the road, in the rain, while you went on to lead the company to Wealdhold without him."

Had they really not talked about this before? Yes. Jame hadn't wanted to bring up the embarrassing details, and Harn hadn't asked her.

"Well, that last at least is partially true," she said. "It was raining. He wouldn't move. We were running out of time."

"I understand that. Others have reported to me even if you didn't. And you humiliated him in combat with that rathorn of yours."

"Only with his help."

"Huh. His stories of the wolver hunt, the Burnt Man, and the rout in the Weald are harder to believe."

"Agreed. What do we Kencyr know of such things? But the Burnt Man let us go and the Deep Weald wolvers escorted us out of the wilderness. Beyond that, what can I say? Jurik panicked."

"And in his mad scramble to escape he left troops behind."

"That too."

Harn sighed, his broad shoulders slumping. "If only he could be truthful about something. But note: he hates you."

"I gathered that. What can I do about it, though?"

"Stay out of his way."

"So, we are sent traipsing off to Karkinaroth."

"Yes. But a word of caution. We haven't fought the Caineron since the White Hills, unless you count Tiggeri's attack on Tagmeth."

"Believe me, I haven't forgotten it."

"Still, he wasn't acting then on his father's orders. That was personal."

Tiggeri had thought that Jame was sheltering his sister Must and their child Benj, born of rape, but Must was dead by then in childbirth and her infant son had been taken for safety behind one of Tagmeth's gates. He was still there. Tiggeri had missed that. He had not, however, forgiven Jame for interfering.

"Surely Tiggeri isn't at Karkinaroth."

"I didn't say that he was. The thing is, what stories has he told his father? Then too, Caldane has gotten more and more unstable, and it affects his Kendar. I don't know what we will find in Karkinor."

With that she had to be content.

II

THE GAMES, or whatever Prince Uthecon had in mind, were scheduled to start on the 12th of Winter. In some ways, they were like those at Transweald, most notably in that no program had yet been announced. Therefore, the Knorth had no idea what skills they were supposed to display or what trials they must undertake. Harn thought that the prince had made the initial arrangements, and then had become too ill to be more specific. Subsequent correspondence had been vague and signed by Uthecon's chamberlain, Malapirt, a name Jame remembered from Gothregor without fondness.

On the other hand, this was a much smaller expedition consisting of twenty contestants with twenty assistants and a much smaller baggage train. There would also be no hangers-on. The Transweald expedition had scared all such off, not that they would have been welcome in any case. Instead, all the participants were Knorth randon or sargents, whose backs stiffened whenever Harn Grip-hard passed. This was to be the military excursion that it should be, not the pleasure party to Transweald that Jurik had planned.

What else? thought Jame as she arranged her own affairs and worried about them.

The Danior, for one, had been recalled from Nether Bashti to serve in the army at the capital. Mordaunt apparently trusted them, and some Knorth. Mint and Dar, at least, were still employed as royal guards.

Who, however, trusted the king? The Council was still enraged by his increased call for taxes, even though he claimed that they were for the greater glory of the city.

Pensa challenged that, and the Council supported her. At last she had found her voice, and her audience. So far, however, she hadn't mentioned the contract for her father's murder. Jame supposed that she was biding her time. It added a note of uncertainty to Jame's own plans but, on the whole, she was glad that she had passed on the parchment. What happened next was up to Pensa.

III

THE EXPEDITION left two days later on the 60th, the last day of Autumn, to no cheers or bands playing *umph-pah-pah* but with a purposeful stride. The roads were good, the weather better, enough for them to make at least forty miles a day down Thyme Street to the River Road. That was perhaps three hundred miles—seven or eight days.

Some thirty miles down the Silver, Karkinor had recently rebuilt a bridge across the river that allowed travelers to take a shortcut across the toe of Karkinor to the capital of Karkinaroth. They came to this on the 9th.

Harn crossed first, to demonstrate that it was safe. No bridge across the Silver was completely trustworthy thanks to the frequent writhing of the River Snake. Jame followed as the second in command.

She had asked about that.

"You have at least three dozen randon senior to me. What will they think?"

"That you're the Knorth lordan," he had said, "arguably the highest ranking Knorth with the Southern Host. Also, that you saved the Transweald expedition from disaster. Maybe they could have done as well, but they weren't there, and it was a tricky situation."

So Jame rode second. Was it only her imagination that the stones beneath her horse's feet quivered under the pressure of the rushing water? Currents sucked and swirled at the piers below. The horse stepped warily.

Bloop, said a minor maelstrom, with a flash of silver scales, and the span above it shivered.

On the eleventh day of their journey, they crossed a more secure bridge over the River Tardy with Karkinaroth looming ahead of them.

Jame had last seen it in ruins, crouching down within itself as the Kencyr temple inside had collapsed. Lower and lower it had gone, drawing in on itself. The rumble had gone on and on, in the air, in the ground, in one's bones, until at last it had died out of each in turn.

Silence.

Then below in the city, shouting had begun, and the howl of dogs.

That was then. This was now.

Prince Uthecon had rebuilt, nearly as grand as before. Walls, towers, turrets, banners . . . what lacked but the patina of age and, perhaps, of substance? To Jame, the whole structure felt misty, ephemeral. She wondered if she should enter it at all given that compromised architecture tended to collapse when she was around, but here she was, with no place else to go, following Harn.

They rode into the palace's main courtyard, where baggage was reclaimed and the horses were led off by liveried grooms to the stables. A flight of steps led up to the gilded front door. On the threshold above stood Malapirt, clothed in a robe of orange and puce swirls that stood out vividly against the palace's pale pink walls. So did his white teeth against a face nearly as dark as Brier's. Around his neck, in further contrast, he wore the ornate golden chain of a chamberlain.

"Welcome to Karkinaroth!" he said to Harn, spreading his wide-sleeved arms in greeting. "His Highness, Prince Uthecon, regrets that his health does not permit him to express his salutations in person."

"And Lyra?" asked Jame, stepping forward.

Malapirt's mouth twitched, as if jerked up at one corner. "Ah, lady. How pleasant to see you again, and once again fully clothed. What delight is denied me. The princess attends His Highness, as any good consort should. I doubt if she has either the time or the inclination for idle chatter."

"For that matter," said Harn, bulking large at the foot of the stair, "where is the Commandant?"

"You refer, I assume, to your esteemed colleague, Sheth Sharp-tongue. He has spent most of the summer and fall at the Forks, tending to the prince's business. We expected him back for your arrival, but some matter has called him to the northern border of Karkinor. Our business here will commence when he returns. In the meantime, you are our honored guests."

They followed him into the cavernous entry hall and were directed from there up a sweeping flight of stairs to their second-story quarters. Jame noted that the plaster walls were cracked here and there, with dust dribbling down onto the steps.

"I don't like this," she said to Harn under her breath as they went. "Too many people are missing, and I don't trust our dear chamberlain."

"Huh. Eyes wary, ears open."

Most of the company was assigned to a spacious dormitory, reached after many curving corridors farther back in the structure. Harn had a suite next door which he was to share with his servant Secur. Jame and Rue were lodged in the room opposite.

By now, it was late afternoon with a formal dinner soon to come. Before that, however, there was time for a hasty bath in a more luxurious tub than Jame had seen in years, fitted with lion's feet which she half expected to walk off with her.

When she emerged, Rue ruthlessly toweled her down despite her protests, then shoved her into a chair and attacked her wet, black mane of hair. After hard travel, the Merikit braids for which she had become famous were frayed. It took both Rue's horse-comb and Jame's claws to disentangle them, then their combined efforts to braid them up again slick and intricate enough for company— not that anyone here was likely to know that the twenty braids on one side represented men she had been credited by the Merikit with having killed and seven on the other with daughters that she had presumably sired. Merikit society was complicated.

After that, Rue presented Jame with clean underclothes, then shrugged her into her court coat, a rich patchwork of heirloom fabrics donated and stitched together by her fellow cadets, a treasured possession.

There was a full-length mirror in the room. They both looked at her reflection.

"You clean up good," said Rue gruffly, and slapped her on the back.

The dinner warning sounded below in the banqueting hall with horns and a commanding rattle of drums.

The Knorth descended. All, including Harn, at most other times slovenly, looked their best. He, Jame, Malapirt, and various minor Karkinoran nobles sat at the high table. Down the right side of the hall were the Caineron participants; down the left side, the Knorth. This, Jame thought, did not bode well. Her people and the Brandan at Wealdhold had mixed. They had understood that they were all Kencyr in league, if need be, against their Central Lands paymasters. These Caineron seemed to have their own scheme. They hunched over their food and traded whispers. Laughter rippled from one end of the table to the other and many sly glances were cast across the hall. They reminded Jame of nasty little boys plotting mayhem.

Sheth's second in command, Marham, was there. Jame hadn't met him before, but he had a good reputation among the randon, as befit anyone in Sheth's favor. However, his gloating expression made her skin crawl. With Sheth absent, he had been let off the leash, and something within him obviously relished it.

The food was sumptuous, if overly rich, and the wine free-flowing. Harn partook sparingly. His troops, observing him, followed suit. Jame herself had only been drunk twice in her life and had no urge to repeat the experience, especially in such company. The Caineron drank, and giggled, and snorted.

The Knorth, eventually, went up to bed.

"That was uncomfortable," said Jame to Rue.

Out in the hall, Harn started shouting for his servant Secur, who had disappeared.

Jame was about to shed the court coat when someone scratched on the door. Before she could answer, it burst open and Lyra Lack-wit rushed in in a swirl of crimson skirts and a tight, pearl-strewn waist-coat.

"Oh!" she cried, throwing herself into Jame's arms. "They said that you had come but didn't want to see me! I couldn't believe that!"

"Of course not," Jame said, returning the girl's embrace.

Lyra burst into tears. "It's been awful! Not the prince. He's ever so kind. But all of his relatives! They swarm and swarm and swarm like so many flies, waiting for him to die, and then they'll eat me up too! I don't want anything to do with any of them. I want to go home!"

Home was likely to be worse than she remembered, thought Jame, given Caldane's decline, but still . . .

Lyra snuffled into a lacy handkerchief, then stuffed it, sodden, into her sleeve. "Oh. I was sent with a message," she said, like a child faithfully remembering a duty. "His Highness, Prince Uthecon, would be pleased to grant you an audience. Now."

"He would? I mean, of course, if you will show me the way."

The way led up more flights of stairs, back into the palace's main tower. Up and up and up. Jame told herself that it was only imagination that made the spire seem to sway, although more plaster dust dribbled on the floor. Who had overseen the rebuilding of this structure anyway—Uthecon or Malapirt?

Here was a spacious tower room rimmed with windows. A cool breeze blew sheer curtains in and out, in and out.

Furious play on the floor froze at their entrance. Six pairs of blue eyes stared at them. Tails twitched and rose.

"Oh," said Jame, going down on her knees. "Ounce cubs!"

A litter of them tumbled into her arms, sniffing, nuzzling, waving their paws in the air. They might be nine or ten weeks old. Their mother, a royal gold, approached with more deliberation, inspected Jame's coat, which probably smelled of Jorin, and retreated with tacit approval.

Lyra scooped up a cub. "This is Smokie, a silver smoke ounce. The prince says he will give her to me when she's old enough, any day now."

The cub was white, dappled and pointed with blue-gray fur—paws, mask, and tail. Her eyes were wide and luminously blue. She licked Jame's nose.

"Oh," said Jame again, cuddling her. "What a sweetheart."

"The prince raises them," said Lyra proudly. "He loves them. They love him."

The chamber, however, was strewn with moldy food, urine-soaked bedding, and feces. Whoever cared for the prince cared less for his pets, or perhaps in equal measure. Lyra led Jame to a canopied bed. Gauzy hangings flexed in the air, but could not contain the stench within. Prince Uthecon lay on silken sheets in his own filth. His eyes were filmy and anxious, his breath labored. One side of his face drooped and drooled. He seemed, however, to smile at Jame, and mumbled something that she didn't understand.

"He says that he is pleased to meet you," said Lyra.

"You can understand him?"

"Oh, yes. No one else can, though. Some of them used to come to me to translate, but they didn't listen. I've told him, oh, so much about you."

He mumbled again, and fumbled at Jame's hand.

"He says that he sent for you, hoping that you will protect me," Lyra reported.

"I will," said Jame.

IV

BY NOW, the eleventh shortening day of winter was drawing to a close. Shadows stretched over the city, reaching eastward away from the setting sun. The city hummed, consumed with its own affairs, while palace towers jutted up into the fading light.

Jame followed the way down to the second floor. Her instinct for mazes, she noted, was still strong, once she had seen the way.

Harn came grumbling to the door when she knocked.

"Have you found him yet?" he demanded, by which she knew that Secur was still missing.

"No, Commander, but there is this."

She told him what she had discovered in the high tower.

"Huh," he said. "Come with me."

The dormitory was full of Kendar preparing for bed.

"Volunteers!" Harn barked.

All rose. This was Harn Grip-hard. One didn't ask questions.

Jame led them up to the chamber where the wind blew in one window and out the other to a billowing of curtains. Here she introduced the commander to the prince, who greeted his visitor with a tremulous, broken smile.

Harn surveyed the filthy room. "Right," he said to his troops. "Clean up this mess."

They attacked the piles of waste and shoveled them out the windows. Lyra shoved the ounce cubs out of the way despite their mother, who hissed and jumped up onto the prince's bed. She meant to protect him. Her cubs scrambled up after her except for Smokie whom Lyra grabbed and held despite her protests.

Harn picked up Uthecon, an armful of bones, while the Kendar chased off the ounce family and stripped the bed.

Soiled sheets fluttered down into an interior courtyard far below. Somewhere, someone had found fresh linens. These were spread, the prince reinstalled. He patted Harn's arm and mouthed his thanks.

"This is horrible," Jame said as they descended. "What can we do about it?"

He grunted. "Only what is possible. D'you think we can save the world?"

Jame sighed. "I rather hoped so, but then who am I to talk?"

V

IN THE MORNING, another two Knorth were missing. It seemed that they had gotten up separately in the night to relieve themselves, and had not come back.

"Could they have gotten lost?" wondered Rue.

"The garderobe is just down the hall," Jame said. "No. Something else is going on."

This was to have been the first day of the games. Instead, the Caineron didn't even appear for breakfast. Neither did any Karkinoran nobles or the servants. The palace seemed to be deserted.

Lyra showed up at this point to announce that she too was hungry. Moreover, no one had fed the prince or the ounces.

"Right," said Harn. "First, we find the kitchen. Then we continue to search for our people."

Lyra brightened. "Oh, I can lead you to the cook rooms!"

Jame assumed that she often raided them. The girl she remembered would do that, as during the rescue of Graykin when she and Lyra had unexpectedly come face to face in Restormir's pantry thanks to a run-away chicken.

"Do you know the palace well?" she asked.

Lyra beamed. "Yes, I've spent a lot of time exploring it. That was what I thought you would do. Besides, I was bored."

Here, as she said, were the kitchens on the ground floor, a complex of pantries for fresh food, storage for nonperishables, roasting rooms, stew pots, bakeries, and butteries. All had been abandoned, it seemed, in haste. Chopped vegetables wilted on the block. Roasts were scorched on one side, raw on the other. Bread crusts blackened in the oven. Soup boiled over.

A meal was scrounged from this chaos and as much as was salvageable was set aside for later in the day. Lyra scraped up porridge for the prince and minced meat for the cubs. A Kendar took these from her and went up into the tower to feed the inmates, also to deal with any residual or resultant mess. No one questioned that the Kencyr had become responsible for the prince, at least as long as they were there.

The palace was complicated, if crumbling. More plaster rattled down. Walls groaned and cracked. It made Jame cringe every time this happened, remembering that previous cataclysmic collapse. Was it her imagination or did Prince Uthecon's labored breath now drive the curtains in and out, in and out?

Lyra stayed below to help the Knorth with their search for their comrades.

"I get the feeling," said Jame to Harn, "that the games have already begun, but no one has told us the rules."

The day progressed. Two more Knorth disappeared. By now, most were going about in five-squad units. Some reported glimpses of flitting, outlandish figures, others of a solitary form in white, wax-face.

What, thought Jame, *are the Deathless involved now too? How and why?*

And who, more worrying, were the other figures?

She went with Lyra and Rue to explore the most obscure hiding spaces within the deep palace, of which there were many. The structure seemed to be full of dead ends, of doors opening on blank walls or onto empty shafts. Windows, likewise, sometimes led outside, but just as often their stained-glass panes faced internal corridors lit with branches of candles where these hadn't burned down to the sockets. The palace had been confusing before. It was worse now.

Low whistles sounded around them as they moved, now before, now behind. Who was signaling? Figures flitted by corners. Then they unexpectedly came face to face with one. It was presumably a Kendar, but with white streaks painted on its face and black kohl around its eyes and mouth. It—he?—rushed them. Jame slipped aside and tripped him. Rue dropped on his back and wrestled his arms behind him to be bound by his own belt. They turned him over.

"Don't cut me!" he cried, cringing. "Don't cut me!"

"Why would we?" Jame asked, puzzled.

They did gag him, however, and left him where he lay, threshing and trying to whistle around the gag.

"We need to get back to our own people," said Rue.

Jame agreed.

At a wrong turn, though, they found themselves in an upper chamber below the prince's suite. It seemed to be designed for intimate dinners, but food lay rotting on the tables, infested with maggots, and flies buzzed over it. Also, there were desiccated bodies sprawled over the plates or tumbled into the floor. Judging by their rich robes, they were nobles, and some wore chains of office similar to Malapirt's. Could this be the rest of the prince's household? If so, who had killed them? When? Why?

"This is a charnel-house," said Jame, stepping back as if from an abomination, which it was.

Otherwise, they found desolation: stale rooms long untended, dust-balls in the halls, cobwebs draping corners.

"How long d'you think it's been like this?" asked Rue.

"Since last summer, when the prince fell ill," said Lyra. "At least, that's when I first noticed it. Chamberlain Malapirt took charge of more and more, and consulted the prince less and less. People disappeared." She shivered. "Now I've seen where some of them went."

"In short," said Jame, "it was a palace coup with murderous intent. Poor Uthecon. He had no way to fight back."

Another turn placed them in a hall which once might have held the royal guard. Tables and benches were pushed back against the walls between meals, the floor cleared for pallets that had never been laid out. Their feet echoed hollowly under a high ceiling. Other feet echoed too. Figures flowed through the door and moved along the walls, spreading out to surround them.

"Eek!" said Lyra.

"Run," Jame told her, and she did.

The intruders parted to let her pass. By that, Jame knew who they were, if there had been any question before: Caineron would not attack their lord's daughter.

"Get help!" Rue shouted after her.

There were perhaps twenty of them with painted faces and knives. They circled the two Knorth, chuckling.

"Here, chickee, chickee, chickee . . ."

Jame drew a deep breath, extended her claws, and screamed. As the rathorn battle cry deepened to a roar, both she and Rue sprang forward, taking their enemies by surprise. Some Caineron tripped over each other, trying to get out of the way. Others, however, closed in. Jame slashed at them, ripping cloth, ripping skin, and slid past them with wind-blowing when they slashed back.

At first she sensed Rue at her back, but then they were separated. Twenty against two were not good odds to begin with. This was worse.

Someone kicked her from behind and she crashed to her knees. Hands seized her hands, nails still out, and stretched them out to either side. She couldn't get free. She couldn't get up. Fingers twined in her braids and jerked her head back by their roots. Straining to turn, out of the corner of an eye she saw the flash of a knife.

"Don't cut me!" the Caineron had cried. "Don't cut me!"

A figure in a pale robe entered the room and approached her, its waxen mask fixed in a smile. A voice spoke softly through its motionless lips.

"Now you will see," it said, "what it means to defy your superiors."

At that point, Harn Grip-hard arrived with a bellow, twelve Knorth behind him. They were outnumbered, but they swept the hall clear of Caineron within seconds.

Harn picked Jame up off the floor and shook her.

"What are you playing at?" he roared in her face. "You little fool, why d'you always go off on your own like this?"

Jame realized that she had scared him half witless and now he was on the edge of a berserker flare. Still, she could only take so much of being man-handled in a day, much less within fifteen minutes. Her own temper flared. She rotated her hands in his grip and put the tips of her unsheathed claws against his inner wrists, over the throbbing pulse.

"Put. Me. Down."

Lyra burst in at the door. "I found them!" she cried. "They're dead. All of them. And . . . and . . ."

But here she fell prey to strong hysterics and made no more sense.

Harn and Jame looked at each other. He still held her suspended in mid-air and she still had her claws poised over his veins. She withdrew them. He put her down. They both turned toward Lyra who had collapsed, wailing, into Rue's arms.

"Show us," said Jame.

Still babbling with shock, Lyra led them to a closet. Five bodies were stuffed into it in a tangle of limbs, with room for more on top. Harn's servant Secur was at the bottom of the heap, identifiable by his wooden foot sticking out. All had had their throats cut. Even more shocking, when they were pulled out and sorted, was that each had been scalped.

"'Don't cut me,'" Jame said. "Was this what the Caineron meant? Oh. I've just realized what game we're playing. It comes early, but this is Tentir's Winter War."

Harn was sitting on the floor with Secur's head in his lap. He kept gesturing as if to stroke the old man's gray locks, but they were gone, leaving red ruin. A massive rage built in his eyes. Jame knelt before him and put her hands on his shoulders.

Ancestors, please, let me deal with this, she thought, even as she felt the berserker surge within him.

He lay his servant down and rose, Jame rising with him, to her feet. The other Kendar drew back.

"I will kill whoever did this," he said thickly. "I will kill . . ."

His hands rose as if to rend. So he might have looked just before he tore apart the Kencyr who had dared to taunt him, so many years ago. The room seemed to distort. Berserkers were the Kendar equivalent of the Highborn Shanir, which also had its problems with rage. Both could warp the world. Now everyone else had backed up to the walls, leaving Harn at the center of an apocalypse about to explode. Jame threw her arms around him.

Hold on, hold on . . .

"Think," she said to him, trying to reach his rational mind. "Think. What is the goal of the Winter War?"

He blinked down at her, his mind finally, reluctantly, engaging.

"To capture the opponent's flag."

"But what else counts in the final tally? Seizing the scarves of the enemy. It's called 'scalping.' It takes cadets out of play unless someone restores their scarves to them."

Harn still looked dangerous. "Are you saying that the Caineron are claiming literal scalps?"

"Wait a minute," said Rue. "Lady, in the war your scarf was worth as much as our house banner. We don't have a flag here, but we have your braids, and your scalp."

"Which they nearly got," Jame said grimly.

A Knorth Kendar skidded into the hallway leading to the closet and stopped short, aghast at what he saw.

"Commander," he gasped, wrenching himself back to his message. "The Commandant has just ridden into the courtyard. He brings company."

VI

THEY ARRIVED in the entry hall just as Sheth Sharptongue entered it. In recognition of the warmer clime, the Commandant wore a coat of black silk, elegantly figured, flowing. He smiled at the welcomers, with only a twitch of the lip at the absence of Malapirt or the prince. With him, several paces back, came a young man with golden hair and a rich if dusty coat.

"Timmon!" cried Lyra, and rushed to embrace him.

"Here now," he said, enfolding her, "has it been so bad?"

"Yes! Yes! Yes!"

His eyes found Jame. "I entrusted her to you."

"You shuffled her off on me. I'm glad to see you, though, as she apparently is too. What happened?"

He smiled crookedly. "I slipped my mother's minders and came south. The Ardeth randon let me through Hathir. The Randir in Midlands caught up with me at the border to Karkinor. I think my mother sent a rider to the Randir there. She still has some influence with Lady Rawneth, or perhaps vice versa. They would have packed me back home, but then the Commandant arrived and ordered them off."

"One should not," said the Commandant mildly, "treat a randon officer so dismissively. Not even a mother."

"So here I am," concluded Timmon with an engaging smile.

He still trusted his charm to win him all contests, Jame thought. Would that ever change?

Harn had advanced into to hall carrying Secur's body. The party bearing the other four mutilated corpses followed him. Sheth saw him, saw them, and frowned.

"Old friend. What has happened?"

"You tell me. Your people did this."

The Commandant touched Secur's face with his white fingertips, closing the man's dull, staring eyes.

"Not with my will," he said.

"But under your watch." No longer with rage but with sorrow, Harn spoke almost in tears. "How could you let this happen?"

"All summer, all autumn, I was at the border. Orders came from Restormir to obey the prince; orders came from the prince's chamberlain to stay where I was. But I feared . . . I feared . . . then, when Lord Ardeth fell into my hands . . ."

"Who?" blurted Timmon. "Oh, I thought you meant my grandfather Adric."

Lyra thumped him in the chest with her small fist. "Timmy. Grow up."

"...I used that as an excuse to return to Karkinaroth, to find this."

Painted Caineron poured out of the palace.

"Commandant!" cried Marham. "We won the war! At last, at last!"

Following him came the Caineron banner, a golden serpent on a field of crimson, devouring its young. The flag was trimmed with five mops of hair.

"Why is your face painted?" asked Sheth.

Bewildered, his second-in-command smeared a hand across his brow and stared at the resultant black and white streaks.

"I don't know. He told me, 'Honor my name,' but what does that mean? 'Obey me,' he said. 'Do this. Do that.' Heh, heh, heh."

His blurred face contorted into a sly grin. "Can do anything I want, can't I? Who's to tell me otherwise? You, you Shanir half-breed? Oh, the great Commandant this, the great Commandant that. I have more grandeur in my little finger than you do in your whole, long, lanky body. Who obeys whom, heh?"

Jame felt the hair prickle on her scalp. Sheth was talking to his lord Caldane through his unfortunate subordinate. Marham's grin widened, bearing white teeth. The corners of his mouth cracked and bled.

"You will do as I say, yes, even you. Everyone will. It is inevitable. Obey now."

Sheth swayed. For a moment, he covered his face with both hands. Then he let them fall, drew a deep breath, and straightened. The entire hall seemed to breathe with relief.

"These bodies, these scalps, will be given to the pyre at dusk," Sheth said. "Commander Harn, do you agree?"

Harn nodded with a grunt.

"Marham . . ."

But the Kendar had turned away. "I'm sorry, I'm sorry, I'm sorry," he babbled, and bolted back into the palace.

VII

HARN ASKED JAME INTO HIS QUARTERS, although he didn't seem to know what to say to her when she got there. It was something to do with the pyres. She listened, and tried to make sense.

A rap on the door announced Sheth Sharp-tongue. He nodded to Jame and turned to Harn.

"So," he said. "You feared that you would rule in favor of Jurik in the Transweald games."

"I didn't say so," Harn protested, turning away, gruff. "I only said that he should be given a fair chance."

"How fair could that be, given his training?"

"I trained him as best I could, but he grew up in High Bashti, in the king's court. Its morals are his. I didn't even know that he existed until I returned to the court thirty years later."

They spoke as if Jame wasn't there, but both had acknowledged her presence and neither had told her to leave. She sat on Harn's bed, cross-legged, elbows on knees, fists under her chin, listening. It felt to her as if she had been called upon to bear witness. A randon, a

Highborn, a potential Tyr-ridden—how much did they understand? Enough that she was here.

"Queen Vestula claims you as his sire."

Harn turned, a baited bear. "I don't deny that."

"She also claims that you raped her."

Harn beat his fists together. "I don't deny that either, but I don't remember any of it."

"So, you don't know. She has had other lovers, and has pulled other such tricks before, but without issue. Ah, I thought that would surprise you. Her position depends on having provided Mordaunt with an heir whom he can at least pretend is legitimate."

Harn glared at him. "Jurik is my son," he said. "I know it. But I don't have to be proud of him or responsible for him. I see that now."

And that, thought Jame, was as fair a judgment as he was likely to make. The mission on which Torisen had sent her was complete. Now one only need deal with the aftershocks.

A rumble came from the core of the palace and plaster dust rattled down from a cracked ceiling. As the disturbance subsided, someone knocked on the door. The Commandant answered it. One of his Kendar murmured a message to him. When he had gently closed the door and turned, his expression was unreadable.

"The pyre is ready," he told them, and began slowly to pace.

Harn got out of his way. Jame watched. The Commandant kept his emotions close, behind a sardonic mask, but they were there, and they stirred the room like the passing of some great, dire cat.

"One more will join it," he said over his shoulder. "Marham has taken the white knife. Others had to be talked out of it. To most, the events of the past few days are a nightmare from which they are just awakening. Marham was a good man, until m'lord Caldane fouled his soul."

He laughed, a terrible sound. "All of this time, we have worried about the lost clause that would protect us against our paymasters here in the Central Lands, but we were looking in the wrong direction. The contracts that really matter are between a lord and his people, between Kencyr and Kencyr. Is that not so, lady?"

They both looked at Jame.

"Yes," she said, and felt her answer resonate in the very fabric of a tortured Kencyrath. Would Tori agree? She thought so.

Some things need to be broken.

What was that but another way to say that change must come?

The mass pyre was laid in the palace courtyard. Much of it came from shattered furniture doused in oil. Five Knorth bodies and one Caineron were placed on or under combustible layers, and more oil was poured on top. The sun set behind the western mountains. Shadows climbed the palace's central tower. The curtains there must be going in and out, in and out, Jame thought as she watched the Commandant insert a burning brand into the wooden pile. Flames kindled and licked up its sides, over kindling, over bodies. Firelight flared up the palace's pink facade.

A rumble came from within. The tower swayed. It was

crumbling, falling. Wood and stone and shoddy plaster—all collapsed inward with the sullen internal ruction of a flawed architectural body giving way to gravity.

Dust belched out the front door.

Lyra emerged from it, clutching Smokie. The royal gold queen followed her, carrying her smallest cub by the scruff of its neck. The rest of her family tumbled after her.

"Oh!" Lyra cried, falling into Jame's arms, pinning a protesting ounce cub between them. "My poor prince is dead! He died on clean linen, though, smiling, so that's something, isn't it?"

"I would like to think so," said Jame, watching the spires fall.

A crowd of nobles and commoners pressed against the outer gate. Now it gave way and they spilled into the courtyard, ignoring the Kencyr and the flaring pyre.

"Prince Uthecon is dead!" they cried. "Long live the new prince!"

But who was he?

Claimants rallied their supporters, there, on the threshold of desolation. Some apparently were related to the lost, poisoned councilors. It had taken them all of this time to work up concern? Kencyr held them back, or in their enthusiasm they would have fallen into the pyrrhic flames. Some surged forward as if to seize Lyra as their prize, but Caineron troops held them off while Timmon retrieved her from Jame's arms and held her tight.

"These people are animals," said Harn, swatting one of the most persistent.

"They have a reputation for sophistication," said Jame. "Ah, ambition."

Another figure descended the stair, feet crunching on debris. It wore a pale robe and the waxen mask of the Deathless.

"Ah, people, dear people," said Malapirt, taking off the latter and smiling at the faces turned upward toward him. "Have I not served you well? Who else should you choose to lead you forward after this tragic occurrence?"

A growl answered him. The crowd bore him backward into the entry hall, into the palace's ongoing collapse, and left him there.

"Well," said Harn. "Maybe they aren't so bad after all."

VIII

IT REMAINED TO DECIDE what to do about Lyra.

"I would take her back to Omiroth," said Timmon uncomfortably, "but I don't think my mother would welcome her. Most likely, she would contrive to send her to Restormir, or to Wilden."

"And you, as Lord Ardeth, couldn't say 'no'?" Jame asked.

Timmon squirmed. "She's very persistent, my mother. Not smart, you understand, but stubborn."

"I should think," Jame said, "that she would welcome a Caineron as your consort."

"But, you see, according to her standards Lyra is used goods. Never mind that no man has touched her. She's been the consort of two Karkinoran princes, both now dead. I don't know what Mother wants for me, but it isn't that."

Jame threw up her hands. "Timmon, you have to sort this out for yourself. My advice? Send Lyra to the Women's World at Gothregor. The Matriarchs will have conniptions, but Tori won't force her to do anything she doesn't want. And let her take the ounces with her."

⊰⊱ Chapter XVII ⊱⊰
In Defense of the Gods
High Bashti: Winter 24

I

TWENTY-FIVE DAYS after their departure from High Bashti, the expedition returned.

Once back across the Silver, they had seen mostly local traffic on Thyme Street and on the river—few wagons full of fruit, vegetables, and grain bound westward toward the capital, few herds of swine or cattle, few laden barges.

"We hear stories," said the innkeeper darkly when they stopped to water their horses and to drink warm cinnamon cider at his wayside hostelry. "The city is in chaos, the Council against the king, the king against the citizens. Everyone is fighting. Food is short. So is money. If supplies go in and aren't heavily guarded, one faction or the other seizes them. So we stay here, safe. We hope. The gods only know where it will all end."

The travelers entered the Necropolis at sunset. Skeins of smoke drifted under the now skeletal trees and wreathed the monuments, here draped over a marble neck, there flowing around the flanks of a stone lion. On the ground below, fumble-fingers of mist shifted through the fallen leaves of autumn, stirred by a fitful breeze.

Here was the Tigganis sanctum, mostly rebuilt. On its threshold crouched the suggestion of a misshapen figure, perhaps the late Lord Prestic, animated by love and by vengeance? Not dead. Not alive. Where did he belong? So many questions remained unanswered.

Beyond the crypts, within the outer city wall, was the Thyme river valley. It had been a vast garden. Now it was not so much harvested as stripped.

And then there was High Bashti.

With sunset, the shadows of the Snowthorns lay over it, and with these came a distant rack of clouds laced with lightning, shaken with muted thunder. The wind turned. Now the breath of fire gusted in the riders' faces, rising from dozens of lesser conflagrations within the city. Lights flared here and there, painting this wall or that, then sank, then leaped again, untended. A growl of many voices rose from the Grand Forum. More fires there cast a ruddy glow on the watching statues of the gods, on the surrounding buildings including the ornate facade of General Suwaeton's temple.

The Kencyr regarded all of this from afar.

"No," said Harn, in answer to Jame's questioning look. "Before we go there, we have to find out what's happening."

With that, they rode through the looted fields to the main gate, through that into the smoldering city.

II

"**...AND THEN,**" said Lady Anthea, "Mordaunt stopped the dole. And so, of course, the citizens revolted."

Jame and Harn were in her apartment at Campus Kencyrath, along with the randon officer whom Harn had left in charge of the garrison.

"The urchins are our eyes and ears in the city," the latter had explained. "Snaggles captains them. They report to him, he reports to the lady, and she, graciously, shares that information with us. So does your agent Graykin, although not as regularly, nor do I trust him as much."

"Let me get this straight," said Harn, and began to count on his fingers. "Mordaunt demands more money from the Council. They say no. He raids the dole fund, depleting it. The citizens riot. The Council sends the city guards to help them. Mordaunt declares martial law and calls in the army as well as his ruffians, led by Jurik. He also draws on us to protect him, personally, which is where most of our troops are right now, on the palace mound. Meanwhile, there's widespread looting and arson. And you, lady, open our campus as a refuge for those citizens fleeing the violence, rooms, halls, steps, arena and all. You think I didn't notice that they're using our fences and furniture for firewood? Go on, tell me: Have I missed anything?"

Anthea's wrinkled lips twitched into a smile. "One does what one can."

"How are we feeding them, by the way?"

"By my patrimony and by the thieves' market. What, you didn't know that I am one of the richest women in the city?"

The door burst open and Snaggles tumbled in, exclaiming, "It's gotten worse!"

Mordaunt's ruffians and the army had seized the major temples in the Forum, he reported. City guards had tried to take them back, but the king's forces threatened to destroy the deified bodies within if they persisted, also if the Council didn't pay Mordaunt what he demanded by midnight. Then they would go after the domestic saints. They were, in effect, holding the entire Pantheon hostage.

"What, even General Suwaeton?" Rue asked.

"Especially him."

"Mordaunt hates and fears his grandfather," said Jame, thinking out-loud. "Whatever he's planning, it involves Suwaeton's destruction."

Why, though, should she care? These gods had virtually nothing to do with the Kencyrath. They predated even the Four in their archetypes, although not in the individuals who currently enacted them. Yes, that latter change seemed to have coincided with the activation of the Kencyr temples, but their current power pertained wholly to Rathillien. Maybe that was it: this world needed all of its souls to oppose Perimal Darkling. To lose the Central Lands Council of Gods, especially its king, would weaken it, perhaps fatally. That must be forestalled at all costs.

Besides, she liked the man.

Jame stood up. "I'm going back to the Forum," she

said. "What I can do there, I don't know, but I have to do something."

After a quick visit to her quarters through hallways jammed with fugitives, she, Rue, and Damson left. Harn and the rest of the garrison went part way with them, then turned west toward the palace to check on the Knorth troops there. A clutch of civilian guards drawn from among the refugees remained to protect the campus on what promised to be a turbulent night.

Storm clouds rolled closer, lightning flickering in their bowels. Thunder cleared its throat.

On the way in, the expedition had skirted the forum on back streets to its north, between the Tigganis mount and that to the north, nameless, abandoned, blasted. Now Jame and her small company took a more familiar route southward between the Floten and the Tigganis hills. Here was the market reduced to ashes, circled by frantic pigeons. Then there were the apartment buildings with smoking roofs, their bottom stories on fire. Citizens crowded the street between them with their families and possessions. Dogs ran in circles, barking. Children cried. Parents looked distraught. High Bashti was falling apart.

"This is not good," said Jame.

"Well," Snaggles said, "what are you going to do about it?"

By now they were in charred Thyme Side, not far from where the Guild fire had started. The urchin made Jame jump as he popped up at her elbow.

"What are you doing here?" she demanded.

"It's my city, isn't it? Followed you, didn't I?"

"Apparently. Now keep out of our way."

They arrived at the Forum, which seethed with people.

Mordaunt's ruffians and random elements of the army held the temples, fending off the growing crowd. Jame recognized Jurik strutting behind the lines before Suwaeton's sanctuary, loomed over by the broad, simpering thug already familiar to her from past encounters. Both, as Harn had said, were bedecked to the eyebrows in lace, sequins, and glitter. Less gaudy, compared to the rest, was Jurik's perennial golden brow band, now shoved back on a sweaty forehead, barely a cover for his receding hairline.

Oh, little boy, she thought. *Will you ever grow up?*

One of the army detachments was Danior from Nether Bashti, looking disgusted. Jurik paused, apparently to give them orders. If so, they showed no sign of having heard him.

The city guards faced these troops but held back due to the threat that the latter posed to Bashti's gods. Citizens piled up behind them, more and more filling the Forum as the midnight deadline approached. Standards waved as they had on Autumn's Eve, beacons to the faithful of each house. The threatened, after all, were not only deities but family. Some began defiantly to sing:

> "What is, will be.
> We are the heart of this world.
> Our ways endure."

But an armed legion stood before them with its hand, as it were, at their throats.

"How do we get in?" asked Damson.

Snaggles tugged Jame's sleeve. "There's a side door especially for priests."

One by one, they angled through the crowd, then darted between the front lines, then passed between Suwaeton's Floten temple to the right and the Tigganis to the left. The Danior commander saw Jame, but looked the other way, her troops likewise. Jurik didn't notice.

Here was the door, or so Snaggles said. It was almost indistinguishable from the wall, and locked. Jame extended a claw to pick it open, to Snaggles' avid interest. The mechanism within clicked. They crept inside.

The interior was as elaborate as Jame remembered—room after room of votive offerings, shining stone floors, thick columns, walls adorned with tapestries and murals, high ceilings inlayed with mosaics.

At first it seemed to be deserted. Then they heard the murmur of a voice echoing through the halls. It wheedled. It cajoled. It was utterly, smugly, self-confident.

Believe in me, its tone said, under whatever words it spoke. *I alone know what you truly want and can give it to you.*

Jame shivered.

This seduction was what she had always most feared, this call to the unfallen, uncertain darkling within her, to what had betrayed her mother. To yield. To belong.

But she was no longer a child huddled alone in a lightless room, listening to darkness speak.

Now it was the king of the gods who lay helplessly coffined within.

They followed the voice, up and up internal steps, to the inner sanctum. There was the General's rock crystal sarcophagus on its altar, its lid slid off and lying shattered on the floor. Over it bent a pale figure. Smiling waxen lips spoke, but did not move.

"I ask such a little thing from you," they murmured, with the lilt of light-hearted enticement. "You will not even miss it. Only your soul, freely given to me. Admit: it has always burdened you. The weight. The responsibility. Why continue to carry it? You are dead. You long for oblivion. You know you do. If not this way, well, your soul will be set free from this carrion mass regardless. With fire. Look."

He waved a languid gloved hand toward the back of the room. There stood a half dozen of the Deathless in white robes with featureless waxen masks. In their hands were oil jugs and glowing fire pots, which they raised in salutation or in menace.

"Oblivion or immortality. Choose."

"Which is which?" Jame asked, stepping forward, dry mouthed.

The smiling mask raised to regard her through the black holes of its eyes.

"I am immortal. All who oppose me die. You still have that choice, little girl, even after all the times that you have disappointed me."

Jame gulped. "I don't accept that. Even so, I would rather be dead than be what you are."

The smiling mask seemed to laugh.

"Power," it said. "Immortality. Final victory over Perimal Darkling. Yes, I oppose the Shadows. They would swallow me."

"You bowed to them."

"But I never crawled before them. I am greater than that. I am omnipotent."

"Gerridon. Uncle. I will not call you Master of Knorth again, for you are delusional. The souls you fed upon are gone. You have failed to harvest new ones. Like the shadow assassins, you can kill but not reap without consent. Have you not found that so here, in your court of last resort?"

He rose. She hadn't realized that he was so tall—enough, it seemed, almost to scrape the ceiling. Wisps of luminous mist writhed about his unseen feet and swirled up his pale robes as they had in the White Hills. They looked almost like weirding. Oh, chilling thought: Had she been wrong about his current access to power?

"Never say that I am finished," he said, looking down his nose at her as if from a great height. His mask cracked at one corner. It appeared to sneer and then, in a trickle, to bleed. "Never dream it. More souls await me among our own kind than you or your hapless brother can count. He will fall. So will you. So will that weakling whom perforce I must call my son. I say again, wait." He drew up his cloak. "This conversation no longer amuses me."

Again he gestured to the Deathless, and they advanced.

Damson dived at the nearest, knocking him sideways into his fellow. Oil splashed from the former's vessel onto the latter's robe, into his fire pot. Flames enveloped them both and spread. Rue yelped. Damson watched with speculative eyes, as she had done at Vont's pyre, until Jame pulled her back. Robe after robe kindled and the Deathless floundered about the room, beating at themselves, setting fire to the tapestries. Cloth blackened and fell. Beneath it was—nothing, until skin charred and *mere* ink boiled away from seared flesh.

"They're shadow assassins!" Snaggles cried, almost in tears. Jame remembered that he had expressed admiration for the Deathless, who promised eternal life to all classes.

"Not all of them," she said. Malapirt came to mind, although he would probably not have welcomed someone like this grubby urchin into his brotherhood, any more than the so-called Master aspired to immortality for everyone.

Fire climbed the walls to the rafters and licked across the floor. Shimmering veils of heat rose.

Gerridon had disappeared. If he really had stood on a patch of weirding, he could potentially go anywhere.

Suwaeton's body remained.

"We have to get him out of here," Jame said, a sleeve raised to protect her face from the scorching heat.

Her first thought was that the General could be resealed in his sarcophagus, but the lid was broken. Besides, if the fire spread the heat might bake him inside like a ham.

Rafters began to crack and fall. Mosaics shattered, tiles crashing down in a many-colored rain. Below, rich offerings burned or melted.

Snaggles tugged her sleeve again. "There's a garden behind the temple."

"Right. Damson, Rue, help me."

They lifted the General's corpse out of its coffin. It was limp, which they hadn't expected, but heavy. He might have been sleeping. One almost expected to hear him snore. The side door remained open. They carried the body through it, back into the autumn-swept garden where they laid him under a tree and buried him in a mound of fallen foliage.

Leaving, at the temple's front they found their way blocked by Jurik and his brigands.

"Always in the thick of things, I see," he said, with a smirk. "Shall we explain this to my father? I think so."

Damson stepped forward, pugnacious, but Jame held her back. "I meant to visit Mordaunt next anyway," she said. "Let's see how that goes."

Smoke began to boil out from under the temple's eaves. People noticed.

III

JURIK AND HIS THUGS hustled them back to the palace mound, pushing, shoving, sneering. One of them tried to cuff Snaggles, who wisely ducked away and disappeared into the crowd. The hill's lower slope was guarded by Knorth Kencyr. When they saw Jame, a troop of them closed around Jurik's party, bringing it to a halt.

"Let us through," Jurik demanded, trying to push past. "I am the crown prince."

Mint stepped forth. "In that garb," she said mildly, "you could have fooled me."

His hulking shadow snorted and charged. Mint side-stepped with wind-blowing, tripping the brigand as he passed. The circle made room for him to fall and regarded him as he sprawled on his face, taking up half the width of the steps, knocked cold. Then they looked away and closed ranks.

"Lady," Mint said to Jame, "what is your wish?"

"To see the king."

"Then you shall."

Kencyr escorted her, Damson, and Rue up the stairs that led to the royal hilltop compound, Jurik sulking at their heels, his retinue straggling behind him. They climbed, then passed through the outer buildings and courtyards, which were lit with a host of mural torches and scattered with more Knorth guards. Here at last was the frieze-bedecked palace with the new temple next to it. Firelight crawled across the former's facade, making its figures seem to twitch within their frames. The latter was nearly finished. Quite grand it appeared, all white marble and colonnades without, the interior gilded with golden regal coins and mosaics of lapis lazuli. The heroic statue seated on its marble throne that Jame had last seen in the workshop was now set in place before the temple's door. However, it still lacked its head. This lay to one side, judging by the shape under a sheet. Before it paced the king.

Jurik joined him, gesturing to Jame as if to claim credit for having retrieved her. Mordaunt impatiently waved him away.

"Look," the king said to the solid, obdurate phalanx of workers who faced him behind their foreman. "Finish the job and I will pay you."

"You have that backwards, Your Majesty," said the foreman, polite but unyielding. "When you pay us, we will finish the job."

Mordaunt stomped. "I will have the money tonight. Don't you trust me?"

"We've trusted you so far, sire, and not a penny have we seen. We owe the quarries and the stone masons and the sculptors and the laborers. You owe us. Pay."

"How dare you speak to me like that!" Mordaunt almost screamed. He turned on Harn who stood nearby, Dar and a Knorth ten-command behind him. "Make these sluggards work. By the contract between us, I order you!"

Harn looked uncomfortable: service in the Central Lands had never before included intruding on trade disputes.

Jame crossed over to his side.

"For that matter," she said to Mordaunt, "you haven't paid us either."

Mordaunt laughed in her face. "And yet you obey anyway. Weak, weak, for all your vaunted reputation. Should I reward such frauds as you? Never, never, never!"

"Then I declare our contract void."

Harn stirred, but didn't speak.

Mordaunt gaped, then laughed again, contemptuously. "You don't have the authority. Now, do as I say. Make them work, or damn well hoist that head onto this statue yourselves!"

"Neither. I have leave to speak for my brother, the Highlord of the Kencyrath. We say that this farce is over."

Harn cleared his throat. "It's true. She has the right. Blackie told me so."

So Torisen had passed his judgment on to his commander. Jame hadn't known that, but should have guessed. Was that why Harn had looked to her for judgment in Karkinaroth?

Lightning glared to the west, illuminating the inner recesses of roiling clouds, throwing shadows across the court. Thunder growled as the storm advanced.

Another group came into the courtyard, led by a stocky young woman clad in black. Pensa. Following her was the City Council, a gaudy array of patricians in a nervous, huddled clot.

Mordaunt spread wide his arms to welcome them. "At last you have come to your senses! Where is my money with which to pay these good folk?"

Pensa faced him, implacable.

"Forget that. You contracted the Shadow Guild for the murder of my father."

He stared at her. "What proof do you have to make such a ridiculous charge?"

She produced the parchment that Jame had given her. "I have already shown it to the Council. They do not approve."

Mordaunt's lips twitched. Then he smiled crookedly and shrugged as if to shake off something of little importance. "What if I did? It was only politics."

"It was his life."

Flash. Boom.

Two of Mordaunt's ruffians emerged from the crowd. Between them they dragged the actor Trepsis, so frightened that his legs had failed him. He was dressed as if for the stage, in gilt armor, an ornate helmet that tipped over his brow, and a theatrical red cloak that dragged at his heels.

"Ha!" said Mordaunt, advancing on him. "You preening fool. You dare pretend to speak for my grandfather, do you?"

"S-sometimes he speaks through me, your highness," quavered Trepsis. "I can't help it."

Mordaunt slapped him. Jame and Pensa both stepped forward but checked themselves. The ruffians had bent the actor's arms behind his back, fit to break them, and had lifted him, painfully, onto toes that scrambled to touch the ground.

"You act in his filthy farces!" the king shouted in Trepsis's face, spraying him with spittle. "You spread sedition!"

"I-I-I can't help it!"

Someone else slipped forward and whispered in Mordaunt's ear.

"Ha!" he said again, much louder, with a note of triumph. "Suwaeton's temple is in flames. So much for him."

The Council members swayed, murmuring.

"That is the founder of your house," said Pensa. "The link to your ancestors and to kingship."

"He is nothing, I tell you! Damn you, grandfather, you are gone, forever and ever. At last!"

A gust of wind scoured the courtyard. Leaves swirled and side torches flared. The sheet over the stone head stirred. Trepsis's cloak billowed.

The actor bent his head, gathered himself, and seemed to swell. Before, he had cowered in the hollow armor of a giant. Now he began to fill it out. The brigands struggled to hold his arms behind him, but he slowly drew them forth as his sandaled feet came down solidly on the pavement. Then he flexed, and his captors tumbled aside.

General Suwaeton drew himself up, now fully inhabiting clothing more fitted to the battlefield than to the stage. He coughed, spat out a mouthful of sodden, chewed foliage, and wiped his mouth.

"You had to bury me in leaves?" he demanded of Jame. The echo of thunder rolled in his voice, shaking her bones.

"It was the best we could do," she said. "Sorry. I'm glad that you survived the fire."

He cleared his throat and spat again. "Hah-whoom! Even now it ravages my sanctuary. Boy." He turned on Mordaunt. "You owe me a temple. This new toy of yours will do until my worshippers can build me something better."

It was hard to tell by the flaring light, but Mordaunt's face seemed to congest with fury. "Well, you can't have it!" he snarled, stomping his feet. "This is mine, mine, mine!"

Another stronger blast of wind stripped the stone head bare, its sheet flapping away like a frightened ghost. The sharp features revealed did indeed belong to Mordaunt, not to the General. Everyone stared.

"What is this?" Suwaeton rumbled. "Foolish boy, do you pretend to claim godhood?"

Mordaunt glared at him. "Why shouldn't I? It's just a matter of faith, isn't it? Who should the people believe in except for me when all their other gods fail? After tonight, I will reign alone, supreme. Do you think, at this late hour, that you can defeat me?"

"I always could. You are weak. You always were, even as a child. I told your father so, but he was weak too."

"You over-bore him!" Mordaunt shrieked. Foam flecked his lips. He licked it up with the dry rag of a tongue. "What could he do against you? What could any of us do?"

Suwaeton looked both incredulous and taken aback. "I never meant to run rough-shod over anyone, least of all my own family. Someday, you would have taken my place if only you had been patient. How not?"

Jame had been listening. "Oh," she said to Mordaunt, partly enlightened but also still puzzled. "You want to become a living god."

Mordaunt bared his teeth at her in a ferocious grin. "Yes! Why should I die at all, ever?"

"That sounds like something Gerridon would say to his followers. Death itself shall die. Did he give you this idea, maybe also hint that reaping souls might help?"

"Why not? He is immortal. Now I will be too, after I destroy the rest of the Pantheon through its preserved bodies and its temples. Only this one will remain. Then the people will turn to me and give me the immortality that I deserve through their faith. I will reign forever and forever—from my palace, from my temple, over the living, over the dead."

With that, he fetched up breathless, glaring, panting.

Jame suspected that what he really didn't want was to face his grandfather in life or especially in death. While he remained defiant, shouting, his spindly legs shook under him and his teeth chattered. There was some courage in that, at least, if only that of a cornered dog.

The storm flashed and shook, painting the courtyard with intermittent bursts of light. The Council members huddled together. The sculpted figures on the palace facade seemed to cavort, the stone head on the ground to grimace.

Jame gingerly approached General Suwaeton. His beard snapped with sparks. The air around him seemed charged.

Dangerous, dangerous...

"This belongs to you," she said, and handed him the second contract that the shadow assassin Smeak had given to her, which she had retrieved earlier that night from her quarters at the campus.

He took the parchment. His eyes raked over the eloquent blank spaces left by *mere* dye. He blinked. Then he turned on Mordaunt.

"You," he said, more astonished than, so far, angry, as if he couldn't quite believe that his grandson had had the guts to do such a thing. "You contracted the Guild to poison me? This life in death is all because of you?"

"And what if it is?" the king shrieked at him. "You... you bully, taking up all the air, rolling over everyone like cartwheels to crush our souls.... How were we supposed to breathe, much less to live? Yes, I took out a contract on you! I did on my own father. He was weak, as you said. I was destined to be king, yes, of everything. My friend told me so."

"That would be this Gerridon," growled the General, his wrath at last kindled. "You loved him, didn't you? More than your wife. More than any of your children or concubines. He told you what you wanted to hear. I smelled his rot when first he appeared with his Deathless cult. I told you he was poison. You didn't listen. You knew better. Now here we are, thirty years later, with the city in flames. All because you feared death. People die, you fool. It happens. It happened to me, before my time, because of you."

Mordaunt gibbered at him.

At his elbow, Jurik looked uneasy.

With a gulp and a sheer act of will, the king collected himself. "You said that you survived the fire because you were buried in leaves. That suggests to me that your body was carried into the garden behind your temple. Jurik!"

The prince jerked to attention, although his eyes rolled white under their gilded lids. Did he stand next to inspiration or to madness?

"Take the guard and reclaim that body. Destroy it. Utterly. You see, grandfather, I will triumph after all!"

As he spoke, the sky roiled and spat. Jame felt the hair rise on her arms and tasted metal.

Oh schist, she thought.

Suwaeton raised his black staff with its silver knob. (Where had that come from?) Lightning lanced down toward it, a jagged flash of light with a simultaneous ripping, thunderous retort. Jame saw it strike the knob and arc toward Mordaunt. Then her muscles locked and she was falling.

It seemed to take forever to hit the ground. During that eternity, images crawled before her stunned eyes which could not blink:

—Mordaunt lightning-struck, convulsed. His eyeballs boiled white. His mouth gaped and smoked.

—the stone head split in two, the halves rolling apart.

—the Council sagged where they stood, each kept from collapse, perhaps from death, by the support of their representatives in the Pantheon. Only Pensa stood alone although swaying, a painted woman disdainful and aloof behind her. The Tigganis queen of the gods? Her mother?

My mother may have been a monster, Jame thought, still dazed, *but at least she loved me.*

Why should that idea come now, as such a revelation?

—Suwaeton faced the dispossessed soul of his grandson, which mouthed at him from the shadows gathering around it.

"Run," he said. "Trust me: I will follow."

The ghost turned and fled.

—in his place, wax-faced Gerridon stood on his nest of weirding tendrils. He raised his head, framed in its hood. His lips seemed to smile.

"You are the cause of this boy's damnation," the General said to him. "Leave this world forever. By the power invested in me, I command you."

The other hesitated a moment, then bowed ironically and disappeared.

Jame hit the ground with a gasp. Her entire body hurt, all extremities twitching as the lightning's energy dispelled. The soles of her boots smoked. The ends of her braids twitched. But now she could breathe again. And blink.

The courtyard took shape around her.

Others too close to the strike had also been felled. Damson and Rue were gathering themselves up, shaken. Mint and Dar had been far enough away to escape the lash. Trepsis huddled on his knees, nursing his scorched hands. A body as scrawny as a child's lay convulsed on the ground at his feet, smiling blindly upward through clenched teeth. All of the clothes had been burned off of it.

Bojor, thought Jame.

She suddenly wondered if the boy actor had been yet another of Mordaunt's bastard sons. He had the build. He had the flare. He might have turned to Suwaeton for support as his grandfather. Tonight, had it been he all along and not the rest of the Pantheon, playing his favorite theatrical trick one last time with fatal consequences? Mundane and sacred space could overlap. This poor, doomed boy had been one such link.

Suwaeton had undoubtedly been here, but now he was gone. The storm rumbled off eastward, chasing sputtering clouds, having dropped no rain.

Jurik stood over Mordaunt's smoking ruin.

"Er," he said, speechless, aghast. "He's dead."

Clearly, he had forgotten Mordaunt's last command, if he had understood its import to begin with. Something else preoccupied him now.

"I am the crown prince," he said, drawing himself up, raising his chin. "I claim the throne of High Bashti, heir to Mordaunt Sharp-teeth, as the first of my name."

IV

JURIK'S PROCLAMATION was received with a stunned silence. Perhaps that was because he had embraced the king's grisly death so much faster than anyone else, perhaps because no one could imagine him in control of the oldest kingdom on the western bank of the Central Lands. But what choice did they have?

Harn cleared his throat. "They should know," he said gruffly. "You aren't Mordaunt's son. You are mine."

Briefly, Jurik looked pleased; better a legendary randon officer than a pence-pinching, despised monarch. Then he recognized the end to all of his own regal ambitions and his countenance fell.

Flutes and harps sounded afar, moving closer through the compound. Queen Vestula entered the courtyard followed by a nervous retinue of Amalfia's priestesses. She herself was dressed in finery as the princess. Around the temple she danced, kicking up the hem of diaphanous skirts with glittering heels, tapping on a tabor with long, painted nails.

Jurik looked unnerved as she circled him, humming a nursery rhyme while also seeming to flirt:

"Bye, baby Bunting
The queen's gone a-hunting
All to catch a Kencyr skin
To wrap a baby Jurik in . . ."

"Please, Mother," he said, abashed. "Not now."

Then she turned on Harn.

"My king," she crooned, reaching up to trace his ear with a long-nailed finger-tip as she passed. He shivered. "My love. Have you come back to me at last?"

Harn looked desperately uncomfortable.

Jame stepped between them. "Leave him alone," she said.

Vestula sneered at her. "I have heard about you. No man is good enough for you, is he? No woman either. Try that as you age, cold, alone. I at least had one great love, and here he stands."

"Leave him," said Jame again. "We are more than the use that we make of each other. He was never more than a tool to you, to deceive, to use, and then to abandon. Is that love? One of us, at least, has been greatly mistaken."

The queen made as if to slap her. When Jame dodged out of her way, she rushed past and seized Harn's arm.

"Come . . . with . . . me," she panted, trying to tug him toward the palace.

However, she might as well have attempted to shift the towering, headless statue of her dead husband. Her ornate heels skidded out from under her. Flushed and furious, she fell to the pavement from which she glared up at Harn as if to say, "Men!"

Pensa had gone to bend over Bojor, but he was beyond help.

Then she turned to help Trepsis, who was attempting to stand on shaky legs, still nursing his burned hands.

In her absence, the Council consulted. Their conference soon concluded, perhaps along lines on which they already agreed, they turned back to the general assembly. One of their number stepped forward. His white robe embroidered with words reminded Jame of the judge's costume stitched up out of linen legal briefs in the god farce. Was this Lexion, the head of that house, Trepsis's birth lord?

"Now, lady," he said soothingly to Vestula, reminding

Jame even more of a jurist. "We of High Bashti have other ways of choosing our king. The direct line of Floten has ended with the death of our late king." He glanced at the still smoldering remains. "Our very late king. Let all here bear witness. His grandfather, of course, remains well regarded and, I am pleased to tell you, intact. As are the other gods. Our society remains whole, if shaken."

"'What is, will be,'" murmured Jame. "'We are the heart of this world. Our ways endure.'"

"Er . . . yes." He gave her a look as if unsure if she dared to make fun of him, if so not approving. "The army and the city guards are helping to fight fires. Mordaunt's minions have fled. I see that the Kencyr are here, no doubt to protect you, my dear."

This last was addressed to Jame with a touch of sarcasm. She had already noticed that the margins of the courtyard were filling up with Knorth. Should she thank the randon bond for such support, or her role as lordan? Probably both. Rue and Damson had come to stand behind her. Now they were joined by Harn, in flight from an enraged Vestula.

"As I was saying," said Lord Lexion with a soft smile that made Jame want to slap him even more than his reference to her as "my dear" had. "We have long debated how to face such a crisis as this. Other houses before now have claimed to be descendants of the true founder, whoever he was. Floten's house has failed. Where do we turn next, and must it be to a king?"

Jurik had been seething. Now he burst forth. "Where else," he demanded, "and why not to me? I am the queen's son. She brought more to this marriage than he did, and to this country!"

"Yes!" Vestula said, stomping, tottering on her broken heels. "Much more!"

"Lady, dear lady."

Now Jame really could have hit him for that dismissive note, even though she had no interest in supporting either Jurik or his mother.

"In millennia we have never before had a change of ruling family or a queen regnant. Why not now? I nominate Lady Tigganis."

He meant Pensa.

She looked up, startled, from where she bent over her actor mentor. "What?"

Lord Lexion knelt before her and extended his hands. "Will you rule over us as our queen?"

She gulped. "Yes."

Vestula drew herself up, glaring. "I have held that honor for twenty years."

"Thirty-five," muttered someone among the Council's ranks.

"Be quiet! What fault do you find with me?"

"That you were born a foreigner, lady, and are no longer married to the king," said Lexion. Besides, he might have added, echoing Dar, no one trusted her. "Go back to Amalfia's sanctuary, as the princess's high priestess. No one begrudges your service to your Hathiri kinswoman."

"I should hope not!" she snapped, and flounced off, trailed by her hieratic retinue, which looked relieved to get away.

Jurik gazed after her, bereft, then pulled himself together.

"Have you stopped to think," he demanded of the Council, "how Hathir will respond to this move? My mother, as you say, was Hathiri, her dowry an offering of peace between the east and west banks of the Silver. They will take this as an insult."

"They may," said Pensa. "What, though, if as my first act as reigning monarch I should take you, her son, as my consort?"

The Council murmured over this.

Jurik goggled, at first aghast. Then, considering the alternatives and the possibilities, he looked pleased.

"Yes," he said, huffing out his chest. "That would do."

"Then so let it be done."

"Are you sure about this?" Jame asked Pensa under cover of more exclamations from other houses who had hoped to secure unions of their own with the new queen, followed by a general realization that at present they cancelled each other out.

Pensa gave Jame a tight-lipped smile. "Yes. Trust me.

"My second act," she continued, raising her voice, "is to guarantee that the Knorth mercenaries are paid in full for their good service up to now and here after. Immediately. Or at least as soon as civil order has been restored, which I expect within days. I trust that other houses will contribute to this effort. Also, I declare a forgiveness for any Knorth who has gone into debt because of the late king's failure to pay."

Mint punched Dar in the ribs. He grimaced, then heaved a guilty sigh of relief. Would he keep to that abstemious regime, though? That remained to be seen.

There was more muttering at this, but a general resigned consensus: new rulers required concessions to keep them sweet and, the patricians hoped, compliant.

Jurik, on the other hand, glowered. "Why should we pay them at all? Father . . . that is, Mordaunt . . . didn't."

Pensa smiled at him, diamond hard. "Are you at least his son in that? I will remember it. That settles everything, except for my poor father."

Trepsis tottered out of the crowd, cuddling his hands. They were now seen to be seared to the bone, immobile. Would he ever be able to use them again? Perhaps as his divine patron decreed.

"Lady, the General left you a message. What happened to Prestige is without remedy, he said, but perhaps not beyond justice. Take him as he is into your house. He is to be recognized as a saint."

Pensa bowed her head. "I will."

Jurik started up. "I will not! If we must share a house, why should we have such an abomination within our halls? What is he but a walking corpse, sewn together with your misguided devotion? Where, in life, in death, does he have a place?"

"With us," she said.

No yielding there. Perhaps she remembered the cruel laughter, the torn clothes, the scorn with which she had been dismissed as "dark, squat, ugly" at her aborted engagement party. All of that had indirectly led to her father's murder. Yes, Pensa had more scores than one to settle with her soon-to-be spouse.

"You will welcome him as your father-in-law," she added, to drive the point home. "Do you think that I care about anything you say? A mere consort has no power. Ask your mother about that and then be quiet."

"You wait," he cried in frustration. "Your father had ambitions in life. Why not in death? Where is your precious general then?"

A mutter rose in Jame's memory: *"I'm hungry. I'm hungry."*

"We will see," said the new queen, and turned to her duties.

⋘᠁᠁ Epilogue ᠁᠁⋙
High Bashti
Winter 25

TORISEN BLACKLORD didn't communicate well by letter. When he was worried, he tended not to write at all. The last time this had happened, he had been very sick and had thought that he was dying. While not anticipating that again, Jame had hoped to find a missive waiting for her when she returned from Karkinaroth. However, there was none. She sat in her quarters for some time thinking about this, missing what was no doubt a lively breakfast as the garrison discussed the night's events.

At last, she sent word down to the mess hall.

"I think that we've done all we can here, for good or for ill," she told Damson when the former cadet arrived.

Damson frowned. She often did when presented with a question that seemed to involve morality. "Why do you say 'for ill'?"

"By force of habit, mostly. Wherever I am, things tend to happen. Not that I'm sorry Mordaunt is dead, or that Pensa is the new queen, or that the General perseveres."

Thinking of Suwaeton reminded her how easily he had seemed to dismiss Gerridon from Rathillien. Did it really work that way? If so, coming to the Central Lands had been worthwhile for that alone. If not, well, time would tell.

Also, Harn had come to grips with his past.

Also, the Knorth garrison was to be paid and, by extension, Gothregor, to keep it over the winter.

Also, the Knorth ladies had been avenged, at least as far as the Shadow Guild was concerned. As to whom had paid the Guild's hire, ah, that was another matter.

And she had learned that an internal threat, the lords of her own people, was more dangerous to the Kencyrath than any lost clause in a Central Lands' contract.

What had the cadet officers sung at the muster, so long ago?

"New foes, new lands, now do we seek,
Our lords to please, in worth our trust.
But doubt stands forth among our ranks.
Contrariwise, who stands by us?"

Now, something was wrong in the River Land.
"It's time," she said, "that we went home."

✣ The Beginning of the End ✣

Appendix I

People, Places, and Things

Adiraina	Blind Ardeth Matriarch.
Adric	Lord Ardeth, Torisen's mentor.
Amalfia	Primary figure in the Princess cult (dead).
Anthea	Bashtiri lady living at Campus Kencyrath.
Ardeth	One of the nine Kencyr houses.
Arrin-ken	The third people of the Kencyrath; judges; huge cats who withdrew from the Kencyr world after Gerridon's Fall.
Arrin-thar	Combat with clawed gloves.
Artifax	Artist/craftsman/god: Bashti house, lord, god. *See Appendix II.*
Ashe	Haunt singer of Mount Alban.
Awl	Former Randir war-leader (dead).

Bashti   The ancient seat of power on the west
                  bank of the Central Lands.

Bastolov   An ancient crown prince of Bashti,
                  betrothed to Amalfia, now the Burnt Man
                  (very dead).

Bear   Brain-damaged, clawed randon; Jame's
                  teacher or Senethari in the Arrin-thar.
                  Also known as the Monster in the Maze.

Bel-tairi (Bel)   Jame's Whinno-hir mount.

Belacose   Warrior god: Bashti house, lord, and god.
                  See *Appendix III*.

Benj   Infant son of Must and her half-brother
Tiggeri

Binding   Sufficiently strong Kencyr lords and
                  Highborn can bind followers, which
                  means accepting them into that person's
                  service and in exchange giving them a
                  place in said Highborn's soul-image.

Blood-binding   Certain Shanir can bind anyone body and
                  soul that tastes their blood.

Blood-kin   Close relatives, down to first cousins.

Bo   Infant Kendar son of Merry and Cron.

Bojor	Trepsis's assistant actor.
Bone-kin	One step below blood kin, e.g., distant cousins.
Brandan	One of the nine Kencyr houses.
Brant	Lord Brandan.
Brenwyr	The Brandan Matriarch, Brant's maledight sister.
Brier Iron-thorn	Jame's marshal at Tagmeth.
Builders	A mysterious race of small people who built the Kencyr temples.
Burnt Man	Rathillien's fire elemental; once Prince Bastolov.
Burr	Torisen's Kendar servant.
Caineron	The largest of the nine Kencyr houses.
Caldane	Lord Caineron.
Cervil	Jurik's half-brother.
Chain of Creation	The universe is comprised of dimensions that overlap on key threshold worlds.

	Rathillien is the last one accessible to the Kencyrath, attacked by Perimal Darkling.
Changer	A Kencyr infected by Perimal Darkling, capable of changing its shape. Can be an innocent victim.
Char	A Knorth randon from Tagmeth.
Cheva	Horse-mistress at Tagmeth.
Chingetai	Gran Cyd's consort in the Merikit village.
Chirpentundrum (Chirp)	A Builder stranded at Tagmeth.
Citizens	The common class of High Bashti. *See Appendix II.*
Coman	One of the smallest Kencyr houses.
Commandant	When spelled "commandant," it is a title of respect to a randon leader. When spelled "The Commandant," it refers to Sheth Sharp-tongue.
Conillion	Ardeth replacement for Aden on the Randon Council of Nine; Distan's brother; Timmon's uncle.
Corrudin	Caldane's uncle and chief advisor, who keeps backing out of windows.

Council   Can refer to the Kencyr High Council of
                lords, the Nine of the Randon Council,
                or the High Council of High Bashti
                comprised of the ten major patrician
                houses including the king's.

Cron   Kendar mate of Merry, father of Bo.

Cult figure   Someone in Bashti who is worshiped
                as a divine figure, but not deified or
                sanctified. Usually dead.
                See Appendix III.

Damson   One of Jame's Knorth randon.

Danior   One of the smaller Kencyr houses,
                bone-kin to Torisen.

Dari   Adric's grandson and marshal at Omiroth.

Dark Judge   A blind, vengeful Arrin-ken who hunts
                Jame and keeps watch in the Riverland
                for Gerridon. Allied to the Burnt Man.

Death's-head   A nasty-tempered rathorn blood-bound
to Jame

Deified   One of the Bashti nobles who on death
                has been promoted to godhood.
                See Appendix III.

Delectica   Goddess of love: Bashti house, lady, god.
                 See Appendix III.

d-hen   A knife-fighter's jacket from Tai-tastigon,
                 which has one tight sleeve and one full,
                 reinforced, to catch an opponent's blade.

Dianthe   The Danior Matriarch.

Distan   Timmon's lady mother.

Dreamscape   Kencyr can sometimes interact through
                 dreams. Below this lies the soulscape.

Drie   Timmon's half-Kendar brother,
                 once bound to a carp, now beloved of
                 the Eaten One.

Dunfause   A Caineron scrollsman.

dwar   A deep, healing sleep.

Earth Wife   Rathillien's earth elemental,
                 also known as Mother Ragga.

Eaten One   Rathillien's water elemental.

Edirr   One of the smaller Kencyr houses.

Ennobled   Bashtiri rich enough to elevate
                 themselves from commoner status.
                 See Appendix II.

Essien and Essiar	The twin lords Edirr.
The Exile	Ganth Graylord's flight to the Haunted Lands after the Knorth massacre, which left the Kencyrath leaderless for thirty years.
Falconer	Tentir master who trains Kencyr bound to animals such as Jame and Shade.
Falkirr	The Brandan keep.
The Fall	This refers to Gerridon's betrayal of the Kencyrath to Perimal Darkling, which precipitated their flight to Rathillien three millennia ago.
Falling Man	Rathillien's air elemental; also known as the Tishooo and the Witch King of Nekrien.
Farmer Fen	Jame's agricultural expert.
Fash	Once a Caineron cadet, then Tiggeri's servant.
Floten	Cult founder of Suwaeton's regal house.
Ganth Graylord	Former Highlord, father of Torisen and Jame.

Gari   Coman randon who can bind insects.

Garr   Brandan commander at Wealdhold.

Gates   Tagmeth, an abandoned keep since
of Tagmeth   reclaimed by Jame, has a ring of step-
                forward gates that open onto other
                parts of Rathillien.

Gen   A Kencyr board game.

General, the   Suwaeton, king of the Bashti gods.

Gerridon   Also called the Master Master of Knorth
                and the Prophet, who betrayed the
                Kencyrath to Perimal Darkling for the
                sake of immortality. To maintain this,
                however, he has to feed on souls reaped
                by someone else.

Girt   Benj's Kendar nurse.

Gnasher   Once the leader of the Deep Weald
                wolvers, also Yce's sire (dead).

Gorbel   The Caineron lordan, also a randon
                and Jame's friend.

Gothregor   The Knorth keep.

Gran Cyd   Queen of the Merikit hill tribe.

Granny Sits-by-the-fire	An ancient story-teller, linked to forgotten, primordial gods.
Graykin	Jame's servant and spy.
Gray Lands	A spiritual wasteland between death and life where unfortunate Kencyr souls may go.
Grimly Wolver	Tori and Jame's friend from the Grimly Holt, a werewolf poet.
Harn Grip-hard	Torisen's randon war-leader, a berserker.
Harward	King of Hathir.
Hatch	A Merikit youth, beloved of Prid.
Hathor	Ancient seat of power on the east bank of the Central Lands.
Haunted Lands	The northeastern corner of Rathillien, where Perimal Darkling overshadows the land. Ganth went there into exile where Jame and Tori were born.
haunts	Neither alive nor dead, these inhabit the Haunted Lands.
Healer	A Shanir healer like Kindrie interacts

with his patients' soul-images, setting right whatever is wrong with them.

High Bashti — Capital of Bashti.

Highborn — Upper-class Kencyr.

Highlord — Leader of the Kencyrath, traditionally Knorth.

Holly — Lord Danior, Jame and Tori's bone-kin cousin.

Honored — Bashti citizens who are remembered but only preserved in their ashes. *See Appendix II.*

Jame — Also known as Jameth, Jamethiel Priests'-bane, or the Talisman. Twin sister of Torisen Highlord although she is ten years younger than he is. Becoming That-Which-Destroys.

Jamethiel Dream-weaver — Gerridon's consort, who danced out the souls of the Kencyr host, but who was also the mother of Torisen and Jame (dead).

Jaran — One of the nine Kencyr houses, closely associated with Mount Alban.

Jedrak, the	Generic name for Lord Jaran.
Jelly	Kallystine's changer baby, sired by Lord Randir (Kenan).
Kencyr	Anyone who belongs to the Kencyrath, Highborn, Kendar, and Arrin-ken.
Kencyrath	Also known as the Three People, chosen by their god to confront Perimal Darkling.
Kendar	The most numerous of the Kencyrath, larger than the Highborn and more creative.
Jorin	Jame's blind ounce, to whom she is bound.
Jurien	Jaran randon of the Nine.
Jurik	Crown prince of High Bashti.
Kallystine	Lord Caldane's daughter, Lord Randir's consort.
Kantir	A set patterns of moves in one of the Kencyrath's martial arts.
Kedan	Lord Jaran, granduncle to Kirien.
Keep	A Kencyr lord or lady's fortress in the Riverland.

madness and the slaughter in the
White Hills, precursor to Ganth's exile.

Kouri   A game similar to polo, but played either
with sheep-skin ball or with a headless
goat carcass.

Kraggen   The Coman keep.

Lexion   God of Judges; Bashti house, lord and god.
See Appendix II.

Lordan   A Kencyr lord or lady's heir apparent.
Traditionally male, but that is changing.

Lyra Lack-wit   Caldane's daughter, contracted to Prince
Uthecon of Karkinor.

Malapirt   Steward of Prince Uthecon of Karkinor.

Maledight   A Shanir who can kill with a curse.

Marcarn (Marc)   Jame's steward at Tagmeth and
Long-shanks   her oldest friend.

Marham   Sheth's second-in-command
at Karkinaroth.

Mercanty   God of merchants; Bashti house,
lord, and god. *See Appendix III.*

mere

A plant dye that can be used to make fabric, documents, or bodies invisible. Used by the Shadow Guild. When injected for tattoos, it can also drive people insane.

Merikit

A hill tribe.

Merry

A Knorth Kendar; mother of Bo.

Mint

One of Jame's randon; a regal guard in High Bashti; Dar's partner.

Mount Alban

The Scrollsmen's College. Also home to the Kencyr singers.

Mordaunt Sharp-teeth

King of Bashti.

Mother Ragga

The Earth Wife, Rathillien's earth elemental.

Mustard (Must)

Benj's mother; Tiggeri's half-sister (dead).

Noyat

A northern hill tribe.

Nutley

Torisen's master-baker.

Omiroth

The Ardeth keep.

Ort   King of Ordor.

Ostrepi   King of the Midlands.

Ounce   A big cat weighing about 40 pounds,
               used primarily for hunting.

patrician   Bashti's upper class. *See Appendix II*.

Pensa   Prestige's daughter; subsequently
               Lady Tigganis.

Perimal   A malignant force spreading down the
Darkling   Chain of Creation from threshold world
               to world, digesting them and their gods
               as it comes. The Kencyrath was created
               by the Three-faced God to stop it. So far,
               they haven't.

Pereden   Adric's son; Timmon's father (dead).
Proud-prance

Prestige   Lord Tigganis, father of Pensa,
               rival of Mordaunt.

Prid   Jame's Merikit lodge-wyf.

Priests'   Home and training ground of the
College   Kencyr priests at Wilden.

Pugnanos   Duke of the Transweald.

Quill	Damson's second-in-command.
Rachny	Master cook at Tagmeth.
Randir	One of the nine Kencyr houses.
Randiroc	The "lost" Randir Heir, a Shanir randon also known as the weapons-master.
randon	The officer class of the Kencyrath's military, trained at Tentir.
rathorn	An omnivorous equine plated with ivory armor, armed with two horns.
Rawneth	The Randir Matriarch; mother of Lord Randir (Kenan).
regals	King Mordaunt, his family, and his attendants; also, a gold portrait coin. *See Appendix II.*
Restormir	The Caineron keep.
Riverland	The Kencyrath's home on Rathillien.
Rothurst	King of Mirkmir.
Rowan	Torisen's steward.
Rue	Jame's self-appointed Kendar servant.

Rush	Agricultural agent sent by Torisen to Tagmeth to open the gates.
Sanctified	Bashti dead who become domestic saints through their families' faith in them. *See Appendix III.*
Sanctor	Priest god; Bashti house, lord, and god. *See Appendix III.*
Scythe-arms	Two swords, one long and one short, which are strapped to the wielder's arms.
Schola	Scholar god; house, lord, and god. *See Appendix III.*
Secur	Harn's servant, a retired randon who has a wooden foot.
Sene	A combination of Senetha and Senethar; while a flute plays, contestants dance; when the music stops, they fight.
Senetha	Slow dance form of the Senethar.
Senethar	Kencyr fighting based on Wind-blowing, Fire-leaping, Earth-moving, and Water-flowing moves.
Senethari	A teacher or master of various Kencyr fighting forms.

Shade Lord Randir's half-Kendar daughter, a randon and a Shanir changer.

Shadow Guild A Bashti association of assassins who depend heavily on *mere* dye, and *mere* tattoos, and blackmail.

Shadow Rock The Danior keep.

Shanir Kencyr with special powers, sometimes known as possessing "the Old Blood." They are seen as close to their god, whether they want to be or not.

Sharp A scrollswoman and commander of the wandering Jaran.

Sheth Sharp-tongue Caldane's war-leader, also known as the Commandant.

Smeak Junior archivist for the Shadow Guild.

Smokie Lyra's silver ounce cub.

Soul-image Kencyr have a sometimes unconscious idea of what their soul looks like in a literal sense, often as a building like the Master's House or Torisen's Haunted Lands keep. Damage to the soul-image reflects physical or mental damage to the physical body.

Soulscape	On this level, all Kencyr soul-images relate to each other.
Storm	Torisen's quarter-blood Whinno-hir warhorse.
Snaggles	An urchin living at the Campus Kencyrath.
Stennen	A Transwealdian noble.
Stubben	Rue's post pony.
Suwaeton, the General	Mordaunt's grandfather, former king of Bashti, current king of the gods (dead). *See Appendix III.*
Tagmeth	Jame's keep.
Talisman	Jame's nickname in Tai-tastigon within the Thieves' Guild.
Taur	Blind director of Mount Alban.
Tentir	The Randon College.
Thorn	The female offspring of a rathorn stallion and a domestic mare.
Three-faced God	The mysterious deity who brought together the Kencyrath to fight Perimal

Darkling, and then apparently abandoned it. He/she/it is expected to return as the Tyr-ridan.

Tigannis — Queen of the gods; house, lord, goddess. *See Appendix III*.

Tiggeri — Caldane's youngest established son, also his favorite.

Timbuk — Snaggles' honored ancestor.

Timmon — Now Lord Ardeth; a randon, also Jame's friend.

Tirresian — Jame and Gran Cyd's "daughter," of uncertain gender.

Titmouse — A Kencyr priest whom Jame met in Tai-tastigon.

Tomtim, Timtom — Shanir twins rescued from the priest's college by Kindrie.

Torisen Blacklord (Blackie) — Highlord of the Kencyrath; Jame's twin brother (although ten years older), Kindrie's cousin; becoming That-Which-Creates.

Trepsis — The elderly farceur actor who plays Suwaeton on stage and sometimes channels him.

Trishien	The Jaran Matriarch; a scrollswoman.
Tungit	A Merikit shaman.
Tyr-ridan	All of this time, the Kencyrath has been waiting for their god to return in the form of three Shanir who personify creation, preservation, and destruction, known collectively as the Tyr-ridan.
Uthecon	Elderly prince of Karkinor.
Valantir	The Jaran keep.
Vestula	Mordaunt's queen, Jurik's mother.
Vont	A cadet who threatened Jame at Tentir, whom Damson killed.
Wealdhold	Capital of Transweald.
Weirding	A mist or fog that can transport anyone or thing that encounters it anywhere.
Weirdingstrom	A giant rolling bank of weirding that can shift the earth itself.
Whinno-hir	A near-immortal equine mare linked to the Kencyrath since the beginning.

Wolver	A sort of werewolf, but with faster transitions and sometimes a strong poetic tendency.
Wolver Grimly	Wolver prince of the Grimly Holt, an old friend of Torisen's; loves Yce.
Wort	One of Jame's randon from Tagmeth.
Yce	Leader of the Deep Weald wolvers; Grimly's mate.
Yondri	Kendar who have no lord or home.

Appendix II

The Mortal Order

High Bashti was founded by ten patrician families, each of which now occupies one of the city's ten hills and has a representative (usually its lord) on the High Council. One of them, traditionally the Floten, reigns over all as king, to some extent counter-balanced by the other nine. Young patricians are allowed to change houses to fit their nature if their lords permit them.

The social ranks are Regal (the king and his family), Patrician (noble), Ennobled (middle-class raised by wealth), and Citizen or common (everyone else).

◈ Appendix III ◈

The Divine Order

The Council decides who among the recently dead will be considered for godhood or sainthood. Success in either case depends on who attracts the most worshippers, as proven by the incorruptibility of his or her mortal body.

Saints go back to their houses as minor domestic deities as long as their family continues to honor them.

Gods become part of the Pantheon, replacing older gods of the same name who have lost favor and followers. There are always ten gods in the Pantheon, one from each house. Each god and each house tend toward a certain role, for example the king (Floten), the queen (Tigganis), the warrior (Belacose), the judge (Lexion), and the actor (Thespar). House, lord or lady, and god are known by the same title, but with a distinction between the mortal and the divine tiers.

The divine ranks are Deified, Sanctified, and Honored. Cult figures also feature, but they are too old and too dead to belong to the above ranks.